Crime Plus Music

NINETEEN STORIES
OF MUSIC-THEMED NOIR

Crime Plus Music

NINETEEN STORIES OF
MUSIC-THEMED NOIR

EDITED BY
Jim Fusilli

THREE ROOMS PRESS

New York, NY

Crime Plus Music: Nineteen Stories of Music-Themed Noir
EDITED BY
Jim Fusilli

ISBN 978-1-941110-45-4(trade paperback)
ISBN 978-1-941110-46-1 (ebook)
Library of Congress Control Number: 2016936895

ACKNOWLEDGEMENTS

"Long Black Veil" © 2006 by Val McDermid, first included in the anthology *A Very Merry Band of Murderers* published by Poisoned Pen Press 2006. Used by permission.

"Unbalanced" ©2012, 2104 by Craig Johnson, from *Wait for Signs: Twelve Longmire Stories* by Craig Johnson; used by permission of Brandt & Hochman Literary Agents, Inc and Penguin Random House LLC.

COVER AND BOOK DESIGN:
KG Design International
www.katgeorges.com

DISTRIBUTED BY:
PGW/Ingram
www.pgw.com

Three Rooms Press
New York, NY
www.threeroomspress.com
info@threeroomspress.com

TABLE OF CONTENTS

FOREWORD
BY JIM FUSILLI

I don't suppose it would be much of a surprise to discover that there's a dark and deadly side to the world of popular music.

Fraud, embezzlement, and larceny. Institutional stupidity. Rampant deceit. Money vanishes, backs are stabbed, careers are crushed. Art? Er, no. The album is a product to be commercialized; the concert a chance to move drinks and merch. Better you should have gone to Wharton than Berklee. The promise of a fabulous meal at sunset on a gorgeous island turns into a bologna sandwich to eat in the back of the bus. As Hunter S. Thompson said, "The music business is a cruel and shallow money trench, a long plastic hallway where thieves and pimps run free, and good men die like dogs. There's also a negative side." What's surprising is that musicians in droves haven't taken up the simple art of murder. Yet.

Welcome to *Crime Plus Music*, the anthology that offers exactly what it claims: crime stories that are inspired by music, in particular rock and pop. If, as the ancient maxim goes, music hath charms to soothe the savage beast, in *Crime Plus Music* it stirs in the souls of men and women the savage beast that will awaken with murderously foul intent. You are warned: Songs familiar and not so will be brought to mind, yes, but there will be blood.

I'M BLESSED TO LIVE A bifurcated life: I'm the author of eight mystery and crime novels; and the rock and pop critic of the *Wall Street Journal*, as well as editor and founder of ReNewMusic.net. My worlds collide when I meet other authors of crime, mystery, and suspense novels and short stories at writers' conferences, luncheons, bookstores, and social events including, but not limited to, weddings, funerals, and card games. Inevitably, the conversation turns to music. As you may have noticed, most people not only like music, they also like to talk about the kind of music they like. Given that most writers think creatively and understand the artist's mindset, they have insight into music that makes the conversations a pleasure. You'd never know that, while you're talking to them, they are scheming up ways to kill and maim characters in the stories they're working on. The spark for the idea for *Crime Plus Music* came out of these conversations with many of the writers who appear in this anthology.

I'd written a few short stories that were set in the music world and I found them a pleasure to do: As noted, bad guys abound; and you can give your tale a soundtrack. After proposing the idea for the anthology to the publishers, I set out to invite as participants many of the best crime and mystery short story writers of our time. It is our great luck—yours and mine—that so many agreed. The crime and mystery community, comprising fans, authors, editors, publishers, critics, and bloggers, is about the most welcoming and supportive that you'll ever find. But even knowing that, I was thrilled at the response. I hope you will be too.

Some of the names in this book are stars in that community: Craig Johnson is the gifted writer who gave us Walt Longmire, the Wyoming sheriff you know not only from Craig's deeply satisfying books, but from the TV series, *Longmire*; Val McDermid, whose intense novels featuring the psychologist Tony Hill were the source for the TV series, *Wire in the Blood*; and Peter Robinson, whose tales featuring Inspector Alan Banks are as delightful (and occasionally terrifying) as the TV series *DCI Banks* that emerged from them. With Val and Peter, our relationship has as much to do with music as books: on several occasions, I played guitar as Val sang, ominously, the song that inspired her short story in this collection, "The Long Black Veil." I once traveled to a gig in Ontario without my guitar and Peter allowed me to use his. As I said, a welcoming and supportive community.

The other writers in this anthology deserve better billing than "the other writers" in this book. I'll leave it at this: their stories will tell you why they are so admired by readers and authors alike. If you've yet to read some of them, you're in for a treat—and you may find that you'll be seeking their books in order to continue your flight with their excellence.

I want to draw your attention to two writers who haven't been associated with the crime and mystery community until now: Galadrielle Allman and Willy Vlautin. Galadrielle is the author of *Please Be with Me: A Song for My Father, Duane Allman*, which is a miraculous combination of memoir and biography of one of rock's great musicians. As for Willy, as his work with his band Richmond Fontaine shows, he is a master storyteller, a skill that is amply evident in his novels of the hardscrabble life in the American West. Their contributions raise the level of quality in our collection.

With that, welcome again to *Crime Plus Music*. Enjoy not only the wonderful tales told by some of our best writers, but also how, every now and then, the clenched fist of fate gives some of the music world's bad guys the cosmic beating they deserve.

—*Jim Fusilli*

THE LAST TEMPTATION OF FRANKIE LYMON
BY PETER BLAUNER

HE WALKED INTO THE BAR wearing the jacket that Sam bought for the *Ebony* photo shoot last year. A mostly wool blazer with two rows of brass buttons, that must have cost—what?—like forty to fifty dollars at Blumstein's. He felt bad because Sam was living on about two hundred a week as food inspector in the Bronx, while trying to manage the comeback for him. But what could you do? All the star clothes he used to have in his grandmother's closet were either child-sized and long ago outgrown or had holes in them because he'd nodded off with a cigarette in his mouth.

So now the jacket felt heavy as a burden on his shoulders as he eyed his surroundings and tried to get comfortable. The bar was around the corner from his grandmother's and he half recognized some of the people from the neighborhood, where he hadn't lived since back in the day. There were mailmen and bus drivers wearing turtlenecks or open-collared shirts with jeans. Doormen and janitors in T-shirts and growing out their hair into bushy naturals as they rapped effort-lessly to short-skirted former double Dutch girls from the block with sleepy eyes and soft mouths, who kept going "uh-huh, uh-huh, right on" as that Gladys Knight "Grapevine" song played on the jukebox.

He felt like a square by comparison, with his blazer, his rep tie, and the perfect part in his processed hair, but he put up a front and strutted by like he was on his way to play the London Palladium again. But from the corner of his eye, he could see the stray looks in the smoked mirror; people kind of half recognizing his squished-angel's face and dice-dot eyes from before his voice changed. Or maybe just wondering if he *thought* he used to be someone.

He half wished he'd stayed in tonight. But it had been so long since he'd done anything worth celebrating. This afternoon in the studio, something had happened. He didn't know if it was the band or the melody or the lyrics. For one take, though, he'd found a way to get inside that song. It was just some trifle about a town called Sea Breeze where a man could see the lights and finally find peace. But for three minutes and twenty-two seconds, he was completely himself again, after all these years. For that alone, he deserved some little reward. Didn't he?

There was a Wurlitzer jukebox at the back, a lit-up mini-cathedral made of glass, walnut, grinding gears, and vinyl. He went to it and scanned the titles. They had a couple of tracks by the Supremes that even the Flintstones could have turned into hits; "Respect" by Aretha Franklin, which he literally would have killed to get his hands on; and something called "Green Tambourine" by the Lemon Pipers. Weird white people music by boys who relied on studio tricks and probably couldn't carry a tune in a bucket if their lives depended on it. And there, near the bottom of the fourth column, at P-9, was "Why Do Fools Fall In Love?" by Frankie Lymon and the Teenagers.

The quarter was in his hand before he knew what he'd do with it. He was torn between wanting to play his own hit to remind everyone who he was, and being embarrassed about the potential for more soul-scouring humiliation.

Three songs for twenty-five cents. The coin dropped and he pictured a ball bouncing between the slots of a spinning wheel.

Round and round she goes, where it stops . . . He punched in that "Dock of the Bay" song that just came out and then "Wonderful World" by Sam Cooke, who he'd envied to the point of sickness until Sam got himself shot to death by a pissed-off lady in a motel room. Which left one more choice. As the needle found the groove for his first pick, he hit the button for "Fools" and stepped away like he'd just lit a fuse on a stack of dynamite. Giving himself just enough time to make a quick exit if the shame got to be too much.

"What song you put on, Frankie?"

A woman was sitting at the end of the bar, grinning at him, with her purse on the counter, next to an empty martini glass with an olive at the bottom. She wasn't young and it didn't look like her first drink. When she opened her mouth, her front teeth were a little irregular. But when she blinked her long lashes made him think of the way a drummer's brushes softly touch the skins when the music gets slow and sad and sweet.

"Do I know you?" he asked.

She, too, looked vaguely familiar. But there had been so many. He used to brag that by the time he was twelve he'd learned everything there was to know about women, and had kept going anyway. Pimping since he was ten. Dating ladies twice his age when he was on the road with the Teenagers. Shooting skag with a woman old enough to be his mother when he should have been in high school. Married three times by the time he was twenty-five, but never formally divorced from any of them.

"Do you think you know me?" she said, as lapping waves ushered in Otis Redding sounding all mellow and elegiac over a lightly strummed guitar.

"If I don't, I'm about to get to know you." He claimed the stool beside her.

Here it was again: the game. He only hoped it wouldn't be over too soon. The distance between "Oooh, Frankie, Frankie" and "Get out my life, you washed-up little motherfucker" seemed to be getting shorter and shorter these days.

He snapped his fingers twice to get the bartender's attention, but got nothing but a blank stare. She batted her lashes once and the man came right over.

"Give me another In and Out Martini and use the Noilly Prat gin this time." She looked at Frankie. "He's paying."

"I'll have a Rum and Coke," Frankie said.

It sounded like a little kid's drink. Or worse, a drink for a junkie with a sweet tooth. "Use the Bacardi," he said, trying to class it up. "And a lime if you got one."

"Where you been, Frankie?"

UP CLOSE, SHE HAD THE kind of face that was mature and interesting at certain angles, and a little dissolute and scary at others. Under those long lashes, her eyes were more sunken than they first appeared and her smile had heavy brackets.

"Oh, you know. Just to the stars and back."

"I heard you were living in Georgia."

"I was." He leaned against the counter. "But how you gonna keep a boy down on the farm after he's seen the farm? Know how I'm saying?"

"I do."

In fact, he'd gone AWOL from the army, trying to hustle club gigs, and had gotten himself dishonorably discharged. Lucky not to be court-martialed and in the brig by now.

"Who's paying for you to be back up here?" she asked.

"I still got some bridges I haven't burned. I did a session for Roulette Records today."

"Oh yeah?"

"Song called 'Sea Breeze.' I think it could do something."

"Roulette? Isn't that Morris Levy?"

"What you know about Morris?"

She showed him a bit of her crooked teeth again. Apparently even people who weren't in the music business knew about Morris by now. About his office full of gold records and his bloodsucker contracts, about the songwriting royalties he got for music that he'd never heard, about the way people around him got dangled out of windows or stabbed in the stomach with shards of glass. The man was so mobbed up that the Mafia killed his brother and he kept working with them anyway. But he was pretty much the last man in the industry who would still take Frankie's calls and pay for his studio time, so why let pride set the terms?

"I know you're playing Russian Roulette by being on Roulette again," she said.

"Baby." He shook his head. "My whole life is Russian Roulette."

If he wasn't taking a chance on another comeback, he was taking a chance on another woman. And if he wasn't doing that, he was putting a needle in his arm, knowing that one of these days he was probably going to hit one of those bad batches that were always going around. Just a matter of time. Like Johnny Ace putting a pistol to his head backstage on Christmas Day when he had "Pledging My Love" on the charts. Everything eventually came around.

The bartender put down their drinks and went away, as Otis Redding rolled off with the tide and Frankie started to get a little unnerved by the steady way she was looking at him.

"Hey, why you asking so many questions?" he said.

Normal people, in his experience, usually weren't that interested in anyone else. Even around celebrities, they found a way to make the conversation about themselves.

"You're still Frankie Lymon, ain't you?"

"If anybody remembers."

He looked around at the other customers deep in conversation, bobbing their heads and swinging their legs as Sam Cooke came on, all suave and seductive.

"Who's gonna forget 'Why Do Fools Fall In Love?'" she said. "How did you write it anyway?"

"I'm an artist." He shrugged. "I got inspired. That's what artists do."

He took a quick sip off his drink, without taking the little red straw out first, trying to sand the edge off his growing nervousness. He'd always been a jumpy kid, eager to get out of the crowded house he grew up in and into more worldly business. Which was a fine thing when he was a teen idol in a white varsity sweater, singing to the rafters, dancing like Sammy Davis Jr.'s bop-crazed little brother, and working the lip of the stage. And less fine once his voice dropped.

"Thirteen years old." She shook her head. "You're singing, 'Why do birds sing so gay?' That sounds like some Emily Dickinson shit, doesn't it?"

He shrugged. "Just wise before my time, I guess."

"I read how you said it started as a poem you wrote for school and then you turned into a song."

"Yeah. I guess I said that."

He'd said a lot of things, to a lot of different people. And some of them were true, sometimes. He wondered if this could be some kind of lawyer set up, meant to pry his name off the song completely. When they first cut it, the producer George Goldner copped half the composer credit and put his name next to Frankie's on the label. Then George got in deep to gamblers and had to give the credit to Morris, to get out from behind the eight-ball. So maybe this lady was a plant to help Morris get the rest while he was pretending to still be Frankie's patron by paying for the studio time.

"We went down to Times Square to audition for Gee Records— Herman, Jimmy, Joe, Sherman, and me," Frankie said uneasily, trying to stick to the story as he'd told it a million times before. "I wasn't even the lead singer then. I was just an annoying little kid with a high voice. So we sang them all these songs the Jacks and the Spaniels did. But they said, nah, make that little one the singer and give us a new song. So I came up with 'Fools.' And then it went on the radio. And then we went on tour with Alan Freed and Little Richard and the Platters, and the rest is rock and roll history."

"You know what I think?" Something at the corner of her smile cut him more than it should have.

"What do you think?"

"I think you're a lying motherfucker, Frankie Lymon."

He stuck his chin out. "Yeah, why is that?"

"You never could have written that song on your own."

"Why not?"

He looked around at the other patrons to see if they were listening. But they were all deep in their own bags, either lost in each other or listening to Sam Cooke's smooth insinuations with half-closed eyes.

"Because I wrote those words," she said. "And you took them."

"How could I do that? I never even met you before."

"The letters," she said, reaching for her purse on the counter.

"What letters?"

"You know the damn letters I'm talking about." She put the purse on her lap. "Before you made it big? When your friends were practicing in the hallway of that building on 165th and Edgecombe? Singing 'Goodnight Sweetheart' and 'Why Don't You Write Me?' over and over? Who do you think was upstairs?"

"Who?"

"The answer is *me*." One of her lashes stuck together. "That's where I was living. When I was in love with a man across the hall. Mr. Kenny Tyrone. Who made me feel things that no woman has ever felt before. Do you understand what I'm saying?"

He drained half his drink. "I don't know why I'd care."

"Because I taught poetry to little punk-ass students like you and I knew how to put my feelings into words. And I put those words into letters. And I gave those letters to Mr. Kenny Tyrone. And he gave those letters to your friends because he didn't want his wife to find them and because he got sick of hearing you all sing the same damn words over and over. And then you put them in your song."

"This is a lie." Frankie shook his head, refusing to look at her.

"It's not a lie." She used her fingers to peel off the misbehaving lash. "Because at dawn every day, Kenny's wife would go to work early at Presbyterian Hospital. Then I'd go across the hall. Because I had an hour and a half before the first class I had to teach at Stitt Junior High. And I lived for those mornings, because my life was so lonely the rest of the time. I'd sit by that window looking out over 165th Street, waiting for the sun to rise over Highbridge so she would go and I could live again. And I'd listen and I'd ask myself, 'Why do lovers await the break of day?'"

"That's just one line." Frankie finished his drink.

"That's the whole damn song, Frankie. It's all about waiting for the break of day. It's not about *being* in love. It's about *falling* in love. Dumb as you are, even you understand that. Otherwise you couldn't have sung it the way you did."

He looked away from her with a sinking feeling. Of course, it was true. He was reminded of it every time he heard the song. It wasn't about the thing when it happened. It was about imagining what it would be like just before it happened. Like when he was standing backstage at the Apollo, listening to all the girls scream, like they were promising all the love in the world. Before he realized it would never be enough.

"You taught at Stitt?"

"For ten years."

"I ever have you?"

"Only as a substitute. And you were a fresh-mouth lying little motherfucker even then."

He stared at her until the fog of years parted and she became faintly recognizable as Miss Brooks, the seventh-grade English teacher. Hiding behind her glasses with her hair up in a bun and her pigeon-toed walk with her flat shoes and long skirt that made a seething sound when she walked.

She looked completely different now. The glasses were gone, along with one of her eyelashes. The sunken eye looking back at him had seen to the bottom of too many things. Of too many high-ball glasses, of too many lies, of too many men who couldn't live up to their own promise. She didn't believe in homework or steady diligence or poems or love songs that could change your life anymore. She was just looking for something to take her away for a while. And the thing that bothered Frankie the most was that it was like looking straight in the mirror.

"What happened to you?" he said.

"You're not the only one who's had a hard time, Frankie."

"You're not teaching anymore?"

"I got depressed. Especially after Kenny gave you all those letters and then moved away. He betrayed me. And I had to think about that every time that song came on the radio. And that's why I cursed you."

"You cursed me?"

"Let me tell you something, Frankie." She slid to the edge of her stool, so he could smell the rancidness of her breath mixing with lavender. "I went to City College, and I studied romantic poetry. I wrote my thesis on Keats. But some of my people were from the islands. And they know all about Voodoo and Yoruba. I lit a candle to try to get Kenny to come back to me. And when that didn't work, I lit a candle to put a curse on all of you."

"I don't believe in any of that." Frankie took the little red straw out of his drink and put it in an ashtray.

"Ask yourself. Doesn't it seem like everyone who touched that song got cursed?"

He smirked and raised the drink to his mouth, even as his mind started revolving. Morris's brother stabbed to death at Birdland. George Goldner broke and on his last legs with gambling debts. Alan Freed disgraced, forgotten, and dead with cirrhosis at twenty-three. And Frankie himself an addict since fifteen, in and out of rehabilitation ever since, living his life like the Furies were after him.

"You may have cursed everyone else but it doesn't look like you're not doing too well yourself."

"That's how it goes with some curses." She looked down at the purse. "You call forth the darkness, it overtakes you too. I got so down about what happened with Kenny and that song that I stopped being able to get out of bed in the morning to go to work. So they fired me. And then the same curse I put on you got put on me."

He saw now that her hands were swollen and her arms were unnaturally skinny in her puffy sleeves. If he rolled them up, he knew she'd have almost as many track marks as he did.

"That's not a curse," he said. "That's drugs."

"There's a difference?"

"Look." He spun away from her on his stool. "I'm broke too. If you know anything about me, you know it's true. If you want a piece of my song, go talk to the lawyers. Because I haven't seen a dime off it in years. And most of what I had I put in my arm, like you did."

The Sam Cooke song had ended and the next song started. And there was Sherman doing the deep bass intro. "Ehh-de-doom-wopa-de-doom-wop-de-doom wop duh-duh . . ." Before Frankie came in with the other fellows, his high voice all velvet and brass, with streetwise choirboy sass. "Ooo-wah. Ooo-wah . . ."

She started rummaging through her bag. All at once, he realized there were no accidents. Curses were real. She hadn't just seen him randomly in the bar. And he hadn't just randomly picked Sam Cooke on the jukebox. The purse bulged as she put her hand in it and he thought he discerned the shape of a gun.

"You owe me something, Frankie. And you know it."

Ever since Sam Cooke died, he'd had a premonition that he'd go the same way. But he thought that it would be one of his wives who pulled the trigger.

"I'm sorry." He put his hands up, his voice cracking in the wrong way. "But I don't have anything left to give you. It's all been took or given away."

In the background, his young voice seemed to mock him. Young Frankie wailing, "Tell me why, tell me whyyyyy" before giving way to the bodacious blare of Mr. Wright's dirty hot sax solo, which promised decidedly adult pleasures just down the pike.

She pulled a crumpled Kleenex from the purse. "I want you to acknowledge me."

"Okay, you're acknowledged." He dropped his hands. "Now let me be."

"That's not enough. I know Morris Levy must have put a few dollars in your pocket when he brought you back up here."

"Barely enough to put a song on the jukebox."

She bunched up the tissue in her hand. "I know a spot around the corner where they say Charlie Parker and Billie Holiday used to score."

"Uh, Miss Brooks, I'm supposed to be trying to stay clean, case you hadn't heard."

And God knew, it wouldn't take much to get him chipping again. His doctor at Manhattan Psych said he never saw an addict more determined to get a hypo in his arm.

"Come on, Frankie. I'm just trying to get what I need, same as you."

"And what is it you think I need?"

She sighed. "We both know that if you had another verse, it wouldn't be about fools in love, or rain from above, but 'why's someone in pain put a stick in his vein?' Some things just got to be."

He watched her blow her nose and in the dim light of the bar, he almost reached out to touch her tracks. She was right. They were the same. Chasing that feeling they once had. She'd gotten it when she was sitting by the window waiting for Kenny Tyrone's wife to leave so she could go across the hall. He'd gotten it when he was waiting to hit that seraphim-clear high note that would make girls scream. And less and less these days, when he was waiting for the powder to stir up his blood and bring on the rush.

As the sax break finished and his old voice came back in with Herman, Jimmy, Joe, and Sherman, he saw a couple of the other patrons look at him, bop their heads nonchalantly and smile. And he had the strangest sensation that he was here but already gone. The people were taking the song and making it their own, like the guy who sang it wasn't standing among them like a ghost. It was part of their stories now. His presence was irrelevant. He was just a vague memory to them, not significant for who he was, but for how he reminded them of how it used to be in their own lives.

For a half second, he thought about what it would have been like if he'd never gotten his hands on her letters. Then there never would have been that song and they wouldn't have gotten past the audition. He would've stayed in this neighborhood, working as a delivery boy at the grocery down the block and occasionally picking up two dollars for steering white men to the whores across the street. He would've limped through high school and maybe caught on with some crappy little civil service job or wound up driving a truck. There would've been no "Fools Fall In Love," no Alan Freed Tour, no rock and roll. He would've been just like these other people in the bar, drinking his wages and trying to forget his troubles. Or, just as likely, shivering through withdrawal for the umpteenth time and awaiting trial in a Rikers Island cell.

What was the difference? It was over now. "Sea Breeze" would never chart, and he knew it. He'd never play the Palladium or the Apollo again. He would just keep trying to hit that high note until he wound up face down on damp tiles, a fallen junkie-angel crashed out on a bathroom floor.

Maybe it wouldn't happen tonight, but it would be another night and soon. He'd hang up the jacket Sam had bought for him and roll up the sleeve his grandmother had ironed, and he'd let this woman—or someone else—stick a needle in and that would be that. And then the legend wouldn't just be That Song anymore but The Bag of Heroin that Killed Frankie Lymon.

Meanwhile, the young Frankie was still on the record, and would always be, full of light and hope, singing his heart out in a voice full of promise, taking a breath to make that one last daredevil acrobatic leap into the upper register as the other guys' vocals gathered to cushion him in case he slipped off the note, but he held it and held it until the engineer started to fade him too soon and the band hustled to get the triumphant last beat in under the wire.

"Don't look so sad, Frankie." Miss Brooks closed her bag and stood. "We got up there once, didn't we?"

"I know that." He nodded, somehow relieved that it was over. "It's just everybody else I feel sorry for."

THE BLACKBIRD
BY PETER ROBINSON

IT ENDED WITH A HEAD floating down the river. Or is that where it began? You never could be certain with The Blackbird. I should know. I've known him for years, and I was with him until the end. Well, almost.

His real name was Tony Foster, and once, quite early in our relationship, I asked him how he had acquired his nickname. Tony drew on his cigarette in that way of his, cupping it in his palm like a soldier in the trenches, as if he believed it would be bad luck to let anyone see the glow. He turned his blue eyes towards me, a hint of a smile lighting them for a moment, then he looked away and told me it came about when he was a teenager growing up on a rundown council estate in the mid sixties.

Tony and his parents lived at the far end of the estate, and there was a ratty old tree a bit further on, by the main road. It had hardly any leaves, even in summer, and the ones it did boast were a sickly sort of yellow. Somehow, though, like Tony, the tree survived.

One spring morning he was woken early by the most beautiful birdsong. He thought it was coming from the tree. All he could do was lie there transfixed and feel himself tingle all over, the hairs on the back of his neck standing on end. He had no idea what kind of bird it was. Being a city boy, he only recognized the sparrows that fought over crumbs on the pavement and the pigeons that made a hell of a racket across the street.

Mr. and Mrs. Fox lived next door in a house that smelled of pipe smoke and boiled cabbage. Tony used to drop by sometimes to see if they were okay and if they needed anything from the shops. Mr. Fox never said much. Tony's dad told him it was because the old man had fought in Burma, where he got captured by the Japanese and sent to a prison camp. Mrs. Fox had shown Tony some medals and photos of men in uniforms smiling in a jungle clearing, but Mr. Fox wouldn't talk about what they did to him there. He just clamped his mouth down on his pipe and stared at a fixed spot on the opposite wall, his jaw muscles so tense they quivered. But Tony had seen *The Bridge on the River Kwai,* and he didn't lack imagination.

The Foxes seemed to know a lot about most things, Tony had discovered, so after he had been listening to the strange bird singing for a few days, he asked them what it was. Mrs. Fox told him it was a blackbird and went on to tell him that it had made its nest in the old tree. She could see it from her bedroom window. The nest was rather messy, she added, and the tree itself was hardly the most suitable environment for a blackbird, which surely must be choking on all the exhaust fumes. And as if all that wasn't bad enough, the poor creature had a damaged wing, too. He flew slightly off-kilter and was very wobbly on his landings. He looked lopsided, too, she said, when he was perching on a branch—the wing not folded up quite right. But for all that, Mrs. Fox concluded, he did have a beautiful song.

Then Mrs. Fox asked him if he knew why the blackbird was singing. Tony admitted that he didn't. It was then that Mrs. Fox said what he thought was a very strange thing. She told Tony it was because the blackbird was looking for a true love to share his nest. It was because he was trying to attract a *mate.*

TONY TOLD ME THAT HE was enthralled to hear about this black-bird with the gimpy wing sitting in its messy nest and singing a beautiful song. Somehow, it struck a chord deep inside him. He had lived a very sheltered life, dominated by illness, and the only kind of *mate* he knew about was the kind you had at school— friends, pals—though he didn't have any friends, himself. Even so, the more he listened to the blackbird, the more he identified with it. They had so much in common, except the singing. Tony said he began to believe that if only he could sing like that, then maybe he would have pals and mates, too. Maybe they would over-look his limp and his sick room pallor.

From then on, Tony thought of himself privately as "The Blackbird." Not very long after, he began to feel all sorts of con-fusing emotions about girls that he had never felt before, and when he learned what a true love and a mate really were, he set about learning with a vengeance and a passion. Despite his game leg, he got a part-time job at a mushroom farm as well as morning and evening newspaper rounds, and with the money he made, he bought a beat-up acoustic guitar from a pawnshop and paid for singing and music lessons. His voice had a touch of Tim Buckley with a hint of the more bluesy Van Morrison thrown in for good measure, and though the guitar was hard for him at first, he worked at it and developed a fine, individual style.

Tony was wise enough to realize even so early that a human singer needs more than just a fine voice and a pretty melody; he needs good words, too, so he started to write his own songs. Luckily, he had hardly been to school, so teachers hadn't had a chance to knock the love of poetry out of him. He had spent many of his days in his sickbed reading Tennyson and Kipling and Wordsworth, even as a child. He loved the magic and the music of words, so in many ways he was a natural. He started out with the simple boy-meets-girl pop songs of the times, though he had never been out with a girl, let alone kissed one, and as time went on his songwriting developed into that more complex mix of myth, social comment, angst, and mysticism that became the hallmark of his later years. He loved the old sixties guys best—Bob Dylan, Leonard Cohen, Paul Simon. These were his heroes, his models. These were the poets he imitated when he hit his stride in his late teens.

I only heard him later, after the lessons, but I guessed that he must have had natural potential from the start. After all, you can't improve on what's not there in the first place, can you?

THE FIRST TIME I SAW Tony perform was in 1969 at a folk club held in the upstairs room of a pub. He was about eighteen or nineteen, and it seemed to me that he already had an enthusiastic audience. One of the young female folk singers on that night's bill told me that he was a regular, and he performed there most weeks. People just couldn't seem to get enough of him, she said. I also noticed an odd kind of wistful yearning in her eyes when she looked at him.

He was certainly nothing to look at. There he sat on a stool on the stage, all dressed in black, skinny as a rail, always half in the shadows, lock of dark hair hanging over one eye, misshapen foot propped on a cushion, eyes on the floor, face pale with that strange, haunted consumptive look he seemed to retain all his life, yet he could have had his pick of any of the girls in the room. His voice and words took them to places where he was whole and handsome and virile and just a little bit dangerous. And at the same time, there was an aura of sadness, of innocence, and vulnerability about him that the girls seemed to find irresistible. He hurt, and they wanted to make it better.

I went back to the club week after week and found that every set strengthened my original conviction that here was a talent to be reckoned with. I was a good ten years older than Tony, and I prided myself in already knowing a bit about the music business. I had briefly managed a couple of folk bands some years back, and I thought I could at least get this kid a start. I didn't fool myself that I could hang on to someone with his kind of talent, and if anyone had told me then I'd be his manager right to the end, I wouldn't have believed them.

And if they had told me how that end would come about, I wouldn't have believed that, either.

NATURALLY, THE FIRST FEW YEARS were a slog. People seem to think that stars appear out of nowhere, come fully fledged off *Britain's Got Talent*, for example, and some do, no doubt about it. But even with talent, you have to have luck, and with luck you have to have passion and drive. Tony had all these, but it wasn't until he put the band together and took them on the road about three years after I first met him that things started to move ahead quickly. Word of mouth is a wonderful thing, and people were already singing the praises of this weird guy with the unbelievable voice. He mentioned the blackbird that had inspired him in an interview with *Melody Maker* and so the legend of The Blackbird was born.

Tony was always a hard worker. He was willing to gig every night and spend the rest of his time in the studio. Soon there was a debut album in the works, and that opened a lot of doors. Some of his songs were obvious single material and made the charts, but it was the albums that did the most for him. The early seventies was still very much the age of the album. Then there were the live concerts. Word was getting around fast that you simply had to see this guy live. Be there, or be square, as they used to say in an earlier age.

As for the girls, they couldn't stay away. Tony may even have succumbed to one or two—he was only human, after all—but I noticed an odd reticence about him, a sort of deep inner reserve, as if he were waiting for someone. The right someone, I suppose, though it sounds corny to say it. Tony was *saving himself* for the true love, the real *mate*. Like the blackbird he had told me about, he was singing his song, and when it was good enough, she would come.

And I was there when she turned up.

IT HAPPENED AT A RARE solo acoustic gig in one of those banquet halls where you can have dinner before the act and keep on sipping your champagne or nibbling at your Black Forest *gâteau* during the performance. It wasn't Tony's normal sort of gig, but he was doing a favor for the club manager, who had given him a lot of support in the early days and had fallen on hard times. The tickets were expensive, the crowd hip and wealthy and primed for something special.

Tony sang mostly his own songs, but he did do the occasional cover, homage to his heroes, and I remember that night he sang Dylan's "Eternal Circle." Perhaps the song cast a spell on the evening, but it describes almost exactly how things went. Perhaps he even performed it with her in mind, as it wasn't exactly in regular rotation on his set list.

She was sitting at a table with some friends, and there might as well have been a spotlight on her. Their eyes met and held. For once, Tony's gaze wasn't fixed on the floor. I could feel the waves of desire and attraction pulsate between them. At the end of Tony's set, she was still there, whereas the girl in the Dylan song had left. And I have to say that I have never heard Tony sing so well, so soulful and heartfelt. He wasn't showy at all, but actually quite subdued, and absolutely spot on. His voice soared effortlessly into places it had never been before, and he took the audience's emotions wherever he wanted to take them.

After the set, Tony couldn't just walk off the stage into the audience and take her hand. They'd tear him to bits, civilized as they seemed. The applause seemed to go on forever, then there was the obligatory encore. And another. But some sort of signal must have passed between the two of them, because when Tony got back to his dressing room, she was waiting for him.

HER NAME WAS CONNIE, AND perhaps it's stating the obvious to say how beautiful she was, to mention the luster of her tumbling auburn hair, those large dark eyes and the full lips just crying out to be kissed. And her figure—slight, but curved in all the right places. That night she was wearing a satiny green dress, I remember, fairly low cut and ending halfway down her thighs, showing off her long slim legs to perfection. But her beauty was more than just her looks. It went deeper. I could sense that even on our first meeting. She had an inner intelligence, beauty, and calm; she had *soul*, and she made an immediate and electric connection with Tony.

Connie was in her early twenties, like Tony, and in no time they were chatting away as if they had known one another all their lives. Tony later told me that after I'd left, they went back to her flat and did nothing but sit up and talk about art and books and drink wine and listen to Roy Harper, Al Stewart, and Bert Jansch until dawn. The closest they came to anything sexual was holding hands and looking into one another's eyes. There was certainly no lack of desire between them, he said, but that night, talking and wine and music were enough.

I liked Connie. People have said that I was jealous, among other things, that I felt she came between Tony and me, or Tony and the band, but that's simply not true. I loved her like a sister, and she was good for Tony. She was wise beyond words. If ever he got upset about anything, all she had to do was touch him gently and he calmed down right away. She was also a very talented artist and had paintings hanging in famous collections and galleries. I liked her stuff well enough, but to me it was abstract art, and it always surprised me that her most loyal fans saw so much more in it, a reflection of their own desires and struggles and images of the enslavement of women over the ages. I never saw any of that; they were just colored shapes to me. Beautiful shapes, and expertly arranged, but only shapes and colors, nonetheless. Still, she had her loyal followers, and she had ties with a loosely knit group or movement of female artists who wanted to lift up the art world by the scruff of its neck and shake it.

With Connie in his life, Tony's songs got even better, his stage presence more assured, more confident. Even though The Blackbird had attracted his mate, that didn't diminish the beauty of his song. Now Tony looked audiences in the eye, and even his game leg didn't seem such an encumbrance any more. His skin was still pale, though, and its whiteness still burned with that consumptive fire.

Tony and Connie got married the following April. It was a joyous occasion followed by a wonderful party, during which the bride and groom slipped away for a brief honeymoon in Paris. The band had a new album coming out in May, and he would be out on the road promoting it when they got back. For now, everything was hunky-dory.

For now.

DRUGS IS A SUBJECT THAT comes up a lot when people talk about rock music. It's hardly surprising, given the number of musicians who have succumbed to excess over the years. Jimi Hendrix, Janis Joplin, and Jim Morrison had all died just a short time before Tony became famous. And the list goes on. Tony smoked a bit of dope occasionally, but that was all, as far as I knew. I was with him on that. I didn't mind the occasional joint, but I had seen far too many talented people fall afoul of the hard stuff, or end up with their brains short-circuited by hallucinogens. Perhaps more than anything, Tony became fond of wine, especially now that he could afford the really good stuff. When he let his hair down—which wasn't as often as the media made out—you'd more than likely find him drinking Château Latour or Château Margaux. But the hard stuff, never. Not coke or smack. Not even scotch or vodka.

Connie was a different story. Despite her inner calm and wisdom, a part of her was strongly attracted to the dark side. She read Thomas De Quincey, Coleridge, Huysmans, Gérard de Nerval, Rimbaud, Burroughs. She loved Bosch, Goya, and Dali. The whole idea of a rational derangement of all the senses fascinated her and, she believed, nurtured her art. If there is any truth in the media rumors about a conflict between Connie and me, this is where it has its origins.

In the early days of their life together, Connie would accompany Tony and the band on tour. She got to see the world that way: America, Australia, Japan, South Africa. But she didn't like touring, the hanging about waiting, lengthy sound checks, crowds, long hours in hotel rooms, then the constant rush to a new city every day, with little or no real chance to see anything or meet anyone. And her painting was suffering, too; she wanted to get back to her studio. Even her followers and group members were complaining of neglect. She began to stay home more often, but as the lonely days dragged on, she would become restless. She and Tony had recently moved into an Elizabethan mansion on a country estate, and the large empty rooms and grounds only seemed to emphasize her isolation. She painted a lot and had her artist friends over to visit her, but it just wasn't enough.

Mostly, as far as any of us knew, she kept her drug use under control, and when Tony came home, everything would appear as much as normal. Certainly there were no dawn police raids, no naked women wrapped in fur rugs and rumors of obscene acts with Mars bars. But we found out later that Connie was taking uppers and downers just to maintain the semblance of normality. When Tony was away, especially for lengthy periods of time, she began to drive down to London more often and fell in with some very shady characters on the fringes of the art world, with whom she delved deeper into the darkness, into the world of coke, hallucinogens, and the drug that became her favorite of all: heroin.

ONE DAY, TONY ARRIVED HOME late from the a long studio session and called Connie's name. Getting no answer, he went from room to room and finally found her in their bedroom. She was lying fully clothed on the king-size bed, pale and still, a needle and spoon on the bedspread beside her.

Tony felt frantically for a pulse on Connie's wrist, then her neck, but he could sense no signs of life. The muscles around her throat and jaw felt stiff. He grabbed for the telephone and dialed

999, then he picked Connie up from the bed. Her skin was cool to the touch, and he felt her dead weight in his arms. First he tried to get her on her feet walking around, but she was like a heavy rag doll in his hands and her feet just dragged along the carpet. He tried to perform CPR as best he could, imitating actions he had seen on television, but he found that he couldn't even get her mouth open to breathe air into her.

They weren't far from the county town, and soon he could hear the sound of an ambulance approaching. Laying Connie gently back on the bed, he dashed down and practically pushed the attendants up the stairs in front of him. They kept him well back as they got Connie on a stretcher and took her to the ambulance. He noticed one of the attendants shake his head and cover her face with the sheet before closing the doors.

As Tony had suspected, he had been a few hours too late. There was nothing more he could have done, the doctors said. The heroin Connie had injected came from an unusually strong batch. She had hardly had time to get the needle out of her arm. The stuff had already killed two junkies in town, and warnings were out, but nobody listened. Needless to say, the police searched the house from top to bottom, took blood samples from Tony and then "interviewed" him for hours without pause—they had no Police and Criminal Evidence Act to hamper their style back then—but in the end they had to let him go. The media made much of Connie's death, of course—from the screaming headlines in the tabloids about the sick and immoral culture of rock music to more carefully written and thought out pieces in the quality press by establishment figures educated at Eton and Oxford.

So began a long dark period of grieving for Tony, a period he thought at times would never end. And perhaps it never really did. For over a year he wrote no songs, performed no concerts, did very little, in fact, except stay in his room or, when the mood took him, go for long walks around the estate. On one of these walks, he came across three women trespassing on his land. He said nothing, as he didn't really care about property rights, but as he passed, one of them threw something at him, and he heard another hiss, "Murderer!" He ran back to the house, and when he got to the bathroom he saw that he was covered in red paint.

After that, Tony hardly went out at all. He also never watched television, listened to the radio, or read the newspapers, so he could have no idea of the storm brewing, of Connie's followers and group members desecrating her grave with anti-Blackbird graffiti and insisting that Tony was responsible for Connie's death, that he had murdered a far more talented and important artist than he would ever be. According to them, he had introduced her to the drugs lifestyle, then abandoned her for his rock-and-roll life on the road with groupies after every gig. It wasn't true. Tony had always shied away from groupies every bit as much as he kept clear of hard drugs, but even if he had known what they were saying about him, any attempt he made to defend himself would have only dug him deeper in the hole.

I handled most of it by ignoring it, issuing the occasional blanket denial and keeping it from Tony, which wasn't difficult. I didn't take the matter seriously. I thought it would all blow over soon enough. During these months, I spent a lot of time at the mansion just keeping an eye out. Tony didn't always know I was there, but I was. For him. We rarely spoke on those occasions when we did see one another, but I will never forget the time he came running downstairs with his hair wild and his cheeks burning, dashing from room to room shouting my name.

I calmed him down and offered him a Mandrax. As usual, he wouldn't take anything but a glass of wine. He put his fists to his temples and shook his head, groaning. I asked him what the matter was, and he told me he'd had a dream, the most vivid terrifying dream he had ever had. It wasn't the first time. He'd had it about three times since Connie's death, but it was getting worse every time, feeling more real. I asked him if he wanted to tell me about it, and he was silent for so long that I assumed he didn't. Then he refilled his glass and mine and leaned back in his chair. His voice was a monotone, his eyes fixed on one of Connie's abstracts hanging on the wall behind the grand piano.

"I'M LOOKING FOR CONNIE," HE said. "In the dream. Looking everywhere. She's not in the house, not under any of the beds, not in the stables or the guest house. Then I'm in a strange city at night where the buildings are all old, dark, and decaying. There are noises all around—rumblings, echoing voices, children crying—but I don't know where they're coming from. There's a river nearby, and a stinking mist seems to be rising from its surface, threading its way through the gloomy cobbled streets. I arrive at a big house made of black stone with gargoyles hanging out high up on the walls, some sort of dark viscous fluid—not water—spurting out of their mouths. I'm feeling nervous, in the dream, but I go inside. There's no furniture and very little light, just shadows, dust, dark corners and whispering voices. Every time I think I've got as far as I can go, there's another room beyond. Finally, I arrive at a big ornate door, and I go through it. There are people spread about on the floor. It's too dark to make out their features clearly, but I know that Connie is one of them. I can see the glow of opium pipes and matches heating spoons, and there's a smell, even in the dream, acrid but sweet somehow, like pears and ammonia. I think it's death.

"Connie is lying next to someone who is wearing strange clothes. Edwardian, or something like that. Mostly he's in the shadows. I have no idea who he is. Connie looks up at me, and I can see the pleading in her eyes. 'Get me out of here!' She wants me to save her, to rescue her, take her away. When I reach out for her hand, a voice tells me I can't leave with her.

"There's a guitar propped against the wall. A Fender Stratocaster. I pick it up and strum a chord. It's out of tune and the volume is deafening. I can't see any leads or amps but it's definitely plugged in somewhere. I sing a song because I think that's what they want. The first song I ever wrote for Connie. It's all very hazy, but I get through it somehow, and then all the people lying around are clapping and saying how great I am and how Connie can go back with me now. I reach for her hands and pull her to her feet. She's a bit unsteady, but she can walk. The voice says, 'Remember don't look back,' as we set off. I'm confused. I don't know why he's talking about the Dylan movie, what he means by that. I'm in a hurry to get out of there, and my feet seem to remember their way back through room after room, though there's a heaviness that slows us down, as if we're squelching through mud. You can never run fast enough in dreams. I see ghosts of people I've known long ago flitting through the shadows: my parents, Mr. and Mrs. Fox, a blackbird with a damaged wing. A disembodied voice whispers, 'It is always afternoon' and then echoes and echoes until all the words blur into one another. The journey seems to last forever. Connie is behind me now, and I can see a glimmer of light ahead. The outside world. Daylight.

"When I get to the door, the sunshine beyond is almost blinding. I turn to look back at Connie, to make sure she's still close behind, but when I do, it's as if the room and Connie are moving further and further away from me and becoming smaller and smaller. The more I reach out, the further away they get. The next thing I know, I'm out in the street and the heavy door has slammed behind me. I hammer on the wood calling out for Connie, but nobody comes."

It sounded pretty terrifying to me, and Tony had worked himself up again in telling me about it. I poured him more wine and made soothing noises.

"I've lost her forever," he said. "You know that, don't you? That's what it means. I've lost her forever."

HE *HAD* LOST HER FOREVER, of course. There's no way you can get someone back from the other side, no matter how good a singer you are or how much you plead.

But the dream marked a kind of watershed for Tony. As the months passed, his condition slowly improved. I don't think he was ever quite himself again—he'd lost something too important for that to happen. Not just Connie, but a part of his soul, perhaps. What made him who he was. The Blackbird. The voice was still there, but it wasn't the same. He wrote sad songs, heartbreaking songs. The next album, a solo effort, sold millions, mostly to pale and lovesick youths eking out their existence in student bedsits.

But none of us had reckoned on the lengths to which Connie's supporters would go.

I wasn't with Tony at the time, but I pieced events together as best I could later.

On one of his latenight city rambles, he was walking across a patch of waste ground when three women started throwing stones at him and calling him a murderer, just like the three he'd found on his estate during his period of mourning. He stopped to talk to them, to try to tell them he had nothing to do with Connie's death, with her drug addiction, that he knew how they loved her, but he had loved her, too, and he wasn't the one responsible for destroying the life of their spokeswoman, their heroine, that it wasn't his neglect or infidelity that had killed her. But it was no use. One of the stones hit him on the head and blood started to flow down his cheek. He crumpled to his knees. More stones hit him, then the women, sensing victory, rushed forward as one and enveloped him.

THE POLICE COULDN'T FIND ALL the pieces, but a courting couple walking by the river saw Tony's head floating downstream the following day.

The three killers were easily found, partly because they had been charged before with desecrating Connie's grave. They delighted in their confession. One of them, it turned out, had a history of violent mental disturbances, and other two were followers, weak and easily manipulated—or *inspired*, as they claimed in court. During the trial, they kept jumping to their feet and disrupting the proceedings, raising their fists in the air, shouting slogans and proclaiming victory, to the extent that one commentator said it was like the Manson trial without Manson.

Of course, most of Tony's fans were devastated. Record sales hit the stratosphere, and in death The Blackbird became, if anything, an even more potent figure than he had been in life. Tony Foster was just twenty-seven years old when he died.

As I sat by the riverbank smoking a cigarette after the police and everyone had gone that day they found his head, I had the strange thought that if we managed to find all the pieces of Tony and somehow put them together, The Blackbird would live again. I believe in transformations.

Then I recalled a day not so long before, when Connie was still alive, and she and Tony were in love. I asked him what happened to the blackbird in his story, the one with the damaged wing and the messy nest. Had he found a mate? Did they live happily ever after?

And Tony told me that the blackbird had simply disappeared. One day he just wasn't there any more. His nest was empty and his song was silent.

But whenever I hear a blackbird now, I always think of Tony. And if I can, I try to get a look at it, especially its wing. Just in case.

THE MISFITS
BY NAOMI RAND

WHERE WOULD YOU HAVE BEEN without me, go on, tell me that why don't you, you ungrateful bitch. I made you.

THAT WAS HIS PARTING SHOT to me. Johnny O believed that until the minute he cast his eyes upon you, you didn't actually exist. My ex-manager thought I was some piece of clay he breathed that lousy cigarette breath into to coax into life.

I believed otherwise. My version is that when we met, I had already been alive and well and living in Calabasas for seventeen years. I, Julie Weston, was a senior at Calabasas High. I'd already been accepted to my first choice school, UCLA. And why not? I had a 4.0 average. Plus, I was captain of the girl's swimteam, lynchpin of the debate team, and to top it off, I was dating the boy most likely to be crowned prom king. So really I did exist before. Not only did I exist, I was well on my way to making my doting parents proud. But you be the judge.

LATE MAY, BUT THERE'S JUNE gloom in the air. I cut class and head east from the boring suburbs to the City of Angels. I drive straight to Tower Records and park. Walk inside and comb the rack to find the new album filed under S for Smith. On the cover, Patti wears a wife-beater tee and a locket. She looks like she's pretending to be demure, her eyes look down and a little to the side, while really she's saying, good luck, you'll never know me.

Patti Smith is the girl I wish I could be pretty much every minute of every day. In reality, I'm her polar opposite. Not just in attitude, as in I give my parents no trouble at all, but of course in looks. I have straight blond hair that falls almost to my waist, winning blue eyes, and a natural tan.

The title of the new album is *Easter*. I think how genius that is comparing herself to Jesus because of course, she's risen again after falling off the stage and breaking her neck.

She's so brave.

I'm such a coward.

This is what I think as I walk to the register and stand in line to pay. Then the guy behind me asks, "Is that really for you, luv?"

The first thing I notice is the English accent. When I swing 'round to see who he is, I see a guy who's way on the wrong side of thirty. They say clothing makes the man. If so, his outfit is questionable. He's wearing a leather fringed vest over a washed-out Stones concert T-shirt. Strapped round his hips, a thin leather belt with an oh-so-expensive Navajo hammered silver buckle, and to finish off the look, worn-out jeans and lizard-skin cowboy boots.

A sleazebag, I decide.

"Are you buying it for your boyfriend then?"

"No, I'm not." Though how is it even his business?

Luckily it's my turn to pay. My boyfriend? Josh thinks the Bee Gees are what music is all about. At the prom he'll want to do one of those dance routines with me. I squirm at the thought. A few months ago, I lost my virginity to Josh in the backseat of his car. We've had sex pretty regularly since then and I wish I could say the groping and fumbling has turned into something desirable. But it hasn't. I have already decided to break up with him as soon as I leave for college.

Enough of Josh, he's annoying to think about at best.

I grab my yellow Tower bag and head out to my car. It's an ancient orange VW bug and by ancient I mean you can see the road passing if you look down, due to the rusted floorboard.

"So you're a fan then, are you? Do you play anything?" The guy has followed me. Jesus, he's persistent. In fact he's leaning on the car as he talks to me. "If you're in the mood, swing by Thursday, I'm having tryouts."

He's giving me a business card.

"Come by at six."

I read *Johnny O, Musical Impresario*. What does that even mean? But there's an address and phone number.

He walks away. Gets into a retro Thunderbird convertible and drives off in a blaze of glory and gas fumes.

OUR HOUSE IS A ONE-STORY ranch on Susan Drive. Susan Drive ends at Eve Court. The developer who built every one of these ticky-tacky houses named the streets after his daughters and sisters and mother and, when those names ran out, about a zillion cousins. When I pull into the driveway, the sprinklers are whirling away. But the garage is empty.

Perfect!

In my room, I turn up the sound on my KLH to blast. Then lie prone on the shag carpet and shut my eyes. I forget where I am, my pretty-in-pink bedroom in the middle of what used to be a desert. My perfect home in a perfect town filled with perfect people and their perfectly tedious and predictable lives. I'm where she is. Where she lives. I picture New York City, which is hard since I've never actually been there. It's more of theoretical construct, an amalgamation of images that I've seen in movies and photographs.

I've listened to the record three times through by the time my mom yells, "Julie!" I leap up and turn down the sound and can hear her asking herself her favorite rhetorical question: "How can anyone call that din music?"

THURSDAY FINDS ME HEADING SOUTH. My mom thinks I'm with Stacy. Stacy thinks I have a hot date and am two-timing Josh. I slide my tape of *Horses* into the eight-track and chant along, slamming the palm of my hand against the steering wheel in time to the beat.

When I get there, my heart sinks. The address is for a garage, smack in the middle of two working auto body shops. The joke is clearly on me. I look around surreptitiously, wondering if it's some humiliating version of *Candid Camera*. But I see no one filming, so I force myself to get out and walk up to the door. Sure enough, there's his name next to the buzzer. Johnny O.

What does the "O" stand for anyhow, I wonder? I hesitate, but I've come all this way, so I force myself to ring. The lock is released. When I pull the door open, I see a dark hallway. What comes to my mind is that quote, "Abandon all hope, ye who enter here." Still, I walk inside and the door shuts behind me with a harsh click.

"We're down here, luv," a voice calls out.

WHEN I GET TO THE end, I find a rehearsal space. In it, there's a piano and a drum kit and a bunch of mics. And on the far side, I see an actual office. It's not high class, but it looks legit.

"Put your name down," Johnny O says to me, handing me a piece of paper. "We'll get started in about fifteen, ladies," and he saunters away into the office and shuts the door.

There are a bunch of other girls there. Thank God!

I've lugged in my Guild in its sad cardboard case. Some of the other girls have theirs out, tuning up. I sit down on a folding metal chair and do the same. What I wonder is if he approached all of them on line at Tower, but then a girl says to me, "I was sure no one else would come," and shows me the ad. He put a notice in the *LA Free Press. Do You Have What It Takes to become Rock and Roll Royalty?* It says whoever passes the audition is going to be a member of a brand new, all-girl band. He's even picked out our name for us.

We're going to be called The Misfits.

Just then he emerges and says, "Shall we get started then?"

JOHNNY AUDITIONS THE DRUMMERS FIRST. The rest of us sit and watch and wait. It's no contest, there's one girl who's far and away the best. He says, "Thank you for coming," to the rest and then uses that girl to keep the beat. He chooses two of us to play together with her, one plays lead, the other bass, and he puts up sheet music in case we don't know the songs. I can read chords, but not the notes.

I start to really panic. I think about leaving. But that would be humiliating too. Lethargy sets in, and so, I stay.

Johnny O looks even more dubious than he did two days ago. He's thin and twitchy and a cigarette perches perilously in the corner of his mouth. Yet not one of us questions that he can deliver on the advertised promise of fame and fortune.

IT TAKES ANOTHER HOUR AND he selects the bassist, dismisses a bunch more. Now there are only four left. That I'm among them is a total shock to me. The other three go first, and they're all much better guitarists than I am. They can all carry a tune as well. When it's my turn I'm so nervous, I literally bang my lips against the mic. "Sweetheart, please, it's not your boyfriend up there, it's a mic."

I blush. Extensively.

The song he picks for me to sing is the Stones, "Sympathy for the Devil."

First stroke of luck, I know it by heart.

When Patti first showed up, all they could do was compare her to Mick, which I find insulting. She was herself, wasn't that enough? I strum the first chord a few times and then the drummer hits the beat and we start in.

I don't know what happens, because I'm nervous as hell but somewhere along the way the music takes over and by the time I'm in St. Petersburg I've forgotten where I am.

Then, just like that, it's over.

"All right," Johnny O says and he turns around and dismisses the other girls.

OUTSIDE, THE THREE OF US stand in the parking lot. We are The Misfits.

Tara, the bassist, is spark-plug short with dark hair, cut just at her shoulders. She looks kind of boyish. Eileen, our drummer, is really tall. I'm five eight and she looms over me but like a lot of tall girls she hunches her shoulders to try and hide. She's got this mop of curly red hair and a lot of freckles spanning the bridge of her nose. It turns out Eileen's from Woodland Hills and Tara is from right nearby; she lives in an apartment complex two blocks from Griffith Park. They're both living with their moms, as in children of divorce. I come from a happily married family, so I'm the odd girl out. Also Tara's already been in two other bands and Eileen learned how to play because her older brother is a drummer.

"How about you?" Eileen asks.

I admit that I've basically only played alone in my room.

"Really?" I can't tell whether they're impressed or horrified. Changing the subject, Eileen says, "That guy Johnny O is pretty weird, right?"

"No kidding," I say.

"Do you think he can really do something for us?" Tara asks.

"I hope so," Eileen says.

I nod. We all have the same dream glittering in our eyes.

Eileen stubs out her cigarette and then she turns to me and says, "You really killed that song by the way."

"Yeah, you totally did!" Tara agrees.

They both seem to mean it. I don't think I've ever felt this happy.

THUS, I BEGIN TO LIE big time. I invent a new job, a new friend, tutoring after school, anything that sounds even halfway real. We have to rehearse every day.

I get away with being the queen of deception for seventeen days. On the eighteenth, Johnny O introduces us to Trish who he says is going to perfect our look. When she's done with me, my hair is cut short and dyed jet black. Not to mention the makeup. "You'll have to stop sitting out in the sun so much," Trish tells me as she works to accentuate my eyes, dark slashes of eyeliner and coral pink eye shadow.

"What on earth?" My mother's jaw could not fall further south and the horror is etched on her face. "Oh my god, your beautiful hair." She is almost crying as she grabs my hair in a last-ditch attempt to believe that somehow I'm playing dress up.

"I'm in a band," I tell her.

"What?"

I explain, a little. My father comes home. They're both aghast. They announce I'm officially grounded.

"You can't do that," I say.

"Yes, we can. We're your parents."

Wrong. That night I sneak out with a backpack full of a few essentials and head for Tara's. When her couch gets old, I move into the back room at Johnny O's.

FOR A GUY WHO LOOKS tubercular, he is a real babe magnet. Most of the women are blowsy, with big teased hair and way-too-tight tube tops constricting their massive chests. At first, I'm polite but honestly. What's the point, it's like Union Station in there. I stuff my ears with Kleenex at night. And yeah, there are plenty of times when I wonder what I'm doing. I even call home, but my mom just breaks down sobbing and my dad gets all tough love with me, so I

NAOMI RAND

give up on that. Then one night I'm resting on the mattress on the floor and listening to the sirens and the whir of the helicopters and I realize I'm doing just fine. Not just fine, better than that. I feel a rush of elation. "I'm free," I say aloud.

In July, Johnny announces he's booked us our first gig. He doesn't believe in starting small either; we're playing the Roxy. "If you don't think you can manage ladies, then you've been wasting my time." We all know a warning when we hear one.

To celebrate what will either be a huge mistake or the first day of the rest of our lives we go to this funky tattoo parlor on Sunset and have the word "Misfit" tattooed on our left upper arms in Gothic script.

We're the opening act, as in the background noise for everyone getting buzzed. The three of us step out on stage to complete our sound check, and I look out at all the people in the room and I just panic. I stand there, frozen. But then Eileen does this snappy little drum roll and calls out, "Hey, Julie?" and that brings me back. You can do this, I tell myself.

It may be bluster but it helps.

By the time we're playing our third song, I can feel the difference in the room. The sound of talking has died down and there are a lot of people close to the stage, watching. The drumming is savage, the guitar solo stinging, and is that really me? It is, I'm screaming, then purring, hitting the notes or purposely swerving around them. The stories we're telling are true; girls want just what boys want.

When we step off, Johnny O is grinning. "Fabulous," he tells us. We get to watch from back there and the headliners surprise everyone when they call to us, "Come on out here," and reintroduce us. We sing along with their big hit.

After the show, there's a party and we're invited. Johnny O drives us up into the hills. It's like someone sprinkled pixie dust on us, I think as the gate opens and we ride up a curving driveway and come to a huge mansion. When I step out, it smells like jasmine and evening primrose.

This is absolutely the best night of my entire life.

Which is even better after Johnny O breaks the news to us. Two different A&R people were there in the audience and he's cooking up a deal. "As promised. Rock-and-roll royalty!"

We walk past the house and there's a kidney-shaped pool. Music blasts. Tons of people are drinking or smoking or snorting coke. We toast each other with Champagne.

"ARE YOU OKAY?" JOHNNY O asks. I think I should have eaten something because I'm feeling kind of sick. "Let me help you," he says. "Let's get you some fresh air," and he walks me away from the pool, toward a guesthouse at the end of the path. "You just need a good lie down," he tells me.

I WAKE UP AND IT'S morning. The sun is blazing. My head feels like it's about to split apart. It takes me a while to realize that my jeans and underwear are missing. I find them in the corner of the room on the floor.

"Johnny?" I call out.

But there's no one there but me.

I stumble out and into the day. The maid is there cleaning up the mess; she lets me use the phone to call a cab. "Where to?"

Why, to Johnny's. I walk past his room to get to mine and as I do, his door opens. A strange woman emerges. I have such a splitting headache I can barely look at her.

In the bathroom I open the cabinet to get the aspirin and shut it and see myself. Only then do I notice the red half-moon prints on either side of my neck. That's when it comes back to me in a rush, someone on top of me. His fetid breath and his nails digging in, choking me until I black out.

"Is that you, Julie?" I hear Johnny asking just outside the door.

I blink. It is, and it isn't. I tell myself it couldn't have been him.

He's here, I was there, he has someone with him, and he's never even looked at me that way.

I'm shaking when I emerge. "How did you sleep?" he asks. "You looked so peaceful, I didn't want to disturb you."

"When did you leave?"

"The party? Late. You could use some coffee," and he is heading for the kitchen to make it for us. I hear him relaying the good news. As promised, Capitol Records wants to sign us.

I go back inside and shower. I clean every pore twice. By the time I step out, I decide that if it happened, it couldn't have been him. And whatever happened, it was my fault for getting so drunk and passing out. I decide, the best thing I can do is forget about it.

THAT FIRST DAY IN THE recording studio is surreal. Like Christmas in July, that is if Christmas means you get to try out every guitar you've ever dreamed of playing. I pick an aqua-and-white Fender Stratocaster. And we rehearse endlessly. They want to release a single with a B-side and it's all incredible, including the producer who has worked with all these famous musicians and is full of compliments, what a unique sound we have, how talented we are, what a privilege it is.

I learn later on, that's what they tell everyone. It's called grooming the artist. As in, sucking up so you can get the most out of them.

At night, to get to sleep, I get drunk and high and finally drift off. But in the middle of the night, I wake shivering and shaking. It's summer in LA and Johnny doesn't have air conditioning so it's stifling in that room. Yet, for me it might as well be the Arctic Circle.

IT TAKES A MONTH FOR them to get the single polished and perfect, and then they release it and we go out on tour in support. We are booked into pretty decent sized clubs in the Midwest to begin with. The label backs us up; there's radio play and a ton of interviews. They keep adding dates to the tour.

As for Johnny, he finds a new girl in every port. Meanwhile, Eileen hooks up with Nick, one of our roadies. Tara prefers the groupies, or as we call them, Tara's boys. They all have the same kind of look: long hair and sensitive, slightly hangdog expressions. I can't bear the idea of having someone touch me. I lie and tell them I met a guy back in LA and I'm staying true.

BY THE TIME WE ROLL into New York, it's December. It's freezing. I can see my own breath. And the city is even crazier than I imagined. All this traffic and noise and grime and all the people walking intently, they are clearly on the way to somewhere important.

"Are we staying at the Chelsea?" I ask Johnny eagerly.

"Sorry, no can do."

The Chelsea might be historic but it's also been getting some bad press, what with the sad tale of Sid and Nancy. He's booked us into the Hilton in midtown. Boring. Bland. But it's the last stop on our tour and that night we're playing the Palladium.

OUR SET LASTS FORTY MINUTES and we come back for three encores. The last one is a surprise to me, Tara and Eileen have come up with it without saying anything. I know it, of course: "Sympathy for the Devil."

I let loose and it's wild, the bouncers are dragging kids off the stage but they're like jumping jacks, they keep popping right back up.

Afterward, there's a party at the Factory in Union Square only a few blocks away. When we leave by the side door, it's snowing. What could be more perfect, I think. I open my mouth and a flake lands on my tongue and melts away. I follow along at the back of the pack and then, it's easy for me to slow down and peel off without anyone else realizing.

The Chelsea is right nearby. No one will miss me.

I STAND IN FRONT OF the hotel and gawk. To get inside I would have to buzz and I don't have a reason. So I crane my neck and try and imagine which one was Patti's room. There's a black metal latticework that looks like a row of balconies. The snow is really coming down and crystals catch in my eyelashes. The clothing I'm wearing is soaked in sweat. My mom would admonish me: "You'll catch your death." Is it possible to actually catch death, can you trap it in a net then tuck it into a jar like a lightning bug?

And then, without warning, I start sobbing. And can't get myself to stop. My vision blurs. I'm gasping. "Please oh please," I manage to get out, and I have no idea who I'm saying it to.

I'm losing it completely when two women step out of the bar next to the Chelsea. One of them shoves the other. Hard. She totters, but regains her footing, "What did you do that for?"

"I saw you making eyes at him."

"I wasn't."

"Yes, you were!"

They are both wearing leather mini skirts and high heels and one of them has on this white fur coat.

"Slut!"

"Says who?"

Wait, their voices. I realize those aren't women just as one of them turns and sees me, and says, "What the fuck are you gaping at?"

"Yeah, bitch, what's so funny?"

"Nothing," I mutter and hurry away.

ALL I CAN THINK OF when I get back to the hotel is running a hot bath and sinking into it. So, it's a surprise when I open the door to the room and find Johnny sitting, yogi style, on my bed.

"Where were you?"

"I just went for a walk," I say.

"A walk?"

"To the Chelsea," I admit. "I just wanted to see it," though I'm embarrassed. It all seems to silly, my devotion to her. And the way I broke down.

"You should have told someone." Johnny is up and he's moving toward me. "I was worried. We all were. You can't just run off like that, Julie."

"I'm sorry," I tell him.

"Are you?" he asks and that's when I realize he's really pissed off at me. "It was fucking embarrassing not to have you there."

"Look," I begin which is when he slaps me. I put up my hand because it stings.

"Don't you ever do that again, do you hear me? I'm supposed to be in charge of you, you understand?"

"Okay," I say.

"Okay?"

I can smell the funk coming off of him, the sour smell of sweat, the sweet smell of pot, the burnt smell of cigarettes, and of course, the alcohol. I try to move away, but he has me flush up against the wall. He's leaning over me, and then I blink and it comes back, all of it, him on top of me, him breathing hard, choking me, and then jamming himself inside of me.

"It was you!" I say, as much in wonder as in horror.

Which is when he punches me in the stomach, once, twice, three times and I crumple and slide down onto the floor. They're not stars you see, they're little slivers of your brain floating away. He drags me by my feet across the rug and then he pulls off my jeans and rips off my underwear, one of his hands is over my mouth as he does it. I'm smothering and I try to squirm away, but I can't.

I give up. I tell myself he'll be done and when he's done it will be over and then, and then, and finally he grunts and pulls off of me, stands up, zipping his jeans and says, "You won't forget now!"

I wait till the door shuts. Then I manage to stand and get myself over to the bathroom and sink down next to the tub, pulling off the rest of my clothes. I run the bath and get in. My body protests. There are stabbing pains, cold meeting heat but then it stops and I turn as red as a lobster. I put my feet up on the wall and slowly, surely lower myself until my head is under the water. I wait until I can see bubbles drifting up and finally I open my mouth and the water pours in. There's a moment when I think I can do it.

That then it will be over.

I hold on for what seems like forever.

Only then, I can't. Something else takes over and my body lurches upright and I'm retching, and coughing and wheezing and hanging over the side of the tub. It turns out I'm just another pathetic Lady Lazarus, rising from the dead.

THE RECORD COMPANY BOOKS US a private plane for the trip back. "They love you girls," Johnny says. He has one of his women with him. Eileen has her roadie. Tara has Zach. "Isn't he adorable?" she asks anyone and everyone as he gets her drinks and lights her joint and rubs her feet.

The entire flight west is one big party. Lots of coke being snorted and all that goes with it. But I don't imbibe. I stay stone-cold sober. I sit by the window and stare out at the clouds.

WHEN WE LAND, JOHNNY O announces he has a huge surprise for all of us. The record company has rented us a house in Malibu. It has a practice room in it. Just wait till we see.

"It'll get all your creative juices going, girls," he tells us in the limo. "It's just like I said. Johnny keeps his promises."

IT'S QUITE A HOUSE. IT'S got a pool and private beach and a whole wing for Johnny. He buys himself a waterbed and has it installed and the ladies come and go. He gets a dozen pairs of authentic snakeskin cowboy boots. And a new classic ride, a British import, a Triumph convertible. He seems to have an endless supply of coke as well.

We are supposed to be working on some new material, or as Johnny puts it, "making us a hit." He tells us that what we've been doing is great, but to get to be in the top ten on the radio? "Soften it up a bit is all." A steady beat, nothing too driving; a catchy chorus, nothing too demanding; and of course the lyrics have to be extra special, clever without being so smart they go above the listener's heads. "I'll leave you to it then, ladies."

ONE AFTERNOON WE'RE SITTING IN there working and Eileen says, "Has he ever talked to either one of you about the money?"

We shake our heads.

"We should ask him, I guess," Tara says.

And we look at each other. It becomes clear that none of us wants to do that.

"Maybe we should find someone else to check on it for us," Eileen suggests.

So we do. We find a lawyer. He has his investigator do a little discreet digging. He tells us the size of our advance. He shows us the Xeroxes the investigator has found, contracts we supposedly signed giving Johnny O complete control over all of our finances.

"But we didn't sign those," I say.

"It's your word against his right now. Of course, once we go to trial . . ." His retainer is paid up front. It's $10,000 to begin with. We don't have access to our money, and I'm the only one who even has a family I can turn to. Or could. I think about my parents, I think about going back to them and asking for a loan. As if I can do that. I have to admire the genius of it; he's got us exactly where he wants us.

ON THE WAY BACK FROM the lawyer's office, we park at the Santa Monica pier and walk out to the far end where there's a metal railing and a view of the ocean.

"What are we going to do?" Tara asks.

"We could quit," Eileen says.

"And let him get away with it?" I counter. I stare at the horizon and I think about all of it, about chance and fate and how I could have been somewhere else, anywhere else, but no, I was there, that day and he found me. It was for a reason, it has to have all been for a reason. Then I take a deep breath and turn to them and say, "It's not just about the money." I tell them the rest.

Eileen goes pale.

"You too," Tara says dully.

It's like the nursery fable only in reverse. Three blind mice have been given back the gift of sight.

DID YOU KNOW THAT YOU can make daiquiris at home in a blender? All you need are the proper ingredients. For fun, pop in a festive paper umbrella. Then it's like you're really on vacation on some Hawaiian beach.

We lift our glasses and make a toast. "To us, Johnny."

From our deck, the sunset turns the water blood red.

We clink, all four of us and drink to the dregs.

"We're going to rule the world we are," he proclaims loudly.

We agree.

"We have a surprise for you," I say. Then we lead him back inside, right down the hall to his bedroom. We strip him down to his underwear. He looks happy, thinking he knows what's coming next. He pats the bed vaguely. It rocks underneath him. Eileen and Tara step back. But I don't. I lean in and ask him, "Why did you talk to me that day?"

His eyes can't quite focus by then.

"What?"

"That day you met me, at the record store. Why me?"

He grunts. There's that lizard-like smile. "Because I did."

"Because you did? That's it?"

I get nothing more.

"By the way," Eileen tells him, "you're fired."

"You can't fire me." Only it doesn't come out cleanly, the words slur and then he hears himself and asks, "What is this? What did you give me?" And the panic sets in. I start to back up but he's too fast, he grabs me by my wrist and pulls me down to him. Hisses it at me. "Where would you have been without me, go on, tell me that why don't you, you ungrateful bitch. I made you!" There's spittle on the side of his mouth. His tongue darts out and freezes and I unlock his fingers as he falls backwards.

TARA WASHES THE GLASSES AND the blender, though what could they really find in it? His drink was special, still. We put them all away. We sit out on the deck and watch the moon rise.

One by one the lights in the other houses go out.

Captain of the swim team and Red Cross certified as a senior lifeguard. I worked at the local pool every summer, didn't I? It takes all of us to get him down to the water's edge. But once he's in I use the fireman's carry. There's no need to keep his head above water. I swim out past the end of the rock wall. And let go.

HIS BODY WASHES UP TWO weeks later. The toxicology is inconclusive, but Johnny O's reputation precedes him. No one's surprised when they find the cocktail of downers in his system. It's clear he went for a midnight swim and succumbed.

It's a terrible tragedy. We are all beside ourselves with grief. We can hardly stand to talk about it. But somehow I manage to say a few words at his funeral.

After that, the requests pour in. Everyone wants to manage us but we tell them no. We say that none of them could ever match our Johnny. We prefer to take the reins ourselves.

THESE DAYS, INTERVIEWERS ALWAYS WANT to know the secret to our longevity as a band. "We like and trust each other" is what I tell them. "And we love playing music together. There's no other secret than that."

But honestly, the way musicians get taken advantage of it's surprising more bands don't do what we did.

Eventually they always come 'round to Johnny. I smile as I imagine Johnny writhing in that special corner of hell that is reserved for him and I say, "I'm not a big believer, but I like to think that wherever he is, he knows and he's happy for us. It was his vision that pulled this band together in the first place and we owe him so much. I mean, honestly, where would we be if not for him?"

SHADEROC THE SOUL SHAKER
BY GARY PHILLIPS

OH FOR THE DAYS WHEN he could snort him a line of flake while some groupie was down on her knees, her head buried between his spread leather-clad legs, pleasuring him like he was a visiting pharaoh. Goddamn, that time in his room backstage at the Forum . . . the two big-titty blondes. Sheeet, the top of his head damn near blew off that night as they sexed him up, down, and sideways.

Churchill "Church" Gibson shook his head, regretfully cycling away from the glorious past into the stone-cold reality of now. He glared at the screen of his laptop as if it were an adversary. He put aside his coffee and tapped the keyboard and the music app replayed his most troubling track through external speakers. The green audio readout traveling from left to right as the music filled his compact home studio space.

He tapped a key again midway through to bring silence. The track was all right but it wasn't killer. It merely filled space. None of the tracks so far were killer. No, that wasn't quite right, two of them he was happy with . . . not in love with, but their shine only highlighted how lackluster the others were.

"Motherfuck," he muttered. There came a momentary gurgle in the middle of his chest and he closed his eyes, centering his chi, breathing in and out slowly, summoning his mindfulness. He took hold of his crutch, sliding his arm through the bracket, latching onto the T-handle, and rose from his seat with a grunt. He walked over to his wet bar that no longer was stocked with Johnnie Walker Black, Majesté XO cognac, and blunts thick as a big mama's clit and trés potent, as if laced with jet fuel. Now it was an assortment of bottled green and red concoctions of blended fruits and vegetables, vitamins and his various pills for blood pressure and what have you. He sighed and checking his Tag Heuer Carrera watch, a gift from Quincy Jones, took his meds. He swigged it down with some kind of kale-and-berry smoothie that while he would never actually like the taste, at least his tolerance for the stuff had grown.

"Those were the days, weren't they, Church?"

Licking green foam from over his top lip, Gibson turned and gaped. There in his studio stood Shirley King. She'd been one of his backup singers once upon a time, one of the few who managed to make it across that twenty-foot expanse to the spotlight. He'd produced her first hit album. Then it got messy when they got involved. But, he frowned, hadn't she died in that car crash in Paris? Higher than a 707 in '02?

"Shirley," he muttered.

She always had a body to make a sissy hard and she was rockin' it in a lavender dress with a slit up her shapely thigh. She sat before his laptop, swiveling toward him on the chair's ball bearings.

"I must be trippin'," he said. After the stroke four years ago, these days he barely had imbibed any booze or what they called controlled substances. Okay, sure, there was a blast of Macallan 25 he'd had last Christmas, alone, but it was only one drink and that was months ago.

"Maybe I'm your subconscious talking to you, baby," she said. King crossed those magnificent legs. "Maybe the mother ship beamed you up and deposited you in the cosmic slop you could be swimming in, or could be I'm the constipation you got sneaking that bacon cheeseburger yesterday."

He grinned. "I'm weak."

"That was your excuse when I caught you wiggling your finger in Jeanie on the tour bus."

"Yeah," he agreed.

She smiled sweetly, crooking a finger at him. "Come here."

He did, feeling more spryness in his steps than in some time. Like when he was a youngster staying ahead of the Five-O and the competition. He'd amassed enough slangin' rock to finance dubbing his first effort, a cassette tape of his songs he sold out of the trunk of his hoopty and at swap meets.

She turned back to his laptop and after a few taps, brought up the clips from *Shaderoc the Soul Shaker*. This was a new version of the Stagolee inspired, "super bad" brother persona created by a comedian friend of Gibson's named Renaldo Redd. Redd had parlayed the character into a couple of low budget actioners in the eighties—*Shaderoc vs. Dr. Funkenstein* and *Shaderoc: Seekers of the Pimp Cane*. Both had done well at the box office. Enough so that Redd had been preparing a third outing, the bigger budget *Shaolin Shaderoc*. But he died of a heart attack as he panted while peeling off the panties of a percussionist named Sheila Ramirez.

Even before Redd's body was interned at Inglewood Cemetery, complete with six Amazon honeys in gold hot pants and matching top hats as honorary dancing pallbearers, Gibson had made his bid for the character. He'd recalled coming up with the Shaderoc moniker as he and Redd drove up the coast one day, passing a bottle of Jack back and forth while Redd told him about his idea. But through various legal and who-knew-what-all-else twists and turns, Ramirez eventually secured the rights to the character.

"Wasn't there a Shaderoc graphic novel out in the early oughts?" the King apparition said. They both watched the actor playing Shaderoc as *Crouching Tiger, Hidden Dragon*-like, he sailed through the air delivering a devastating kung fu kick to three bad-guy ninjas, scattering them like bowling pins.

"There was. There was also a talk of a limited series on cable but that didn't happen. Until . . ."

"Until Thomlinson."

She meant the cult director/writer Nic Thomlinson known for giving grindhouse the A-picture treatment. He worked out the rights with Ramirez and the flick was scheduled to drop on Netflix. Going full bore on the retro vibe, he brought Gibson out of semi-retirement to do the soundtrack.

"But it's not flowing like it used to, huh, Church? Like the notes were singing their song in your head."

"I felt it when I worked out the title song and recorded with Marie and Sylvia," he answered, the two old friends of both of them.

"Meaning they knew where to fill in where you left holes."

"True," he admitted. For the big love scene between Shaderoc and Xtal, the Queen of the Aztecs, he'd scrapped the dopey lyrics he'd written and went with an instrumental version, which had come out pretty good he'd concluded. But since then, he was running on fumes and Thomlinson and the suits would know it.

"I've already pushed back the deadline," he said, knowing such increased expectations or dampened them in some quarters.

Elbows on the desk, King leaned forward, her fingers with their gold twinkling nails pressed before her face as she looped the scene again. This time with the lackluster track Gibson had been listening to underneath. "Speaking of fingers, stud, yours still work, right?"

"About the only damn thing that does."

"Figures. Get your guitar."

He shrugged and, turning, reached for his Fender Telecaster. He pulled a stool close and turned on the amp as King swung the mics attached to adjustable arms into position. She smelled good, Gibson noted as he plucked the strings while he tuned it. How could a ghost have a scent? But then again, how the hell did a ghost have solid form?

If a gun was pressed to Gibson's head, later he couldn't recount how it all went down. How Shirley King dusted off the Yamaha keyboard in the closet and played the thing like when he first heard her in that night spot on Florence in the 'hood. He worked his fingers and thumbs on the strings like he too was in his twenties again, standing before thousands in the Sports Arena, his licks moving through them like current. He was sweating and rasping the songs that used to make the honeys swoon and the men bop their heads. The music like a cocoon around him as he and his band, Rhythm Pulse, did their thing and there was no one who could touch them.

Head back, the Telecaster a blood-pumping part of his body, was a thing alive that didn't make music, but rather the music channeled through it from the Source. He was plugged in and the crowd was with him. Looking across the sea of faces he saw his ex-manager Sandy Igar. Smiling. Into it. What the hell . . . ?

Head back in the gloom, Gibson's eyes came open.

"About time, ya goddamn lazy bastard."

Igar was standing over him in Haggar flared slacks, that porno-actor mustache and those two-tone aviator shades—a look he sported well past its prime.

"Dreaming about pussy your sorry self ain't never gonna get you can do any time. Right now we got to lay down some sound, son."

With effort, given his left leg was the one with the strength, he sat up on the couch in his studio. "I'm in purgatory, is that it? I have to earn my way out by completing this soundtrack?" The real Igar was still alive but had been ensconced, some said entombed, in his Bel Air mansion for years. He was said to be suffering from a short list of long-suffering ailments.

The fit Igar before him had his hands on his hips like an NFL coach judging his new prospect, a sour look on his face. "Look, crip, you gonna sit there and wallow in self-pity or you going to earn?"

"Carrot and stick I see," Gibson muttered, slipping on his crutch. He must have sued Igar at least three times during his music career. "Or better," he huffed, getting to his feet. "That stick up your ass."

"My job is not to stroke your fragile ego," Igar began. "That's what groupies and your hangers-on are for."

"'My job is to get the best out of you, and that takes sweat and blood,'" Gibson finished. He knew all the Igarisms. The two settled in, trading insults and verbal jabs back and forth, as Gibson reworked two other tracks. As had happened to him in the past, he was annoyed and envious that Igar knew his shit only too well. He couldn't sight read like Gibson and at best could keep time banging a cowbell, but the sumabitch knew how to pace, where to emphasize this riff over that one, what to bring up and what to bring down. More in the role of engineer than musician, Gibson worked the mixing board cutting and remixing tracks at Igar's direction.

"I'm going to grow tulips out of the shit you spread," Igar said.

"I'm'a put my two lips on ya mama tonight," Gibson replied, but followed the other man's cue.

Finally, as dawn approached, they took stock. "Okay, that's not too bad," the Igar simulacrum allowed, sitting on the stool, his ear turned toward the playback monitor speakers.

A spent Gibson was back sitting on the couch. "It's great. The best I've done in I don't know how long." He said in a whispery tone as if his vocal chords were made of some gossamer material.

Igar turned his head toward him. It was a stuttering, mechanical motion, as if there were gears in his neck and they slipped slightly with the effort. He removed his glasses revealing all-white eyes with red glowing outlines. This did not rattle Gibson.

"About my end," the Igar thing said.

"I got your end, bitch." Gibson grabbed his crotch, managing a chuckle.

Igar returned the insult but Gibson's attention was on a framed original artwork print on a near wall. It was the cover for his

Dominoes with Selassie album. The more he stared the more he was drawn into the scene—that of a man and woman warrior back to back with futuristic-looking weapons in their hands battling half-monster-reptile and half-machine creatures. He blinked, and it was if he were floating away.

"About time you go here, brother man."

Gibson blinked again. Before him was Shaderoc the Deifier, the Demolisher, the Defender, the Soul Shaker. He was a big cat as Gibson had always imagined him. Six four or five and built like Mike Strahan back when or J. J. Watt now.

"Sheeet," he muttered.

Shaderoc wasn't real. That is, Gibson looked down at his hands and they looked like . . . his hands. But this construct before him was hyper-idealized, like a live pencil drawing by comic book artist Jack Kirby, inked with fluidity by Gil Kane and colored in a combination of a bold primary palette.

"We've got our back up against it, Church," said Shaderoc in his, of course, bass voice. He was hefting a retro kind of space rifle like what Dr. Funkenstein's minions used in that movie. The weapon looked like it was made of tin and plastic. In a scabbard attached to his belt was a sword.

Gibson realized they were in a good-sized cave and a group of people were crowded in here too. There was the fine mus-cled sister from the album cover in a kind of modified tiger-skin bikini with breechcloth, heavy gravity boots slinging a large, curved knife weapon like the Klingon's bat'leth. There was Miles Davis in his *Kind of Blue* phase, sharp in a sharkskin suit, shades, and wielding a onyx samurai sword, the blade phasing in and out of solidity. Near him was a hunched over Chet Baker who worked the valves of his horn and out of the music end swirled color tendrils that snapped as they lashed and licked the thick air. Big Mama Thornton was in a svelte aquamarine space suit while she expertly loaded a magazine into a World War II-era Thompson submachine gun. Like a character in a Sam Fuller movie, she rolled the dead cigar stump around in her mouth.

"Are you ready?" Shaderoc asked Gibson.

Given he was unarmed and unprepared, he said, "What can I do?"

Shaderoc looked bemused. "Bring it home, baby, bring it home."

"I want you bad," the wet-dream woman said as she threw her body roughly against Shaderoc's. She kissed him with lustful ferocity as he kneaded a handful of her incredible backside.

Looking away, Gibson was handed his Telecaster by Stevie Ray Vaughan. Charlie Christian sparked a cheroot behind him. Gibson heard a screech and turning around, flying into the cave were musical notes the size of greyhounds. They undulated as they spread about, the strains of Muzak and smooth jazz. Miles was visibly shaken but rallied as an F note rushed at him, a jaw full of razor-like teeth opening in the note head. Those teeth closed in on Miles's face but he executed a spinning move, his sword cleanly severing the note head from the stem.

"Take that, motherfuckah," he rasped.

All about him, Shaderoc, the Tiger Woman and the musicians did battle against the invading notes. Invaders and defenders experienced losses. A ravenous note dove for him and a panicked Gibson strumming his axe on reflex. To his surprise, the sonic waves the guitar released burst the demon note into tiny pieces. A hand clamped on his shoulder. It was Shaderoc.

"With me," the big man said, already in motion.

Down a dark tributary to the cave they went. Gibson still was on his crutch, but he somehow kept up with Shaderoc's long strides. From up ahead in the half-light came a blast of sound that sent Gibson onto his back and Shaderoc to his knees. Growling, venal notes swarmed about them, their teeth lunging for them and a jumble of off-key singing assailing their ears.

Gibson had managed to sit up but he felt nauseous.

"Come on, follow me, Church." Shaderoc was back on his feet, aiming and firing his rifle, disrupting some of the notes that died screaming. More of them filled the tunnel. The soul shaker went prone and started belly crawling forward. Gibson imitated him, using his arms to propel himself forward. He was glad he'd been diligent in his workouts.

"We got to get to the source," Shaderoc said over the cacophony.

Apparently they were heading toward the origination point of the attacking notes. They began to travel down an incline and soon found themselves sliding through dirt and loose rocks into another chamber.

"Shit," Gibson swore as they came to a halt.

Before them was a giant pulsing entity, sort of like a gigantic cocoon or hive from which knobby, exoskeleton-like shell material protruded. There were also thousands of undulating feelers wiggling from the mass. The hive construct was lit from within and the demon notes squirted into life from the ends of the feelers. A rhythmic drone beat pounded at their bodies as well. Shaderoc crawled over to Gibson.

"We got one chance," he said. "I'm going to rip open a seam in that mutha and in that moment she'll be vulnerable."

"Shaderoc, I—"

"No, this is how it must be. I told you, only you can bring it home."

Before he could object again, the big man was up and seeking handholds invisible to normal men, scaling the rock wall. Hundreds, thousands of notes swirled about him. He unlimbered his rifle strapped across his back and blasted the notes to hell. Others he wrung their stems in his bare hands. But they were overwhelming him, their racket and jagged teeth opening countless wounds and gashes on his mighty body. His clothing was ripped to shreds and his rifle had been torn away from his hands. But Shaderoc kept on.

Then in position, he looked over his shoulder at Gibson and winked. The notes battering him, he unsheathed his sword, but it wasn't a saber. It was the fabled pimp cane and was resplendent, made of dark burnished wood with a jeweled head in the image of a pitbull's skull. He jumped from the small ledge he'd gained.

The pimp cane was arched high over his head, held in both hands as he yelled "Die, nasty mothersucker, die." Shaderoc came down at the Hive Mother, his body engulfed in her musical killer note children.

But the beasts couldn't halt Shaderoc's momentum. Out blazed a laser blade from the end of the cane, crackling with cosmic gravitas. The white-hot beam opened a deep gash in the rutted hide. "Now, man, now," he yelled as the notes engulfed him, stilling his words forever as he fell away.

"Shaderoc," Gibson yelled. Getting upright, the fizz and pop like toxic carbonated water flooded his chest again. But he rallied and his fingers worked the strings feverishly, his thumb thumping a ferocious funk attack. His fingertips bled, sweat blinded his eyes. He sent his sound spears at the opening even as it healed itself shut. The wound closed, most of his sonic javelins bouncing away impotently. But hadn't one or two gotten through? Hadn't he been able to pull it off? Agonizing moments crawled by and Gibson could see no change as the notes zoomed around his body like a cyclone, those hungry teeth nipping at and sampling his flesh.

But as he sunk down, as his consciousness left his torn body, even as he watched his arm ripped off and eaten, the hive burned brighter from within. Its pulsations increased and as if too much water was being streamed into a balloon, its sides stretched beyond tolerance and burst. In one collective earsplitting wail, the notes died. Some of their bodies slammed into each other, the cavern walls, or simply fell to the earth, writhing in their death agonies.

One-armed, Gibson, his stub miraculously cauterized, crawled to Shaderoc. His form was getting soft, his hard distinct Kirby lines dissolving. In his outstretched hand with the squared-off fingers was a squarish block with miniature tubes and knobs all over the surface of it—a gadget straight out of the Fantastic Four.

"Take it, you earned it."

"What?" he stammered.

"Make me proud," Shaderoc said and died.

Gibson rolled onto his back. He held tightly onto the gizmo, which was warm and hummed in his hand. Overhead was black, yet in that void he could see the distant twinkling stars. The dark vault got lighter and lighter, Gibson's face placid in satisfaction.

"Oh, jeez, hey, Mom, Dad, better come here."

"What is it, Cory?" called the middle-schooler's father anxiously.

"Is he dead?" said Cory, not sure what he should feel.

"Tell your mom to call 911, okay, buddy?" Nic Thomlinson bent down to the body splayed across his doorstep. "Tell them we need an ambulance." He felt for a pulse in Church Gibson's neck but could detect none. Looking about for a clue as to how long the musician might have been out here, Thomlinson saw something sticking out of the dead man's fist. He knew from those *Forensic Squad* episodes he helmed a decade ago he shouldn't remove evidence but he did. It was a thumb drive.

"Huh," he said, pocketing the item.

SEVEN MONTHS LATER, THE SOUNDTRACK album of *Shaderoc the Soul Shaker* would be the number one download for three weeks running. Church Gibson would be nominated for a posthumous Oscar, and there was interest in a biopic about him. While different people had their favorite track from the film, the complete score on the thumb drive recovered from his stiff fist, was a track of what was presumed Gibson yelling "Shaderoc" over and over, with a haunting, evocative guitar instrumental underneath. Thomlinson used it on the ending credits.

THE LONG BLACK VEIL
BY VAL McDERMID

JESS TURNED FOURTEEN TODAY. WITH every passing year, she looks more like her mother. And it pierces me to the heart. When I stopped by her room this evening, I asked if her birthday awakened memories of her mother. She shook her head, leaning forward so her long blond hair curtained her face, cutting us off from each other. "Ruth, you're the one I think of when people say 'mother' to me," she mumbled.

She couldn't have known that her words opened an even deeper wound inside me and I was careful to keep my heart's response hidden from my face. Even after ten years, I've never stopped being careful. "She was a good woman, your mother," I managed to say without my voice shaking.

Jess raised her head to meet my eyes then swiftly dropped it again, taking refuge behind the hair. "She killed my father," she said mutinously. "Where exactly does 'good' come into it?"

I want to tell her the truth. There's part of me thinks she's old enough now to know. But then the sensible part of me kicks in. There are worse things to be in small-town America than the daughter of a murderess. So I hold my tongue and settle for silence.

Seems like I've been settling for silence all my adult life.

It's easy to point to where things end but it's a lot harder to be sure where they start. Everybody here in Marriott knows where and when Kenny Sheldon died, and most of them think they know why. They reckon they know exactly where his journey to the grave started.

They're wrong, of course. But I'm not going to be the one to set them right. As far as Marriott is concerned, Kenny's first step on the road to hell started when he began dating Billy Jean Ferguson. Rich boys mixing with poor girls is pretty much a conventional road to ruin in these parts.

Me and Billy Jean, we were still in high school, but Kenny had a job. Not just any old job, but one that came slathered with a certain glamour. Somehow, he'd persuaded the local radio station to take him on staff. He was only a gofer, but Kenny being Kenny, he managed to parlay that into being a crucial element in the station's existence. In his eyes, he was on the fast track to being a star. But while he was waiting for that big break, Kenny was content to play the small-town big shot.

He'd always had an eye for Billy Jean, but she'd fended him off in the past. We'd neither of us been that keen on dating. Other girls in our grade had been hanging out with boyfriends for a couple of years by then, but to me and Billy Jean it had felt like a straitjacket. It was one of the things that made it possible for us to be best friends. We preferred to hang out at Helmer's drugstore in a group of like-minded teens, among them Billy Jean's distant cousin Jeff.

Their mothers were cousins, and by some strange quirk of genetics, they'd turned out looking like two peas in a pod. Hair the color of butter, eyes the same shade as the hyacinths our mothers would force on us for Christmas. The same small, hawk-curved nose and Cupid's bow lips. You could take their features one by one and see the correspondence. The funny thing was that you would never have mistaken Billy Jean for a boy or Jeff for a girl. Maybe it was nothing more than their haircuts. Billy Jean's hair was the long blond swatch that I see now in Jess, whereas Jeff favored a crew cut. Still does, for that matter, though the blond is starting to silver 'round the temples now.

Anyhow, as time slipped by, the group we hung with thinned out into couples and sometimes there were just the three of us drinking Cokes and picking at cold fries. Kenny, who had taken to drifting into Helmer's when we were there, picked his moment and started insinuating himself into our company. He'd park himself next to Jeff, stretching his legs to stake out the whole side of the table. If either of us girls wanted to go to the bathroom, we had to go through a whole rigmarole of getting Kenny to move his damn boots. He'd lay an arm across the back of the booth proprietorially, a Marlboro dangling from the other hand, and tell us all about his important life at the radio station.

One night, he turned up with free tickets for a Del Shannon concert fifty miles down the interstate. We were impressed. Marriott had never seen live rock and roll, unless you counted the open mic night at the Tavern in the Town. As far as we were concerned, only the truly cool had ever seen live bands. It took no persuading whatsoever for us to accompany Kenny to the show.

What we hadn't really bargained for was Kenny treating it like a double date right from the start when he installed Billy Jean up front next to him in the car and relegated me and Jeff to the backseat. He carried on as he started, draping his arm over her shoulders at every opportunity. But we all were fired up with the excitement of seeing a singer who had actually had a number one single, so we all went along with it. Truth to tell, it turned out to be just the nudge Jeff and I needed to slip from friendship into courting. We'd been heading that way, but I reckon we'd both been reluctant to take any step that might make Billy Jean feel shut out. If Billy Jean was happy to be seen as Kenny's girlfriend—and at first, it seemed that way, since she showed no sign of objecting to the arm-draping or the subsequent hand-holding—then we were freed up to follow our hearts.

That first double date was a night to remember. The buzz from the audience as we filed into the arena was beyond anything we small-town kids had ever experienced. I felt like a little kid again, but in a good way. I slid my hand into Jeff's for security and we followed Kenny and Billy Jean to our seats right at the front. When the support act took to the stage, I was rapt. Around us, people seemed to be paying no attention to the unknown quartet on the stage, but I was determined to miss nothing.

After Del Shannon's set, my ears were ringing from the music and the applause, my eyes dazzled by the spotlights glinting on the chrome and polish of the instruments. The air was thick with smoke and sweat and stale perfume. I was stunned by it all. I scarcely felt my feet touch the ground as we walked back to Kenny's car, the chorus of "Runaway" ringing inside my head. But I was still alert enough to see that Kenny still had his arm 'round Billy Jean and she was leaning into him. I wasn't crazy about Kenny, but I was selfish. I wanted to be with Jeff so I wasn't going to try to talk Billy Jean out of Kenny.

Kenny dropped Jeff and me off outside my house and as his taillights disappeared, I said, "You think she'll be okay?"

Jeff grinned. "I've got a feeling Kenny just bit off more than he can chew. Billy Jean will be fine. Now, come here, missy, I've got something for you." Then he pulled me into his arms and kissed me. I didn't give Billy Jean another thought that night.

Next day when we met up, we compared notes. I was still floating from Jeff's kisses and I didn't really grasp that Billy Jean was less enamored of Kenny's attempts to push her well beyond a goodnight kiss. What I did take in was that she appeared genuinely pleased for Jeff and me. My fears that she'd feel shut out seemed to have been groundless, and she talked cheerfully about more double dating. I didn't understand that was her way of keeping herself safe from Kenny's advances. I just thought that we were both contentedly coupled up after that one double date.

All that spring, we went out as a foursome. Kenny seemed to be able to get tickets to all sorts of venues and we went to a lot of gigs. Some were good, most were pretty terrible and none matched the excitement of that first live concert. I didn't really care. All that mattered to me was the shift from being Jeff's friend to being his girlfriend. I was in love, no doubting it, and in love as only a teenage girl can be. I walked through the world starry-eyed and oblivious to anything that wasn't directly connected to me and my guy.

That's why I paid no attention to the whispers linking Kenny's name to a couple of other girls. Someone said he'd been seen with Janine who tended bar at the Tavern in the Town. I dismissed that out of hand. According to local legend, a procession of men had graced Janine's trailer. Why would Kenny lower himself when he had someone as special as Billy Jean for a girlfriend? Oh yes, I was quite the little innocent back in the day.

Someone else claimed to have seen him with another girl at a blues night in the next county. I pointed out to her that he worked in the music business. It wasn't surprising if he had to meet with colleagues at music events. And that it shouldn't surprise her if some of those colleagues happened to be women. And that it was a sad day when women were so sexist.

I didn't say anything to Billy Jean, even though we were closer than sisters. I'd like to think it was because I didn't want to cause her pain, but the truth is that their stories probably slipped my mind, being much less important than my own emotional life.

By the time spring had slipped into summer, Jeff and I were lovers. I'm bound to say it was something of a disappointment. I suspect it is for a lot of women. Not that Jeff wasn't considerate or generous or gentle. He was all of those and more. But even after we'd been doing it a while and we'd had the chance to get better at it, I still had that Peggy Lee, "Is that all there is?" feeling.

I suppose that made it easier for me to support Billy Jean in her continued refusal to let Kenny go all the way. When we were alone together, she was adamant that she didn't care for him nearly enough to let him be the one to take her virginity. For my part, I told her she should hold out for somebody who made her dizzy with desire because frankly that feeling was the only thing that made it all worth it.

The weekend after I said that to her, Billy Jean told Kenny she wasn't in love with him and she didn't want to go out with him anymore. Of course, he went around telling anybody who would listen that he was the one to call time on their relationship, but I suspect that most people read that for the bluster it was. "How did he take it?" I asked her at recess on the Monday afterwards. "Was he upset?"

"Upset, like broken-hearted? No way." Billy Jean gave a little "I could give a shit" shrug. "He was really pissed at me," she said. "I got the impression he's the only one who gets to decide when it's over."

"You know, I've been wanting to say this for the longest time, but he really is kind of an asshole," I said.

We both giggled, bumping our shoulders into each other like big kids. "I only started going out with him so you and Jeff would finally get it together," Billy Jean said in between giggles. "I knew as long as I was single you two would be too loyal to do anything about it. Now I can just go back to having you both as my best friends again."

And so it played out over the next few weeks. Billy Jean and I hung out together doing girl things; Billy Jean and Jeff went fishing out on the lake once a week and spent Sunday mornings fixing up the old clunker her dad had bought for her birthday; we'd all go for a pizza together on Friday nights; and the rest of the time she'd leave us to our own devices. It seemed like one chapter had closed and another had opened.

Jess turned fourteen today. Seems like yesterday she came into our home. It wasn't how we expected it to be, me and Ruthie. We thought we'd have a brood of our own, not end up raising my cousin's kid. But some things just aren't meant to be and I'm old enough now to know there are sometimes damn good reasons for that.

I remember the morning after Jess was conceived. When Billy Jean told Ruthie and me what Kenny Sheldon had done, I didn't think it was possible to feel more angry and betrayed. I was wrong about that too, but that's another story.

It happened the night before, when Ruthie and I were parked up by the lake in my car and Billy Jean was on her lonesome, nursing a Coke in one of the booths at Helmer's. According to her, when Kenny walked in, he didn't hesitate. He came straight over to her booth and plonked himself down opposite her. He gave her the full charm offensive, apologizing for being mean to her when she'd thrown him over.

He claimed he'd missed her and he wanted her back but if he couldn't be her boyfriend he wanted to be her friend, like me. He pitched it just right for Billy Jean and she believed he meant what he said. That's the kind of girl she was back then—honest and open and unable to see that other people might not be worthy of her trust. So she didn't think twice when he offered her a ride home.

She called me first thing Sunday morning. We were supposed to be going fishing as usual but she wanted Ruthie to come along too. I could tell from her voice something terrible had happened even though she wouldn't tell me what it was, so I called Ruthie and got her to make some excuse to get out of church.

When we picked her up, she was pale and withdrawn. She wouldn't say a word till we were out at the lake, sitting on the jetty with rods on the water like it was any other Sunday morning. When she did speak, it was right to the point. Billy Jean was never one for beating about the bush, but this was bald, even for her.

"Kenny Sheldon raped me last night," she said. She told us about the meeting at Helmer's and how she'd agreed to let him drive her home. Only, before they got to her house, Kenny had driven down an overgrown track out of sight of the street. Then he'd pinned her down and forced her to have sex with him.

We didn't know what to do. Fourteen years ago, date rape wasn't on the criminal agenda. Not in towns like Marriott. And the Sheldons were a prominent family. Kenny's dad owned the funeral home and had been a councilman. And his mom ran the flower arranging circle at the church. Whereas the Fergusons were barely one step up from white trash. Nobody was going to take the word of Billy Jean Ferguson against Kenny Sheldon.

I wanted to call Kenny Sheldon out and beat him to within an inch of his life. I wanted him to beg for mercy the way I knew Billy Jean had begged him the night before.

But Ruthie and Billy Jean stopped me. "Don't stoop so low," Billy Jean said.

"That's right," Ruthie said. "There's other ways to get back at scum like him."

And by that afternoon, I had started the rumor that Janine from the Tavern in the Town had stopped sleeping with Kenny because she'd found out he had a venereal disease. I don't know how long it took to get back to the shitheel himself, but I do know he'd had quite the struggle to get anyone to sit next to him in Helmer's, never mind hang out at gigs with him. That cheered us up some, and Ruthie said Billy Jean was starting to talk about getting over it. That was so like her—she wasn't the kind to let anybody take her life away from her. She was always determined to control her own destiny.

But all her good intentions went to shit about six weeks after the rape. I'd been helping my dad finish off some work in the top pasture and both girls were sitting on the front porch when I got back to the house. We all piled into my truck and headed out to the lake. We hadn't gone but half a mile when Ruthie blurted out, "She's pregnant. That bastard Kenny got her pregnant."

I only had to glance at Billy Jean to know it was true and the knowledge made me boiling mad. I swung the truck 'round at the next intersection and headed for the Sheldon house, paying no mind to the girls shouting at me to stop. When we got there, I jumped out and marched straight up to the house. I hammered on the door and Kenny himself opened it.

I know that violence isn't supposed to solve things, but in my experience, it definitely has its plus points. I grabbed Kenny by the shirt front, yanked him out the door, and slammed him against the wall. I swear the whole damn house shook. "You bastard," I yelled at him. "First you rape her, then you get her pregnant."

I drew my hand back to smack him in the middle of his dumbfounded face, but Billy Jean caught my arm. She was always strong for a girl and she had me at an awkward angle. "Leave him," she said. "I don't want anything to do with him."

"You say that now, but you're going to need his money," I snarled. "Babies don't come cheap and he has to pay for what he's done."

Before anybody could say anything more, Mrs. Sheldon appeared in the doorway. She looked shocked to see her golden boy pinned up against the wall and demanded to know what was going on.

My dander was up, and I wasn't about to back off. "Ma'am," I said, "I'm sorry to cause a scene, but your son here raped my cousin Billy Jean and now she is expecting his baby."

Mrs. Sheldon reared back like a horse spooked by a snake. "How dare you," she hissed. "My son is a gentleman, which is more than I can say about you or your kin." She made a kind of snorting noise in the back of her throat. "The very idea of any Ferguson woman being able to name the father of her children with any certainty is absurd. Now get off my property before I call the police. And take your slut of a cousin with you."

It was my turn to grab Billy Jean. I thought she was fixing to rip Mrs. Sheldon's face off. "You evil witch," she screamed as I pulled her away.

Ruthie stared Mrs. Sheldon down. When she spoke her voice was cold and sharp. I know I hoped she'd never use that tone of voice with me. "You should be ashamed of yourself," she said, turning on her heel and walking back to the truck, head high. I never knew to this day whether she meant Kenny or his mother or both of them.

What happened that evening must have had some effect, though. A week later, Kenny was gone.

BACK IN THE EARLY '60s, being an unwed mother was still about the biggest disgrace around and most girls who got into trouble ended up disowned and despised. But Billy Jean was lucky in her parents. The Fergusons never had much money but they had love aplenty. When she told them she was pregnant and how it had happened, they'd been shocked, but they hadn't been angry with her. Her father went 'round to see old man Sheldon. He never told anybody what passed between them, not even Mrs. Ferguson, but he came back with a cashier's check for ten thousand dollars.

Nobody knew where Kenny was. His mother told her church crowd that he'd landed a big important radio job out on the coast, but nobody believed her. Truth to tell, I don't think anybody much cared. We certainly didn't.

Jeff and I were married three months later. I guess we were both kind of fired up by Billy Jean being pregnant. We wanted to start a family of our own. We moved into a little house on Jeff's daddy's farm and Jeff started working as a trainee sales representative for an agricultural machinery firm.

Half a mile down the track from us there was an old double-wide trailer that had seen better days. Jeff's dad used to rent it out to seasonal workers. We persuaded him to let Billy Jean have it for next to nothing in return for doing it up. We knew there wasn't enough room in her parents' house for Billy Jean and a growing kid and I wanted her to be close at hand so we could bring up our children together.

Jeff and I spent most of our spare time knocking that trailer into shape. Billy Jean helped as much as she could, and by the time Jess was born, we'd turned it into a proper little home for the two of them. They moved in when Jess was six weeks old, and Billy Jean looked relaxed for the first time since Kenny had raped her. "I can never thank the two of you enough," she said so many times I told her she should just make a tape of it and give us each a copy.

"It was Ruthie's idea," Jeff said, acting like it was nothing to do with him.

"I know," Billy Jean said. "But I also know you did more than your fair share to make it happen."

We settled into a pretty easy routine. I worked mornings on the farm, helping Jeff's mother with the specialty yogurt business she was building up. Afternoons, I'd hang out with Billy Jean and Jess. Then I'd cook dinner for Jeff, and we'd either watch some TV or walk down to have a beer and a few hands of cards with Billy Jean. Most people might have thought our lives pretty dull, but it seemed fine enough to us.

There was one thing, I thought, that stopped it being perfect. A year had gone by since Jeff and I had married, but still I wasn't pregnant. It wasn't for want of trying, but I began to wonder whether my lack of enthusiasm for sex was somehow preventing it. I knew this was crazy, but it nagged away at me.

Finally, I managed to talk to Billy Jean about it. It was a hot summer afternoon and Jess was over at her grandma's house. Billy Jean and I were lying on her bed with the only AC in the trailer cranked up high. "I love him," I said. "But when we make love, it's not like it says in the books and magazines. It doesn't feel like it looks in the movies. I just don't feel that whole swept away thing."

Billy Jean rolled over onto her back and yawned. "I'm not the best person to ask, Ruth. I only ever had sex the once and that sure wasn't what you would call a good experience. I don't guess it's the kind of thing you can talk to Jeff about either."

I made a face. "He'd be mortified. He thinks I think he's the greatest lover on the planet." Billy Jean giggled. "Well, you have to make them feel like that."

Billy Jean yawned again. "I'm sorry, Ruth. I don't mean you to feel like I'm dismissing you, but I am so damn tired. I was up three times with Jess last night. She's teething."

"Why don't you just have a nap?" I said. But she was already drifting away. I made myself more comfortable and before I knew it, I'd nodded off too.

I woke because someone was kissing me. An arm was heavy across my chest and shoulder, a leg was thrown between mine and soft lips were pressing on mine, a tongue flicking between my lips.

I opened my eyes and the mouth pulled back from mine. A face that was familiar and yet completely strange hovered above mine. *Jeff with long hair*, I thought stupidly for a moment before the truth dawned.

Billy Jean put a finger to my lips. "Ssh," she said. "Let's see if we can figure out what Jeff's doing wrong."

By the end of the afternoon, I understood that it wasn't what Jeff did that was wrong. It was who he was.

KENNY CAME BACK A COUPLE of weeks before Jess's fourth birthday. It turned out his mother hadn't been lying to the church group. He had landed a job working for a radio station in Los Angeles. He was doing pretty well. Had his own show and everything. He rolled back into town in a muscle car with a beautiful blonde on his arm. His fiancée, apparently.

All of that would have been just fine if he had left the past alone. But no. He wanted to impress the fiancée with his credentials as a family man. The first thing we knew about it was when Billy Jean got a letter from Kenny's lawyer saying he planned to file suit for shared custody. Kenny wanted Jess for one week a month until she started school, then he wanted her for half the school vacations. If he'd been the standard absent father as opposed to one who had never even seen his kid, it might have sounded reasonable. And we had a sneaking feeling that the court might see things Kenny's way.

Justice in Marriott comes courtesy of His Honor Judge Wellesley Benton. Who is an old buddy of Kenny Sheldon's daddy and a man who's put a fair few of Billy Jean's relatives behind bars. We were, to say the least, apprehensive.

The day after the letter came, Billy Jean happened to be walking down Main Street when Kenny strolled out of the Coffee Bean Scene with the future Mrs. Sheldon. I heard all about it from Mom, who saw it all from the vantage point of the quilting store porch.

Billy Jean just lit into him. Called him all the names under the sun from rapist to deadbeat dad. Kenny looked shocked at first, then when he saw his fiancée wasn't turning a hair, he started to laugh. That just drove Billy Jean even crazier. She was practically hysterical. Mom came over from the quilt shop and grabbed her by the shoulders, trying to get her away. Then Kenny said, "I'll see you in court," and walked his fiancée to the car. Billy Jean was fit to be tied.

Well, everybody thinks they know what happened next. That night, Kenny was due at a dinner in the Town Hall. As he approached, a figure stepped out of the shadows. Long blond hair, jeans, and a Western shirt, just like Billy Jean always liked to wear. And a couple of witnesses who were a ways off but who knew Billy Jean well enough to recognise her when she raised the shotgun and blew Kenny Sheldon into the next world.

That was the end of her as much as it was the end of him.

I KNEW BILLY JEAN WAS innocent. Not out of some crazy misplaced belief, but because at the very moment Kenny Sheldon was meeting his maker, I was in her bed, moaning at her touch. That first afternoon had not been a one-off. It had been an awakening that had led us both into a deeper happiness than we'd ever known before.

If I'd been married to anyone other than Jeff, I'd have left in a New York minute. But I cared about him. More importantly, so did Billy Jean. "You're both my best friend," she said as we lay in a tangle of sheets. "Until this afternoon, I couldn't have put one of you above the other. You gotta stay with him, Ruth. You gotta go on being his wife because I couldn't live with myself if you didn't."

And so I did. It might seem strange to most folks, but in a funny kind of way, it worked out just fine for us. Except of course that I still couldn't get pregnant. I began to think of that as the price I had to pay for my other contentments—Jeff, Billy Jean, Jess.

Then Kenny came back.

They came for Billy Jean soon after midnight. A deputy we'd all been at school with knocked on our door at one in the morning, carrying Jess in a swaddle of bedclothes. He looked mortified as he explained what had happened and asked us to take care of the child till morning when things could be sorted out more formally.

Jess had often stayed with us, so she settled pretty easy. That morning, I drove into town, leaving Jess with her grandma, and demanded to see Billy Jean. She was white and drawn, her eyes heavy and haunted. "They can't prove it," she said. "You have to promise me you will never tell. Don't sacrifice yourself trying to save me. They won't believe you anyway and you'll have shamed yourself in their eyes for nothing. Just have faith. We both know I'm innocent. Judge Benton isn't a fool. He won't let them get away with it."

And so I kept my mouth shut. Partly for Billy Jean and partly for Jess. We'd already made arrangements with Billy Jean and her parents for me and Jeff to take care of Jess till after the court case, and I wasn't about to do anything that would jeopardize that child's future. I sat through that terrible trial day after day. I listened to witnesses swearing they had seen Billy Jean kill Kenny Sheldon and I said not a word.

Nor did Billy Jean. She said she was somewhere else, but refused to say where or with whom. Judge Benton offered her the way out. "Woman, what is your alibi?" he thundered. "If you were somewhere else that night, then you won't have to die. If you're telling the truth, give up your alibi." But she wouldn't budge. And so I couldn't. It nearly killed me.

But I never truly thought he would have her hanged.

I NEVER TRULY THOUGHT HE would have her hanged. I thought they'd argue she was temporarily insane because of the threat to her child and that she'd do a few years in jail, nothing more. And I was selfish enough to think of how much my Ruthie would love bringing up Jess for as long as Billy Jean was behind bars.

Sure, I wanted to make her suffer. But I didn't want her to die. She was my best friend, after all. A friend like no other. I swear, I always believed we would lay down our lives for each other if it came to it. And I guess I was right, in a way. She laid down her life rather than destroy my marriage.

When the sentence came down, it hit me like a physical blow. I swear I doubled over in pain as I realized the full horror of what I'd done. But it was too late. The sacrifices were made, the chips down once and for all.

I saw the way she looked at me in court. A mixture of pity and blame. As soon as she heard those witnesses, recognized the conviction in their voices, I think she knew the truth. With a long blonde wig and the right clothes, I could easily be mistaken for her.

There was an excuse for the witnesses. They were a ways off from Kenny and his killer. But there's no excuse for Ruthie. She was no distance at all from Billy Jean that afternoon I saw them by the lakeshore. She could not have been mistaken.

Why didn't I confront her? Why didn't I walk away? I guess because I loved them both so much. I didn't want to lose the life we had. I just wanted Billy Jean to suffer for a while, that was all. I never truly thought he would have her hanged.

JESS TURNED FOURTEEN TODAY. SHE'S not old enough for the truth. Maybe she'll never be that old. But there's one thing she is old enough for.

Tonight, there will be two of us standing over Billy Jean's grave, our long black veils drifting in the wind, our tears sparkling like diamonds in the moonlight.

ME UNTAMED
BY DAVID LISS

SHE COVERED THE BLACK EYE with makeup, but I could still see it was there, something alien and unaccountable. Like a vandal's scrawl across a museum painting, the dull outline of her bruise was an outrage. Carla smiled and greeted everyone good morning, defying us to say a word, to let our eyes linger too long. It was, I supposed, how she protected herself.

Jim Baron, the senior partner in the practice, met my gaze and flicked his head toward Carla as she walked past with a stack of case folders under her arm. Carla was getting ready, as we did every Tuesday and Thursday, for surgeries—no office visits on those days, just procedures. The practice felt a bit like a gastrointestinal assembly line, and sometimes I hated how we moved patients in and out, hardly taking the time to look at them, but Jim cracked the whip. It was volume, volume, volume as far as he was concerned. We were there to heal, not to socialize, and the more healing, the better.

Maybe we didn't linger with any patient long enough to know one's face from another's, but they looked at ours, and I knew what Jim was thinking—that it was a good thing this one was of the practice's surgery days. People would be too occupied with their own fears to notice that one of the masked doctors, not even the lead doctor, had a bruise around her eye. Jim was thinking we'd caught a break. No one wanted a victim, someone who would let herself get smacked around, noodling around inside some of the most intimate parts of their body. One quick gesture toward me, a nod of his head, was like a lecture: get her to straighten out her personal shit.

I went into the break room and had the gigantic machine, clanging and hissing like some steampunk contraption, make me a black coffee. It was scalding, which was how I liked it, and I took painful little sips while I had it make Carla a skim-milk latte. I then brought it over to her office, where she sat with her desk lamp on and overhead off, reviewing the day's procedures.

"You looked like you could use some caffeine," I said, closing the door behind me.

She smiled. "I can get my own coffee, Mike."

I knew she was glad I'd gotten it for her, though. A little kindness doesn't erase someone else's cruelty, but maybe it soothes it a little. "Just being friendly."

We sat in silence for a long pause. Carla had just started at the practice where I'd been working for four years. I'd helped her land the spot. We'd met in medical school, though she'd started several years behind me, and I'd taken her under my wing. I'd always been something of a mentor to her—a big brother, she liked to say. Now here she was, with an office just down the hall from mine. We were both doctors and that made us equals. I was three years divorced and Carla was married to a guy who, apparently, liked to hit her in the face. That made us something else.

Full disclosure: I'd never thought of Carla as a little sister. If anything, my kindness toward her, back in the early days, had been kind of parental, maybe avuncular. She had been this clueless, desperate thing, and it had made me feel a little more wise and doctorly to help her out. I was newly married, and she hadn't interested me sexually, not at all, but over time, Carla had gotten under my skin with a slow creep.

She wasn't beautiful, maybe not even pretty with her long nose and weak chin and almost imperceptibly uneven teeth, and straw-colored hair pulled into ponytail, but there was a thing about her—a kind of liveliness and humor that transcended traditional notions of beauty. Also, she had a trim, athletic body that she rarely showed off, but I knew was always lurking under her skirt suits or scrubs. In the last, uneasy days of my marriage, my then-wife had accused me of being in love with Carla, but that wasn't true. Maybe it was even completely false, but there was a thing there, maybe more for her than for me, and I liked the charge that hung in the air when we met in the hall or went out for lunch or sat in my office with the door closed.

I could no longer say that I didn't think about Carla, but now she was married, and I wasn't going to be like my ex-wife and play fast and loose with the rules. That had always been my position, anyhow, but now I began to think of my morals as a bit more plastic. It was better to live within a range of options rather than sticking to one point inflexibly. I'd met Carla's husband a bunch of times—a big guy who owned a sizeable portion of a local roofing company. He did pretty well, but he he'd always seemed sort of a brute, maybe a little beneath her. Maybe a lot.

"Carla, if there's something you want to—"

She smiled—tight lipped and broken hearted, shyly concealing her teeth. Her eyes sparkled with sadness and maybe gratitude. I don't know. She looked about perfect to me in that moment. "There isn't. I just need—I need to get some work done."

"If Steve is—"

She cut me off. "Steven," she reminded me, her face as devoid of expression as a human face can be. Less readable than a mask. Steven, I was reminded, did not like nicknames. He didn't like people who refused to own guns or eat pizza without pepperoni. He did not think highly of electric cars. He didn't like doctors, who thought they were smarter than everyone else. *This little lady's the exception!* he would bark. *You, Mike, are not,* was implied. Every time I was forced to have a conversation with the guy at a party or barbecue, all he could talk about was how much money he was making—more than a doctor!—how he could only do one thing at a time. He wasn't like some con man who could schedule eight patients for the same time slot. What he did, he explained to me, was honest work. He didn't spend his days with his thumb up his ass, or, he would say with a grin, up someone else's.

"Whatever his name is," I said, "you can't put up with him hitting you."

She looked away. "I never said that."

"Carla, come on. You don't have to."

She sighed and pushed some hair from her pale hazel eyes. She forced another false smile, and she was as close to objectively beautiful as she was ever going to get. It broke my heart a little. "You'd think, taking all those martial arts classes, I'd be able to look after myself."

"You don't have to do everything by yourself," I told her, keeping things vague, because I had no idea what I was supposed to do here. "Your friends can help you."

She shook her head. "You don't understand."

"I know that," I said. "I know that for sure, but I don't have to understand in order to help you be safe."

She shook her head. "Life is funny, you know. We spend all these years learning about how the human body works. We have this authority, and we advise people on decisions that affect lives. Sometimes we make calls that affect whether or not people live or die. You'd think with all that, we could have more power in our own lives."

"Carla, you do have power," I said. "Whatever you want to do, you can do. I can help you."

"You can't," she said.

After I left her office, I thought about that. I'd taken her words to mean that she didn't think that anyone could help her, but maybe that wasn't it. Maybe she'd meant "*You* can't." Maybe she didn't think I was up to it, and maybe I wasn't, but I wanted to be the sort of person who was. And I knew she was right. I was a doctor and that meant something. I was not going to let her suffer.

I'M A LITTLE ON THE short side and I've been losing my hair since high school. I shave my scalp pretty close these days and make up for the absence with a neat little goatee. I wear glasses because contact lenses make my eyes tired. I could change some things around, knock a few years off my appearance, but my patients think I look like a doctor, like someone they can trust to advise them. They are almost all older than I am, so conforming with their idea of the platonic doctor saves us all time. Maybe it even saves lives. If people are more inclined to listen to me, to do what I advise, they just might live longer. That's the kind of position I'm in.

I run regularly and hit the gym three times a week, and I'm in pretty good shape for thirty-nine, but I know that once I hang up the white coat, I give off a harmless vibe. Strangers on airplanes always guess that I'm a university professor because I strike them as bookish and introverted. One guy once called me dweeby, right to my face. I wanted to bloody his nose for that, but I just laughed agreeably, which maybe proved his point.

I know that the people in my life, those who know my story, think I'm weak and that's because of my ex-wife. It turns out that while I was logging long hours and earning the money that paid for our nice house and our exotic vacations, she was cheating on me with the guy from Home Depot who was redoing our kitchen. Maybe it was more than just animal attraction because she's living with him now. On an abstract level, I get that. Emotions are tricky things, and often beyond our control.

Still, I know what the world sees. She left a successful doctor in a lucrative practice for a guy who works for Home Depot, so clearly I was fucking up. They don't conclude that my ex-wife was a cheater who couldn't stand stability and domesticity, who didn't want kids when I did, and that maybe my silent disappointment chipped away at her own contentment. She told me that's what drove her to Eduardo, and I had no trouble believing it. She didn't do responsibility well. She liked mess and surprise and lighting itineraries on fire. That's how things boil down, but to the spectators in my life, she was a good-looking and charming woman, a trophy wife, and she'd left me for a tattooed wage slave who rides a motorcycle.

I'd never felt particularly unmanly before she left me. As a kid I'd gotten along with everyone, so I'd never had to fight. I'd played violin, and primarily listened to classical music, and the other kids still didn't pick on me. That's how easy I was to get along with. When I started noticing girls, some noticed me back. I got by on my personality, and I always did pretty well. I put myself through all those years of schooling, I paid my debts and helped out my friends. I always felt I was on top of things, but now I found myself thinking all the time about the ways people thought I was lacking. I couldn't keep my wife. I didn't start a family. I'd sold the house, which was too big and full of memories, and was now in a two-room apartment. I was going to be forty soon, and I was living like a kid almost half my age.

Lately I'd begun to suspect that the people who knew me didn't think I was all that competent. Carla, I was now sure, was one of those people.

EVEN BEFORE THE BLACK EYE, I'd been dwelling on this. I dwelled on it all that day, through the various endoscopies, sigmoidoscopies, and hemorrhoidal bandings that made up a typical Tuesday. I needed to be more assertive. I needed to make my life what I wanted it to be. The song—stuck in my head through every procedure—was a prodding and a reminder.

When I was in high school, an older kid I really admired, Charles Randall, had introduced me to all kinds of music—things I wouldn't have listened to otherwise. I'd have stuck with Haydn and Beethoven if he hadn't gotten this idea that he was going to make me cool. He gave me lists, generated mix tapes, dragged me to shows. One of the bands he'd pointed me toward was Beat Happening. At the time I hadn't heard anything like them—they played and sang really badly, the production values were poor and yet somehow it all came together as an engaging and unlikely pop confection with jagged edges, a dessert tray sprinkled with broken glass.

I'd forgotten about the band for years, but a few months before Carla's black eye, I'd been going through my CD collection, looking to get rid of things that reminded me of the marriage. I threw away less than I kept and I put on a lot of music I hadn't listen to in decades and most of it seemed to me better forgotten, but when I put on the Beat Happening CD *Dreamy* something clicked. The opening track, "Me Untamed" felt like a wakeup call. It's guitar and drum driven and catchy, and Calvin Johnson's vocals, flat and base, sound as much like a deathbed convulsion as a performance, but there was an urgency to the song. It was like a revelation. I had been tamed my entire life, by my marriage, by my divorce, by my niceness, by my inoffensive looks. The song, I realized, needed to become my anthem. I wanted to become untamed.

I'd have the song stuck in my head while sitting alone in my apartment after work, watching a baseball game, eating a sandwich I'd bought on the way home from a late night at the office or, as Carla's husband would put it, sticking my thumb up someone else's ass. The song, twitchy and urgent, was a prodding, but it was one thing to determine you wanted to take more risks, live more fully, be a more daring version of yourself, but it was another to know how to do it.

Most of my friends were married and had kids. It wasn't like I could recruit anyone into a dangerous adventure. I had no interest in going out to bars and trying to pick up women. I was a doctor and still of marriageable age, so the reality was I met plenty of women, but that wasn't the kind of adventure I was looking for. I wasn't after sexual conquest, I was looking to assert myself, to become the sort of person who people took seriously. I wanted to be untamed.

Carla didn't think I was up to it. "*You* can't," she'd said. So maybe it was time to show her that I could.

I KNEW HOW TO FIND Steven. That part wasn't hard. He and I went to the same gym, and I had picked up on his schedule, noticing it mostly so as to avoid running into him. He liked to check out how much I was bench-pressing, or if we were in the locker at the same time, he would sometimes glance at me and smirk. Tamed Mike wanted to avoid the scrutiny. The untamed Mike did not give a shit.

Okay, that wasn't true, but before I might have fantasized about manufacturing an encounter. It was that song, looping through my head, that prompted me to actually do it. The edgy sound of the drum hammered in my head, driving me forward.

I couldn't focus on my workout, but I did catch up with Steven after my shower. He must have been running late because he was coming into the locker room when I was on my way out. He had a good six inches on me, and he was broader in the shoulders. He had a full head of blond hair and a wispy soul patch that he thought made him look youthful and cool. In fact, it made him look like a moron.

He nodded at me as he passed. That was how it was with us. He figured I was into his wife, so he regarded me with polite contempt. Ours was a battle he had already won, and he liked to swagger past me in a fog of perpetual conquest. I usually let him get away with it.

"Hey, Steven," I said. I stopped, forcing him to stop. I was taking command of the conversation, not letting him call the shots.

He looked at me, puzzled.

"I saw Carla today," I told him.

He cocked his head. "Yeah? She works in your office, so that doesn't seem like such a big deal."

"No, what I'm saying is, I *saw* her. You know what I mean?"

He was now staring at me. He took a step closer. "No, what do you mean? What exactly are you trying to say about my wife?"

"I'm not saying anything about her," I said. "I don't think she's the subject of this conversation at all."

He was now moving his head back and forth, like he was studying some kind of oddity he couldn't quite figure out. "I don't know what you're talking about, man."

I shrugged. "Okay, Steve."

He walked away, not bothering to correct me about his name. He'd gotten the message, I decided. He was on notice.

I sat in the car after, my hands trembling so badly I could barely work my phone as I synched up the Beat Happening song to the sound system. The music washed over me while I thought about doing things that, just a few weeks ago, would have been unimaginable. I was a doctor, I told myself. I make decisions of life and death. I am untamed.

CARLA DIDN'T SAY ANYTHING TO me at work the next day, but she was much less walled off. The bruise was barely visible under her makeup now.

Before the onslaught of patients began, she came into my office to talk about nothing in particular, and laughed at some jokey things I said, maybe more loudly than they deserved. The next day she asked me if I wanted to go to lunch, and while we were waiting for the check, she briefly put her hand on mine.

Talking to Steven had somehow shaken things loose. All my life I'd avoided making enemies, avoided conflicts that weren't necessarily my own, but now I began to wonder how much I might have missed by not sticking my neck out more. I'd always liked being low-key and laid-back. Maybe I liked being untamed even more, and that meant I needed to consider taking things to the next level. It was one thing to think about doing something that had once been inconceivable. It was another to make a plan, to figure out how to cover my tracks.

Carla's touch, that fleeting brush of her fingertips against the back of my hand, seemed so full of promise. What was she doing with a guy like Steven, anyhow? Even if he hadn't been the kind of person who hit his wife, he would have been beneath her. She needed to move on, find someone more worthy, and I wasn't afraid to help her.

I was sure she was prepared to help me, which was why I was surprised when she asked me if I wanted to go out that weekend with her and Steven and a woman she thought I might like. Were my attentions making her uncomfortable? Was this her polite way of getting me off her back?

More likely, I decided, it was her way of spending time with me outside of work in a way that would be acceptable to her husband.

We met on Friday night at a Thai restaurant. The woman, whose name was Patti, seemed nice enough. She was closer to my age than Carla's, and pretty in a generic best-friend-on-a-sitcom way, but she didn't seem terribly interesting.

"I like trying lots of different things," Steven announced after we sat down. "I'm for sharing."

This was not the first time I'd had to have this conversation with him. He did it to get on my nerves, to see if I would push back. "Sharing's fine with me," I said, "but remember that I don't eat meat."

"You want to make all of us eat tofu?" Steven asked, squinting at me.

"I don't want to make you do anything," I told him. "I'm just letting you know that if you order food with meat, I won't have any."

"Less for you then!" Steven said with a laugh.

"I can order something vegetarian," Carla volunteered.

He turned to her. "You want to change how you live for this guy? Let him be flexible for once and eat meat."

"It's not really the same thing," Patti mused. "I can get something vegetarian too."

The three of us ended up sharing. Steven ordered something with pork, maybe because it was the most offensive meat he could think of—at least two major meat-eating religions shunned it.

The ordering debacle was the highlight of dinner, but the rest of the meal didn't go as well. I tried to steer the conversation to politics, mostly because I knew Carla followed current events closely and Steven did not, but Patti wasn't very skillful at hiding her boredom.

"I don't keep up with that stuff," she said to me. "It's so depressing!" She mostly wanted to talk about the popular reality shows—the ones with the singers and the people who are competing to get married—but I didn't follow those. Everyone else did, so I checked out while they talked.

When Carla reached for some hot sauce, her sleeve rode up, and I noticed a dark bruise on her forearm. Maybe it had been there a while, but it looked raw and new. Her eyes met mine for a moment, and she looked away.

Steven was watching us. He grinned at me with a *What are you going to do about it?* look. I stared right back, hoping to convey that I knew precisely what I was going to do about it even though I had not the foggiest idea. I dared a look over at Carla, and her eyes met mine, only for a second, but I knew she was begging me for help. She needed me to do something. She couldn't leave him without my help.

We went our separate ways after the meal. It was pretty clear I hadn't clicked with Patti, and it seemed easier to end things. I needed some time to figure out my next move, anyhow. Or, at least, I had to go over the details of my next move, which had been taking shape in my head. I knew what I had to do, and I'd been preparing to do it. I just had to pick my time.

It turns out the time picked me. The next day Steven called me up. He said Carla was going out of town to visit her sister, and maybe I wanted to come over for a few drinks. He said he wanted to clear the air between us. I did not want to have some sort of confrontation with him. In Steven's mind, this was going to end with a fight or with a bro hug, and neither of those appealed to me. The old me would have refused, but I had Beat Happening grating discordantly in my head, so I told him it sounded like a great idea.

He told me to come by at five. He said he'd crack open some beer and order up some pizza. I had no doubt the pizza would come with pepperoni. I wasn't going to eat pepperoni to show I was a good guy, and I wasn't going to pick the meat off daintily like a bitch. I had a third option in mind.

He was wearing workout clothes when he answered the door, but he didn't look sweaty. Maybe he just wanted to show off his muscles.

I came in and he put a bottle of beer in my hand. There was a college football game on the television, and I pretended to make small talk but Steven wasn't even trying, and after a few failed attempts I gave up. I finished my beer, and when Steven didn't offer me another one, I went to the refrigerator and helped myself.

A few minutes later, the pizza came, and of course it was sprinkled with pepperoni. "Help yourself," Steven said.

I smiled. "I'm okay."

"What? You watching your girlish figure?"

"I don't eat meat," I told him, like we'd never had this conversation.

He shrugged. "You can just pick them off and give them to me. I'll eat them."

"I'm fine," I said.

He grinned at me. "Not eating meat. Does that help you get pussy? Because the only other explanation is that you are a pussy."

I set down my beer. "Steven, you're being hostile."

"I love the fancy talk," he said.

"I'm not being fancy, I'm being straight. You were hostile last night, and you're hostile today. You said you wanted to clear the air, so go ahead and clear it."

"Fine," he said. "Let's talk about how you're looking to fuck my wife."

"Hold on," I began, but he cut me off.

"Don't try to deny it. Your own wife fucked around on you, and now—what? You're looking for some cosmic payback? Do it on your own time. Play your games somewhere else. You and Carla have to work together, and we can be chums, but I want you to stop trying to get her into bed with you, because it's not going to happen. Your flirting is embarrassing to you and insulting to me. I can't let it stand."

"I'm not looking to sleep with Carla," I told him, not knowing if this was true or not. "I'm trying to protect her." This was definitely true.

"From what?" he sneered. "Life with a meathead?"

I held up my hands. I was about to excuse myself, say that this was none of my business and get the hell out of there. That's what I wanted to do, and it's what I knew I should do, but I had that song telling me I couldn't stop. This was me untamed, not the old me. So I lowered my hands and I got ready.

I'd thought about this, played it out in my head over and over again until it felt like a memory. It was what I intended to do, but I never really believed it would happen. Yet the moment was here. Wheels were turning and gears were grinding, and I had to go forward. It was like the first time I operated. I knew, on some level, that I could walk away, but I also knew I couldn't retreat and live with myself. Carla needed me to step up.

"I know you're hurting her," I said.

His face went red like I'd slapped him. Maybe no one had ever dared to speak it aloud before. Maybe it was a dark secret, even between the two of them. He took a step toward me. "I'm doing what?" he demanded. He tossed his beer bottle against the wall. It exploded in a spray of glass and moisture. "I'm doing what?"

"You think people don't know?" I stood my ground. I wasn't going to be intimidated by a wife beater.

"I'm going to give you a chance to walk this back," he said through clenched teeth. "Because what you're saying is not something I can let you get away with, so you damn well better unsay it."

"You think somehow it's not obvious?" I asked. "You think I'm the only one to see it?"

"You'd just better shut the fuck up," he said through clenched teeth. "My father beat my mom, and as a kid, as a little kid, I vowed I would not hurt a woman. So let me tell you that what you're saying is complete and utter bullshit."

"This sort of thing runs in families," I said "That's probably why you're doing it. You can't help it. It's like hardwired in your DNA. Isn't it, Steve?"

He took a step toward me, his fist curled into a ball, and this was where things were going to get tricky. If I made a mistake, I was going to get worse that beaten, I was going to get caught. This would be the end of everything. I'd put my life on the line for Carla. It's what she needed from me.

Steven was coming at me, ready for me to run or face him or try to talk him down. I don't know what he was expecting, but it wasn't that I would drop and leap forward, tackling him by his legs.

He didn't fall, and he didn't need to. I only needed a second to get the hypodermic out. It was in my hand, with the cap off, in a second. I rammed it into his Nikes, getting him in the side of the foot, and I plunged the lethal dose of succinylcholine into his blood. Maybe it would leave a mark, maybe not, but I doubted anyone would be hunting for signs of foul play.

Steven glanced down at me. He looked at the needle in my hand, trying to comprehend what I was up to. Did he think that I was just trying to calm him—that doctors carried sedatives at all times in case of emergency—or did he begin to realize how far I was willing to go to protect Carla? He staggered back, the drug already taking effect, or maybe it was just the shock. If the succinylcholine hadn't kicked in yet, it would only be a few more seconds. I collected the cap for the needle and then went out went out back with the kitchen garbage. I knew they kept their trash in the alley behind the house, along with the rest of the neighbors. I put the needle in a tangled mass of aluminum foil and placed the trash bag in a neighbor's can. It wasn't a foolproof plan, but succinylcholine is hard to detect, especially if no one is trying to find it. If they figured out what got him, then I was pretty much toast anyhow. They wouldn't need the needle to pin it on me. Putting it in the neighbor's can was more to soothe me than cover my tracks.

By the time I got back to the house, Steven was dead. I performed CPR on him to make things look good, and then I called 911. I stood in the quiet house, Beat Happening pounding in my head, thinking about how it had been a pretty serious mistake for him to hurt someone I cared about.

The cops suspected nothing. Steven was young for heart failure, but he ate badly and drank a lot of beer and while these things were unusual, they weren't unheard of. Cops saw this sort of thing every day. Carla was called back from visiting her sister, but I was long gone by then. I left a few messages on her phone, but she never called me back. She texted and said that she couldn't see anyone right now, but she knew I'd done all I could. I guess that was her way of saying she knew it was me. It was her way of thanking me.

She announced she'd be taking some time off from the practice, but that was to be expected. She wanted her privacy. Did she regret that I'd done it for her? Was she angry? I couldn't guess, and I decided there was no rush in finding out. Maybe I could never have her. Maybe things were tainted now, but I'd saved her. I'd allowed the untamed me to get her out of a bad situation and stop a man who was cruel and vile. That was good enough.

At least it would have been if I hadn't seen her exchanging sly looks with a strange man at the funeral. He was tall and athletic and movie-star handsome. I made a point to talk to him after the burial. He wore a dark suit that looked a little threadbare. He was clearly the kind of guy who didn't wear suits very often. The kind of guy Carla likes, I couldn't help but think.

"Hey, I'm Mike," I told him.

"Alexander," he told me.

"A relative?" I asked.

"A friend," he said, "of Carla's."

"How do you know her?"

He shook his head shyly. "You work with her, right? I can't believe she didn't mention me. How did she explain that black eye?"

I looked at him. "You?"

He held up his hands as if to show he meant to no harm. "Total accident. I've got a karate studio. Carla is one of the best in my adult class, but that means things can get a little aggressive. I thought she was going to block, but I made contact. Felt like shit."

He must have seen me looking horrified. He laughed and put a hand on my shoulder. "I'm sure she keeps it under wraps on the job, but trust me. Carla can be pretty violent when she wants to be."

I didn't move when Alexander walked on. Carla was with her sister and her mother, where she was deliberately not looking in my direction.

1968 PELHAM BLUE SG JR.
BY MARK HASKELL SMITH

WHILE ONE OF US WAS fucking the middle-aged goth chick against a dumpster in the alley, we went and got beer. We didn't think it would be a big deal. This kind of thing happened all the time and we tried to give each other space for a quick bang whenever we could. It made being in the van easier and gave us stories to share. For some of us, the sex was the main reason we played these gigs. It wasn't for the money.

We found a bar a block away. It was one of those places that calls itself a tavern and has a list of beers written on a chalkboard behind the bar. They had mismatched sofas and coffee tables scattered around the room and shitty electro-groove music dripping out of the speakers. Maybe this is what people are into these days. It's not like anyone came to our show. We had seventy-nine paying customers and one horny soccer mom wearing vintage Hot Topic. Maybe everyone else was sitting in thrift-store living rooms listening to laptops make music.

We took a couch, put our sweaty Docs up on the coffee table and drank beers that were so fancy they weren't called beer. It was the French or German or Flemish name for something that tasted a lot like beer. But it was tasty, we all agreed on that. We also agreed that the one of us banging the chick against the dumpster was the designated driver for the night. Then we ordered another round. Someone said something about the importance of proper hydration, especially after a show in a tiny sweaty shithole, and we quickly came to the understanding that we would dedicate the night to replacing lost electrolytes.

We told jokes that maybe we'd told before but we laughed like it was the first time we'd heard them. A few of us told versions of events that didn't seem like the way we remembered them but we laughed anyway. We talked about bands we liked and how new music sucks. We agreed that drum machines have no soul and that anyone who played a Rickenbacker was a dickhead. Except Lemmy. But then we couldn't figure out why he would play a Rickenbacker. It just doesn't make sense.

We chatted with some hipster girls, hoping that they might want a quick fuck in the bathroom or out in the alley, but they just wanted to talk about how the beer on the chalkboard was brewed two blocks away by a cool young guy who always wore T-shirts from old cult bands. He had one of our T-shirts. The hipster girls made it sound like he was one of those guys who digs up dinosaur bones.

We started to feel tired.

One of us politely asked the bartender to turn off the shitty music and put on something else and another of us threw our empty glass at him when he put on the Red Hot Chili Peppers. We all agreed that the Chili Peppers were a band that should be playing Rickenbackers.

We were asked to leave. We didn't leave a tip.

Some of us were pissing in a parking lot when we began to shout. We knew something was wrong. The middle-aged goth was gone but so was our gear. The back door of the van was open and we'd been cleaned out. Guitars, drums, amps, our clothes, gone. Everything but a box of old merch we'd been trying to sell at the gig.

The drums weren't that big a deal. It was a cheap Tama kit that we found online. Neither was the Fender bass. Those things you could find on Craigslist. The other gear hurt. A new Mesa/Boogie amp and a seriously badass Ampeg bass rig. Some vintage FX pedals. It sucked that they were gone, but at least they were replaceable. The same couldn't be said for the sunburst Les Paul from the early seventies and a bright green Gretsch Country Gentleman. Those were really sweet guitars. But the real mind-fuck, the thing that caused our blood to boil, was that a super rare 1968 Pelham Blue SG Jr. was gone. The purchase of the SG had caused a divorce, so maybe it was cursed, but whatever it was, it was more valuable than all the other equipment put together and multiplied by a thousand. We're only kind of exaggerating about the value. Our signature sound came from that guitar. It defined us.

The first thing we thought was that someone had come to our show and cased our gear. The second thought we had was that we couldn't call the police because one of us was supposed to be home with an ankle monitor strapped to our leg. It had been tricky to slide it off without cutting into the fabric and alerting the authorities, but the genius move was to strap it around the neck of a Chihuahua named Manny. Manny just thought it was a cool new collar. We couldn't put the monitor on a chair because they monitor the movements and if it didn't move then they might think we were dead. Manny was perfect because he wandered around the house like a stir-crazed parole violator anyway. Sometimes he went out the doggie door to poop in the backyard. It was a good setup because one of us was definitely not supposed to be two hundred miles from home playing a rock show in a shitty little bar.

We sat on the bumper of the van and shared a joint. We were upset. We wanted justice. We wanted revenge. Mostly we wanted our shit back. Then we could take our revenge.

It was agreed that we needed a plan. It was getting late and we realized that we would also need to continue hydrating.

We regretted not tipping the bartender at the tavern and spent some time discussing whether or not he might accept our apologies and maybe some of this excellent White Rhino as a peace offering. We decided to take this approach and maybe throw in a couple of T-shirts from the merch box.

While a couple of us went to get the beer, it occurred to one of us that one of us was missing. Was he kidnapped? Would we receive a ransom note? What would we write on the Missing Person report? Last seen fucking a middle-aged goth chick against a dumpster?

We sent a text message to his phone asking if he was okay. We did not get the courtesy of a reply.

A couple of us came back from the tavern with four giant bottles of beer called growlers and some plastic cups. We smoked another joint and rehydrated.

The manager of the club came out into the alley and gave us our cut of the door. He then suggested we move the van. We told him about the robbery and he gave us another two hundred bucks and said we should ask a guy named Alfonso at the twenty-four-hour donut store if he'd heard anything. Alfonso supposedly knew everything about anything that was going on in the area.

We finished our beer and relieved ourselves on the back wall of the club. It wasn't a tradition with us, not like some bands, but it is satisfying to mark your territory.

We drove a few blocks to the donut shop. On the way we talked about bands that have road crews and big rigs and fancy tour buses with bunk beds and big-screen TVs and minibars and a personal chef to make you whatever you wanted to eat whenever you wanted to eat it and WiFi and chocolate fountains and nurses that would give you B vitamins and antibiotics and painkillers. We were never that kind of band. We traveled in two vans, an equipment van with a couple of roadies, and a van for us. We did our own driving. We didn't have bunk beds but we had sleeping bags and most of the time some fans or the promoter would let us sleep in their living room, but sometimes we stayed in cheap hotels. We didn't get rich, most of us have regular jobs now, but we had fun back in the day and some of our fans still remember us. That's why we play gigs like this. The oldsters come to relive their youth, the youth come because they think it's ironic to relive a past they never had, and some people like a couple of our songs that were big in the nineties on college radio. Most us of have no regrets. We are not complaining. Except about the herpes. That could've been prevented.

The donut shop was bright. Blasting florescent light at glazed circles of fried bread must do something to the human brain because when we walked in we temporarily forgot about asking Alfonso about our gear, we just ordered a couple dozen mixed donuts. There were classic cake donuts with powdered sugar and yeasty glazed ones. But this donut shop wasn't your average donut shop, they had crazy donuts. Peanut butter with marshmallow fluff glaze. Coconut cream with mango filling. Lemon donuts with iced tea frosting. Bacon maple logs. A strawberry cruller with Sriracha sauce.

We had eaten the first dozen when one of us went up to the counter and told Alfonso our story. Alfonso was a sympathetic guy. He said he'd once made out with a girl while one of our songs was playing on the radio and he didn't think she would ever make out with him but she did and he even got to second base so he felt like he owed us. He went to make a call.

Back in the day it was easy to see when we got cocaine on our faces, but now the powdered sugar just blended in to the gray of our goatees and mustaches and soul patches. Nowadays we could do a lot of cocaine if we had any.

The hipster girls from the tavern came into the donut shop and acted like they were old friends. We let them sit with us, because why wouldn't we, and told them about the 1968 Pelham Blue SG Jr. and our missing bandmate.

Alfonso came over and said he hadn't heard anything from his sources which meant it was probably someone from outside the area. He said that was not good news for recovering our stuff. We worried about our gear. We worried about our bandmate. We drank some coffee with our donuts to keep our spirits up. We did not know what to do. We are not detectives.

One of us checked our smartphone to see if our missing bandmate had replied to our text and one of the hipster girls said we should use the Find Friends App to see where he was. This is the kind of thing we don't like about the new generation. No privacy. Auto Tune. Pro Tools. Soulless mechanization. We'd rather break a guitar string, play out of tune, and feel alive. Still we recognized it as a good idea. Especially because it worked.

We followed the coordinates on the phone but we were scared. We didn't know what we might find. Would one of us be tied up in a warehouse? Would he be dead? To calm our nerves we passed around another joint and, because the donuts made us feel dehydrated, we drank the rest of the beer.

Even though it was three in the morning the lights were still on at the house. We walked up to the front door and peeked in. Through a gap in the curtains we could see all our gear stacked up in the living room. We were trying to figure out how to approach the situation when a pizza delivery guy pulled up. We said hi to him and he nodded at us and rang the doorbell.

We were surprised when one of us opened the door. He was surprised to. He said he could explain and paid for the pizza.

The middle-aged goth chick was there. It was her house. We sat on her couch and ate the pizza while one of us told us a really long story about how he needed the money for an operation to cure the tinnitus in his ear that was making him crazy. But all we heard was that the middle-aged goth chick was his cousin. It meant he'd fucked his cousin. We would never fuck our cousin and told him so. The middle-aged goth chick didn't seem to care. She reminded us that it wasn't like they were getting married and having kids so it was none of our business and could we kindly get the fuck out of her house.

We carried the gear back to the van and, once it was loaded, one of us wanted to make sure the 1968 Pelham Blue SG Jr. was still in its case and we opened it. Then one of us swung the guitar around just like Jimi or Kurt and hit the cousin fucker who had been one of us in the head. We don't know why it happened. Maybe Alfonso's donuts have too much sugar. Maybe it was the stress of almost losing our most valuable instrument or the sting of betrayal. Maybe we just don't think cousins should have sexual relations. We didn't know if it was the guitar hitting skull or the subsequent skull hitting curb that caused the most damage. We are not Crime Scene Investigators although we have watched the show.

We put some plastic over his head so he wouldn't bleed on the gear and threw him in the back of the van with the amps and drums.

The highway was empty, not even any big rigs rumbling down the road, so we smoked another joint. We knew we had a lot of work ahead of us. One of us mentioned that we would need to audition a new drummer.

ALL AGES
BY ALISON GAYLIN

WE STARTED WITH THE HAIR. Bret said that was where all adventures started—*Great hair, great music, great buzz.* And so the first thing we did on the night of the all-ages X show at The Whisky was to lock ourselves in her upstairs bathroom with two cans of Aqua Net, three boxes of Midnight Raven temporary dye, and an assortment of pics and combs, gels whose names I can no longer remember but whose colors I do—battery acid green, radioactive yellow. . . . Each of them with an epoxy-like consistency and a sickly chemical smell. We teased the mercy out of each other's hair and took swigs from a bottle of peach schnapps we'd found at the back of her parents' liquor cabinet and we played X albums—*Under the Big Black Sun, Los Angeles,* some bootleg tape recorded live at one of their local shows. Bret's trifecta in action. And it was working. Exene's steely voice grew more and more beautiful with each gulp of schnapps, John Doe's growl a cloud I could float on. My hair turned stiff and black and defiant and before long I was a star, a punk rock star. I felt like dancing.

We were sixteen years old. It was my first show at any Hollywood club, and to my San Gabriel Valley mind there was no Hollywood club more punk rock than The Whisky. Bret's parents had gone out that night. Even though they thought we were simply having a sleepover, they'd left behind wheels—the Karmann Ghia that used to belong to Bret's older sister, broken down for years but recently restored to working condition. "Use the car only if there's an emergency, girls," her mom had said. And we'd managed to keep straight faces. Both of us.

When we were done with the hair, Bret and I looked in the mirror. Dueling Exenes stared back at us. . . . Well, from the scalp up, anyway. Quickly, we put on our makeup—dead-white skin, blood-red lips. We troweled kohl around our eyes and sucked in our cheeks and winked at our reflections like we were posing for an album cover.

"Now," Bret said, once we finished. "Now we look like we belong at an X show."

"We look so different," I said. I felt different, too—scary and grown-up. Invincible.

I CAN TASTE THE PEACH schnapps now. I feel the tacky pull of the gel and spray in my soft, sensible hair thirty years later as I approach Bret's coffin. I can't figure out why I'm experiencing the memory this palpably, but then I understand. . . . It's the song that's playing over the funeral home's speaker system, so quietly you can barely hear it—moaning vocals over a jangly, urgent guitar riff, two chords like footsteps moving closer. An X song. "Johnny Hit and Run Paulene."

"Why, Bret?" I say it out loud, even though I've come to the wake alone. I feel a small hand on my back and turn to see a sweet-faced lady of about my mother's age, steel-gray hair shaped into a shiny bob, lips a neat red slash. She smells of jasmine, a scent my own mother used to favor when she was alive, and for a moment, I truly am sixteen again, about to embark on my first and last adventure and everything that came with it.

"Some things," the woman says, "are just unfair."

She is talking about Bret dying at just forty-six of course, about Bret's mother outliving both her daughters. She's talking about the nature of Bret's death—a suicide by pills, just like her older sister's thirty-five years earlier. All of it unfair, yes. But that isn't what had made me ask why. It had been the song.

"They did a lovely job with her makeup," another woman offers. She's a bit younger—my age, maybe. She's wearing a chic black suit and heels, chunky custard-colored highlights in her ash-blond hair.

"Yes," I lie. "She looks beautiful."

It's an open casket. Bret is lying on her back, arms crossed over her chest like Snow White in her glass coffin. She's wearing an ivory dress with a high collar, under a hairstyle I'd be shocked if she had ever favored in life. People change, of course. I only knew Bret as a teen, a lifetime ago, and I understand this. But still there is something about the way her body looks, the enforced primness. The way it has been styled beyond her control, her hands arranged. . . .

I remember her telling me how much her sister's wake had scared her—how unfair it was that she'd been forced to look at something that was no longer Trina, just a stiff outer covering, painted to look human, posed like a doll. *Trina's shell*, she had called the body. I remember this. I can hear her say it in my head and it makes my throat clench up. A tear slips down my cheek.

"Did you know her well?" says the custard-streaked woman.

"I haven't seen her in a long time," I say quietly. "Not since we were kids."

"Nice of you to come," she says. "I know Bret from church. We ran the Christmas toy drive together. I had no idea she was so. . . . She always seemed quite happy, actually." She gives me a probing look, introduces herself as Georgette.

"I'm Lara."

"Her mother's over there." Georgette gestures at a delicate woman standing at the far end of Bret's coffin, talking to a big bear of a man who keeps shaking his head. She peers up at him, says something. It looks like "thank you." Though her hair is white and cropped close now, Mrs. Raines otherwise is much the same as I remember her. Very small, with sharp features, a tiny pointed nose that looks as though it was pinched from clay.

She's full of tension, always has been. Squinting eyes, pursed lips. Hands that keep clutching each other. I think about Bret's father, how hard he'd try to smile. "Have fun, kids!" he'd said once after dropping us off at a movie, "Don't get into trouble!" I used to wonder what they had been like before their older daughter had died, if they had ever been able to relax their faces or if they'd always been this tense, as though they were bracing for a fall. Mr. Raines was dead now too, according to Bret's obituary.

"Bret should have had children," Georgette is saying. "Single women adopt all the time."

I turn to her. "Do you think children would have made her happy?"

She shrugs "It would have been something."

I have no idea what that means.

We weren't Facebook friends, Bret and me. We have never sent each other Christmas cards. She wasn't invited to my wedding, and I wasn't invited to either of hers. I have two boys now, aged twelve and fifteen. I have no idea if she knew this about me; if she had ever seen the birth announcements I sent to our school's alumni magazine.

"Who is Bret Raines?" my husband said yesterday morning, when he saw me reading her obituary online.

Married twenty years, he's never once heard me say her name.

"We used to be friends," I said.

BRET AND I HAD MET at the beginning of junior year. She'd come to my town from Beverly Hills, four years after her older sister's suicide—a news event that had made the papers because of her family. Her dad was a producer who'd worked with some of the

top names in Hollywood. And so, even though we high school-
ers from Pasadena might not have remembered the story from
when it happened, our parents had. By the time the school year
started, we all knew about the tragic Raines family and how
they were escaping to our quiet town to build a new life.

Death is so attractive when you're young, so romantic and rare.
And Bret was beautiful—a golden California girl—which added
to the allure. Senior boys stared after her, the popular girls in our
class passed her notes, inviting her to parties. Everyone wanted to
help her, to talk to her, to be her friend. But for some reason, she
spoke only to me.

Our last names were close—that was part of it. Hers was Raines,
mine Ramsey, and so we sat next to each other in homeroom. But
really it was more the way we looked at the world—both of us
bored, bookish, not very happy. "Is this place as lame as it seems?"
she had said to me on the first day of school.

"Lamer," I'd replied. And things had taken off from there.

That first Friday after school, she had invited me to her house.
I'd expected some kind of castle, celebrity that she was. But really,
it was just a clean, two-story house a lot like mine. All over the living room, there were pictures of Bret—as a toddler in a ballet
outfit, in a puffy white dress at a debutante party, in a Girl Scout
sash dotted with merit badges, as Wonder Woman for Halloween.
A couple of shots of Bret's parents, too, but nothing of her dead
sister. You'd think she was an only child.

After dinner, she'd taken me up to her room and pulled a box
out from under her bed. Inside were several pictures of a girl with
huge brown eyes and silky, pale blond hair like Bret's own. In one,
the girl was about seven and held a toddler Bret in her arms. In
another, she was in a formal dress, standing stiffly beside a dark-
haired boy much shorter than herself. In one of the more recent
ones, she'd shaved off part of her hair and wore a ripped T-shirt
held together by safety pins and heavy, Cleopatra-like eyeliner. A
punk-rocker.

"My mom thinks she threw all of these pictures out, but I stole 'em out of the trash. They're all I have left of her."

The night of the X concert, I was aware of that box under Bret's bed as we put on the bad-girl clothes we'd bought at a thrift store the previous week. I kept wondering what Trina would think of us, sneaking around like this without her parents knowing, wearing fake leather skirts that we'd hidden in the back of Bret's closet. I hoped she would approve. I didn't have a sister of my own and so the closer Bret and I became, the more I began to think of Trina as my sister too—a guardian spirit watching over everything we did, approving and disapproving. Helping us. Trina's favorite movie had been *Somewhere in Time*. Her favorite book, *Forever*. She had discovered punk rock when she was sixteen, like us. As with us, the music had saved her from the boredom of growing up. She loved the screaming, the swearing, the impatience of the sound. Her favorite bands had been the Dead Kennedys, Black Flag and, most of all, X. I knew these things about Trina because Bret had told me, doling out each piece of information quietly, reverently, unwrapping them for me like gifts.

Trina had taken all those pills because a boy had hurt her terribly. I didn't know the details. But Bret wanted revenge. We both wanted revenge. *It's my whole life's purpose*, Bret would say. *And you're the only one who knows it.*

Once we were all dressed, I crouched down, looking for the box, thinking maybe I could get a clue as to how Trina would feel about what we were doing if I looked hard enough at the face in the Mohawk photo. Most punk rockers scowled in pictures, but in that shot—a shot taken by the hurtful boy—Trina had been smiling.

"It's gone," Bret said.

"Huh?"

"The box," she said. "It's gone. My mom found it."

I pulled myself to my feet. "Oh no," I said. "Oh Bret."

But she was busy gazing into her full-length mirror, examining herself from every angle. "You know what, Lara?"

"What?"

"I don't think I've ever had a better friend than you."

Beneath the caked-on makeup, my skin warmed. "Same here," I said.

Bret took another pull off the bottle of peach schnapps and handed it to me, her words slurring a little. "You ready for our adventure?" she said.

I took a big swig. It tasted like furniture polish. "You bet your ass," I said. We both started laughing.

THE MEMORY GROWS STRONGER IN my mind as I kneel in front of Bret's coffin—the heat of the alcohol in my throat, the feel of fishnet stockings and a too-tight skirt, the way everything blurred and my words slurred and I weaved on my feet. The dizziness of that night. The thrill.

This song is about a drug that makes guys need to have sex every hour.

I hear Bret's voice in my head, that song playing on and on in the funeral home like it did on the tape deck of Trina's Karmann Ghia as it sped along the Pasadena Freeway on its way to the X show back in 1984. I feel as though I'm trapped in time. I shut my eyes tight, wishing somebody would turn it off. "To shoot all Paulenes between the legs," John Doe sings. I remember Bret saying, "He thinks all girls are named Paulene" and I can't even think enough to pray.

"Lara? Lara Ramsey?"

I know Bret's mother's voice. It sounds the same. I'm surprised she recognizes me. I'm glad I'm here without my family because I don't want them to see me like this, reacting this way. But it feels so strange, being here at all.

I stand, move toward her. "Mrs. Raines I'm so sorry." I say it too loudly, trying to drown out the song.

"God, it's been such a long time." She hugs me. I feel her ribs through her black linen dress. "How did you find out?"

"Facebook," I say. "Our high school has a page and it posted her obituary."

"Technology."

"Yes." There is an envelope in my purse, Bret's name on the return address. It came in the mail after I saw the obituary and I haven't been able to open it. I have no idea what it could be, but the possibility scares me. The timing. She had to have sent it right before taking the pills.

I came here to the wake because I thought it might give me the strength to open the envelope. I thought it might give me some closure. But I can't tell that to Mrs. Raines. I can't tell her about the envelope and anyway I hate that word. Closure.

"There's something I need to ask you, Lara," she says.

I swallow hard, taste bile in my throat. I may as well be sixteen again. It may as well be the day after. "Yes?"

"That sleepover you and Bret had. The summer between junior and senior year."

"Yes."

"Why did you two stop talking after that?"

Funny. I must have imagined her asking me this question a hundred times when I was a kid. But in my mind back then, she'd always sounded so angry. Now, she sounds sad, defeated. *Bret is gone. What's the point in lying anymore?* For several seconds, I teeter on the brink of telling her the truth.

"Bret told me you fought over a boy that night."

My jaw tightens. "Right," I say, giving in to the lie. "Now I remember."

She places a hand on mine. It's cool and dry as a dead leaf. "You were a very good friend to her. I wish you two hadn't fought. Sometimes I think her life would have been happier if you'd stayed close through the rest of high school."

I close my eyes for a few moments, listen to the song still playing, to John Doe singing about the last Paulene, the one who wouldn't cooperate. When I open them again Mrs. Raines is looking up at me, thin lips trembling. I put my arms around her and hug her. I want to start sobbing, but instead, I tell her the only truth I can. "Mrs. Raines," I say. "I wish that sleepover had never happened."

"You know what this song is about?" Bret said.

I didn't answer right away because my heart was in my throat. We were in the Karmann Ghia on the Pasadena Freeway, all treacherous bends and Bret behind the wheel, X's *Los Angeles* pounding on the tape deck. She'd just dived head first into a sharp curve at full speed and I saw now for the first time how drunk she was to be driving. "Jesus, Bret," I breathed. "Be careful."

"Don't be such an old lady." At least she slowed down a little.

The music blasted. I tried listening to the song, but everything sounded like it was under water. It was hard to make out the words.

"It's called 'Johnny Hit and Run Paulene,'" she said. "It's about a drug that makes guys need to have sex every hour."

"Need?"

"Uh huh, so the guy in the song takes it. He shoots it up with a needle and for twenty-four hours, he is like attacking every girl he can find. He's pulling them off of busses. He's not taking no for an answer. . . ."

"Why would a guy take a drug like that?"

Bret shrugged. "He calls all girls Paulene, too," she said. "And he spells it weird. . . . Hey, there's the off-ramp." She cut across three lanes fast and swung onto the ramp that took us to the Hollywood Freeway.

I gasped. "You're going to get us arrested."

She ignored me, driving faster. She shifted into the fast lane, nearly cutting off a Porsche. Its horn blared.

"Arrested or beat up or dead."

"I vote for dead," she said. Trying to be punk rock.

"Shut up, Bret. We're from Pasadena. We wear uniforms to

school." I took another swig of the schnapps and closed my eyes. *Best not to even look at the road*, I thought. So I didn't.

"WE'RE HERE," BRET SAID.

I'd fallen asleep for a few minutes. I had to blink a bunch of times just to get my eyes focused. Bret was checking herself out in the rearview mirror, re-applying her dark lipstick. Out the window, I saw the Whisky, the legendary Whisky, X's name on the white marquee, a long line in front. I wanted to squeal over it, but I was too drunk to get excited, too queasy. Bret handed me the lipstick and tilted the mirror my way. Again, I was startled at my own image and the schnapps buzz made it hard to put the lipstick on straight. "I can't believe we're in Hollywood," I tried.

"I need to tell you something," Bret said.

"Yeah?"

"I need to tell you why Trina killed herself."

I turned to her. "Now?"

"Yes," she said.

"Why?"

"Because it happened here."

"What?"

"At the Whisky. At an X show."

"She killed herself here?"

"No," she said. "No, listen. That boy I told you about. The boy who . . ."

"Hurt her terribly."

"Look at me, Lara."

I had been watching the crowd out the driver's side window. I shifted to Bret. Her face was perfectly still. She stared into my eyes with all her death makeup, and I felt as though I was dreaming and would never wake up. "He did it to her here," she said. "Took her out to a show and did it to her in his van. In front of other guys. With other guys."

"What did he do?"

She gave me flat eyes.

"But . . . but he took that picture of her. She was smiling."

"So?"

"So . . . I thought they were in love." I cringed at the sound of my voice, the words I'd chosen, but still I couldn't stop myself. "I thought he just broke up with her. I thought that's what you meant by hurting her."

"He gave her a bunch of pills and then he wrecked her," she said. "He *shared* her, Lara. She told me." Bret stared out the window at the line outside the club. Her eyes burned through the glass. "It took hours."

"Oh," I said. "Oh my God."

"She never told our parents. But she told me. Three days later, she locked herself in her room. Put *Los Angeles* on the tape deck. Took the pills. . . . That song, 'Johnny Hit and Run Paulene.' It was the last song she listened to."

"How do you know?"

"She stopped it, right after the line about the Paulene who wouldn't cooperate." Bret leaned over me and snapped open the glove compartment. Her words weren't slurring anymore, and I noticed how smooth and calm her movements were, the drunkenness gone, as though she'd pushed it off. "Lara," she said. "He's the bouncer at The Whisky. He does all the X shows. He's there."

I turned. She was watching my face.

"We can get revenge," she said.

I swallowed. *Revenge.* The word pulsed through me.

Bret removed something from the glove compartment and placed it in my hand—a pocket knife. She held up another one of her own.

Are you serious? I wanted to say. But I knew she was.

"We can hurt him," she said. "We can scare him, at least."

I opened my mouth, closed it again. I wasn't sure if it was all the schnapps or the story itself or that picture of Trina, the trust in her smile. But I liked the idea. I liked the feel of the knife in my hand, solid and real as a drumbeat. "We could get caught," I said.

"Are you kidding me? Look in the mirror, Lara. No one will recognize us."

I looked at her. "You planned this."

She put her hand on mine and smiled at me with blood-red lips. "I've been planning it for four years."

HE WORE A TIGHT BLACK T-shirt with The Whisky's logo on the front and he leaned against the club's door as though he owned it. I had the strangest feeling when Bret pointed him out—a mixture of anticipation and dread, as though he were a dangerous animal we were hunting. As we approached the door, Bret told me his name was Johnny. "For real," she said. "Like the song." Then she waved at him. Winked.

"What have we here?" he said.

Johnny was thicker than I'd imagined he'd be, with beady green eyes, dumb, pouty lips, and a fat head. I couldn't imagine Trina wanting to be with someone like that, but Bret insisted it was him, so who was I to doubt her? I hung back while she sidled up to him, the crowd streaming past, jostling for a place inside. "Do you have black beauties?" she said in a shy voice. "I heard you did."

He grinned. "I can get some for you."

"Yeah?"

"They're in my van."

My van. My heart pounded. I pressed my purse to my side and thought about the knife.

"Can my friend come along?"

He glanced at me. "Why not?" he said. I looked at the kids in line, laughing and shoving each other, shouting to be heard. Inside the club, I could hear an electric guitar being tuned, someone banging on a cymbal. For a few moments, I was filled with a longing I couldn't quite name. . . . A longing to be a kid, I suppose, going to an all-ages X show. A longing to be thinking about nothing but the music like all those kids were, like I would have been if I hadn't swallowed so much schnapps and if Bret hadn't told me what had happened to Trina.

Johnny led us away from the door, both of us. "My lucky night," he said through his thick lips, his fingers at my waist, my skin shrinking from them. "What's your name, baby?"

"Paulene," Bret answered.

"What about—"

"Her name's Paulene, too."

"Wow," he said as we rounded the corner, "What are the odds?"

THE NEXT PART IS FUZZY in my mind and keeps changing each time I remember it. Sometimes he's pushing Bret up against the side of a black van, other times, she's pulling him to her. Sometimes, she's slapping him across the face or calling him a murderer and he's pulling out clumps of her hair, just like Johnny does to the last Paulene in the lyrics of the song. She's screaming, he's clamping his hand over her mouth. There are so many variations. Keep in mind, this all happened in a matter of seconds and I was very drunk. And drunk or not, all memories fog over with time.

The one part that's consistent, though, is Bret's head slamming into the side of the vehicle—the sound of it, a loud crack. And the next part too. The next part, I have never been able to forget.

"Stop it!" I screamed. "Stop hurting her."

He didn't turn. He threw his weight into the side of the van and she squirmed against him and told him to stop and his hands went where I couldn't see them, making some kind of awful adjustment. I heard Bret whimper and I thought about how this wasn't the way we'd planned it and I thought about history repeating itself and about how he was supposed to be scared and sorry, how he was supposed to apologize and why wasn't he apologizing and some-how, the knife was out of my purse, clutched in my sweaty hand. I flicked it open and rushed at him and jammed the blade into the small of his back and yanked it out again, feeling nothing beyond adrenaline and anger. Blood dripped from the knife's blade. I stared at it and for a few moments, everything seemed to move in slow motion—Bret heaving on the pavement, Johnny whirling around like an animal, blood spraying out of him, blood on my hands, a timed streetlight humming to black. . . .

He lunged at me. I couldn't see his features, just the outline of him on the dark street, a shadow coming at me, grabbing me by one wrist. My eyes started to adjust, just enough to see him, the funhouse-mirror face, the gritted teeth. *A bad dream. Trina's bad dream.*

"Bitch," he said. With my free hand, I slashed him across the throat.

I REMEMBER THE GURGLING SOUND now as I hug Mrs. Raines, the sound of a man dying. I remember how he fell to the sidewalk and Bret and I had stared at him until he went still and quiet, without helping, without thinking to help. I remember how we'd looked down the row of quiet houses, how none of their lights had gone on and how in my dim, shocked mind, I'd rationalized that into some kind of tacit approval. *They saw what he was doing to her,* I had told myself. *They wanted me to kill him.* I remember how calmly Bret had taken the Kleenex out of her purse and wiped my prints off the knife and dropped it on him. How she'd plucked his wallet out of his pocket and tossed it into the bushes and called him scum, a piece-of-shit drug dealer, how she'd held her ripped blouse to her chest and told me I'd done the whole world a favor.

We'd walked back to our car in utter silence. I remember how slowly and carefully she'd driven home, using her blinker for every turn. How we'd taken turns in the shower, washing off the hair dye and make-up and blood before stuffing our bloody thrift store clothes into three sets of garbage bags and throwing them in the dumpster at the gas station down the street, how we'd jumped into our sleeping bags just as Bret's parents pulled into the driveway. "I'll never tell anyone," Bret had whispered.

"Thank you," I had said, thinking of that dying noise he made and, for a few moments, trying to feel bad about it.

The next day, she'd given me a ride back to my house, and returned home telling her parents we'd had a fight about a boy and that we were never speaking again. It was for the best, we had decided, talking it over in the car. If we cut ties and stayed apart, we'd be less likely to give each other away. Really, though, I think there was another reason. We were different, now. Everything had changed. But so long as we stayed apart, it was easier to pretend it hadn't.

As I pull away from Mrs. Raines, I remember my last conversation with Bret—a phone call, two weeks after the X show, when her parents weren't around. "It wasn't him," she had said. "It wasn't Johnny."

"I'm so sorry," I say it again, again too loudly.

Mrs. Raines gives me a weak smile. "That song is horrible, isn't it? Bret specified they play it at her wake."

"When?"

"Funeral home said she spoke with them about it years ago," she says, a sigh in her voice. "My daughter always did love to plan things in advance."

NEITHER ONE OF US WAS contacted by the police. Bret's parents never even asked if we'd left the house that night. My parents didn't notice a change in my behavior because my behavior didn't change. It was part of a survival plan and we both stuck to it. It scared me a little, how easy that was to do.

Once school started again, we moved in with different crowds, me joining the school newspaper staff, Bret assuming her rightful place among the popular girls. We'd pass each other in the hallway, barely exchanging a glance. Alone in my room, I still listened to my punk-rock records. And I could only assume that Bret did the same.

Just before graduation, I heard two boys talking about a murder near the Whisky that had happened over the summer, a bouncer knifed in what looked like a drug deal gone wrong. "My brother bought weed off that guy," one had said. "Chuck something. Real asshole." It was the first and last I ever heard of him, the man I had killed.

I DUCK INTO THE FUNERAL home's reception area, weaving my way past groups of mourners I've never met and thinking of Bret, sixteen-year-old Bret, her sad voice on the phone during our very last conversation. *I'll find him, Lara. I'll find the real Johnny someday. . . .*

I spot the ladies' room and slip inside. Once I'm in a stall, I slip the envelope out of my purse, open it while listening to two women washing their hands, one of them saying how pretty Bret was, what a tragedy, what a waste.

"She was so sweet too," whispers the other. "She never wanted to bother anyone with her troubles. When she got into a bad mood, she'd just escape by herself for a few days. Go to the beach or the mountains, who knew where?"

Inside the envelope is a small newspaper clipping—a story of a fifty-four-year-old lawyer found stabbed to death at his home in Monrovia—a suspected robbery. I stare at the picture—a heavy, benign-looking man in a Dodgers cap, flanked by two skinny, smiling teenage sons. *People can change. But only if no one remembers who they used to be.*

His name was John Samuelson. And when I look closely at the photo caption, I notice the *n* and the *y*, penciled in at the end of his first name in Bret's small, careful writing.

ARE YOU WITH ME, DOCTOR WU?
BY DAVID CORBETT

SHOCKER TUMBREL FIRST ENCOUNTERED THE loving Buddha inside a padded holding cell at San Francisco County Jail.

Twelve hours earlier, a SWAT team had dragged him out of a shooting gallery two blocks from the Bottom of the Hill, the club where his band had joined a handful of other outfits in a benefit to save the venue, one of the few left in town to offer live music, now targeted for condo gentrification at the hands of the usual cabal of city hall sellouts and bagman developers.

The night had ended with a beautiful mosh-pit frenzy unlike anything the locals had seen in years: multiple swan dives off the stage monitors from dervish girls and acrobat boys, not just fans but band members too. Pinball aggression. Brothers and sisters united in pain.

At night's end, stoked from adrenaline, Shocker stowed his gear in the van and headed off to mellow the edges with his best friend and bandmate, Mousy Tongue.

The two had met through sheer dumb luck in middle school, all but inseparable since: skateboarding, tagging, paint sniffing, runaway odysseys to Portland and Vegas and Burning Man, multiple stints in juvie detention, moving up the buzz ladder to reefer and meth and smack as they formed and dissolved a slew of bands—Molotov Snot, Flaming Citadel, Deathwagon Ponies—culminating finally in the latest, the truest, the fiercest, the best: Acid Prancer.

Shocker writing the songs and playing bass, Mousy up front on guitar and vocals, Clint Barber on drums—they remained true to the poverty-fueled rage, the misfit love, the howling anarchy of punk. They promised themselves they'd never succumb to the soul-sucking über-capitalist fame machine, never cave to money. They started their sets screaming, "This ain't no fucking White Stripes," then kicked into their signature cut, "Shopping Mall Shootout."

Seriously, when 5 Seconds of Summer, an Aussie boy-band rehash of One Direction pop schmaltz bullshit gets crowned as the latest messiahs of hardcore, what could you do but drop trou, moon the power, and hit the spike?

Which was exactly what he and Mousy did after the gig, trundling over to a long-familiar nod pad, scoring from an obese albino named Jelly Stone, and heading upstairs to the playroom. The shit Jelly sold them was powdery and fine, a fresh batch of china white, he said, new to the street. Mousy fired up first, passed the gear, and Shocker tied himself off, slapped up a vein. He eased back on his first hit, figuring he could bump it up if need be. Hearing a deep, chesty sigh beside him, he figured Mousy had slipped into the haze, and settled in to do likewise.

By the time it dawned on him Mousy hadn't spoken or even stirred in far too long, no amount of shouting or shaking could bring him back. Neither one of them had brought along naloxone, the thinking man's OD antidote, because, well, they hadn't been thinking. Jelly hadn't offered any, either—I'm your connection, he'd say, not your mother. The Free Clinic and the needle exchanges handed out injectable vials to any dope fiend who bothered to ask—Christ, they practically forced it on you.

But that argument was over. Mousy had wandered across that invisible line where your lungs forget to breathe. All things considered, a gentle death.

Born Robert Sean McFadden, Hayward, California. Twenty-three years old.

Shocker didn't exactly remember stacking the moldy couch and two broken chairs in front of the door, or screaming at anyone standing outside that he had a gun and would shoot to kill any motherfucker dumb enough to try to force his way in.

The clearest thing he recalled was dragging Mousy into the corner, sitting there curled up with him, the lifeless head in his lap, that handsome, waxy face staring emptily up into his own as the SFPD busted their way in—battering ram, follow-up kicks, a final shoulder or two—suited and booted in storm-trooper black, aiming their AR-15s in his face and screaming like Warg riders: "On the floor! Show your hands, asshole! Do it! Now!"

TIME SWIRLED IN AND OUT—he sat cocooned in a straitjacket, entombed in his quilted cell—until finally the lock clattered open, the door swung back.

Even if given a thousand lifetimes of lovely dreams, he could never have imagined the person who entered, sat beside him, and said gently, "Would you rather I call you Shocker or Lonnie?"

It wasn't how she looked that made her sitting there astonishing—just another tall, slender, California blonde: center part on the pulled-back hair, fat brown eyes but prim lips, a dusting of mustard-brown freckles. Her voice had a clipped warm twang—Midwestern vowels wrapped in tortilla consonants—but that too seemed irrelevant. She wore an ID card on a lanyard that read simply "Visitor." Given his savage state of mind, though, where the edge of the universe felt intimately close, he misread the word as "Visitation." And that seemed perfectly right. She wasn't just someone from beyond the locked door. She'd been transported here from a totally different plain of existence.

"How did you know that name?"

"You mean Lonnie?"

He nodded, thinking: *I probably look like a missile went off inside my head.* Nerve endings were crackling back to life. His blood had started to itch.

"It's on your booking sheet. They printed you on intake, remember?"

He didn't. Suffering a sudden wave of shame that quickly metastasized into utter self-loathing, he dropped his eyes, studied the straitjacket's crisscrossed sleeves, the security loop pinning them to his chest. He caught a whiff of bleach off the white cotton canvas.

"My name is Katy," she said, leaning a bit closer. "I'm a counselor here at the jail. I've come to help you feel better."

Good luck with that, he thought, even as, from somewhere beyond the oily skid at the bottom of his mind, he sensed a feeble hope that it just might be true.

She sat back, folded her hands in her lap, and crossed her ankles, as though in sympathy with his bound arms.

"I'm going to guide you in some breathing exercises, very simple stuff. It's the principle aspect of Buddhist meditation. I think it might help calm you."

He considered spitting back: *What fucking makes you fucking think I'm not fucking calm?* His skin felt like a carpet of chiggers, the air in his lungs had been set on boil. *And there's this guy they found with me*, he thought, *fella named Mousy, sweet skinny fuckup with a chain-lightning mind—we grew up in the same stinking shithole—maybe you've heard of him?*

"Close your eyes," she said, "not completely, you don't want to fall asleep."

By way of demonstration, she dropped her eyelids to half-mast, while Shocker flashed on trying to bitch slap his only real friend back to life. Yeah, he felt pretty sure he didn't want to fall asleep.

"Be present," she said, "but focus on nothing except your breath. Inhale . . . let the air fill your lungs, drop your diaphragm. Gently, gently. Then just let it go, exhale . . ."

She did it herself a few times, as though to show him how, and he figured, why not? What other miraculous plan is in the works?

"If thoughts enter your mind, don't dwell on them. Let them go. Return to your breath. Focus on that. There's nothing so important it can't wait."

He couldn't imagine such a thing could be true. *My* brother-from-another-mother *died a few feet away and I was too loaded to save him.* There was a thought to latch onto, cling to, like an anchor dragging him down to the bottom where he belonged.

Except maybe he didn't. Maybe, just maybe, he belonged here, with this woman named Katy, nothing to do but breathe in . . . breathe out . . . breathe in. . . .

He wasn't sure how much time passed, but the freedom to let go, the simplicity of nothing in the world to do but breathe, felt strangely forgiving. He imagined her hand on his chest, just above the solar plexus, creating a kind of radiance, a warm rush not unlike heroin, and all the nagging, bitchy questions of his life seemed answered, or answerable.

He opened his eyes a little and looked at her, wondering if it could be true. This stranger, this visitor—could she possibly be the person who might save him?

He whispered, "I don't want to die."

She glanced up—no expression at first, like she was waking from a dreamless sleep—then offered a smile.

"We all want to live and keep living," she said. "Unfortunately, that's not a viable long-term option."

AFTER THAT, HE LET HER call him Lonnie, a name he'd long associated with a mother drowning in self-pity, a father too focused on being pissed off to make a living, a ratty house in a crap town. But Shocker would no longer do. Shocker died with his unlucky friend.

From an investigator at the public defender's office he learned that the stuff he and Mousy booted that night wasn't heroin at all, but fentanyl, and there'd been a flood of overdoses all across town. Useless knowledge in retrospect. Meanwhile, Jelly Stone had disappeared, haunted by hindsight or just run out of Dodge by an angry mob of fist-shaking junkies. *That won't last long*, he thought. The strung-out are notoriously indulgent.

Katy's visits continued. His parents had split up and moved to their separate redneck havens far away and out of the picture—happy chance, to his mind—and no one from the scene, not even Clint, bothered to come by, no doubt meaning they all blamed Guess Who for Mousy's death. *Get in line*, he thought. Regardless, for all intents and purposes, Katy became his world.

She and the center she worked for helped liaise with the public defender handling his case, offering to provide housing, oversee and monitor his diversion to rehab. He took heart in that show of confidence. Besides, he felt no inclination to backslide. The very idea, in fact, came to terrify him.

But being an addict by nature, and having discovered something that made him feel good, he couldn't help but want to do it relentlessly. So within the confines of his cell he dove into not just meditation but the dharma, memorizing the Four Noble Truths and the Eightfold Path, devouring every text Katy provided: the Mahayana Sutras, the *Dhammapada* (Treasury of Truth), the *Visuddhimagga* (Path of Purification).

By the time he walked out of the detention facility into the foggy burn-off of a mid-winter morning, carrying his shoebox of books and dressed in the spanking new jeans and sweatshirt Katy had brought him (the better to obscure the freakish ink scrolled across his skin from knuckle to neck and down to his skinny flat butt), he felt reasonably ready to confront the monster he'd always pretended didn't exist: the future.

SHE DROVE HIM TO A quiet street on the edge of the Presidio and parked outside a sprawling three-story Shingle Victorian with a brick façade—an anomaly in a town known for its earthquakes. It seemed to suggest either reckless optimism or uncanny luck, and that struck him as only too apt for a rehab center.

Banyan trees shaded the pebbled walkway, and Lonnie half expected to spot a smiling monk perched beneath one of them plucking an angular banjo. Similarly, he wondered what kind of wistful muzak might be playing inside the house, and whether with its flutes and singsong chants it would conjure a spa or a noodle house.

Neither, as it turned out. As Katy led him through the thick front door, nothing but silence greeted them.

The place resembled a professor's home, or what he imagined one might look like from movies and TV. Katy introduced him briefly to a couple other residents shelving dishes in the kitchen—both twenty-something, strangely scrubbed and ruddy for recovering addicts, no piercings, no tats, no scarification—then led him up two flights of stairs to an office at the back of the house.

A black-haired man in a cardigan and slacks sat at a desk with his back to the door. Through the giant windows along the north wall, Lonnie spotted, beyond the tops of the eucalyptus trees in the near distance, the Golden Gate, the Marin Headlands.

Katy knocked gently. The man did not move.

She didn't speak or knock again, just patiently waited. Finally the man removed his glasses and set down the book he'd been reading, rose from his chair, turned, and approached the door. He was Asian, trim with an athletic gait, handsome if a bit sharp-featured, the angles of his face accentuated by the impeccably combed-back hair. Scholarly eyes, a careful smile. Two red discs on the bridge of his nose marked where his glasses had rested.

"Welcome to Metta House." Hint of an accent. He extended his hand. "I am Doctor Wu."

The ensuing handshake was clumsily formal and gratefully brief.

As though sensing the awkwardness, Katy interjected, "'Metta' means 'loving kindness.' It comes from the Pali word *mitta*, which usually translates as 'friend.'"

Doctor Wu nodded. "More accurately," he said, "'the true friend in need.'"

Lonnie shrank a little, feeling their eyes on him.

As though reading his mind, Doctor Wu said, "Your friend, the one who died, I believe he called himself Mousy Tongue?"

Lonnie swallowed what felt like a burr. The floor seemed to buckle. *It wasn't meant as an insult,* he thought, *to Mao or you or anyone else. The kind of thing white people always say.*

Finally, he managed to whisper, "Yeah."

Doctor Wu clasped his hands behind his back and stared a hole through Lonnie's skull. Then, ever so gradually: a mischievous smile.

"That's rather clever."

THE FOLLOWING DAY LONNIE COMMENCED his daily routine, which involved the usual recovery *diktat*—making a fearless inventory of people he had injured, preparing to make amends—though without the self-flogging he'd expected.

Instead, the practice focused on cultivating *bodhicitta*, the arousal of the compassionate heart, and each day ended not with groveling prayers of contrition but a vow of empowerment—to live as a *bodhisattva*, dedicating this life and all subsequent lives to help alleviate the suffering of others.

Every morning Doctor Wu led the residents in an hour of sitting meditation, followed by a session of *tai chi chuan*, another of *qigong*, moving meditations that gave Lonnie a sense of his physical presence he'd never before known. He'd previously thought of his body as nothing more than a machine of meat, an animated coffin waiting for its corpse. Now he came to recognize the flesh and the spirit as mirror images, deepening his resolve to stay clean.

His energy normalized, without the crazed swings between mania and lethargy. The monkey in his head began to settle quietly in the branches of his mind.

Where he'd once flaunted his tattoos, they came to embarrass him as hopelessly crass, but that too evolved into humble acceptance: they were him. In fact, as his skin and muscle tone improved, the ink seemed to flare more vividly, like the plumage of a wild parrot.

Afternoons were spent in more meditation, some with chanting of mantras focused on healing or transformation, then study and discussion of Buddhist texts and concepts. He came to learn that Doctor Wu had once been a prominent biochemist, whose work—to the extent Lonnie understood it—concerned revealing how both classical Newtonian mechanics and quantum physics were necessary to explain the workings of a living cell. But then some kind of scarring inside his retina began to cloud his vision, making it all but impossible to read the small print in most scientific journals, and two operations only made it worse. So he elected for disability retirement and, needing to redirect his life, chose to dedicate himself to teaching Americans the benefits of Eastern traditions.

Not just any Americans. He found he had a special calling, a particular aptitude for helping those whose talent had only created chaos. The gifted but broken, the brilliant but lost.

That explained, Lonnie realized, the peculiar breed of cat inhabiting Metta House. Unlike the losers, skeeves, and derelicts he'd only recently considered his tribe—and whom he'd reasonably imagined would reappear in rehab—everyone here had been successful, some insanely so.

Victor Mazur had been a hired gun in Silicon Valley specializing in network penetration, exploitation, and defense. Eleanor Tosh had been the assistant director of research for the Pacific Stock Exchange. Jonathan Adler had taught both political philosophy and economics at Stanford. Even Katy had a hotshot resumé—she'd been the youngest faculty member ever at the San Francisco Academy of Ballet.

Sure, they'd all had their problems, cocaine mostly, pharmaceutical uppers, nothing so white-trash as crank. To ease the inevitable crash or just mellow their buzz they'd used Nembutal, Seconal, good old reliable booze. A few had toyed with pharmaceutical opiates, Oxy and Percocet mostly, the occasional flirty snort of heroin. None had mainlined like Lonnie, or sniffed paint from a paper bag or raided a neighbor's medicine cabinet and swallowed literally everything he'd found. None of them had gone on a week-long meth binge only to wake up in a truck-stop toilet in Cheyenne, swatting at invisible bats, no idea how he'd gotten there. Their addictions hadn't been a lifestyle choice so much as self-medication, stress management, the dark underbelly of American mojo.

Leaving Lonnie with the nagging question: What in the name of God-and-weasels am I doing here?

That became clearer as he got better acquainted, not just in class but performing the daily chores. And the answer, again, surprised.

Household duties were performed communally, shoulder-to-shoulder, care of the house and garden, preparation of meals. Only illness excused you. And as he joined in with everyone else to rake leaves and weed flowerbeds and trim back trees, empty the trash and wash the dishes and sweep the floors, change beds and, yes, scrub out shower stalls and toilets, he learned that he wasn't alone in feeling a profound disaffection with the Land of the Free.

The others may have avoided the bitter grind of growing up working class—coming from presentable families, enjoying an actual shot at prestige and money—but they'd come to see the trap in that. Each of them shared Lonnie's utter contempt for the capitalist shell game, the perpetual hustle of working people, the naked rape of the poor. And they'd earned that disaffection not from the outside like him, but from deep within the system. They could genuinely claim the mantle of traitor, to their kind if not their country. Lonnie admired that.

ONE NIGHT, AS THEY SAT around shooting the breeze over white tea and sesame brittle, he got a deeper sense of what *bodhicitta* and the vow of empowerment meant among these people.

In contrast to the usual silence that characterized the house, a CD of classic chants crooned softly in the background, performed by Shi Changsheng, the former pop star turned Buddhist nun.

"This may not be your kind of thing," Katy had said with a shrug when she'd slipped in the disc, "but I find it kind of soothing." Lonnie took note of the title, *Mantras for the Masses*, wondering why dancers so often had such sentimental taste in music, then tried to ignore the syrupy, over-sincere production, focusing instead on the weightless melodies.

Meanwhile the conversation ambled from this to that, until Victor, the former cyber-warrior, casually kicked it into a different gear.

"You hear all this stuff about Chinese hackers." He was burly, stern, wild-haired, clean-shaven. "How on a daily basis they're raiding not just military and intelligence databases but corporate ones, even hitting small businesses. They're probing utility networks to fine-tune a potential crash of the power grid, stealing patent applications, pirating software."

"Planting rootkits and Trojans in stock market computers," Eleanor, the finance maven, added. A comfortably plump woman, disheveled in earth tones, sensible shoes.

"Don't forget the Sony hack." Jonathan, the philosopher, finger-tapped his mug of tea like an ocarina—cowboy handsome but eerily tall, slouching in his armchair, stretched out like a ladder. "Seventy percent of the company's hard drives trashed, handiwork of the scurrilously named Dark Seoul."

Eleanor shook her head. "All for a Seth Rogan movie. Bad? Meet worse."

"What they never tell you?" Victor again, leaning into his message. "We're doing the same damn thing, only ten times worse."

"God forbid," Jonathan said, "the rest of the world defend itself."

"We're the good guys." Eleanor bit off a morsel of sesame brittle. "You know, because we're us."

"Beware the inscrutable Asian." Jonathan glanced inside his mug as though distressed by its emptiness. "Yellow Peril 2.0."

Finally Katy spoke, directing her words to Victor, nodding toward Lonnie. "Tell him about Site M."

"Site M?" Eleanor chuckled acidly. "Christ, tell him about MonsterMind, Treasure Map."

Victor smiled and edged a little closer to the others, like Uncle Buddy preparing to tell the kids their favorite story, but he focused his gaze on Lonnie. In the background, Shi Changsheng sang in prayerful monotony: *"Om mani padme hum . . . Om mani padme hum . . ."*

"There's a wastewater pump station that just got built deep in the woods along the Little Patuxent River outside Fort Meade, Maryland. County officials told reporters that the National Security Agency made anyone working on the project sign a piece of paper agreeing that if they ever talked about the job to anyone, in any way, they'd go to prison for life."

"Amerika über alles," Jonathan said.

Lonnie glanced back and forth between them. "I don't get it. Wastewater—like what, a sewage treatment plant?"

"The pump station," Victor continued, "will provide around two million gallons of water a day to this huge, top-secret lair codenamed Site M. Located right next to NSA headquarters. Guess why."

"Here's a hint." Eleanor waggled her fingers. "It's not for flushing toilets."

"Site M," Victor said, "is the $900 million center that houses the US Cyber Command."

"More specifically," Jonathan said, "High Performance Computing Center-2, which all would agree sounds far less ominous."

"Think of it as a missile silo," Victor said, "only there's a computer inside, not an ICBM."

"Not just any computer," Jonathan said. "A gargantuan cyberbrain that consumes 600,000 square feet."

"That's about ten football fields," Eleanor said, "assuming you share the average American's fondness for sports analogies."

"A computer that large," Victor said, "needs perpetual cooling, which means it has an insatiable thirst for water. That's why the NSA spent $40 million on a nearby pump station that no one who helped build it can talk about."

"Unless they want to disappear," Eleanor said.

Jonathan added, "Which segues nicely to Treasure Map, no?"

Victor tented his fingers thoughtfully. "The purpose of this massive computer is essentially to track every single person on the planet connected to the web—mainframes, laptops, tablets, phones—an almost real-time map of every Internet user in the world."

"Not just to know where they are," Eleanor said. "You know, send a friendly email, cute little emoji—*Hey, just checking in, hope everything's lovely.*"

"We'll be able not just to access, but to attack. An operation code-named Turbine will allow us to infiltrate any device in the world with malware."

Katy made a face. "I'm not entirely comfortable with the word 'we.'"

"It's our tax money," Eleanor said. "Over which we have zip control."

"Ah yes," Victor said. "Lack of control. Which brings us at last to MonsterMind."

He turned once again solely toward Lonnie, the focus of his gaze even more severe. Shi Changsheng and her mantras for the masses seemed to fade further into the background.

"This cyber center will not only be tracking incoming attacks, singling out suspicious algorithms as they flash through communications links. There's going to be an automated strike-back capacity, where the computer, with no human input can, in a microsecond, launch a counterstrike at the source of the intrusion."

"Too bad if the source computer's a proxy," Eleanor said. "Or a zombie."

Jonathan: "Some kid in Slovenia hijacking an Iranian computer."

"And Obama has refused to rule out nuclear retaliation for a massive cyber attack," Victor said. "We're talking the reincarnation of Mutually Assured Destruction. With robotic computers in charge of the nukes."

"The infamous Doomsday Machine." Eleanor tilted her head toward Lonnie and smiled: "I'm assuming you've heard of Dr. Strangelove?"

Jonathan raised a cautionary hand. "But we all agree the problem isn't technological. It goes a great deal deeper than that. It goes to the self-destructive nature of what the West considers freedom."

"The freedom to be miserable," Eleanor said. "The freedom to ruin your life."

"To be greedy and cruel and self-idolizing," Katy said.

An addict, Lonnie thought.

"When most Americans think of freedom," Jonathan said, "what they mean is power."

"I don't entirely agree," Victor said. "Yes, I get what you mean. But some just want to be left alone."

"In a trailer somewhere in Idaho." Eleanor struggled forward in her chair to set her empty cup down on the coffee table. "Head off with the guns and dogs, get away from the niggers and spics and chinks."

Lonnie thought: my parents.

"Money is power," Jonathan said. "Money is liberty. This is America."

"I am free to ride the dragons of want," Katy said, paraphrasing one of the sutras. "Free to chase my illusions."

From which Lonnie inferred the dharma *is* freedom, feeling too timid to say it out loud.

Jonathan rose to stretch his spidery limbs, his fingers almost reaching the ceiling. "The world isn't a mess because we're denied opportunities to discover the truth. We already know the truth. It lies in virtually every spiritual and philosophical system in the world. Abandon the ego. Still the mind, calm the passions, look within. Do unto others as you'd like to get done."

"Simple to state, hard to live by," Eleanor said. "Much easier to be free, which is to say lazy and frightened and restless."

"Speaking of rest," Katy said, "perhaps it's time to turn in."

After turning off the music and joining hands for the vow of empowerment, dedicating themselves to the end of suffering for all living things, they headed up to their separate rooms.

Katy, touching Lonnie's arm, suggested they linger downstairs for a moment.

"Doctor Wu wanted me to let you know he'd like to speak with you tomorrow after morning practice." A puckish smile. She took his hand. "Don't worry. It's a good thing."

ALMOST INSTANTLY UPON RISING AT 5 a.m., Lonnie became plagued by a state of doubt so fierce it swelled to the level of panic as he pulled on his square-necked tunic, tied the draw-string on his loose-fitting pants, stepped into his rubber-soled slippers.

Throughout the hour of sitting meditation his mind hissed with negativity and self-doubt. During *tai chi* his attempts to perform even the simplest movements of the *kata*—Cloud Hands, Parting the Wild Horse's Mane, Grasping the Sparrow's Tail—created such uncontrollable trembling he all but lost his balance, and he actually fell attempting Snake Creeps Down. As for *qigong*, the Five Animals never frolicked more miserably.

He wasn't surprised when Doctor Wu, at the conclusion of the morning's final session, all but fled the garden patio without so much as a glance back. The ensuing sense of foolishness tinged with devastation only broke when a hand settled gently on his arm.

"You look like you could use something cold to drink," Katy said.

Until that moment, he'd barely noticed the sheen of sweat covering his skin, soaking his armpits and the back of his tunic.

In the kitchen she withdrew a pitcher of water from the fridge, filled a tumbler, and passed it to him. Parched by a thirst that felt greedy and small, he downed the entire glass in one go, only realizing at the end what she'd so clearly intended. Words from the *Tao*:

> *True goodness*
> *is like water . . .*
> *It goes right*
> *to the low, loathsome places*
> *and so finds the way.*

Taking the glass from his hand, she said, "Doctor Wu is waiting in his office."

Lonnie climbed the steps to the third floor with the deliberation of someone unsure whether he was ascending an altar or the gallows. Wondering as well: did it matter?

The office door stood open. Doctor Wu, smiling, gestured him inside. "Have a seat," he said in a voice both calm and pleasant, then closed the door for privacy. Lonnie doubted he had ever felt more scared.

He chose a rocker near the bookshelf, thinking movement might ease his jitters, while Doctor Wu wheeled his desk chair over, like a physician preparing for a consultation—eyes with their usual imperturbable focus, now graced with something not unlike warmth.

"I must admit," he began, "I did not know much about your world until Katy recommended you join us."

"My world," Lonnie said. He was gripping the rocker's arms like the railing on a boat about to capsize.

"The music business," Doctor Wu explained. "Specifically, the form I believe you refer to as 'punk.'"

The word had never sounded so cheesy, so petulant.

"I believe there is a recording company," he continued, "that takes a particularly spiritual perspective on the form."

Lonnie bit back a chuckle. *The form.* Like concertos, the minuet. "Equal Vision," he said, thinking: lightweight boojie pseudo-angst. Not quite as lame as Christian metal, but who wants nihilism with a melody, let alone a message. "I know about them, yeah. Based in New York?"

"I was wondering if you would be interested in developing something of that sort out here on the West Coast."

Lonnie, unaware up to that point that he'd indeed been rocking, stopped.

Doctor Wu leaned a bit closer, grazing one hand pensively across the other. "Much of Buddhism focuses on the wisdom of emptiness, the perfection of silence. But the arts, when practiced with right intention, can be useful as teaching tools. Stories excel at demonstrating moral truths. Are you aware of the *Shasekishu*, the Collection of Stone and Sand?"

"Not . . ." The rest of whatever his mind had hoped to say abandoned him. He shook his head, swallowed. "No."

"It's a collection of Zen stories from the thirteenth century, written by a master named Muju." He glanced around the room. "I'm sure I have a copy somewhere. I can loan it to you."

"Okay."

"It's a wonderful example of how stories can enlighten and guide."

Almost imperceptibly, Lonnie resumed rocking.

"As for music, nothing so touches the heart, ennobles the mind."

Yeah, Lonnie thought. Same thing occurred to me last time I slam-danced.

"The popularization of the traditional chants, such as I heard all of you playing downstairs last night, is one such example. Though I must admit, to my taste, Shi Changsheng, for all her good intentions, is a bit . . ."

Slick, Lonnie thought. Cloying. Sanitized.

Doctor Wu reached out, set his hand on Lonnie's knee. A gaze to cut glass. "I realize that what I'm saying may seem outlandish in the context of . . . 'punk'. But as you've already admitted, there is a spiritual side, and certainly a political side, to the music as well. It is not all swagger and attitude."

"No," Lonnie said. "It's not."

Doctor Wu withdrew his hand and sat back. "I've read the lyrics to some of your songs."

Lonnie crossed his legs, feeling a sudden, overpowering need to urinate. "How—"

"Katy sought them out, found them online, your musical troupe's website. They are very powerful, very true to the spirit of anti-materialism, the quest for truth."

"Thank you . . ."

"Most of what one hears and sees in this culture is commercialist propaganda. Advertising for excess and vanity. An ironic pose masquerading as wisdom. I gather you agree."

"I . . ." Lonnie felt a sudden mysterious weightlessness—and feared he might pass out. *Breathe, fool.* "Yeah. Sure."

"So." Doctor Wu laced his fingers together. Two hands joined as one. "Do you know of anyone to whom we might turn to help us with our enterprise?"

TWO HOURS LATER, DRESSED IN a crewneck sweater and jeans, a simple blue windbreaker, Lonnie found himself, courtesy of several bus transfers, seven miles south of downtown outside a ramshackle row house along the Islais

Creek Channel, the borderland between Hunter's Point and
Dogpatch.

He knocked on the door. Middle of the afternoon, he thought,
hard to know if anybody'd be up yet.

No answer, he knocked again—not louder, though. Why be
a dick?

Finally, muffled footsteps thumped down an inner hallway.
The door swung open. An immediate waft of tobacco, reefer, and
something sweet, Jack and Coke maybe.

"Hey, Clint."

He hadn't been sure what to expect. What he got was a stunned,
brutal stare, eyes blasted—Clint shirtless, shoeless, just a pair of
black leathers worn low on his hips, boxer mushroom at the waist.
Pipe-thin torso, ropey arms, every inch blazing with tats. Barbell
studs in the nose and lip. His hair, as always, shaved away on the
sides, madly disheveled up top.

Lonnie said. "Been a while."

Clint crossed his arms, leaned against the doorframe, glanced
quickly up and down the street, like Lonnie might conjure a posse
of narcs.

"Just me," he said. "Sorry I've been out of touch. Been stuck
way across town."

Silence.

"I've gotten clean, been—"

"The fuck you want?"

So this is how it'll go, Lonnie thought. *I'm the stooge. The one to
blame.*

"I just wanted to see you. Thought we might talk."

"About?"

"What happened." Lonnie swallowed. "What's going on. I
dunno . . ."

Clint's eyes tightened, like he was trying to get Lonnie a bit
more in focus. "I got something going on right now."

"Sure, I understand."

"No you don't. That's not the point. I'm tied up the next hour. Come back then, we'll sit and . . . you know." He nudged off the doorframe, stood upright. "That work for you?"

"Yeah," Lonnie said. "I'll come back."

He turned to go. Clint called him back with, "Hey, Shocker."

It took a second for Lonnie to remember: That's me. Over his shoulder: "Yeah?"

That tight-eyed stare again, like there was just too much to take in. "You look good."

LONNIE FOUND A SANDWICH SHOP, feeling too shaky even to risk a café on the off chance they'd have beer and wine on hand. He couldn't risk a relapse. Cardinal rule of rehab: avoid all triggers, like former friends.

He ordered a Snapple and took a seat by the window. A processed, instrumental version of "The Ballad of John and Yoko" simpered through an overhead speaker, as though to remind him that nothing is sacred.

Focus, he told himself. Three months you've been at Metta House, a devoted student, steady and strong. Worthy of trust. Why else would the man in charge send you on this mission?

And yet, having now seen Clint eye to eye, he felt groundless. Maybe this is what they mean, he thought, when they talk about No Self. An anxiety-tinged emptiness.

It was way too soon to bring up starting a production studio, no matter how he pitched it. Sure, he could make the case that they'd weed out the listless cutesy poseurs so typical of the scene now: Doom Dirge, Bitch Pop, Sad Core, Lo-Fi Bedroom Grunge. He had no intention of selling out, going mainstream, becoming the Shi Changsheng of punk. They'd restart true hardcore, give a voice to the angry, young, and poor, speak the ugly fucking truth to power.

Clint would laugh in his face. How many times had he said it? *The minute you think you have something to say, you're on the path to asshole.* Kind of thing you expect from a drummer.

But jacking the system was righteous—what did punk mean if
not that? And what better way to answer back to the sniveling
greedy horseshit than selflessness? Not groovy peacenik sniveling,
that's not what I mean—I'm talking defiance of the emperor, like
the venerable Tano and his warrior monks of Shaolin.

Buddha is true revolution. Buddha is the real Mao Tse-tung.

Which brought him back around to the real problem. They
had to talk that out, Mousy's death. He had to own the rage, the
spite. Cop to the guilt. All grand plans for anything else lay on
the far side of that. Regardless, this was the place to start, for a
thousand and one reasons.

CLINT MET HIM AT THE door, now wearing an Evil Conduct
T-shirt—admittedly not a positive sign—and gestured him toward
the back of the flat. "We'll talk in the kitchen."

From somewhere on the second floor, a stereo blasted "Slave
State," one of Acid Prancer's signature numbers. Lonnie stopped
in his tracks and glanced up the smoke-hazed stairwell. Mousy's
vocals stitched through the air:

A sweat-soaked bed
Then daylight and dread
Stuff whatever you're dreaming
Back inside your head

How many lifetimes ago, he thought, *did I write those words? How
many eternities have come and gone since I showed them to Mousy,
watched him make that wicked, lopsided grin. "Let's work up a tune,
Shocker McRocker." So full of faith. So present.*

Clint, standing hallway down the hall, snapped his fingers.
"You coming?"

"Yeah." Lonnie shook off the moment. "Sorry."

It wasn't till he passed the first doorway that he sensed the
other presence in the house. Two presences, actually.

One had a ball bat, but by the time Lonnie noticed the thing
coming at him all he could make out was a blur. The wood shaft

crashed across his temple and ear, knocking him down like a bag of cement. Instantly all but deaf. Blinded by pain. Wetting himself.

The three of them kept him down with kicks to the kidneys, the groin, the head. He curled up like he had with his father so many times, making out little by little that the other two were Mousy's sister, Jordan, and her old man, Gearhead Greg, who continued chipping in with the bat.

A voice for the angry young. Speaking the ugly truth.

About the time he was choking on blood and his right knee felt on fire, Greg and Clint got down on the floor to hold him down, one pinning his legs, the other his shoulders, while Jordan knelt beside him, leaning close to be heard over the music from upstairs, everything swathed in hiss.

"You remember what you said, cocksucker?" Her breath smelled rank from cigarettes, Southern Comfort and Coke—the sweet smell he couldn't quite make out earlier. "I'm outside the room, pounding on the door, trying to get inside—see my brother, see if he's okay, see if he's fucking alive—you remember that?" She grabbed his chin, squeezed like she wanted to rip it off. "Remember what you fucking said? 'He don't want to know you, you smokehound cunt.' But those weren't his words. That was you. My beautiful little brother was already dead."

Even with it pressed so close he could barely make out her face, his vision fragmented from the pounding, blood streaming into his eyes. But despite the angry buzz inside his brain and the thundering music upstairs he could suddenly make out nearby sounds with eerie clarity. What he heard was a match scrape a friction strip, the whisper of the flame, the singed tobacco of the cigarette. And he could smell: not just her breath but the billowing exhale smothering his face. Just beyond the smoke, in the haze, the red tip of ash glowed like the eye of an angry angel.

Two strong hands gripped his head and Jordan's thumb pushed back his eyelid. Even then, he couldn't see, but that was the least of his problems just then.

She said, "He didn't belong to you, asshole. He was mine, too. He was everybody's."

He wasn't sure whether he merely thought the words or screamed them—*He died quiet, he died peaceful . . . if you wanted in so bad why didn't you force the door, why leave it to the cops?*—but he also realized none of that mattered. This was the price of finding his way. This was the low, loathsome place.

HE SHUFFLED UP THIRD STREET toward Mission Bay, bent over like he'd been gut-shot and dragging one leg. A bus was out of the question: one, Gearhead Greg had taken his money. Two, the driver would no doubt call the law. And that just wouldn't do. They could have killed him, that would've been just and fair, but they hadn't.

So, as best he could, he walked.

The dragged knee buckled every time he tried applying weight, the joint a grinding, boiling knot of gristle. Given the stab in every breath, at least one broken rib seemed likely. As for the eye, an oyster couldn't clench shut tighter, and the scalding pain sent sickly orange flashes throughout his body, crackling and sparking along every nerve.

He crossed Lefty O'Doul Bridge where China Basin narrows into Mission Creek and kept trudging up Third, ballpark looming to the right, downtown a mile ahead. Avoiding eye contact as pedestrian traffic intensified, he continued across Market with its trolleys and traffic and crowds, aiming almost unaware toward Chinatown, sensing somehow he could find a place there to sit, rest. No one would trouble over him. For all intents and purposes, he'd be invisible.

He passed through the pagoda-style gate on Grant Avenue and dragged himself up the steep hill, maintaining his balance any way he could, bracing himself on cars or delivery vans along the curb, latching onto parking meters, grabbing lampposts entwined with dragons, trying not to tumble into the vendor tables mounted outside every storefront.

Somehow he managed the two long blocks to California Street and planted himself breathlessly on a wooden bench in the shaded square across from Old St. Mary's. Rest here, he thought, not long. Once you've got your strength back and can talk without choking, maybe ask a lady with a kind face if you can use her cell, call Katy at the center. Say you were mugged, which is true after all.

Wiping tears from his good eye, he glanced up at the cathedral's bell tower and felt a sudden, powerful sense of release. He'd reached a place of reckoning, acceptance, and felt ready to surrender. If he could only decide: to whom?

IN TIME HE SPOTTED A familiar figure at the corner, waiting for the light. A slender man in a sport coat, a scarf knotted at his neck. His appearance seemed incongruous, even impossible, and yet not. Excluding Metta House, where else but here to encounter Doctor Wu?

Lonnie scrambled from the bench and headed toward the corner. He didn't make it in time for the light, and he lacked the strength to call out, but he watched Doctor Wu continue down Grant, deeper into old Chinatown.

Traffic was light so Lonnie crossed against the red, shambling as quickly as he could. He spotted Doctor Wu turning into an alley and hurried to catch up, forgetting his pain, his weakness, his savaged eye and ribs and knee. When he reached the corner where Doctor Wu had turned he found himself facing a narrow cul de sac cluttered with nondescript shops and restaurants at street level, tenements overhead, towering above the damp pavement.

He went storefront to storefront, glancing through steam-fogged windows. At last he spotted the telltale sport coat vanishing up a stairwell inside a crowded dim sum tearoom. Totally Asian clientele, not a round eye in the place—it worked to his advantage. Nothing but stunned glances tried to stop him as he plowed through the dining room to the doorway that led upstairs.

His good fortune ended at the top. A wide, thick-necked, short-haired guard in a black suit manned the door at the hallway's end, the one just now closing. He stood with his open left hand covering his right fist, as though ready for a Bao Quan bow.

"I need to speak with Doctor Wu."

It came out slurred—the damage to his face, the stabbing lack of breath from his stairway climb. Bracing himself with one hand against the wall, he shoved off with each step, pushing himself along. The guard simply stood there, eyes front, the empty gaze of a temple dragon.

"I need to speak with Doctor Wu!" Bellowing now, as best he could.

That brought the door guard forward, ready to wrap Lonnie up, pitch him back down the stairs into the clamor of voices and hissing oil, clanging pots. Lonnie slammed his palm against the wall, pounding against the ancient plaster as he continued shouting, "I need to speak to Doctor Wu! It's me, Doctor Wu, Lonnie, I need to speak with you, please! Please come out, talk to me, please!"

He was thrashing in the guard's vice-like arms when the door opened. Doctor Wu stood there, ashen but otherwise expressionless. Beyond him, inside the room, a number of stern-faced men in suits, white shirts open at the neck, no ties, sat around a conference table in utter silence.

Doctor Wu whispered something harshly over his shoulder to someone inside the room, then entered the hallway, closing the door behind him. He said something in Chinese to the guard who, after a long moment, released his hold.

Lonnie collapsed to the floor. Doctor Wu bent over him, checking the various obvious wounds, specifically trying to look at the shuttered eye.

"You need medical attention," he said.

A SHORT TIME LATER KATY arrived and, with the help of the thickset guard, managed to get Lonnie down to her car. Doctor

Wu had long since vanished back inside the room with the other men.

She turned up California, heading west. Lonnie said, "Don't take me to a hospital."

She didn't respond—just kept driving, eyes straight ahead, hands at ten and two.

"If I wanted to go to a hospital I could've stopped at SF Gen."

"Lonnie—"

"It was on the way. Kinda. Given where I was coming from. Where I . . . ended up."

She stopped at a crosswalk and they watched a gaggle of Asian school kids troop merrily corner to corner, the sound of their laughter dulled by the windshield.

"Why didn't you?" She looked both ways, then accelerated from her stop. "Go to the hospital, I mean."

He sank a little deeper into the car seat. In a whisper: "I don't know . . ."

They continued on in silence for several blocks. "Well, never mind. Doctor Wu feels terrible about what happened—he assumes it had to do with the errand he gave you—and he's already called his personal physician. He's waiting for us at Metta House."

How responsive, Lonnie thought. How discreet.

"Those guys back there at the tea house," he said, "the ones Doctor Wu was meeting. Who are they?"

Katy shrugged. "I'm not sure. Businessmen, I suppose."

Lonnie managed a small laugh. "Think I don't know a gangster when I see one?"

"Lonnie, please." Like she was talking to a feverish child. "You've been beaten nearly to death, who knows what kind of damage you've suffered, shock alone, but that's no reason—"

"The Triads are in bed with the Chinese military."

"According to who—the US press?"

"He's a spy, isn't he—Doctor Wu, I mean."

Katy put her hand to her head. "Lonnie, for God's sake—"

"Christ, for all I know, you're all spies. Mazur for sure. Jonathan?"

"Yes, yes. You've found us out. We're all . . . spies! What better way to end the infinite afflictions of all living beings. You know what bodhisattva really means, right?"

"Secret agent?" He'd never seen her angry before. She looked on the verge of tears. "Have to admit, it's a perfect front. Put a little 'boo' back in Buddha."

She shook her head. A small, miserable laugh. "You ungrateful prick."

"Who says I'm ungrateful?"

"Please, just be quiet." She redoubled her focus on the street ahead. "At least until we get home."

So that's what we're calling it now, he thought. Not the center, not Metta House. Home.

EXCEPT FOR THE DOCTOR, THE place was empty when they arrived. Not uncommon, most of the others still worked. Katy helped Lonnie to the sofa nearest the fireplace and the physician, an affable, melon-faced Asian perhaps ten years younger than Doctor Wu, commenced with the expected Q&A—"What happened, where does it hurt, are you experiencing flashes of light or a buzzing in your ears?"—his voice calm and caring and precise.

Rummaging in his pebbled black bag, he said, "I understand you are a recovering addict. I therefore need to ask your informed consent before administering a painkiller. But I would like to get a better look at that eye. The knee as well, of course, but that may require a specialist."

A painkiller, Lonnie thought. Probably an opiate. Fentanyl, maybe.

He nodded. "Sure. Why not?"

The doctor took out a sterilized needle and a vial, the print too small and far away for Lonnie to read. As the syringe's cylinder filled, Katy came closer, crouched beside the sofa, and took Lonnie's hand. Her grip felt reassuringly cool and dry.

The doctor came close. "I'm going to lift your eyelid, which may be very tender and painful. But I need to anesthetize the area, and the best spot for that is the eye itself."

Lonnie decided not to tell him he'd shot up in his eye before.

"From the needle itself, you'll only feel a pinprick, nothing more. Okay?"

Lonnie nodded again and braced himself and, all things considered, it went quick. He lay back and closed both eyes and waited for the effect to hit, only realizing once the numbing warmth began to spread throughout his body that the doctor had emptied the entire syringe. And, from what he shortly gathered, it wasn't just an opiate. It was a paralytic—at least, he couldn't move. And yet, with Katy's fingers still entwined with his, panic seemed a thousand miles away.

If he were to describe the ensuing sensation to someone, he'd say that it was like wandering into a strange, small church, no one there but you, except for an unseen organist playing up in the choir loft, which you can't see no matter where you look. You can hear the music, though: a hymn you think you recognize, the name right there on the tip of your tongue. But then the music falters, the organist loses the tune—stops, goes back, repeats an earlier phrase, but once again turns into a musical cul de sac. The organist retreats, revisits another beautiful line, then wanders off, stumbles across another hymn, diddles with that, then strays into odds and ends from other songs: "Fools Rush In," "River Deep, Mountain High," "Mary Had a Little Lamb" . . .

And everywhere that Mary went . . .

Someone should wise up the lamb, he thought, as the cool dry fingers he'd been clutching slipped free. Following Mary is not a viable long-term option.

UNBALANCED
BY CRAIG JOHNSON

THE ONLY PART OF HER clothing that was showing were the black combat boots cuffed with a pair of mismatched green socks. She was waiting on the bench outside the Conoco station in Garryowen, Montana. When I first saw her; it was close to eleven at night and if you'd tapped the frozen Mail Pouch thermometer above her head it would've told you that it was twelve degrees below zero.

I was making the airport run to pick up my daughter, Cady, who had missed her connection from Philadelphia in Denver and was now scheduled to come in just before midnight. The Greatest Legal Mind of Our Time was extraordinarily upset but had calmed down when I'd told her we'd stay in Billings that night and do some Christmas shopping the next day before heading back home. I hadn't told her we were staying at the Dude Rancher Lodge, one of my favorites because of the kitschy, old brick court-yard and fifties coffee shop. Cady hated it.

In my rush to head north, I hadn't gassed up in Wyoming and was just hoping that the Conoco had after-hour credit-card pumps. They did, and it was as I was putting gas into my truck with the motor running that I noticed her stand up, a blanket trailing out from her shoulders through the blowing snow to where I stood.

She paused at the other side of the bed and then raised her head to look at the stars on the doors of my truck and me, the eyes tick-tocking either from imbalance or self-medication. She studied my hat, neatly pressed shirt and the shiny brass nametag and other trappings of authority just visible under my sheepskin coat.

I BUTTONED MY JACKET THE rest of the way up and looked at her, expecting Crow, maybe Northern Cheyenne, but from the limited view the condensation of her breath and the cowl-like hood provided, I could see that her skin was pale and her hair dark but not black; a wide face and full lips that snared and released between the nervous teeth. "Hey." She cleared her throat and shifted something in her hands, still keeping the majority of her body wrapped. "I thought you were supposed to shut the engine off before you do that." She glanced at the writing on the side of my truck and the shotgun locked to the front hump, something I was sure she'd already noticed. "Where's Absaroka County?"

I clicked the small keeper on the pump handle and pulled my glove back on, resting my hand on the top of the bed as the tank filled. "Wyoming; Bighorn Mountains."

"Oh." She nodded but didn't say anything more.

About five nine, she was tall and her eyes moved rapidly taking in the vehicle and then me; she had the look of someone whose only interaction with the police was of being rousted; feigned indifference with just a touch of defiance—and maybe just a little crazy. "Cold, huh?"

I adjusted my hat to keep the blowing snow out of my eyes. "Yep."

She was quiet again, and I was beginning to wonder how long it was going to take, and how much nerve it must've taken to approach my truck; I must've been the only vehicle that had stopped in hours. I waited. The two-way radio blared something. The handle clicked off, and I pulled the nozzle, returning it to the plastic cradle. I hit the button to request a receipt, because I didn't trust gas pumps any more than I trusted those robot amputees over in Deadwood.

Without volition, I found words in my mouth the way I always did in the presence of women. "I've got a heater in this truck."

She snorted a quick laugh. "I figured."

I stood there for a moment more and then started around the front so as to not pass her on the way to the driver's side—now she was going to have to ask.

As I pulled the door handle, she started to reach out a hand but then let it drop. I paused for a second more and then slid in and shut the door behind me, clicking on my seatbelt and pulling the three-quarter ton down into gear.

She backed away and then turned and retreated to the bench as I wheeled around the pumps. I stopped at the road, sat there for a moment, and then shook my head at myself, turned around and circled in front of her. She looked up again as I rolled the window down on the passenger side door. "You want a ride?"

Balancing her needs with her pride, she sat there huddled in the blanket. "Maybe."

I sighed to let her know that my Good Samaritan side wasn't endless and spoke through the exhaust that the wind was carrying back past the truck. "I was offering you a ride if you're headed north."

She looked up at the empty highway and was probably thinking about whether she could trust me or not.

"I have to be in Billings in a little over an hour to pick up my daughter—are you coming?"

The glint of temper was there again, but she converted it into standing and picked something up—a guitar case that I hadn't noticed before. She tossed it into the bed of my truck, still carefully holding the blanket closed around her with the other hand, her posture slightly off. "All right."

"You want to put your guitar in here, there's room."

She swung the door open, gathered the folds up around her knees, and slid into the seat. "Nah, it's a piece of shit." She closed the door with her left hand and then looked at some papers, the metal clipboard, my thermos, and me. Her eyes half closed as the waft of heat from the vents surrounded her. "So, are we going or what?"

"Seatbelt." She settled in and looked out the window, her breath fogging the glass, and I placed her age as mid-twenties.

"Don't believe in 'em." She wiped her nose on the blanket again using her left hand.

We didn't move, and the radio crackled a highway patrolman taking a bathroom break. She looked at the radio below the dash and then back at me, then pulled the shoulder belt from the retractor and swiveled to put it in the retainer at the center—it was about then that Dog swung his giant head around from the backseat to get a closer look at her.

"Jesus . . . !" She jumped back against the door and something slid from her grip and fell to the rubber floor mat with a heavy thump.

I glanced over and could see it was a small, wood-gripped revolver.

She slid one of her boots in front of it to block my view. We stared at each other for a few seconds, both of us deciding how it was we were going to play it.

"What the hell, man . . ." She adjusted the blanket, careful to completely cover the pistol on the floorboard.

I sat there for a moment more, then pulled onto the frontage road and headed north toward the onramp of I-90. Thinking about what I was going to do, I pulled onto the highway. "That's my partner—don't worry, he's friendly."

She stared at the 150-plus pounds of German Shepherd, Saint Bernard, and who knew what. She didn't look particularly convinced. "I don't like dogs."

"Too bad, it's his truck."

I eased the V-10 up to sixty on the snow-covered road and motioned toward the battered thermos leaning against the console. "There's coffee in there."

She looked, first checking to make sure the gun was hidden and then reached down, pausing long enough so that I noticed her bare hands, strong and deft even in the remains of the cold. She saw me watching her and lifted the thermos by the copper-piping handle, which was connected to the Stanley with two massive hose clamps. She read the sticker on the side, DRINKING FUEL, as she twisted off the chrome top "You got anything to put in this?"

"Nope."

She rolled her eyes and unscrewed it, pouring herself one. She placed it in the cup holder and settled back against the door, careful not to move enough to reproduce the revolver. She pulled the blanket back off her shoulders and looked at me. "Good coffee."

"Thanks." I threw her a tenuous safety line and caught a glimpse of a nose stud and what might've been a tattoo at the side of her neck. "My daughter sends it to me."

The radio squawked again as the highway patrolman came back on duty, and she glared at it. "Do we have to listen to that crap?"

I smiled and flipped the radio off. "Sorry, force of habit."

She glanced back at Dog, who regarded her indifferently as she nudged one foot toward the other in an attempt to push the revolver up and onto her other shoe. "So, you're the sheriff down there?"

"Yep."

She nonchalantly reached down, feigning an itch in order to snag the pistol. She slid it back under the blanket and carried it onto her lap. "Your daughter live in Billings?"

"Nope, Philadelphia."

She nodded and murmured something I didn't catch.

"Excuse me?"

The eyes came up, and I noticed they were an unsettling shade of green. "Philly Soul. The O'Jays, Patti LaBelle, the Stylistics, Archie Bell & the Drells, the Intruders . . ."

"That music's a little before your time, isn't it?"

She sipped her coffee and stared out the windshield. "Music's for everybody, all the time."

We drove through the night. It seemed as if she wanted something, and I made the mistake of thinking it was conversation. "I saw the guitar case—you play?"

She watched the flakes that had just started darting through my headlights. "You see everything?"

"Keeps me alive." I glanced at her lap to let her know I knew. "Are you in trouble with someone?"

The chromate eyes flicked to me then returned to the road. "Not really." It was a long time before she spoke again. "Your dog sure has a nice truck." An eighteen-wheeler, pushing the speed limit just a little, became more circumspect in his speed as I pulled out from the clouds of snow billowing behind him and passed. "It's funny how traffic slows down around you in this thing."

"Uh huh."

There was another long pause as 362 horses pulled Dog's sleigh up the road, the muffled sound of the tires giving the illusion that we were riding on clouds.

"I play guitar—lousy. Hey, do you mind if we power up the radio? Music, I mean."

I stared at her for a moment and then gestured toward the dash. She fiddled with the SEEK button on FM, but we were in the dead zone between Hardin and Billings. "Not much reception on the Rez. Why don't you try AM? The signals bounce off the atmosphere and you can get stuff from all over the world."

She flipped it off and slumped back against the passenger side door. "I don't do AM." She remained restless, glancing up in the visors and at the console. "You don't have any CDs?"

I thought about it and remembered my friend Henry Standing Bear buying some cheap music at the Flying J truck stop months ago on a fishing trip to Fort Smith. The Bear had become annoyed with me when I'd left the radio on search for five minutes, completely unaware that it was only playing music in seven second intervals. "You know, there might be some CDs in the side pocket of the door."

She moved and rustled her free hand in the pocket, finally pulling out a $2.99 *The Very Best of Merle Haggard.* "Oh, yeah."

She plucked the disc from the cheap, cardboard sleeve and slipped it into a slot in the dash I'd never noticed. The lights of the stereo came on and the opening lines of Haggard's opus, "Okie from Muskogee" thumped through the speakers. She made a face and looked at the cover, reading the fine print. "What'd they do, record it on an eight-track through a steel drum full of bourbon?"

"I'm not so sure they sell the highest fidelity music in the clearance bin at the Flying J."

Her face was animated in a positive way for the first time as the long fingers danced off the buttons of my truck stereo, and I noticed the metal flake, blue nail polish. "You've got too much bass and the fade's all messed up." She continued playing with the thing and I had to admit that the sound was becoming remarkably better. Satisfied, she sat back in the seat, even going so far as to hold out a hand for Dog to sniff. He did, and then licked her wrist.

"I love singer-storytellers." She scratched under the beast's chin and for the first time since I'd met her seemed to relax as she listened to the lyrics. "You know this song is a joke, right?"

"Well, I don't know if it's a joke . . ."

"He wrote it in response to the uninformed view of the Vietnam War. He said he figured it was what his dad would've thought."

I shrugged noncommittally.

She stared at the side of my face, possibly at my ear, or the lack of a tiny bit of it. "Were you over there?"

I nodded.

"So was my dad."

She seemed to want more. ". . . It was a confusing time; we were all kind of uninformed to a degree."

"Like now?"

"Kind of."

Her eyes went back to the road. "That's why I'm going back home; my dad died."

"I'm sorry."

"Me too."

I navigated my way around another slow-moving eighteen-wheeler. "What did your father do?"

Her voice dropped to a trademark baritone, buttery and sonorous. "KERR, 750AM. Polson, Montana." I laughed, and for the first time she smiled.

"I thought you didn't do AM."

"Yeah, well now you know why."

Merle swung into "Pancho and Lefty" and she pointed to the stereo. "Proof positive that he *did* smoke marijuana in Muskogee— he's friends with Willie Nelson."

I raised an eyebrow. "In my line of work, we call that guilt by association."

"Yeah, well in my line of work we call it a friggin' fact and Willie's smoked like a Cummins Diesel everywhere, including Muskogee, Oklahoma."

I had to concede the logic. "You seem to know a lot about the industry. Nashville?"

"Yeah."

"Okay, so you're not a musician. What did you do?"

"Still do, when I get through in Polson." Her eyes went back to the windshield and her future. "Produce, audio engineer . . . or I try to." She nibbled on one of the nails that held the shiny cup. "Did you know that less than five percent of producers and engineers in the business are women?"

"Can't say that I did."

I waited, but she seemed preoccupied, finally sipping her coffee again and then pouring herself another. "It's bullshit. We're raised to be attractive and accommodating, but we're not raised to know our shit and stand by it." She was quiet for a while, listening to the lyrics. "Townes Van Zandt wrote that one. People think it's about Pancho Villa but one of the lines is about him getting hung—the one about the *federales* letting him *hang* around out of kindness I suppose . . . Pancho Villa was assassinated."

"Yep, seven men standing in the road in Hidalgo del Parral shot more than forty rounds into his roadster."

"You a history teacher before you were sheriff?" I didn't say anything, and the smile lingered on her face like finger-picking on a warp-necked fret. "Maybe Townes was smoking in Muskogee, too."

"It's probable."

Silence again, but she continued to watch me drive. "You're okay-looking, in a dad kind of way."

"That's a disturbing statement for a number of reasons."

She barked a laugh and raised one of the combat boots up to lodge it against the transmission hump, but realized she was revealing the pistol from the drape of the blanket before her and lowered her foot. It was another mile marker before she spoke again, her voice a little strained.

"My dad never talked about it; Vietnam. . . . He handled that Agent Orange stuff and that shit gave robots cancer." Her eyes were drawn back to the windshield, and Polson. "He died last week and they're already splitting up his stuff." The mile markers clicked by like spokes. "He taught me how to listen; I mean really listen. To hear things that nobody else heard. He had this set of Sennheiser HD 414 open-back headphones from '73, lightweight with the first out-of-head imaging with decent bass—Sony Walkmans and all that stuff should get down and kiss Sennheiser's ass. 2000 ohm impedance let you plug into a line-level output without loading it down. The big peak was 2 kHz in their frequency response curve and would seriously scour your ears; tough, too. They had a steel cord and you could throw them at a *talented* program director or a brick wall—I'm not sure which is potentially denser."

It was an unsettling tirade, but I still had to laugh.

"You don't have any idea what I'm talking about, do you?"

We topped the hill above Billings and looked at the lit-up refineries that ran along the highway as I made the sweeping turn west. "Nope, but it all sounds very impressive." The power of the motor pushed us back in the leather seats like we were tobogganing down the hill in a softened and diffused landscape, floating on a cushion of air, rushing headlong into the snowy dunes and the shimmering lights that strung alongside the highway like fuzzy moons.

She turned away, keeping her eyes from me, afraid that I might see too much there. "You can just drop me at the Golden Pheasant; I've got friends there doing a gig that'll give me a ride the rest of the way."

Nodding, I joined with the linear constellation of I-94.

I had a vague sense of the club's location downtown and took the 27th Street exit, rolling past the Montana Women's prison, and the wrong side of the railroad tracks as we sat there watching a hundred and sixty coal cars of a Burlington Northern/Santa Fe train roll by. The quiet settled in the cab the way it does when there's so much to say, and like the muffled tires of the truck had been, the wheels were turning.

When she finally spoke, her voice was different, perhaps the most approaching sane of the night. "It belonged to my father. When I was leaving for Tennessee, he gave me a choice of those headphones I was telling you about, but I figured I'd have more use for the gun." She placed her hand on the dash and fingered the vent louvers. She continued talking now, because she had to. "I got picked up by a few guys from Missouri and they tried stuff. They seemed nice at first . . . anyway, I had to pull it."

I waited.

"I didn't shoot anybody."

"Good." I turned down a side street and took a right where I could see the multi-colored neon of the aforementioned pheasant spreading his tail feathers in a provocative manner. I parked the truck in the first available spot—it was still sifting snow—slipped her into PARK and turned to look at the girl with the strange eyes.

"Maybe I should've taken the headphones."

"Maybe they're still there."

She smiled and finished the dregs of her coffee, wiped the cup out on her blanket, and screwed the top back on the thermos. She placed it back against the console as the revolver slipped from her leg and onto the seat between us.

We both sat there looking at it, representative of all the things for which it stood.

"If you take that back to Polson, what are you going to do with it?"

"Probably throw it in the lake up there. It's never done anything but bring me bad luck."

I leaned forward and picked it up. It was a nice one; S&W Chief's Special with not much wear. "How 'bout I keep it for you?"

She didn't say anything for a long time but finally slipped through the open door and pulled the guitar case from the bed of my truck, standing there in the opening.

The plaintive words of Haggard's "A Place to Fall Apart" drifted from the speakers and she glanced at the radio as if the Okie from wherever might be sitting on my dash. "I'd give a million dollars if that son of a bitch would go into a studio, just him and a six-string guitar, no backup singers, no harps—and just play."

I watched her face, trying to not let the eyes distract me. "Maybe you should tell him that sometime."

The eyes sparked. "After I get those headphones, maybe I'll look him up."

"I wouldn't look in Muskogee."

The wind pressed against her, urging departure. "He lives in Redding, California."

She shut the door and clutched the blanket around herself, dragging the guitar case and walking away without looking back. She disappeared into the swinging glass doors with swirls of snow devils circling behind her, and all I could think was that I was glad I wasn't in Polson, Montana, and in possession of a set of Sennheiser HD 414 open-back headphones.

I emptied the pistol into my center console and then carefully wrapped the revolver in a bandana from my liner pocket, placed it beside the loose rounds, and locked the lid.

Twenty minutes later my daughter climbed in the cab. "Please tell me we're not staying at the Dude Rancher."

I didn't say anything, and waited for her to put on her seatbelt.

She pulled the shoulder belt around in a huff, but then smiled back at me. "Oh, Daddy."

"Merry Christmas, Punk." I pulled the truck in gear, as Haggard softened his tone in my stereo with one of my favorites, "If We Make it Through December."

She was now ruffling Dog's hair and kissing his muzzle, and it must've taken a good thirty seconds before she remarked. "Did you get a new stereo in the truck? It sounds good."

I nodded as we held hands over the console, driving down from the airport. "Yep, it does."

A BUS TICKET TO PHOENIX
BY WILLY VLAUTIN

OTIS WOKE THAT MORNING TO Lenny in the bathroom yelling on
the phone. It was past 11 a.m. at Winner's Casino in Winnemucca,
Nevada. Under the covers he shivered in the cold and could see
his breath fall out and disappear into the room. He got up to find
the window open and the heat off.

He set the thermostat to high, shut the sliding glass window,
and looked out to see snow falling. It covered the van and trailer
and the houses behind the motel. He stood seventy-seven years
old, thin and tall with greasy brown hair. He found his clothes on
the floor, dressed, and walked across the street to the casino. He
used the toilet, lost five dollars on video poker, and went to the
casino restaurant for breakfast.

In a booth he sat alone and filled out his Keno card,
ordered a Denver omelet and a draft beer, when Lenny came
in and sat across from him. Lenny was twenty-nine years old
also tall and thin. He had short black hair and his face was
red from the cold and snot leaked from his nose onto his handlebar mustache. He wore a black felt cowboy hat and two
Levi coats on top of each other.

"Bet you got a Denver omelet and pancakes. You gotta be way too hungover for oatmeal and toast."

Otis nodded. "Man, I'm gonna get pneumonia rooming with you."

"Don't you know you're supposed sleep in a cold room?" said Lenny.

"Not in a freezer."

"That's what you get for being born in Phoenix."

"You were born in Phoenix, too."

"But my folks are from Montana," Lenny said and smiled. "The cold is in my blood. I can take anything."

Otis shook his head and waited for his numbers to appear on the Keno TV bolted to the back wall of the restaurant. The waitress came and Lenny ordered drinks, a hamburger steak, three eggs over medium, and a side of French toast.

"I bet you're wondering why I was on the phone all morning?"

Otis nodded vaguely and kept his eyes on the TV screen.

Lenny sunk down in the booth. "The hot water heater in my house broke, and Wendy's having a fit 'cause I maxed out our credit card buying the new P bass. We're flat broke with no hot water and her sister and her three brats will be there in less than twenty-four hours."

"That's rough," said Otis and looked at him. "I hate showering in cold water."

"And who does she call to help her but Dex. He's picking up a new water heater from Home Depot and coming over to put it in."

"Dex is her ex-husband, right?"

Lenny nodded. "You know she'll fuck him and she always fucks best when she's mad or guilty and she'll be both."

"But look at it this way," said Otis. "At least you'll get a new water heater and you'll get it for free."

The waitress came from the casino bar with a Budweiser and a shot of Jägermeister and set it down. Lenny drank the shot and leaned over the table. "Maybe this tour is cursed. Maybe this one's like the time we went out with Bobby Diamond."

"Shit, man, don't say things like that," said Otis. "The van caught fire on that run."

Lenny drank half his glass of beer.

"And remember that guy in the room next to us at the Super 8 shot himself? And Bobby used to give me those three-page lists of fuck ups I'd make. He had to have a perfect memory, son of a bitch. Fuck that guy. Fifty bucks a day and only ten dollars per diem. One beer per set, it ain't human. And don't forget he picked up that retarded gal and had her ride with us for three days. This tour ain't that bad."

Lenny finished his beer. "Even so I'd rather be out with Bobby. At least Bobby didn't make me dress up like a biker with a handle bar mustache."

"What about me?" Otis said. "I have to play metal licks all night. I've spent my whole life trying not to play metal, and now I'm in a country band that plays metal."

Lenny waved the waitress back over and they ordered two more beers and two shots.

"A movie called *The Martian*'s playing at one," said Otis as she walked away. "The front desk lady said the movie theater's barely a mile down the main street."

"What's *The Martian* about again?"

"A guy stuck on Mars."

Lenny laughed. "Man, we're already stuck on Mars. I hate this run. Mesquite, Laughlin, Henderson, then not even Vegas but a truck stop outside of Vegas, Tonopah, Reno, and now this place."

"It's only twelve more days," Otis said. "At least the shows have been good."

"Harlan can sure pack them in. I have no idea how, but he can," said Lenny.

"I'm getting depressed just thinking about him."

The waitress came with their drinks and set them down. They knocked the shot glasses together and drank them.

"You think Harlan takes steroids?"

Otis looked at the numbers coming up on the Keno screen. "He might."

"I've never seen a guy in that good of shape."

"Me neither."

"You hit?"

"No," Otis said and then a Mexican kid came from the back with both meals and set them on the table.

Lenny put a napkin on his lap and shook his head. "I still can't believe I lost my bass."

"Me neither," said Otis and began eating.

Lenny took a drink of beer. "Did I ever tell you the time when I was seventeen and doing a tour with this band called The High Range Rustlers?"

Otis shook his head.

"We were playing a convention in Helena, Montana, and after the gig we drove to a friend of one of the guys to stay the night. Back then I never left my bass anywhere. My dad had lost a couple guitars over the years and he was the one who told me to never let the son of a bitch out of my sight. So I took the fucker in with me every time, no matter what. But that night I'd taken some mushrooms and we were drinking tequila and I was the guy bringing in everyone's personal gear. I took out my bass, set it on the ground, and started making trips. But I forgot the poor fucker in the dark and left her on the front lawn. It was the same time as now, November, and it was like today and had started snowing. Dumped maybe seven or eight inches, not a lot but enough that it covered my bass. We had the next day off. I woke up hungover as shit and didn't think about where it was. I just ate breakfast and walked around Helena. They had a party that night and not once did I think about my poor bass. The next day comes and we're loading out and suddenly it starts raining and it melts the snow and wham bam if my bass isn't there safe and sound in its plastic case. She caused it to rain so I'd find her . . . And then there was that time I went home with that gal and she pulled the knife on me so I ran out of her apartment. Wasn't until I'd gotten back to the motel that I realized I'd forgotten my bass. And the worst of it was I was so drunk I couldn't remember where she lived. But the next morning I went down to the lobby and there my bass was leaned against the front desk in that same case. The crazy chick had brought her back. My bass convinced a maniac with a kitchen knife to bring her to the motel. I got dozens of those stories. . . . Hell my dad gave me the bass for my sixteenth birthday and now I'm twenty-nine and I ain't half as big a fuck up as I was back then. But now, after all this time, she suddenly vanishes at a truck-stop gig outside of Las Vegas. No other gear goes missing, just my Dad's '72 P bass. And don't forget the manager of the room swore up and down he locked every door."

"I don't even like talking about it," said Otis quietly.

"How do you think I feel?" Lenny cried. "Thing's worth a couple grand."

"And it was your dad's."

Lenny nodded and picked up his knife and fork. "My dad's probably pissing on my head from heaven for being such a shit-heel." He broke apart the three over-medium eggs, mixed them in with the hamburger and hash browns, and poured syrup over all of it.

"I really do have a bad feeling about this whole tour," said Otis. "Don't forget Mickey lost his gold watch in Henderson."

"But he left it in the van," Lenny said. "Who leaves a watch sitting in a van on the seat for everyone to see?"

"But we were only gone ten minutes. Remember it was just a piss break. And there was hardly anyone at that gas station."

"Well they won't let us have a key so it wasn't our fault the van was left unlocked. They get mad if we lock it and they get mad if we don't."

"Mickey said his wife gave him the watch," said Otis with a mouth full of food. "It was her grandfather's prized possession.

She inherited it and had it engraved for their wedding day, 'Mickey and Emily forever.' It's worth a thousand dollars plus, of course, sentimental value."

"Who wears a watch anymore anyway?"

"You just hate him 'cause he doesn't like Sneaky Pete," Otis said and laughed.

"What steel player doesn't like Sneaky Pete?"

"That's a good point."

"Why couldn't it have happened to Terry?"

"You just hate Terry 'cause he drags," said Otis.

"And why shouldn't I? I'm the bass player, aren't I? He has three beers and then he drags the rest of the fucking night. When I see him cracking that third bottle I just cringe. He and Harlan do nothing but lift weights and play on the Internet. Maybe Terry should listen to a click and learn how to keep a beat. And just 'cause he's Harlan's brother-in-law he gets keys to the van and gets paid more than we do."

"He has keys 'cause it's his van."

"Still," Lenny said and took the side order of French toast, covered it in butter and syrup, and scraped it off the small plate onto the half-eaten eggs and hamburger steak. "And here's something else. Mickey thinks Harlan's about ready to sign some big Nashville deal."

"Really?"

"He's probably going to be famous."

"Jesus, you think that could be true?"

"I don't know. He sure packs them in. Even in these shitholes."

Otis looked at the Keno screen and shook his head. "I hate to say what I'm about to say, but maybe we should stick this one out for a while."

"That's what Mickey thinks too."

"The problem is he'll fire Mickey."

Lenny nodded and pointed his fork at Otis. "'Cause he's fat and bald, right?"

"Exactly."

"Man, Harlan's an asshole."

Otis nodded.

Lenny took a drink of beer. "As my dad would say, 'Mickey is one sugar-picking son of a bitch.' And that trumps all looks, weight, and most deviant behavior."

Otis laughed.

"You really think a guy like Harlan could hit the big time?"

Otis pushed his plate to the center of the table. "Did I ever tell you about the time I was in that band called the Black Dust Marauders?"

Lenny shook his head.

"It was when I was nineteen or so. All original songs. We put out a couple records."

"What kind of stuff?"

"Like Doug Sahm meets Yes. Prog country," he said and laughed. "It didn't make a lot of sense. Weird time signatures and songs that would go on for ten minutes. But I dug it and the singer-songwriter's mom bankrolled the band. I made twenty grand just playing fifty or sixty nights a year. She must have lost a fortune. Anyway, we were doing a gig in Salt Lake and the band opening for us was Matchbox Twenty."

"I think I've heard of that band," said Lenny.

"They were famous a few years back. But that night in Salt Lake they weren't shit and all we saw was a brand new blue fifteen-seat Econoline with a matching blue trailer taking our parking spot. They were on a major label when labels still had the money. The Black Dust Marauders were topping out at forty to fifty people a gig and driving a fifteen-year-old Dodge. But hell, we brought the people that night. No one knew who they were. Even so, they had a merch person, a sound man, and that new goddamn van and trailer. I watched their set and that's when I was convinced that none of it made sense. That the whole thing didn't make sense. They'd sign anyone, throw money at anyone, even a blown-out tire on the side of the road. 'Cause to me that's what they sounded like. And then you know what happened?"

"What's that?"

"Maybe three weeks later we were in Boston, Massachusetts, and they were on the radio. I went into a mini-mart and heard them mentioned by a DJ. After that I heard them everywhere. They had a hit. I must have heard their song twenty or thirty times during that last week of the tour. What that says to me is maybe Harlan Sudrey will be the next Kenny Chesney."

"We sure have to play enough of that shit."

"Chesney's better than playing Harlan's 'Riding That Wave like a Bull.'"

Lenny laughed and kept shoveling in his breakfast.

Otis finished his beer. "I got to say you look like an idiot with that mustache."

"How do you think I feel?" said Lenny sighing. He put down his knife and fork. "The last thing I want is a handlebar mustache. 'Cause know who else has a fucking handlebar mustache?"

"Who?"

"Wendy's dad, that's who. Every time I go to kiss her she thinks it's her dad trying to stick his tongue down her throat. Man, it's even worse when we get in the sack."

Otis laughed, crumbled his Keno card and put it on his breakfast plate.

Lenny set down a twenty dollar bill and his food voucher on the table and got up from his seat. "I got forty bucks on Arizona State and the game starts in an hour. I'll see you around. Remember he wants to do the Zach Brown song tonight and the Metallica one."

OTIS WALKED DOWN THE MAIN street of Winnemucca towards the theater. Snow fell but wasn't sticking and the main road was clear and a constant stream of cars and trucks passed on the road. He darted across the street to a minimart, bought a large bag of

M&M's and a bottle of Coke and put them in his coat pocket. He could see the theater marquee a block away when a man ran toward him on the sidewalk. As he got closer he could see it was the singer, Harlan Sudrey, dressed in a silver-and-black jogging outfit with matching silver-and-black running shoes.

"How far have you gone?" asked Otis.

"I don't know. I just run for an hour," Harlan said out of breath. He continued to run in place as they spoke. "It's good to see you're getting some exercise."

"Always trying," said Otis.

"It's good I bumped into you. I was hoping to talk. What happened on the intro to 'Tomahawks and Teepees?'"

"My tuner got stuck."

Harlan nodded. "What about the bridge on 'Champagne Sunrise?'"

Otis shook his head. "I'm sorry about that one. I got it confused with 'Tequila, Tecate & Teresa.'"

"Those changes are close, that's true," Harlan said and spit on the ground. "You want me to send you the MP3s so you can revisit them?"

"I have them. I'll look them over before tonight."

"Want me to see if Terry can get you a tuner that doesn't stick?"

"Nah, I figured it out."

"And remember we're doing Zach Brown's 'Chicken Fried' in E and tell Lenny we're not doing just 'Sandman' but a Metallica medley that Terry and I worked out last night after the gig. 'Sandman' into 'Sad but True' into 'Fuel.' 'Fuel' we'll do bluegrass. Gig starts at nine, maybe practice at seven so we can work them out."

Otis nodded.

"And stop by my room sometime before then. Terry and I were thinking about you wearing a mechanic's shirt."

"A mechanic shirt?"

"The kind with the names on them. We picked you up a couple in Reno. And you were wearing regular jeans last night."

"I spilled coffee on my black ones yesterday," said Otis.

Harlan kept running in place. "They have laundry machines at the end of the motel row."

Otis nodded.

"You ever think of cutting your hair?"

"Not really," Otis said. "But look, I'll let you keep running."

Harlan nodded. "Oh, one last thing. How drunk do you think Lenny was last night?"

"Drunk?"

"He seemed off with Terry on the third set. Seemed like he was rushing."

Otis smiled. "Shit, Harlan, Lenny's got the best time of any guy I ever met. He wasn't drunk, it was just Terry dragging."

Harlan spit again. "We're in room 235," he said. "Maybe come before five."

THE MOVIE THEATER WAS EMPTY. He ordered a small popcorn, watched the film, and then walked across the street to the China Garden Chinese restaurant and ate a late afternoon lunch. He called Lenny on the walk back to the motel.

"You know how I hate bad Chinese food."

"Yeah, so?" replied Lenny.

"Well, for a Podunk town they know how to make Chinese . The Kung Pao Chicken was something else and the sweet and sour pork was the best I've had since that place in San Diego."

"Kung Pao is the stuff with peanuts in it, right?"

"That's it."

"Man, I hate peanuts in food," said Lenny.

"That's 'cause you're a dumb fuck."

"Maybe."

"You win on Arizona State?"

"Missed the spread by two points, but I put twenty on LSU and it looks like I'll get that."

Otis walked along the sidewalk and snow continued to fall.

"Harlan thinks you were rushing the third set. I told him it was Terry but who knows what he thinks."

"Where'd you see him?"

"He was jogging when I was heading to the movie."

"Were there any aliens in 'The Martian?'"

"Nothing like that."

"You like it?"

"Good enough," Otis said.

"Harlan should spend more time learning to play guitar than bitching about me."

Otis laughed. "We have practice at seven."

"Shit, man," Lenny cried. "Why we always have to practice?"

"I don't know."

"What are we learning?"

"A Metallica medley."

Lenny started laughing and hung up.

AT THE BACK END OF the motel was a small laundry room with two washers and two dryers. Otis opened his suitcase and put all his clothes, including the pants and shirt he was wearing, into a rusted-out washing machine. In his underwear he walked back to his room, showered, and shaved. He put his clothes in the dryer, watched TV until they were done, and then put on his black jeans and his best black long-sleeved Western shirt. He shined his boots, brushed his teeth, and walked down to room 235 and knocked on the door.

Inside Harlan and Terry had pushed their beds apart. Harlan was doing pushups in the space in between them.

"Forty-four, forty-five, forty-six," yelled Terry. When he got to fifty Harlan quit, stood up, and stepped back, and Terry got down.

"We're almost done," Harlan said, breathing heavily as sweat dripped down his face. "Terry has one more set so hold tight."

Terry went through his fifty and then collapsed on his bed. Harlan walked over to the vanity sink outside the bathroom, took off his shirt, and stood in front of the mirror and stared at himself. He had the abs of a boxer and the arms of a football player. Otis just shook his head. Terry turned the TV onto CMT, opened a Red Bull, and got on his laptop.

Harlan showered, dressed in silk black sweats, and he and Terry talked about Facebook and Twitter. Boxes of Harlan Sudrey T-shirts and hats were stacked in the corner of the room and Terry began doing an inventory of them.

"What we're thinking is black jeans and these mechanic shirts," Harlan said and took two shirts from a Goodwill bag. "You're a medium, right?"

Otis nodded and took them.

"And I know you have your hands full, but do you think you could get more active on stage? You've said you can't move around and play lead but maybe when Mickey takes a lead you can get more active."

"We need to get the audience to groove harder," said Terry.

Otis just nodded.

Harlan sprayed Clear Throat into his mouth and smiled. "We've been packing houses for five months straight. I know we've confirmed the four New Year's shows in Little Rock and then the Texas run, but can you do a Southern run in February and a California run in March?"

"I have nothing planned but this. Count me in."

Harlan nodded. "You're a hell of a guitar player and you're a team player. I like both of those things."

Otis cleared his throat. "I know you said once things got rolling we could talk about a wage increase."

"We will," Terry said and looked up from counting shirts. "We're locked in moneywise until spring but hold tight, brother, we'll set you up as soon as we can."

"Two hundred and fifty a week is tough."

Harlan nodded and looked at his fingernails. He went to his shaving kit and began cutting them with a clipper in the vanity sink. "Don't worry we'll take care of all you guys. . . . Oh, and one last thing," he said. "Did you get my email about 'Son of a Son of a Sailor?'"

"'Son of a Son of a Sailor?'"

"The Jimmy Buffett tune."

"I haven't checked my email for a couple days," Otis said

"We're going to do it at sound check. Maybe we'll put it in second set by the time we get to 'Jackpot.'"

"What key?"

"G," said Harlan.

Otis nodded.

"And listen, since we're talking shop, you made a few mistakes last night," said Terry.

Otis again nodded. "Harlan and I already went over it. My tuner got stuck on 'Tomahawks.' But you're right I blew 'Champagne Sunrise.' I always get the bridge confused with 'Tequila, Tecate & Teresa.'"

"They are close," said Terry. "But you got the MP3s, right?"

Otis nodded.

Harlan set his nail clippers back in his shaving kit and sat on the bed across from Otis. "And you might want to go a different direction on the solo for 'Rolling into Raleigh.' About half as much chicken picking and a little bit more Neal Schon. You know Journey, right?"

"I know who you're talking about," Otis said.

"All right," Harlan said. "So we'll see you at seven wearing the new shirt, okay?"

THE BAND FINISHED THE TWO last dates in Winnemucca and then did a three-day HVAC convention at Cactus Pete's in Jackpot. After that it was four nights in Wendover at the Peppermill. They had two days off and ended the tour with a Wednesday through Saturday stint in Elko at the Stockman Casino.

Otis woke there on the Sunday morning shivering in the hotel room. He got up wearing long underwear and a sweatshirt and walked to the motel window, shut it, and turned on the heat. Outside, snow was on the ground and the morning was covered in a haze of low-hanging clouds. It was fifteen degrees out.

Lenny snored in the bed next to him. It was 10:30 a.m.

"Let's get breakfast," said Otis.

Lenny woke up startled. "What?" he cried.

"I'm gonna die if you keep leaving the windows open all night."

"I get congested with fake heat," he said.

"What kind of heat isn't fake in winter," Otis said and sat down on his bed.

Lenny pulled the covers up to his neck. "You're just pissed 'cause that girl dissed you after you bought her two Long Island Iced Teas."

"I bought her three friends one each, too," Otis whined. "I spent eighty bucks on drinks alone."

"I saw that one coming from ten miles away."

"You're full of shit, you were right there."

"Maybe, but I didn't buy her any drinks."

"I'm gonna get sick if we don't eat soon," said Otis.

Lenny got up from bed and used the toilet. He came out with his face washed and his hair combed. He picked his clothes off the ground and got dressed. "I feel pretty good today considering. I thought I'd be hungover as shit drinking those Lemon Drops, but I'm not."

"Good for you."

Lenny smiled. "Let's go see a double feature and then hit the Sunday night NFL game in the casino. We'll celebrate the end of the tour. Terry gave me his and Harlan's drink tickets."

"Double feature?"

"We'll just leave one movie and go into the next. A modern-day double feature."

THEY SAT ACROSS FROM EACH other in a booth at the Stockman's Café. Otis played Keno and nursed a Coors and Lenny read the

Elko Daily Free Press and drank a Bloody Mary. They were silent until the food came. They ordered two more drinks and Otis glared at the Keno screen on the back wall.

"You hit?" asked Lenny.

"Close, but no."

"What I want to know is what the fuck happened on this tour? All my years touring I've never seen an amp go missing. A few guitars but never an amp."

"I'm out nine hundred bucks," said Otis. "And now I have to play a Peavey that looks like it's been dumped in Sani-Hut. I have no idea where Terry got it so fast but I fuckin' hate it."

"At least you can drop those things out of a van and they'll still play."

Otis nodded. "I know my Fender was just a reissue but I loved that amp."

"Some meth-head probably stole it," said Lenny and poured syrup over his eggs and hamburger steak.

"When we're done eating I'm calling every pawnshop from here to Reno. I have the serial number in my wallet and underneath the reverb tank I keep my address, name, and a hundred bucks."

"A hundred bucks?"

"For when shit really goes south."

"That's a good idea," Lenny said and covered the French toast with butter and maple syrup and dumped it on top of his eggs and hamburger.

Otis watched as the numbers on the Keno screen began to appear. "It just doesn't make sense. It was there when we left the showroom. I heard the doors lock. A lost bass and a lost amp all on one tour."

Lenny pointed his fork at Otis, "And don't forget Mickey's watch."

"An amp, a bass, and a watch," said Otis. "I'm gonna have a shot. You want one?"

Lenny nodded. "But get Jägermeister. The longer I'm awake the worse my stomach feels."

Otis ordered two shots and two beers from the waitress. As she walked toward the bar Terry appeared from the casino floor and came to their table.

"You guys are already up and rolling," he said and smiled.

Lenny nodded. "I got one question for you, Terry."

"What's that?"

"Why we staying an extra night? Why not leave today? I want to get the hell out of here."

"That's one of the things I came by to talk to you guys about. Can you meet in room 422 when you're done with breakfast? Let's make it a half hour. Mickey's coming then."

"You hear anything about my amp?" asked Otis.

"Not a thing."

"I'm gonna check with security," Otis said. "Maybe they'll have surveillance footage."

Terry rubbed his goatee and shook his head. "I already talked with them. We went over the footage minute by minute. Not a goddamn thing. Anyway we'll talk about all that in our room, okay?"

They both nodded and Terry walked away.

"Man, I hate guys who whiten their teeth," Lenny whispered.

"I wouldn't mind him so much but he's the worst drummer since that guy Willis."

Lenny shook his head. "But at least Willis could play, he just couldn't remember songs. It's 'cause he was a glue huffer."

"He was a glue huffer?"

Lenny nodded. "I caught him a handful of times."

Otis laughed. "Shit, I just thought maybe he was building model airplanes or something in his room."

ROOM 422 WAS EMPTY BUT for Mickey sitting on the bed closest to the window and both Harlan and Terry standing near the dresser. Otis and Lenny came in and sat next to Mickey. On a small table next to the TV sat three manila envelopes.

Lenny looked around and noticed the T-shirt and hat boxes and Harlan and Terry's personal gear were gone. "Ah shit," he said to Otis and shook his head. "We're getting fired."

"What?" Otis cried.

Mickey looked at them nervously.

Terry cleared his throat. "You're not getting fired, but he's right our time together is done. We both appreciate the hell out of the last year you've given us. You got us closer to the goal line and we, of course, got you all some good exposure. We were a good team. But there's no point in beating around the bush. Harlan and me are moving on to Nashville. Our wives are heading there as we speak. He's inked a deal but part of the deal was to rethink the band. The look of the band, the sound of it. We're going to start from scratch in Nashville. That's the truth. So in each of the envelopes is a bus ticket to Phoenix leaving tomorrow at 10 a.m., a thousand dollars for the four weeks, and a bonus each of two hundred dollars plus an extra hundred for baggage charges."

Mickey began shaking his head. "I hate the bus. Couldn't you at least fly us out of Salt Lake or Reno?"

"I looked into it but we don't have that kind of money," said Terry.

"What did you do with our gear?" asked Lenny.

"It's in the showroom. We've loaded out our stuff already. Security has a man keeping an eye on it. Otis, you can keep the Peavey."

"You keep the fucking Peavey," said Otis. "I want my Deluxe back."

"I want it back, too," Terry said. "But there's nothing stating it's our liability."

Lenny began laughing and stood up. "Shit, let's get out of here."

MICKEY SAT IN THE MIDDLE nursing a pint of Jim Beam and eating an extra-large pack of Red Vines. To the left of him Lenny was drinking off a pint of peppermint schnapps and eating popcorn, and to the right was Otis drinking off a pint of Jägermeister and eating from a jumbo-sized bag of M&M's. They had seen *Bridge of Spies* and were now watching *Spectre*.

When the movie ended they walked back toward the Stockman and dusk fell on the empty streets.

"There's nothing sadder than a Sunday night in a small town," said Lenny quietly.

"That's true," Mickey said, drunk and depressed. He stopped and pointed down a residential street. "Over there is where all the whorehouses are. Last night I saw Harlan coming out of one. We get fired and he's having a good time getting laid."

"Harlan was coming out of a whorehouse?" Lenny said and laughed. "Were you just walking by or going in?"

"Walking by," Mickey said. "I'm trying to lose weight so I've been walking. Anyway, the last time I checked I had twenty-three dollars in my bank account."

Otis stared down the street and began kicking the ground with his boot. "What was the name of the place he came out of?"

"I think it started with an I. Maybe Ingrid's," Mickey said.

"Well," said Lenny, "it's like my dad always told me, 'If a man don't wear his vice out in the open like a headband then put on your track shoes and run as fast as you can the other way. 'Cause what he's hiding ain't something you want to know anything about.'"

Mickey laughed but Otis was lost in thought and kept looking down the street. He kept kicking his boot on the ground. "Well boys," he said after a time, "I guess this is where we part. I'm heading down to the whorehouses."

"You're nuts, man," Lenny laughed. "The last time you went to a hooker you got so depressed you didn't stay sober for a week."

"I was only drunk for five days," Otis said, grinned, and began walking down the street alone.

HE CAME TO A SMALL row of brothels: Inez's D&D—Dancing and Diddling—Sue's Fantasy Club, and Mona's Ranch. Inside Inez's, he ordered a drink at the bar and waited until an overweight redhead in her thirties sat next to him dressed in a black lace nightgown.

"Are you here to party?" she asked.

Otis nodded. "Last night my buddy came in here. He looks like a model, about six feet tall, has tattoos on both his arms, and is always wearing a black cowboy hat that looks dipped in plastic. He also wears a black leather motorcycle jacket."

"What about him?"

"You remember him?"

"I think so."

"He said the girl he was with blew his mind. I'm looking for her. Do you remember who it was?"

"I'll tell you for twenty bucks," she said.

Otis took twenty dollars from his shirt pocket and handed it to her.

She folded the money and put it between her breast and the nightgown. "It was Amber," she said.

"You mind getting her?"

The woman got up and said to the bartender, "This boy here said he'd buy me a Manhattan. I'll be right back."

The drink was thirteen dollars and the woman was gone for ten minutes before a fat middle-aged trucker came from the hall and shortly after him an Asian woman dressed in a shiny red gown. She was just five feet tall and had immense fake breasts.

"So you want to party," she asked and sat down next to Otis.

He told her he did and she grabbed his hand and took him down a hall to her room. Inside was just a small tract-home-style bedroom. The walls were painted red and it smelled of lemon air freshener and patchouli. There was a red light and a black light glowing in opposite corners of the room.

"So what kind of sugar do you want?" she asked.

"What I really need is some information." He took forty dollars and two joints from his shirt pocket. "There was a guy who came here last night. He had a bunch of tattoos, looks like a movie star. He has a black cowboy hat that looks like it's been dipped in plastic. I was just wondering what he did with you."

She looked at the money and the joints. "Why do you want to know?"

"It's a long story," Otis said. "But he's married to my sister."

She took the money and the joints. "He fucked me in the ass and took a video of it," she said, got up, and opened the door. "Is that it?"

"How much that cost?"

"Five hundred," she said.

"Five hundred dollars?" Otis cried.

"How much would you charge to be fucked in the ass while someone taped it?"

IN THE BACK OF THE casino bar, while the Sunday night NFL game played, Otis sat for two hours with his laptop and phone. Mickey and Lenny ate four orders of chicken wings, drank beer and shots, and watched the game in the near empty bar. Otis called brothels in Winnemucca, Battle Mountain, Carlin, Wells, and Reno and as the night wore on he found a brothel in each area that had seen a good-looking man with tattoos and black cowboy hat come in. Otis even sent a PayPal payment of fifty dollars to a prostitute in Wells, Nevada, who told him the same thing. Harlan fucked her in the ass and recorded it on a digital camera.

"How much?" Otis had asked her.

"Four hundred," she said.

LENNY LOST FIFTY ON THE Seahawks and Mickey puked in his beer glass and had to be carried to his room. As they left him on his bed, Otis told Lenny what he found out about Harlan.

"I'm gonna kill that motherfucker," Lenny yelled drunkenly and threw a full beer bottle against the wall of the hotel and stormed off.

The next morning Mickey beat on their door at 8:30. "I just wanted to make sure you guys are up," he said when Otis let him in.

"Thanks," said Otis.

"Jesus, why is it so cold in here?"

"It's Lenny," Otis said and went to the window, closed it, and turned on the heat. He used the toilet, dressed, and went to Lenny and shook him until he woke up.

"Wha?" Lenny cried.

"We gotta get some chow and be at the bus station in an hour."

Lenny tried to sit up but as he did he began to gag. He sprang out of bed fully dressed and ran into the bathroom and vomited. He came out ten minutes later sweating and pale but clean-shaven.

"You shaved the handlebar," Otis said and laughed.

He nodded and collapsed back on the bed.

THE BUS TO LAS VEGAS was a quarter full and Lenny was leaned against the window glass, passed out in a row by himself. Mickey was in the row in front of him, and Otis was across the aisle from Lenny. They had left the station and were on the outskirts of town when he called Terry.

"You guys get the bus all right?" Terry asked.

"Did you know Harlan was a pervert?" asked Otis.

"What?"

"You heard me."

"We're driving right now."

"You and he stole the bass, the watch, and my amp."

"I didn't steal anything."

"So it's just Harlan?"

"Yes," he whispered.

"I called a bunch of brothels. He's spending four to five hundred a night. He stole Lenny's dad's bass just so he could fuck a hooker?"

Terry kept silent.

"At least tell us where he sold the shit so we can get it back."

"I'll call you in ten minutes," Terry said and hung up. Otis waited a half hour and called back to find his number blocked.

THE BUS STOPPED FOR A lunch break at the Silver State Restaurant in Ely. They had just ordered when Mickey received a call and went outside. He was on the phone for a half hour. Lenny ate a half a piece of French toast and put his head on the table. Otis ate and then put Mickey's food in a to-go container and they left. Lenny stumbled across the street to a minimart, bought a pint of schnapps, and they got back on the bus.

"Who was on the phone?" asked Otis. Mickey got up from his seat, came back to Otis's row, and sat next to him.

"My wife found the watch in Reno," he said excitedly. "She'd been putting notices up everywhere online and found that some old guy had bought it from a pawn shop. Can you believe it? My wife just wired the old guy four hundred dollars. We're getting it back. He's shipping it overnight tomorrow. It'll be home before I am."

Otis congratulated him and Mickey got up from the seat and went back to his row. Otis leaned back, closed his eyes, and went to sleep. A half hour later he woke to Lenny vomiting into a plastic sack.

"Bad chicken wings," Lenny murmured. He puked three times before he went to the toilet. He came back twenty minutes later and sat in the aisle seat across from Otis. His face was drenched in sweat and his skin was gray.

"Bad chicken wings?" Otis said and fell into a fit of laughter.

"I'm serious, man," Lenny whispered sickly. "It was the chicken wings. I remember the exact wing. I can see it in my mind."

"I told you this tour is cursed."

"Maybe, but maybe not. While I was in the can I thought of something."

"What's that?" asked Otis.

"You remember that rockabilly gal from Tucson, from the band Lucky Lucy and the Lariats?"

"The blonde?"

Lenny nodded. "Lucy."

"I always dug her," said Otis.

"Her husband left her and took their band with him. What made me think of her is that she's a puker. Sometimes you see her and she's heavy, sometimes she's not. She's bulimic, has fake teeth and everything. Anyway I heard a few days ago she was looking for a band that was edging more toward country. I didn't think much of it 'cause of Harlan but now . . ."

"She's big in Europe, right?"

Lenny nodded and smiled.

"We'll have to get passports," Otis said and clapped his hands together.

Lenny took the bottle of schnapps from his coat pocket and opened it. He took a quick drink from it, handed it to Otis, but as he did he began gagging and had to run desperately for the toilet.

EARWORMS
BY ZOË SHARP

*"Earworm: ɪəwəːm (noun) A song that sticks in your
mind, and will not leave no matter how much you try."*
THE URBAN DICTIONARY

SHE WAKES FROM THE MAELSTROM of sleep, from a black hole at
the center of darkness. All she hears is the beat of her own blood.
All she feels is the urge to flee. For a few seconds she lies absolutely still, letting her senses stabilize, her logic circuits reboot.

Perhaps it is simply the echo of another nightmare.

They come so frequently she is afraid to close her eyes.
Often she spends the unlit hours sitting upright in a chair,
staring at nothing and hoping, for once, there will be nothing
staring back.

But there is always something staring back.

Something she remembers.

Something that remembers her.

She concentrates on her breathing, on drawing her diaphragm
slowly down and out to fill her lungs to capacity with each breath,
oxygenating her system for primeval response.

It takes another minute before the sound that stretched down through the layers of disturbed sleep comes again. It is close to nothing. No more than a quiet slither.

It is enough.

She slides out from under the covers in one fluid move. Her hand reaches for the Glock hidden beneath a towel on the night-stand, retrieving it without noise or fumble. She knows it will be loaded—thirteen .40 caliber hollow-point rounds in the maga-zine, plus another in the breech. She checks it every night, part of the ritual. But she checks it again now, sliding her forefinger over the loaded chamber indicator as she ghosts toward the bed-room doorway.

As she steps through she recognizes her mistake. The hairs riffle at the back of her neck a moment before the blade touches her skin and the Glock is plucked from nerveless fingers.

They're pros. She knows this even before her legs are kicked efficiently from under her, as her hands are zip-tied, as the hood goes over her head. They have to be good to have gotten this far, past the perimeter sensors and the yard dog and the alarm, not to mention the acres of barren isolation.

They've come in numbers. Probably two on point and another two to manhandle her down the stairs, across polished hallway, front porch, and gravel. It is only then she hears the roar of an approaching engine. Her shiver has little to do with the still night air.

She wonders what has become of the dog. Not through sen-timent but because it is her most effective early warning sys-tem, trained ruthlessly not to take bait from anyone's hand but her own.

As the first vehicle slews onto the driveway she feels the sting of the needle in her arm. The hood contracts as her mind explodes into static and haze.

And then there is nothing.

SHE WAKES DROWNING.

Her gulp for air is a reflex. She finds only water. It binds the cloth to her face, saturating her mouth, her nose, her eyes. She inhales, retches, and drowns a little deeper.

The flow subsides. She feels the excess running down her body in a river of cold. Her arms are suspended out and up, tied so that her feet barely touch the ground.

As she heaves the water up out of her lungs, as the air rattles in, she understands the place they have taken her.

Not where, but what.

And she is terrified.

It doesn't matter that she knows they will not waterboard her to death. Not yet, anyway. If they had wanted her finished quickly there would have been no point taking her from the house. Or she would never have woken from the needle.

So they want something first.

Information?

Or simply revenge?

From the way sound reflects she deduces the room is small and overcrowded. There are at least four of them with her— all male. She can smell their sweat even above the stink of her own fear.

Besides, she knows how this goes. Two to haul her up. One to grip her head. One to pour.

The air oozes with a stifling humidity. As her gasping eases she hears the underlying susurrus of distant insects, like whispers of dissent.

Somewhere nearby comes a scream that ceases more abruptly than it began.

No . . . not here. Not back here . . .

The hood is yanked from her head. For a moment she squeezes her eyes shut. Not just against the brightness, but against confirmation.

"Look at me, Clara."

She opens her eyes and takes in the man standing before her. His arms are folded. His face is hidden behind a ski mask.

Is that good, because they intend ultimately to release her?

Or bad, because someone she has come to know and trust is behind this?

No, in this business she has learned to trust no one.

He steps in close.

"I own you," he tells her. "Every human right you think you have is a privilege here—one that has to be earned. But you know how this goes, don't you?"

"What do you want?"

He shakes his head. "That's not how this works. You know that, too. We'll talk later. When you've had time to realize the . . . reality of your situation."

He nods to the men holding the ropes at her wrists. They slacken so suddenly she jars to her knees. The hood drops over her head once more. Her hands are short-shackled to her ankles so she cannot stand. The men are deft, without malice. She might as well be an animal they're hog-tying for the slaughter.

The headphones go on, positioned carefully so her ears are completely covered. Now she knows exactly what's coming. Not a beating, not rape or more water torture.

This is far worse.

And it won't leave a mark on her.

THEY START WITH HEAVY METAL, of course, played loud enough that it's impossible not to hear the words or blank out the music. The reproduction quality is good, and the irony of that fact is not lost on her. She can't even pray to be struck deaf by distortion.

So begins Metallica's pulsing "Enter Sandman" on constant repeat. After the first half dozen plays the lyrics start to stick inside her head. Lyrics about dreaming of war, of sleeping with one eye open and of never waking up. Who *would* get her blackened soul, she wonders? With no visual distractions, the monsters that might be lurking at the corners of the room—she doubts there *are* any closets, and there certainly isn't a bed for them to hide under—take on shape and mass and venom.

As the single guitar riff cycles endlessly through its series of gradual changes she is overwhelmed by the prominent beat of the drums until she wants to scream. The words fracture into shouting.

Even shaking her head doesn't work. Someone is monitoring. They reposition the headphones every time she jiggles them loose until eventually they tire of the game and duct-tape them to her ears.

ALL CONCEPT OF TIME VANISHES. There is no respite, hour upon hour. Day upon day, for all she knows.

Until, just as suddenly as it starts, the music stops.

She flinches, the silence more frightening than the noise. Either that, or the prospect of what might come next.

She has a right to fear.

The *Sesame Street* theme song starts up in her ears. She has listened to it numerous times over the years. There are no children of her own—her career has seen to that. But visits to aunts and cousins mean a TV set in the background acting as a kind of electronic pacifier, allowing the adults to talk unencumbered in another room.

Now she is scared that the next time she hears the jaunty tune, the children's raucously cheerful singing, she will run amok. The contrast between this and the previous music is well chosen, she knows, for maximum effect. She feels it as a pounding in her chest, the tightness of her jaw, a vibration through her body as it tries to contain the rage.

It is nowhere near over yet.

"WHAT DO YOU BASTARDS *WANT* from me?"

She can't tell how long she has been subjected to Eminem's "The Real Slim Shady," but the repetition in the chorus has her near to breaking. And *Kim* is her. She has become the woman from the song desperately trying to placate her crazy ex. The man who's just slit her second husband's throat—their son's throat—right in front of her. Every time around, she thinks she might be able to escape him. Every time, he catches her.

Every time, she dies.

"You know why you're here, Clara."

"I don't!"

"Of course you do. And every time you lie to me, you go back under."

"No, please! I did nothing!"

"Ah. . . . At last we begin to get somewhere."

For once she is allowed to rest, to lie curled on a blanket. For once the only sounds inside the hood are those of faint weeping, the hot wet night, and her own despair.

"*I did nothing.*"

It is both truth and lie, because she is back there right now, in the vividness of the moment. The moment she is newly arrived, filled with the aggressive energy of self-righteous indignation. She watches hooded detainees shackle-shuffle between their tiny dirt-floored cells and the interrogation rooms. She sees them forced into stress positions, humiliated, half drowned, surrounded by barking dogs and strobe lights. Over the coming months she feels a little more of her humanity slipping from her grasp. She still cannot abide the color orange.

But in the beginning she has no uncertainties. They are the enemy, or why would they be there? They are intransigent, defiant, and all she can see is the towers falling and the blood on their hands.

When, later—she is ashamed of how much later—she voices those doubts to her boss, back home in his air-conditioned office in the five-sided fortress, word passes down the line that she needs to piss or get off the pot. She of all people cannot be seen to weaken. God is on their side.

She hardens, learns to ask the questions she is told to ask without emotion, without empathy. And if she lets others carry out her commands, it is poor distance.

The policy of "no-touch" interrogation seems a salve to what remains of her conscience. She tries to ignore that Bruce Springsteen's "Born in the USA"—initially blared out continuously over the camp speakers as part of the softening-up process—has to be quickly abandoned for the sanity of the guards as much as the prisoners. By some tacit agreement, it is never discussed.

So she does nothing—nothing to protest use of the headphones and the music.

The same headphones—and the same music—that is now being used on her.

"THE HUMAN MIND CAN ITSELF prepare, mentally, psychologically, for physical abuse, but music? Music takes us back to a time in our evolutionary history when reacting to noise was the difference between survival and being eaten. It triggers a response on an elemental level—one against which we have no defense."

Recognizing the truth of his words keeps her silent. That and the guilt which has plagued her ever since she came home. She has left the job behind her but it will not let go.

"Music has been an integral part of war through the ages. The beat of drums and pipes as an army marches into battle. It was designed to strike fear into the heart of the enemy."

She says, "We *were* at war."

"Your so-called 'War on Terror'? Tell me, how can that war hope to be won by inflicting terror on those who might not even *be* your enemy? Is this not like attempting to put out flames with gasoline?"

"We were sanctioned to use enhanced interrogation techniques—"

"Semantics." She can almost hear the shake of his head although by now she is hanging on to reality by her fingernails. "What are your 'enhanced interrogation techniques' except another name for torture? What is 'food manipulation' except another name for starvation?"

"I never starved anybody."

"But the rest you admit, yes?"

"I . . . *we* were under pressure to get results."

"So the end justifies the means, is that it?"

"No. Yes. I don't know."

"Which is it, Clara?"

"I don't know," she repeats dully. "I don't know what this is all for. What do you want from me?"

"If you have to ask, then you are not yet ready."

She hears him shift. She is shaking, her head pulsing to a beat no longer there.

"Wait! Please! Ask me something—anything. What do you want me to say?"

"That you are a liar?"

"I am! I'm a liar. I've lied to you. I'm sorry."

"What have you lied to me about?"

"About everything. But you have to understand, we were under attack. It was vital we obtained intel from detainees."

"It would have been kinder to beat it out of us the old-fashioned way."

"Us" not "them" . . .

"I would not have been a party to physical cruelty."

"But you were under pressure to produce results, Clara. It was 'vital that intel was obtained,' yes? Admit it—there was nothing you would not have done."

"There was nothing I wouldn't have done," she mumbles.

"Just as, right now, there is nothing you would not say in order to stop me placing those headphones back over your ears and leaving you in here another twenty-four hours."

"No, no, please . . ."

"How long will it take you to lose your mind, Clara? Bruises fade. Broken bones knit. How long will it take your mind to heal—if it ever does?"

"You healed."

"Is that what you believe? We have kidnapped and tortured you. Do you honestly think those are the actions of men who are able to forget what was done to them? Men who are able so easily to let go of the past and move on with their lives?"

Any response will be the wrong one. She says nothing, hears him sigh.

"What you subjected us to was not simply an auditory onslaught, you also denigrated our culture by playing music that was filled with Western dominance and posturing, which was sexually offensive."

"I tried to get them to stop! I tried . . ."

"Not hard enough, Clara. You were the one with influence— the one with a friend in the hierarchy. If anyone could get them to change what was going on there it was you, but you didn't try hard enough, did you?"

"I did try! I was told we had to—"

"Still you cling to this as justification. 'Had to' for what? Did you ever get *any* significant piece of intelligence about *any* high-value target, by the methods you used?"

"Of course we did!"

"Are you sure about that? Did you yourself hear this confession from the very lips of a prisoner or were you merely told?"

"I . . ."

As the headphones go back on she screams. It is not loud enough to overcome the blast of Britney Spears.

THE NEXT TIME SHE SHAKES her head she realizes this time they are the ones who have made a mistake. The headphones are no longer stuck down to her skull and they slip halfway off her left ear. She tenses, waiting for the door to open, for the footsteps, the rip and tear of the duct tape, and the agonizing increase in volume.

It doesn't come.

She takes a breath and thrashes more vigorously, like a dog coming out of water. The hated device flies from her head and goes scuttering across the floor. The sound is tinny now with distance, little more than clicks and hisses.

She waits.

Still no one comes.

She flops and rolls, landing on her side, hands still zip-tied to her ankles. By squirming, she is able to get rid of the hood. It takes her eyes half a minute to adjust to the light before she can see her surroundings.

She is in a small room, a metal box with a dirt floor. Light penetrates through the bars on the door. Her heart plummets, but inside her head a voice is yelling at her to get loose, to get up, to escape and evade the way they trained her.

It takes far too long to get the zip-tie off one hand, by which time her wrists are raw. She keeps struggling, gaze fixed on the doorway for the first indication that they are returning and her attempt is over.

Still no one comes.

More excruciating minutes slip past until both hands are free. More still before she can stand. She sidles to the door, peers through the bars, expects to see the same bare corridors of her memory, the same numbered cells.

Instead, she sees her own living space.

She stares at her sofa, her bookcases, and her fireplace with stupefied incomprehension.

They never took me anywhere at all.

The door opens without resistance and she prowls the empty rooms, going first to the study where she takes her backup piece, a short-barrel five-shot Taurus revolver, from the safe in the floor.

She finds the air conditioning wound up to high heat, a portable humidifier and a loop tape of background effects. The music they used to torment her has been imported onto her own laptop. She can no longer bear to have a hi-fi system in the house.

Bewildered and disorientated, she retreats into an upstairs closet, clutching both the gun and her phone, and calls it in.

"CLARA! JESUS, YOU OKAY?"

She pulls the blanket the medics gave her a little closer around her shoulders. "What do *you* think, Dan?" *No, I'm not.*

It's been nearly two years since she stopped taking his calls, since she started blocking his emails. He's aged—it's a business that puts years on people in months. The once-athletic figure is now blurring into doughy mid-life spread, the jawline beginning to soften, the hair to thin. But he still owns the room the moment he strides in. She waits for the old familiar tingle at first sight of him.

It doesn't come.

Without it she achieves clarity. He is a high-level spook who's sweated through too many weekends in the office or the field to ever know his children. Had it been anyone else in charge back then, would she have yielded so easily to pressure from above?

Perhaps sensing this new reserve, he maintains a distance, scans her with cautious, professional eyes.

"The medics said you were in pretty good shape, considering what you've . . . been through."

"Physically? I guess so."

He doesn't respond to that, just pulls out his signature Marlboro and shakes a couple loose. The two of them bonded over snatched cigarette breaks, but he doesn't offer her the pack. She wouldn't have taken one anyway. She quit the month after she quit the job. The fact that he knows this sends a prickle of unease zigzagging between her shoulder blades.

She wants to tell him not to smoke in her home, but after everything else that's been done there it seems a minor infringement.

"What did they want? Revenge, maybe?"

"Payback," she says. "They wanted to make me appreciate what *they'd* been through."

He waits again. A good interrogator who knows when to let silence exert its own pull.

"The techniques we used—in Cuba, Iraq. . . . Have you ever experienced them for yourself?"

"Of course," he says, on safer ground now. "Started with the S.E.R.E. program back in the Cold War—Survive, Evade, Resist, Escape. Anyone with access to the kind of intel the Soviets might want to squeeze out of them went through it."

"And that included the music?"

"Loud music, stress positions, extreme temperatures, waterboarding, sleep deprivation. The whole nine yards." He takes a long drag on his cigarette, pinches a flake of stray tobacco from his tongue. "We didn't do anything to those ragheads we hadn't been through ourselves. Otherwise, how'd we know how effective it would be to soften 'em up?"

A pulse begins to hammer in her temple. "You went through a what—maybe a twenty-four or thirty-six-hour simulation and you think that makes you an expert? You don't have the *faintest* idea what the *fuck* it's like!"

"Hey, calm down, Clara! Jesus, girl—"

One of the cleanup team appears in the doorway to the study. They moved her out of the living room and she refused to go sit in the kitchen like a good little housewife.

Dan moves across to him and the two confer in murmurs. The guy's eyes flick to her a couple of times. She reads pity in them.

Dan turns back all smiles.

"We need you to come in—debrief," he says. "The boys are finished here. They'll take the cage back to the lab and take it apart—track down the source materials. We'll have you look through some names and faces. See if anything jogs loose."

"Just like old times."

"Yeah, just like old times." He moves in, puts both hands on her shoulders and gives her full eye contact for the required time to create trust. "I'll pull in some favors from Homeland. Don't worry, Clara, we'll run these bastards down."

He indicates the door, that she should walk ahead of him, inclining his head like this is good manners and nothing else.

She stands her ground.

"Why run them down, Dan?" she asks. "What are you going to charge them with?"

"You have to ask? Kidnapping, what else?"

She shrugs. "But they didn't take me anywhere."

"Okay then, they held you against your will. They tortured you, for God's sake."

"How?"

"What? You're not making sense."

"We here in the good ol' US of A do not condone or actively take part in the use of torture on detainees."

"What's that got to—"

"They did nothing to me that hasn't been done to them. By us."

"Yes, but that's different—"

She rides over him again. "We tortured them, Dan. *I* tortured them. And, through me, so did you."

"Clara, I . . . have those fuckers been onto you about the Senate hearings again?"

And then she knows. She's always been a risk to them. Ever since she left—ever since she told them *why* she was leaving. So they've been watching her.

The way you do with a weak link, keeping track, keeping check. Waiting for it to fail. And when it does, you cut out the ruined pieces and rejoin the chain so nobody can tell what once was there is now gone.

He stalls, lighting another cigarette. She doesn't remember him putting out the first.

Eventually, he looks up narrow-eyed through a smoky exhale and says, "Yes, we did, Clara. We tortured them. And you know what? Faced with making the same fucking decision over again, right now, I'd do it over again. In a heartbeat."

"So you can look me in the eye and swear—can absolutely swear—that it was worth it? That whatever intel we forced out of those prisoners was genuine, high-grade, twenty-four-karat gold and not just whatever they thought we wanted to hear?"

But he can't do it. His silence speaks for itself.

She nods as if he's spoken anyway. "Some of them were innocent."

"Bullshit. They were all legitimate enemy combatants, radicals, fanatics."

"If they weren't going in, they certainly were coming out. It wasn't just the sheer acoustic bombardment we subjected them to, was it? Those songs bragged about the supremacy of the West. They were violent, provocative, or just goddamned annoying. We saturated them in an unwanted culture. It would be enough to turn anyone against us."

"Oh, so *now* who's the expert?"

She shoots back, "The one who's been on the receiving end."

She sees him take a pull on his temper, take a breath.

"We need to go, Clara."

Reluctantly, she moves, out along the hallway. By the entrance to the living room she pauses, eyeing the empty space where her makeshift prison cell has been taken down and taken away.

"Have you wondered," she asks, "why they picked on me?"

He shrugs. "They must have known, with the hearings coming up, we need for all of us to hold the line. Anyone breaks and it leaves the rest of us with our asses swinging in the wind."

"But weren't you the one who told me that everyone breaks in the end?"

"Yeah, and some break sooner than others."

"So you thought I'd break."

He sighs. "You were pretty damn close to it before you left."

She leans against the door frame and closes her eyes. The darkness frightens her. The music is back pounding inside her head. She has to raise her voice over it.

"And now?"

Another sigh. "I'm sorry, Clara."

She looks at him. There's a blunt semiautomatic in his hand. She doesn't recognize the model but it looks cheap. A throw-down piece, designed to be used once and left alongside the body.

"So am I," she says.

She sees the realization dawn in his face a split-second before she fires, through the blanket still around her shoulders. The Taurus kicks in her hand and a small dark circle appears on Dan's shirt, just to the right of his tie.

He drops the gun and staggers back, hitting the side wall and slithering down as his legs give way. He lands sprawled against the skirting, touches the wound and stares at the blood as if he can't quite believe she's done it. A half-gasp, half-laugh escapes him.

"You're prepared . . . to kill me for what . . . I made you do to those bastards?"

"No." She lets the blanket drop and stands over him. "I'm prepared to kill you for what you made me do to myself."

LOOK AT ME/DON'T LOOK AT ME
BY REED FARREL COLEMAN

FIVE MINUTES TO STAGE, MR. LAKE.

Terry James Lake remembered a time when his nerves were reserved for the confessional. And for the entire decade of the sixties, with a year of grace and spillage into the seventies, Terry had had much to confess. A darkly handsome man in possession of a bushel full of Southern charm and an *Aw Shucks* country smile, Terry had a way with the ladies and, upon occasion, when the drugs and the spirit moved him, with the men folk, too. The thing was that Terry James Lake—Terry Jim to his fans—was about as country as the D train and his Southern charm was strictly South Brooklyn.

"*Oy gevalt*, we've got to do something about that fucking accent of yours. You sound like an extra from *Guys and Dolls*, for chrissakes!" was the first thing the General had said to Terry over a beer after Terry's set at Folk City. He gave Terry a soft, avuncular slap on the cheek. "Such a *punim*. With a face like that, the chicks, you'll have to beat them off with a stick once we ditch this folk music crap, clean you up, and get you a fancy electric guitar."

Terry was already a bit of a chameleon, so he had no problem with the notion of rearranging himself into any shape if it meant steady money and steady pussy. He'd already done a transformation of sorts from Geraldo Colangelo—Italian father, Puerto Rican mother—to Jerry Cole, the folkie with soul. It wasn't like he really loved folk music, anyway. He found a lot of it to be hokey crap that had as much to do with his life as a pizza pie with a wagon wheel.

He had even less patience for the purveyors and consumers of it. He had no love for the café owners who liked to think of themselves as Bohemian impresarios, but were more like backstreet pimps. They loved you like a son, a younger brother, as a talent supreme. They loved you backstage and on stage. They loved you right up until payday. Then they grew alligator arms and stiff fingers that never quite reached deep enough into their pockets. Every night for them was a rough night. Every week a rough week. Every month rougher than the last. Yet somehow they managed to stay in business.

Then there were the silly goofballs who sat out there in the dark "feeling it" and finding the deeper meaning in the traditional songs.

"'Jimmy Crack Corn,' my balls," he'd once shouted out in drunken disgust at a pal's rent party in the East Village. "And is Michael's boat ever getting to shore or what?" He just couldn't bear all the hushed and phony reverence. It was one thing when Lead Belly sang "Pick a Bale of Cotton," but it was something else when three milk-skinned Princeton grads with matching plaid short-sleeve shirts, chinos, penny loafers, and five-dollar haircuts sang it.

He laughed now, remembering that night in February of '62. Talk about silence. All the people in the cold water flat in Alphabet City turned to stare at him after his outburst, a mixture of shock and contempt in their eyes. But not quite in everybody's eyes. One Beat chick with long straight brown hair that came to the waistline between her black turtleneck and black tights, smiled at him with her eyes. For the benefit of the other partygoers, she'd kept her mouth neutral. But there was nothing neutral about her mouth twenty minutes later in the stairwell.

He reserved his greatest contempt for his fellow performers, those Princeton grads with their standup basses, banjos, and Martin guitars. Them and the girl singer escapees from the Seven Sisters who de-sexed themselves in some bizarre, over-earnest gesture of martyrdom to Woody Guthrie, the Rosenbergs, and the working man. He called bullshit on them.

When his discharge from the service in '60 was greeted with substantially less fanfare than a certain other handsome, dark-haired singer's, Geraldo Colangelo didn't have many prospects lined up. His father got him a job unloading produce trucks at the Brooklyn Terminal Market. On a night off, he went into the Village with this girl from the old neighborhood and they stumbled into an open mic set at Café Wha? Some guy was strumming on a Sears acoustic and croaking out songs Terry used to sing in Thursday morning assemblies at PS 58. It didn't escape Geraldo's notice that the singer, a scruffy, pimply faced stick figure, was receiving enthusiastic applause, female adulation and money in a hat being passed through the crowd. That was the moment Geraldo Colangelo shed his name, his skin, and his sore back for a new name and a used acoustic.

Folk music was a means to an end, a way to get into a holding pattern to see what was what and to figure an angle. The folk scene was strong, though Jerry sensed it wouldn't last. There were limits to its appeal to the wider teen audience, who, as far as Jerry could tell, didn't give a shit about the Bomb or segregation or tradition. But Jerry also knew he wasn't cut out to be a pretty white boy crooner like Paul Anka, Bobby Vee, or Bobby Vinton. He had the looks, but not quite the voice to carry off that type of thing. Besides, those guys struck him as Sinatra wannabes who were more suited to singing at weddings and bar mitzvahs than at a hop. The one thing folk afforded him was the chance to write his own songs. That much, he liked about folk. Not much else.

So when the General, Izzy Gettleman, offered to buy Jerry a beer after his set at Folk City, he couldn't get to Vinny's Tavern on Sullivan Street fast enough. Izzy was a famous manager, the Kike Colonel Parker, as he was called behind his back. Izzy was renowned for picking up talent wherever he could. The thing was that once the General took you on and you put your name on the dotted line, you belonged to him, lock, stock, and amplifier. You sang the songs he told you to sing, dressed the way he told you to dress, dated the people he told you to date. It was a deal with the devil, if a benevolent one.

WE NEED YOU ON STAGE NOW, MR. LAKE.

Terry stared into the mirror in the makeshift dressing room, fussed with his now unnaturally black shag-cut hair, finger-combed his dyed mustache and shook his head at the desiccated, made-up face of the man looking back at him. He didn't like what he saw. Didn't like the ridiculous white polyester suit with the high-waisted flared pants and the red-acetate shirt in which he had been outfitted. Especially didn't like the sparkly plastic stars pasted onto the broad lapels of his silly jacket. He didn't much like the chunky platform shoes either, though they were the least embarrassing piece of his costume.

"And they said sixties' fashion was a joke," he muttered to himself, derisively flicking his left lapel in disgust. "Yeah, right. Fucking clown suit for a clown."

He grabbed his signature guitar, the one Izzy had picked out for him at Manny's all those years ago, a '63 surf-green Fender Telecaster that had taken on a robin's egg blue patina over time. He hated that he wasn't actually going to play it. That he wasn't even going to plug in when lip-synching that hideous fucking song yet again. A song that had come to define him, overshadowing everything else he'd done before or since.

Izzy had done to Jerry exactly what he'd said he would do during that first meeting. They ditched the folk music scene, bought him the aforementioned Fender, recast him as a Southern boy, but not too Southern.

"From the south, sure, but not too country. Anybody asks, you say you don't like talking about your childhood. Just say you grew up poor and hungry. I think we both know from this, so it's not so much a lie." He patted Terry's face as was his wont. "Put some twang in your voice, but not too much twang. You're a white boy who loves Chuck Berry tunes and R&B. You're gonna write maybe some tunes of your own with that kinda feel. We're gonna get you some gigs up here in the north until you perfect that down-home accent because up here they don't know from down there."

And it had worked. It had worked better than either the General or Jerry cum Terry Jim would have believed. It didn't hurt that the Beatles and the rest of the British Invasion legionnaires also loved Chuck Berry and R&B. And Terry Jim proved to be a pretty respectable songwriter. By '66 he was a Top 40 fixture, even making his way into the Top 10 on three occasions: twice with cover tunes and once with his own hit, "Look At Me/Don't Look At Me." It was still the biggest hit he'd ever penned and the single thing he was most proud of. But no one wanted to hear a slow ballad about a facially disfigured war vet writing a goodbye letter to his girl, especially not these days. Vietnam was a recent bad memory everyone wanted to bury and forget. These days it was all disco all the time or that punk rock shit.

No, the only thing people ever wanted to hear from him whenever they bothered to want to hear from him was the stupid theme song from the TV show *Thriller Man*, one of those peculiarly sixties success stories. First a hit in France as *L'Agent Dangereux,* the hour-long show about a hunky American espionage agent named Gabriel and his stunning French sidekick, Gigi, was shot on location all over the world. CBS bought it and showed it on Saturday nights at nine. But because the French title didn't work, neither did the original French theme song. Enter Terry James Lake, his guitar, and a song written by Deptford and Clark. The show lasted one season on American TV, but the theme song had become a radio staple. When he did the occasional sixties rock revival show, the one song they demanded he play was "Thriller Man." No Chuck Berry covers. No hits of his own. Not "Look At Me/Don't Look At Me." Just that one fucking song.

There was a knock at the trailer door. He stepped out onto the metal landing. The stage handler, a pretty girl who looked about sixteen but was probably twenty-five, stared up at him impatiently. She wagged a finger, urging him to hurry up. She looked at him with disdain, like someone else's worn-out shoe, which, he guessed, he was . . . kind of. The kids assembled outside on the sidewalk and inside had no idea who he was other than some old guy their parents listened to.

"Come on, Mr. Lake, we're only a minute or so from the opening credits and your intro," she said, pulling him along.

He stopped for a second outside the place to take it in. So this was 2001 Odyssey, the disco moon to Studio 54's sun, located only a mile or two from his old Carroll Gardens neighborhood. What a freakin' joke! It even had a stupid hand-painted sign. It was probably supposed to have the word "Space" in its name, he thought, staring up at the floodlit placard on the top corner of the white-gray concrete block building, but the yoyo painter either ran out of room or couldn't spell it. Whatever!

Taking this gig was a mistake, though Terry Jim didn't have much choice about taking paying gigs these days. He was good with a lot of things, with women and music. Jimi Hendrix had even sent him a fan letter about his guitar playing and offered to buy his Telecaster from him for an outrageous sum of money. He had had the letter framed and put up on the wall in his Park Avenue apartment. Problem was he no longer had the apartment or the letter because one of the things Terry wasn't good with was money. As long as he had been with the General, things were okay. He had never wanted for anything. The General put him on a generous allowance and invested his money for him.

Sometimes he missed the General. Izzy was more of a father to him than his own father had ever been, but it wasn't like Izzy hadn't fucked him. As Chuck Berry himself had once told Terry, "It ain't a matter of if they'll fuck you. It's a matter of how hard, how often, and where at."

One of the clauses in their contract gave control of Terry's publishing rights to the General's company. Izzy didn't exactly rob Terry blind, but he kept more of the money than he should have. Terry resented that part of their deal. Still, he figured it was a price he was willing to pay for stardom. Not a bad attitude to have if tastes never changed and stardom lasted forever.

"Okay, Mr. Lake," the girl said to him when they got inside the club, "all you have to do when Dante calls your name, is to run onto the dance floor and wave your guitar above your head. Stay in the spotlight." She looked at her clipboard. "Just like in the run-through at the studio, the announcer is going to introduce the show, then Dante. In turn, Dante will intro the guests. First the Tramps, then Vicki Sue Robinson, then you. When you come off the dance floor, I'll be waiting right here to take you back to your dressing room. You'll have fifty minutes until I come get you for your segment. You're on last. Dante, the other acts, and the dancers will join you on the dance floor in the last minute of 'Thriller Man.' We'll lower your playback, so that Dante can thank the guests, thank the audience, and do a promo for next week's show of *Dance Mania*. You just keep pretending to play as the credits role. Got it?"

He nodded, gritting his teeth. Music came up. Heavy on drums and bass, with a scratchy guitar playing what passed for a melody.

"Okay, here we go."

"Live from 2001 Odyssey in Bay Ridge, Brooklyn, the birthplace of disco dancing and the setting for last year's smash movie *Saturday Night Fever* starring John Travolta, it's Dante Ferrara's *Dance Mania*."

"Hello, Brooklyn!" Dante yelled, running out to the middle of the dance floor. He was dressed in a bizarre one-piece outfit of red lamé and sequins. After the applause died down, after the cheers for Brooklyn calmed, he said, "Welcome to a very special episode of *Dance Mania,* live from the mecca of disco, 2001 Odyssey. Tonight's show will feature our two-round elimination dance contest and a bevy of special musical guests. The Tramps . . . Vickie Sue Robinson . . . and an oldie but a goodie, Terry James Lake here to sing his hit 'Thriller Man.'"

There had been no need for the applause to die down after Terry Jim circled the dance floor, a dazzling array of colored lights flashing beneath the soles of his clunky shoes. His name was met with lots of blank expressions and confused whispers, but at least there hadn't been any boos.

When he got back to his dressing room, she was waiting for him. Carla Saroyan, his poison. Carla was, for lack of a better term, his girlfriend-manager-agent. In terms of all three, Terry had run through many of each since the General died of a stroke on August 27, 1967. Not many people noticed the General's passing because it happened the same day Brian Epstein, The Beatles's manager, died. Izzy's son, Bobby, had taken over for his dad, but he didn't have a stomach for the sharp-elbowed, rough-and-tumble managerial aspects of the business. He did, however, have a taste for publishing royalties, a gluttonous, insatiable taste.

Fed up with Bobby Gettleman neglecting his bookings and squeezing every nickel out of his songs, Terry Jim left Bobby and accepted a ridiculously small settlement for his remaining percentage of the publishing rights. But the way Terry figured it, between the investments the General had made for him, his gigs and the settlement, he'd be good. What he hadn't figured on was two very brief and very expensive marriages. He also hadn't figured on Led Zeppelin and Emerson, Lake, and Palmer.

The early seventies had been unkind to Terry Jim. Squeezed out on the one side by Moogs and metal chords and on the other side by the Carpenters and Gilbert O'Sullivan, Terry couldn't get arrested. From '71 to '74, he'd run through a series of managers and agents, many of whom made promises no one could have kept. Still, even the sleaziest of the bunch, which was really saying something, could claim it wasn't for a lack of trying. None of them, not the legitimate ones who'd taken Terry on out of respect for the General or Terry's talent or the ones who had latched onto him to suck him dry of whatever juice he might have left, could create a demand out of thin air. By '75, he was tapped out, living back in the basement of his folks' house in Carroll Gardens and making whatever few bookings he could for himself.

Then he got a call from Lefty Farmer, a bass player with whom he'd done several recording sessions. Lefty, who'd heard Terry was down on his luck, said that he needed a singer and guitarist for a backup band he'd been hired to put together. Some girl singer from Toronto, billed as the Canadian Linda Ronstadt, was doing gigs in the New York area. Terry Jim didn't think twice about it. The gigs and the girl singer were mostly forgettable, but not her manager.

Carla Saroyan had once been gorgeous, a cover girl model with impossibly black hair, perfect dark olive skin, brown eyes so dark they were nearly as black as her hair. Her body had been an amazing blend of curves and sinew, but it was her mouth that men and women alike could never see past. In the business, the modeling agencies used to refer to Carla as "The Mouth." She had made the bulk of her modeling money doing lipstick, lip gloss, and toothpaste ads.

By the time Terry met her, Carla's looks had faded some with age and stress. Modeling, it seemed, had an even shorter shelf life than rock stardom, which is why she decided to go into talent management. Carla and Terry were perfectly mismatched as they shared the same weaknesses: drugs, sex, and spending. Worse for Terry, though, was Carla's appetite for gambling. She had the bug bad. She would as soon bet on cockroach races as the Belmont Stakes.

But for whatever reason, she delivered bookings for Terry where all the others had failed. She had gotten him this *Dance*

Mania spot, though it had taken her a lot of convincing to get him to do it.

"It's a relaunch moment, baby. We're going to remind the older fans of your glory and introduce you to a new generation."

In his darker moments, which were in no short supply these days, he suspected Carla of trading herself for his gigs. He never asked. It wasn't that he didn't care. It was that desperation helped make him conveniently blind.

"Hi, lover," she cooed, tossing her cigarette onto the floor of the trailer and snuffing it out beneath her shoe. "You okay? You look nervous."

"You know the way I feel about this gig, how ridiculous I feel."

Then, before he could say another word, she kissed him hard on the lips, sliding her tongue into his mouth, slipping her hands beneath his suit jacket and pressing her long nails into his back.

"Let me make it all better like I always do," she whispered in his ear, dropping to her knees.

She rubbed her cheeks up against his crotch, reaching for his zipper. When she found the metal tab, she tugged it slowly down, fished out his semi-hard cock and put it in her mouth. He got that jolt as he always did when Carla put him in her mouth, but he clamped his hands around her shoulders, pushed her away and pulled her up onto her feet.

"Stop it! Just stop it!"

"But, lover—"

"No." He zipped up. "We've got to talk."

She lit another cigarette.

"Don't do that. I have to go on. You know what smoke does to my voice."

She cackled at him. "Yeah, and it really kills your voice on an eleven-year-old playback tape of 'Thriller Man.' Next thing you're gonna tell me is that it fucks up your lip-synching."

"Don't be cruel."

"Stealing Elvis songs now, Geraldo?"

"Don't call me that."

"Geraldo. Geraldo. Geraldo. What are you gonna do about it?"

He turned to look at himself in the mirror again. He felt even more ridiculous than he had before the stage assistant had come to retrieve him. And as he stared at himself it hit him that he just couldn't go through with it. That he'd sooner go back to singing "Michael Row Your Boat Ashore" or unloading lettuce crates off trucks at three in the morning than to sing—lip-synch—"Thriller Man" again. That Carla's line about a relaunch moment was a load of crap that he forced himself to swallow one spoonful at a time. That he still had an ounce of pride left somewhere.

She poked him with a fingernail. "I said, 'What are you gonna do about it, Geraldo?'"

Now it was his turn to laugh. "It's what I'm not going to do about it," he said, pouring on his phony down home accent like a ladle of red-eye gravy.

"What the fuck is that supposed to—"

"You know what it means, Carla. I'm not singing that fucking song again. Never. Not ever. Not tonight. Not—"

Her eyes got wide with panic. "But, Terry—"

"What happened to Geraldo?"

She snuffed out her cigarette and threw her arms around him. "I'm sorry, Terry. I'm sorry."

"Me, too, darlin'." There was his accent again. "But I'm outta here." He reached for his Telecaster.

"You have to do it, Terry. You have to."

"No, I don't, Carla. It took this stupid disco dance show to make me see that. Took me having to get so low that I would go out and embarrass myself on national TV. Live TV!" He laughed again. "Live TV, what a joke. I was going to go out there and lip-synch a fucking song I recorded a million years ago. They're not even going to let me plug in, for fuck's sake. I'm ashamed I ever let it get this far."

"No, Terry, it's you who doesn't understand," Carla said, her voice frosty and clear, her eyes narrowing. "People expect you to do this."

"People? Fuck people."

"Wrong answer, Terry. These are the kind of people who fuck you, not the kind that you fuck. How else do you think a washed-up fake with a half-limp dick like you got a gig on a national TV?"

"I suppose if I thought about it, I would say your oral talents and willingness to bed down anyone with a pulse had something to do with it."

She cackled again, only this time it was very shrill and brittle. "No one's that good, Terry. Not even me. You got this gig because I sold your contract to some people."

"Sold?"

"I owed these people, Terry. I owed them a lot and they were willing to let me off the hook if I gave them my rights to manage you and if you would make this appearance. They have power. They can get you a lot more gigs. So you see how it is, right?"

"Explain it to me, honey," he said, his accent all South Brooklyn again. "Explain it so that even a dumb mope from Carroll Gardens can understand it."

She shrugged. "Okay, then. If you walk out of here, they're going to hurt me, Terry. They say it won't be too bad. That they'll just break my legs. They won't touch my face. Not this time."

"That's too bad, Carla. But once your legs heal, you'll still be able to spread 'em again." He wiped the neck of his guitar, then laid it in its case. Stood up. "And to think I really used to love you."

She ignored that. "It's a little late in the game for indignation and jealousy, don't you think? I'll be able to spread my legs, Terry, but you won't have any legs anymore. You don't go out there and do what you're supposed to do, you're dead. And it won't go easy for you. The guys I sold your contract to, they don't fuck around."

"What do they even want my contract for, anyway? I'm barely making enough for you to lose."

"Who knows? You were all I had left to barter. Maybe they think they can launder money with you as a front or maybe one of the old guys liked the way you used to sing. Maybe they want you to be the regular act at the Gemini Lounge on Flatbush Avenue. You ever hear of Roy DeMeo?"

"Why? He the guy who bought me?"

Carla shook her head. "He works for the guys who bought you and he's crazy. He likes killing people. He shoots you in the head, chops your body up, and throws it in the Fountain Avenue dump. And that's if he likes you. If he doesn't like you, he skips the shooting in the head part and goes right to the hacking you up part." She relaxed and came over by Terry again. "So stop being stupid about this and let me make it better the way I always do," Carla said, bending to her knees yet again. "They said I can still travel with you if that's what you want. Let me make you want that, Terry. Let me."

He let her.

IT'S TIME, MR. LAKE.

As they walked once again from the trailer, through the crowd assembled outside and into the club, the stage girl explained once again how it was going to work, but it all sounded like blah blah blah, blah blah blah. Terry was too busy time traveling to listen. He was back at the air base in Germany. Back offloading trucks. Back on stage at Café Wha? and Folk City. Back with the General having deli at Katz's on Houston Street, planning their next moves. Back in his apartment on Park Avenue, showing his Jimi Hendrix letter to everyone who came by. Back making appearances on *American Bandstand*, *Where the Action Is*, *Hootenanny*, and *The Ed Sullivan Show*.

"Okay, Mr. Lake," she said, "get ready. Remember go to the center of the dance floor, watch for the director's cue, and begin playing and lip synching. Try not to actually sing because we don't want the live mics to pick it up. Go!" She clutched him by the biceps and pushed him toward the dance floor, which again was lit from below with an array of flashing colored lights.

The director gave him the cue, but there was a delay in the playback. So he began fingering the chords and plucking his silent strings ahead of the recording. Then came that twangy intro a few seconds behind where he was in the song. His lip-syn-ching was out of synch, so he was mouthing the lyrics—*Gabe and Gigi lived the lives of nomads*—before the vocal playback began. And somehow in the midst of that technical snafu it all came together for him. He realized he didn't give a fuck about Carla's legs or even his own. He didn't care about Roy DeMeo or his bosses or anyone else. He wasn't going to do it. He wasn't going to play this fucking song again, not ever.

He stopped fingering the chords. Stopped lip-synching altogether. Then he started fingering and strumming again. Started singing, loudly. Loudly enough so that the open mics clearly picked up his voice. But he wasn't singing "Thriller Man."

Dante Ferrara turned to the director. "Go to commercial. Go to commercial. What the fuck is he singing?"

Carla, who'd followed Terry in, said, "You don't know this? It was a big hit, 'Look At Me/Don't Look At Me.'"

"Nah, that ain't it," said the pudgy-faced man with the dead eyes and the slick black hair, over Ferrara's left shoulder. "It's a whatchamacallit it. . . . A swan song. Yeah, like that."

Carla opened her mouth to disagree, but when she looked into the man's bottomless eyes, she closed her mouth. She didn't bother trying to run, either. Why piss off the debt collector? She had heard a broken femur was terribly painful. She couldn't imagine how painful two would be. She figured she wouldn't have to imagine for very long. Terry had just seen to that. But like Terry had said, she'd be able to spread her legs again. She laughed to herself. She had never believed him when he said he hated that stupid "Thriller Man" song. She believed him now. You couldn't have asked for more proof.

ONLY WOMEN BLEED
BY GALADRIELLE ALLMAN

ONCE THE CURVING MAZE OF manicured streets that surrounded the Ponte Vedra Country Club was behind us and the wealthiest kids were dropped at their doorsteps, our bus driver, Sherry Walker, began to relax. Each day as she settled the yellow Blue Bird school bus at the long red light between Kmart and the massive used-car lot with the fluttering pennants strung up high, Miss Walker would pull a pair of pink rubber flip-flops out of an Army duffel she kept tucked under the driver's seat, kick off her gray sneakers and groan with relief. Her heels were permanently stained with beach tar and the pink polish on her toes was chipped and dirty. The last half hour of my two-hour ride home from school was shared with only three other kids, all of them boys who also lived at the funky end of the Jacksonville Beaches, near the cheap motels, crumbling condos, drive-thru liquor stores, and tourist gift shops stuffed with dyed seashells and cheap beach towels. Miss Walker told the four of us beach kids we could call her Sherry, as long as all the rich kids were gone, but that never felt right. She told us she lived down at the Beaches too, off Atlantic Boulevard behind the old Pick 'n Save building that had stood empty for years. I thought of her whenever my mom drove by the wrecked store, its broken windows showing the toppled shelves and tangled wires inside.

Sherry Walker was what my mom would have called a "real trip," if I had told her the way she talked to us at the end of our long days. I knew better. Something in the way Miss Walker's eyes shined and bored into mine while she talked made it clear the things she said were between us. She always wore the same grubby mechanic's coveralls splattered with white paint and spotted with grease. She tucked her bleached curls under a battered blue ball cap, the brim cocked back like a proud duck bill, showing her high, damp forehead. As she closed in on the ocean, she rocked us in the hull of her steaming bus, a captive audience of four, and began to talk. She liked to talk to the boys on the bus about guitar players and who was the best and all that, and she saved family stories for me, about her sister who was sick in the hospital all the time, or her husband who crushed his empty beer cans under his boot heel on her kitchen floor while he stared at football on TV. She drove fast but steady the whole time, saying she didn't get paid near enough for how careful she was with each and every one of us, each and every day.

It was a blistering Friday in late May, near the end of the school year, all of us restless and ready for summer to start, and Miss Walker was in a weird mood. She was shifting in her seat more than usual and heaving sighs like she wanted someone to ask her a question so she could complain out loud. I was squirming, too. I got the curse for the third time ever during PE, and it was making me miserable. My back and middle ached and I worried all afternoon it would leak and show. Bleeding just generally makes everything worse. I tried to keep track of when it was coming on my school calendar, but it surprised me anyway. I carried a couple of thick maxi pads wrapped in an extra pair of underwear in my backpack all the time. I never told my mom after the first time it came. We didn't feel close just then and I knew she'd talk about the moon and womanhood and try to hug me. I just slipped pads from her supply under the bathroom sink and hoped she wouldn't notice for a while.

Jesse and the other two boys, Kevin and Davy, sat at the very back of the bus, slumped down with their knees propped against the green vinyl seats in front of them, talking too low for me to hear. I suspect they were looking at the nudie magazines I know Jesse stole from his dad, but they were careful not to get caught. What I heard was the stomping, old timey piano opening to "Bennie and the Jets." It was coming from the little gray radio with the long silver antenna Jesse always carried. It's one of my favorite songs and Jesse knew it, too. We must have spent a million hours listening to rock radio, playing Name That Tune, like the TV show. When we were little, we thought we invented the game where the first person to recognize a song and name the band gets a point, the most points win. I beat Jesse all the time.

Jesse Leander was my best friend for most all of my life, before it mattered that he was a boy and I'm a girl. He lived alone with his daddy in a ranch-style house tucked back in the woods about a mile from me. Jesse's daddy coached football at the Beaches high school and he was hard on Jesse. He yelled that Jesse's soft and he made him do pushups in their driveway for being mouthy or lazy. Jesse would cut his angry eyes at me and blow air out of his nose like a hot horse if he heard me say it, but it was true: he had a tender heart. When we were young, if we found a turtle that had flipped over in the road and starved that way, Jesse would hide his face so I wouldn't know he was crying. Just thinking of all the dogs in the world that had to wander the streets alone because people didn't love them anymore kept him up nights. We'd been in school together since kindergarten, and even when we were babies, our moms were friends, but Jesse's mom died of cancer and we didn't talk about that, but one time, late at night when he was still allowed to sleep over, his feet resting on the pillow next to my head, my feet beside his. That night he let me see him cry. Then his dad started making crude jokes about how he'd be a fool to let us share a bed, now that I was a little woman, and Jesse and I drifted apart.

Jesse stopped sitting with me on the bus this year. We never had to work it out that way, it was just clear from the first day. I sat in the front and he sat in the way back, girls with girls and boys with boys. Last year, he sat in the seat right behind me and even braided my ponytail over the back of the bench seat sometimes, slow and like he wasn't even thinking about it, his hands just working on their own. He would never do that now. He sat with his two idiot friends and listened to music like we used to. Jesse and I both know more about rock 'n' roll than Kevin and Davy ever will, but still he chose them over me.

Just as that ugly thought formed in my mind like a fist, I felt a dry thump on the back of my head and heard the boys laugh. A ball of notebook paper rolled into my lap and onto the seat beside me. I had been beaned in the head, probably by Kevin, the rudest kid I ever met. I shoved the wad into my backpack without opening it up, even though I see black writing on the edges of the paper. I tried to hear if Jesse was really laughing too, but I wouldn't let myself turn around to be sure.

Sherry Walker saw it happen in the long rearview mirror mounted over her head. I could tell by the pitying look in her reflected eyes. They're big and pale blue, smeared all around with black eyeliner and wily, darting between our faces and the road the whole long ride. She just sighed and changed the angle of the window beside her that pivoted smoothly in and out on a hinge, trying to catch a breeze and bring it in. The early summer days were long and over one hundred degrees and that could make a body crazy. That's how Sherry started.

"The freaks come out when it gets this hot, I tell you what. It's a dangerous time, and you best be careful out here," she said pointing her chin at my reflection. She looked a little like one of my sister's baby dolls, her round cheeks splotched pink and her bottom lip poked out in a permanent pout.

"Did y'all hear what happened in Palm Valley, out in the woods? Come up here so I can talk at you and turn that radio off," she said, raising her voice to the boys in the back.

They didn't move right away, but she waved her right hand around like a crossing guard and the boys drug themselves down the center aisle, grumbling.

"It's a real terrible story and I probably shouldn't even tell it to you, but you need to know what's out here," she said, jerking her head toward her window. One corner of her mouth turned up in a sly smile, but her eyes were deadly serious.

"I'm gonna tell you what men are really like."

I looked over my shoulder at Jesse, now sitting across the narrow aisle and one row back from me. His arms were crossed on the seat in front of him, his chin resting on his interlaced fingers. He darted his dark brown eyes at me for a second and rolled them, a look that said *Yeah, right.*

"It was them bikers, that gang that hangs out at Snoopy's Bar?" she said in her low, gruff voice. Sherry was a smoker, and you could hear the damage it's done. "Y'all know about Snoopy's?"

"A gang?" Kevin snorted, like it's a ridiculous idea.

"Yes, a gang. A motorcycle club. We got all sorts of biker clubs out here. Haven't you ever seen 'em, riding all together in their leathers?"

Sherry Walker looked into her high mirror and glared at us, waiting for a response, so we nodded slowly, not sure at all.

"The bikers set their sights on a real pretty blond girl who they always noticed walking down the side of the road by the bar. She worked with her daddy clearing yards and bagging leaves and was out raking and hauling with him most every day. They were way too poor for her to go to school. Do you know how lucky you are just to have school?"

Miss Walker gave her question a little air, then started up again when we stayed silent.

"One of them big mean dudes was drinking at Snoopy's, and first he sees that pretty girl's daddy, so blind drunk at the bar, he can't barely sit up. Then the biker sees the girl walking down the road alone when he goes outside to leave, and he decides to follow her. He keeps his bike back behind her a ways, but she can hear his rumbling engine. She starts walking faster until she gets to the dirt road where her daddy's trailer is parked, then she flat out runs. Just then, with home in sight, that biker goes roaring off, laughing. Well, now he knows her street, and that she's all on her own, and she don't even realize it; she thinks he's long gone. Well, he goes right back to the clubhouse to get his crew."

"Clubhouse? Like Mickey Mouse?" Kevin asked, loud and sarcastic and the boys chittered like monkeys in a zoo. I realized I was holding my breath, and I let it out.

"The gang meets up in an old barn they built out with bunks and a stripper pole. They call it their clubhouse and believe me it ain't nothing to joke about. So, anyhow, the one rider tells his five buddies he knows this sweet little piece of ass and they should go and get her."

I pulled my knees up and stretched my T-shirt over my bare legs, and started double-knotting my tennis-shoe laces while I listened. This story was going nowhere nice, and Miss Walker's eyes were making me nervous. I realized I could smell the rotten scent of blood gathering in the pad under my shorts and I put my legs back down, horrified. I took my sweatshirt out of my bag and unfolded it over my lap.

"So off they go. Now, have you ever seen a pack of bikers riding together down the highway? Forget seeing it, did you ever hear it? They're the loudest bunch of machines you ever heard, like to make you go deaf, and all the hairs on your body just stand up and salute when they go by."

Sherry took her right hand off the wheel and gave a quick salute then laughed so hard she started to cough. After her hacking settled down, she stared in silence at the road in front of us for a long minute, knowing we're hungry for her next sentence. I shifted forward in my seat.

"The bikers found that little silver trailer parked in a clearing, and started to circle it like a pack of starved dogs hunting. They was so loud, that girl thought a plane was about to land on her roof, so she opened her door right up, not even the sense to be scared. She just stands on the little wooden steps her daddy built, watching those bikes stirring up clouds of dust, their engines gunning full blast. The only thing worse than the sound of them bikes screaming is the terrible sound when they cut them engines off. It went dead quiet." Miss Walker went quiet too. "That's the moment that little girl knows she needs to get inside and hide."

"Little girl? How old was she?" I asked, surprised how loud my voice sounded in the hollow bus. My hands had gone cold even though it was so hot sweat was rolling out from under my hair and down my back.

Sherry's smile showed her yellowed teeth and she squinted her eyes at me.

"Just about your age, maybe twelve? Old enough to know better," she said with a bitter laugh.

"I'm thirteen," I whispered, too low for her to hear.

"So, do I need to tell y'all that she couldn't hide? They stomped right up those little wooden steps, kicked that metal door in, broke the lock and yanked her right out of her room by her long blond hair. She was hiding under her bed! Isn't that the first place anybody would look?"

Kevin and Davy both nodded, their eyes glued to Miss Walker's in the mirror. Jesse's face showed nothing; a perfect stillness had taken him over.

"The leader of the pack got the honor of tying that girl up to the back of his bike. He used an extension cord he tore right out of her wall. And off they go, those six bikes cut right through the woods behind her trailer as fast as lightning."

I looked out the window and felt like I couldn't see the strip malls or the tangled green in the empty lots between clearly. My eyes were looking into the woods from the back of a careening motorbike, breaking through low pine branches, engines growling in my ears.

"Them bikers was smart enough not to drag that girl back to their barn. If her daddy sobered up enough to send the police out looking, they would go right to those outlaws' crib. So, they go into the pines, deeper and deeper, riding little dirt horse paths until they get to a spot only they know. They have a secret place where they party and do their worst. They'd hauled a bunch of old moldy couches out there and pulled 'em into a circle around a big black pit for fires."

I was still thinking about the extension cord, and if the girl was tied upright or hung over the back of the seat on her belly, but this new detail interrupted my thought. I wondered how could anybody carry heavy sofas out between the dense trees, especially in secret, but I didn't ask.

"The leader dragged that girl by the cord around her waist and pinned her to a tree. He twisted her skinny little arms behind her back, then hog-tied her wrists to her ankles. She couldn't move an inch. He took a thick buck knife out of his dirty boot and cut off her little white sundress, then her little white panties, until she was stark naked. She's crying and moaning, nearly screaming, until he puts his greasy bandana in her mouth to gag her."

Jesse put his head down on his crossed arms resting on his seat back like he was staring at the floor.

I wondered how Sherry knew what the girl was wearing, and every other tiny detail. I shifted low in my seat and let my legs stretch out, thinking of my own white underwear with the thick pad stuck to them and the blood soaked in. I pressed my palms together and sandwiched them between my thighs. They were still ice cold.

"Then, the bikers just ignored her for a long while, like they had better things to do. They made up a fire and started drinking whiskey and smoking dope. They wanted her to watch and wait, her wrists and ankles bleeding from the bonds. She knows at any time they could turn their sights back to her little naked body tied to that tree like she was nothing but a dog, and waiting is hell." Sherry Walker's eyes were wide and fixed in the mirror.

I wound the scratchy black strap of my backpack tightly around my wrist and pulled it hard. Something strange was happening while I listened to Miss Walker's hoarse voice; my vision was getting darker and tunneling, my heart was beating fast and making it hard to get a full breath. I was stuck in the dark where her story was and it was getting worse by the moment. I'd never heard anything so raw and crazy, from an adult or anybody, nothing even close. A sour smell like an old battery or cat pee in a closed room was coming from my underarms. I felt Miss Walker's eyes on me, and I looked up to meet them.

"She was just starting to develop," she said, "Just like you."

I imagined a Polaroid picture of my naked body developing, my chest coming into focus out of the shiny white chemicals like a lifting fog. Miss Walker was agitated, like she wasn't getting the response from us she was hoping for, but I couldn't imagine what that would be.

Kevin and Davy were on the edges of their seats with their mouths open wide enough to catch flies. Kevin looked excited, but Davy looked scared, even though they mostly looked the same. Jesse's head was still down, refusing to show anything he's feeling.

"First they raped her, one by one. Those guys are huge and hairy and rough. Then they put all kinds of things inside her: bottles, knife handles, the end of a bat, sticks, anything they wanted to. They tore her insides up. One even put out his cigarette on her little tit."

The bus was silent and still, the only sound the murmur of the engine and the creaky whine of the springs that held up Miss Walker's seat. She reached into the breast pocket of her coveralls and pulled out a flattened pack of Marlboro cigarettes and a pink plastic lighter. I thought, *There's no way she will,* but she lit up a strictly forbidden cigarette and took a long drag. She released a stinking plume of smoke that blew right back to our seats.

A hot, sick liquid rose up my throat. I started to cough and Kevin smirked at me.

"Did she die?" Jesse asked.

It was the first thing he'd said the whole time, and his voice was barely a croak.

"No, and that's the saving grace," Miss Walker said in a light way, like happily ever after. "She got herself free after they left her and walked all night to the road. A black gentleman who was taking his son to school in the morning stopped for her and took her to the emergency room."

She heaved a deep sigh. "So, y'all got to be careful. Especially you girls," she said right to me, the only girl on the bus.

"A black guy?" Davy sounded doubtful. "Are you sure?"

"Yes, sir. Don't be a bigot, it's ugly," Miss Walker said.

I pictured an old black man in a bow tie and little round glasses, maybe because of the word "gentleman." I imagined a long white car on the little two lane highway that cut through Palm Valley slowing down when he saw the girl. Her white skin would shine in the new morning light and after what they did to her, there would be blood. Too scared and in need of help to hide your own nakedness from strangers in a passing car? I could even imagine that feeling. My mind was bouncing all over, filling in the gaps of the story, and I knew I'd keep doing it for days and days. How old was the man's son? Was he her age? Did he stare, or did his father have a blanket in his trunk to cover her? Or did one of them give her his jacket? Did the girl have to call her father and explain the whole thing? Miss Walker was done with talking, but there was a tide of details and questions rising up out of her story and I was getting flooded.

I looked over at Jesse again, and he was squinting out the window into the bright sun. A muscle in his jaw moved back and forth like he was chewing on her words, like he hated Sherry Walker now.

Maybe she felt it too, because she suddenly asked us if we'd mind a quick detour to Lil' Champ, the convenience store on the corner before Jesse's stop. The other two boys cheered and started digging coins out of their backpacks in anticipation, and when she stopped the bus, they rushed down the steps and out the door, Jesse ambling behind them, shaking his head.

I was afraid to get off the bus, afraid Miss Walker would keep talking too, but moving seemed harder, so I stayed. I watched the boys through the big windows as they paced up and down the candy aisle, taking their time choosing what to buy.

Miss Walker sucked on her cigarette, leaning toward the small window with the pivoting glass beside her high seat. The heat of the sun was seeping through the still metal body of the bus and sharp light was glaring off the black tar parking lot into every small window. I watched three perfectly round smoke rings rise up over the back of Miss Walker's ball cap, one passing through the next like a magic trick. I couldn't see her face in the mirror anymore, she was leaning too far forward and I was glad.

The boys climbed back up the rubber-ribbed stairs, each mumbling thanks as they passed Miss Walker, clutching chocolate bars and cherry slushies. I didn't even care; I didn't want any of it.

She steered the huge bus smoothly in reverse with her right hand on the wide black steering wheel and flicked her burning cigarette butt out the window with her left hand. We were back on the road with the breeze and almost home.

THE FOUR-BLOCK WALK FROM MY bus stop felt endless and full of menace. I saw three separate motorcycles and their sounds froze me in my tracks on the sidewalk. The clumps of trees that rimmed the empty lot beside Dolphin State Bank held dark places where bodies or bikers could hide. The sun was just beginning to weaken, the air gentle against my bare arms and legs, and it felt strange, like it should have set while Miss Walker was talking. I know I will never forget a word of her story. The white dress, the black fire pit, whiskey breath, and rough pine bark against her naked skin. I will know these details for rest of my life; they flowed through my body like sickness, heavier and more vivid every minute.

Walking up the concrete path to our apartment, I heard the Beatles through the screen door. My little sister Carrie was dancing in the living room with her neighbor friend from downstairs, two little girls in white cotton panties and multicolored Mardi Gras beads making up a dance to "Run for Your Life" from *Rubber Soul*. I stood in the doorway and watched. First they chased each other around the coffee table during the "run for your life if you can" lyric, then they stuck their heads under the toss pillows on the sofa for "hide your head in the sand" and finally they dragged their little fingers across their throats in a slitting motion and stick their tongues out for "catch you with another man that's the end-a, little girl."

"Where's Mom?" I yelled at Carrie, suddenly furious with her. "Put some damn clothes on!"

Carrie shouted "Jim is home!" and jumped up on the sofa bouncing with excitement like it's Christmas.

"Great," I said flatly, heading into the kitchen.

Mom's boyfriend, Jim, was always gone on some job, I don't even know what kind, so when he returned it was treated like a special occasion, as if I cared. He paid no mind to me but he doted on Carrie, always swinging her around by her hands in the front yard and pulling her onto his lap when they watched cartoons. He knows I don't like him or trust him, even though I'm super careful to be polite. Mom changed when Jim came home, splashing handfuls of Jean Nate cologne onto her damp skin after her bath and wearing red lipstick and dresses instead of jeans. It was stupid.

Debbie, our seventeen-year-old neighbor, was straddling the step stool by the kitchen wall phone, the curly beige cord wrapped around her wrist and the receiver glued to her ear. Debbie was "watching us" while Mom and Jim were who knows where, which meant she would hog the phone all night talking to her boyfriend Ron. First her voice would be sweet and high for a while, but by Carrie's bedtime, she'd get annoyed and hang up on him at least two or three times. It was always the same. Debbie had huge boobs peeking out of a low-cut shirt made of terry cloth and a tiny butt smushed into tight bell bottoms with rainbow stitching down the legs. While I looked her over, she started rolling on pink lip gloss, looking into her compact, her mouth in a big O. She snapped her bumble gum, which wasn't ladylike, but she did have on great high-heeled boots. I suddenly wondered if the girl still had her shoes. Did she walk in the woods and down the gravel road all that time in her bare feet?

I heard Debbie say she wasn't ready into the phone, he'll have to wait just a little while longer, and then she caught my eye, and shouted, "Don't be a creeper!"

I slunk back into the living room and found Carrie on top of her friend, slapping their bellies together and saying the word "hump" over and over again, giggling.

"Jesus," I said, and stalked to my bedroom, slamming the door. Seconds later, Carrie, now completely naked except for the bright green and blue beads around her neck, threw my door open and yelled, "Debbie says we get pizza!"

"Get out of here and put on some clothes or I will murder you!" I screamed.

Carrie puffed out her bottom lip and it started to wobble like it did when she pretended to cry, then she slammed the door so hard in bounced back open and I watched her tiny butt running into the kitchen.

I got up to close my door and lock it, even though I'm not supposed to. I laid back on my bed and realized I hadn't changed my maxi pad in hours, but I didn't feel like getting up. I turned on the reading lamp beside my bed and pulled my backpack over to me. As I unzipped it, the crumpled paper Kevin threw at me rolled into my lap. I unfurled the wad and smoothed it out on my thigh, the rough black ink scribbled over the pale blue loose-leaf lines was a drawing of a penis, with big cartoon drops squirting out of the top and a bubble over it like it's talking. It read, "Cum on yer face!" I took the words like punches in my stomach and I felt the blood breaking through onto my shorts. I tore the paper into pieces and threw them behind me while I ran to the bathroom.

Sitting on the cold toilet seat, bent over with cramps, tears came up the back of my throat. I kicked off my sneakers, pushed my bloody cutoffs and underwear down my legs and pulled my stinking T-shirt over my head. I peeled the blood-soaked pad off of my underwear and folded it tightly into thirds, then wrapped it in thick looping layers of toilet paper, making a clean white ball I could leave in the wastebasket. I used up all the paper left on the roll, but I didn't care. While I wrapped it up, I finally let the tears break through, so hot and strong it scared me. It wasn't just the gross thing Kevin wrote. I couldn't stand the thought that Jesse saw that note and didn't stop him from hurling it at me. I folded my chest over onto my lap and rocked myself until I was calm enough to flush and stand. I stepped over Carrie's mangled Barbie with her legs bent in the wrong direction and her hair cut off and landed directly on the bloated belly of her rubber baby doll, almost slipping. I turned on the shower as high as it goes and the heat and steam soon calmed me. I rolled the white bar of soap around in my hands and washed the blood off of my thighs, the water running red, then pink, then clear. As I washed my small, sore breasts, I had a weird thought.

If I did not have these little pink swells on my chest, I wouldn't have gotten that awful note. If I wasn't getting boobs or bleeding, Jesse wouldn't avoid me on the bus. It wasn't so long ago we took baths in this same tub all the time. When we were young like Carrie, we didn't even notice our bodies. Everyone can see me changing now and my tiny boobs are like a signal I can't control, sending out a message that filled me with fear.

I was too tired to eat pizza, too tired to brush my teeth or do my homework. I just wanted to sleep. I pulled on one of mom's T-shirts off the towel rack and went back to my room. Night was finally falling and the fading sun turned my room a hazy, glowing pink. I crawled into bed and watched the warm light disappear.

I woke up disoriented, unable to shake off a dream where I am naked and afraid, walking on sharp gravel in cold bare feet, my legs so heavy I can barely lift them. Without thinking, I pulled my sheet off my bed and wrapped it around me, dragging its length behind me down the hall to my mother's door. I stood with the glass knob in my hand and heard a sound like a howl, then a panting, straining cry. A baby animal was trapped somewhere, back inside my dream, but as I shook off my nightmare, standing in the empty hallway, I realized the sound was my mom and Jim.

I dragged my sheet down the hall to the kitchen, my mind filled with hate. There was no way to reach into her dark room and pull my mother out. There was no way to get comfort from her no matter how much I needed it. She belonged to her boyfriend.

I wouldn't be able to sleep again, I knew it, and I panicked. My mind was filled with naked bodies, with hands and mouths and blood. I walked down the hall, took up Debbie's perch on the step stool by the phone, and punched in the number I knew by heart even though it was maybe a year and a half since I used it.

"Jesse? It's me."

"Oh, hey." His voice was deep and strange, sleepy and grown sounding.

"Can you talk?" I asked.

"What time is it?"

"I don't know. Late. Could we play the game?"

"Huh?" Jesse's voice went higher and I recognized it now.

"You know. The radio? I have to be quiet, but I'll be able to hear yours."

I didn't come out and say I knew his father was probably passed out drunk in his recliner and wouldn't hear his radio.

"Yeah, all right. Hang on."

I heard the muffled sound of him fumbling with his blankets and then his radio came on.

". . . I had to take her upstairs for a ride . . ."

"Stones! Point for me!" he whispered emphatically, like a quiet shout. "Hey, they're coming to the Gator Bowl this summer."

Jesse and I must have started playing this game of Name That Tune when we were seven or eight, in our moms' cars, at the beach with his little transistor radio, and best of all, on the phone after our parents went to bed. I fell back into it like no time had passed. I felt his cheek pressed against his black phone, and saw his dark brown bangs hanging messy over his closed eyes. I remembered how long Jesse's lashes were, and how his nose whistled while he slept, his round cheeks turned pink and hot, and his curls matted into small circles that stuck to his forehead with sweat. He spent the night here when his mom worked late waiting tables like mine. It seemed normal. It felt safe. I listened to the light sound of Jesse's breath and try and slow mine down to meet his. I wanted that young, easy feeling to come back to me, but I had to ask.

"Jesse, do you think it's true? Do you think that could've happened out in Palm Valley and we know nothing about it?"

Jesse didn't answer right away, and we listened to the twangy guitars and bursts of cowbell of "Honky Tonk Woman" for a while.

"I don't know. Probably not. That was totally ridiculous," he said when the song ended. "But, then again, that kind of stuff happens all the time. Not the bikers and the tree and all, but the rest."

"Don't say that. That can't be true."

Jesse heaved a big sigh and rustles his blankets.

"Haven't you ever noticed the fliers outside the grocery store? Missing girls? Don't you ever watch the news?" He was talking louder now, annoyed.

"Not around here, though," I whispered.

"Why not here? The whole world is the same, everywhere you go." Jesse sounded so sure.

The radio let out a watery, warbling sound so familiar it was a thrill to hear, a mix of voices and effected guitar, then drums kicked in and the whole band fired up. Jesse and I started singing at the same time, in perfect harmony just like Steven Tyler and Joe Perry, *"Sweeeeeet Emoooooootion . . ."*

"Aerosmith," I said fast, "My point."

"Too easy," Jesse whispered.

We sang every word to the whole song, but for the first time the lyrics seemed mean and ugly:

"Some sweet hog mama with a face like a gent . . ."

I tried not to pay too much attention. I tried to stay with the lush sounds and keep away from the girl they're singing about. When it was over and the DJ starts talking, the girl in the story came right back to me.

I said, "It's worse than if they killed her."

"That's nuts," Jesse said.

"They put a bottle in her, Jesse." I whispered. "A bat!"

Jesse cracked a mean little laugh, his breath escaping in a dismissive rush.

"You're awful," I said.

"Sorry. I actually think that's physically impossible. Miss Walker saw that in a movie or something. Why would she know all those things about it? Like what she was wearing and all?"

I didn't have an answer. My stomach hurt and the top of the step stool was hard under my bottom. My hair was still damp and clean but my sheet and T-shirt were sweaty. Jesse was all snuggled in his warm bed and I was sitting here, uncomfortable. It all made me mad.

"You don't understand. You don't have to and you never will. Something gets crushed inside that you can't fix when you are raped. That's worse than death." I didn't know how I knew this, and it was like Jesse read my thoughts.

"How do you know? You've never even kissed anybody."

"God, what does that have to do with anything?"

A delicate guitar line, pretty and sad, started a new song.

"Oh, Perfect. Alice Cooper, 'Only Women Bleed,'" Jesse said, "I'm winning."

It's true, I thought. I'm losing and I'm bleeding. I could feel my cheeks go hot with shame when I imagined telling Jesse about my period. We quietly listened to the spooky, pretty song about a man hurting his wife.

". . . he slaps you once in a while and you live in love and pain . . ."

"Do you think the girl could have been Denise?" I asked.

"Who?"

"Denise, from last year. Mrs. Johansen's class. Do you think maybe that's why Denise's mom took her out of school and moved her away?"

"Nah, why would you think that? Her folks just got a divorce and moved."

"But they lived in a trailer," I said. "Not in Palm Valley, but it was out in the woods somewhere. We never did see her again or hear anything after her mom took her out of school. She had a white dress, too."

"Don't you have a white dress? And she said the girl didn't go to school. Why are you making this such a big deal?"

I heard the whirling static of Jesse changing the station, stopping at a nasty guitar riff.

". . . I feel like making love! Feel like making love! Feel like making love to you!"

"Uh . . ." I say.

"You don't know this one?" Jesse asked, sarcastic.

"Yes, I do. It's Sweet, the band not the song. It's dirty."

"Nope. It's Bad Company! I'm still winning." I could hear Jesse grinning, and he suddenly seemed stupid and younger than me. I thought of all the stories in all of the songs I knew and it made me shake inside. It didn't matter if Sherry Walker's story was true or not. There were a million other stories just like it, some true and some made up, but all of them were awful and all of them were about women doing wrong in one way or another. A private, peaceful place inside me was filling up with confusion. From now on, I wouldn't even be able to hide inside of songs.

"Why is every song about sex or women getting hurt or being awful?" I asked.

"Don't be a bitch," Jesse said, flat. He sounded just like his daddy.

"Wow," I said. "Fuck you, Jesse!" I hung up. It was ruined.

I waited for a few minutes, but he didn't call back.

I WENT BACK TO MY room and turned on my bedside light. I opened my closet and slipped my white dress from Easter off its special padded hanger and threw it on the floor. I pulled off mom's T-shirt and smoothed out the sheets on my narrow bed. Laying on my side in my underwear and awkward maxi pad, I stared at the Rolling Stones poster on my wall. Now even the cartoon lips parted by the fat red tongue disgusted me. Why did Sherry Walker plant this girl inside of me? What good would scaring me do? Was her story supposed to terrorize Jesse and the boys too? It didn't seem to. Jesse wasn't thinking about that girl and how she had to live her whole life always thinking of those men hurting her. Every time anyone touched her, she'd remember. Every damn pine tree, every motorcycle or extension cord she ever saw would be like a poisonous snake wrapped around her ankle, rearing back to strike.

I leaned over the edge of my bed and saw a dusty extension cord and yanked it out of the wall. I wasn't really thinking; I had slipped inside the girl's scraped knees. Her bloody thighs and cut-up wrists were mine. I tasted her metallic fear in my mouth and I wanted to feel it. I wrapped the end of the cord around my left wrist and looped it through the iron post of my headboard. I pulled the cord tight and twisted it around my wrist again before I made a double knot. I laid back on my pillow. It hurt. I couldn't straighten my tied arm, but I tugged it a few times just to test it. The plastic coating over the wires pulled at my arm hair like a burn. I wished I had thought to turn off the over head light. I closed my eyes and concentrate. I tried to feel their heavy bodies pressing against me, one after the other, the rough beards scraping my face. I tried to smell their sour breath and hear their hooting laughs, and I tried not to feel afraid.

I knew the end of the story. I knew we get away, the girl and I, so I explored it. I imagined hiding in the deepest part of myself where no one could touch me. I put one finger slowly inside myself to see what it would feel like to be entered, and an immediate warmth rose up through my legs. The men disappeared and the night sky arched over my head, a dizzy dome of clear white stars. I let myself settle against the strong body of the tree and felt the cold piney breeze on my skin. The tight cord melted off of my wrists and ankles and my body was free. Before I understood what I was feeling, a stunning pleasure began in my belly. I kept my finger inside and waited for the sensation to stop, but it built up like pressure. It felt so good. I didn't think about what I was doing and just did it. I let go of the story and went deeper into my body. Behind my closed eyes was an eclipsed, molten sun, a velvety black orb surrounded by wisps of golden light. I was rocking in a warm explosion that made my limbs tingle and sing as the orb moves away and the light became blinding. Every bit of fear and confusion and shame was simply gone: melted, evaporated, vaporized. It was the most beautiful feeling I had ever felt and I rested inside of it for a long time. Then my heartbeat slowed, my breathing deepened and sleep finally took me down.

IN THE MORNING, CARRIE CAME skipping down the hall and threw her little pajamaed body against my door until it swung wide. She had her stuffed blue rabbit in a headlock and something that looks like pink milk was smudged around her mouth.

"What are you doing?" she called to me.

"What time is it?" I said, sitting up straight until my tied up arm pulls me back down flat.

"Who cares? It's Saturday! Jim is making pancakes! Hey . . . why is your hand like that?"

"I was playing a game," I said weakly. Carrie stood above me, leaning her waist against the edge of the bed, looking down at my wrist. It's marked with red streaks, the extension cord still tightly wrapped. I reached up to untie myself and saw that my other hand was covered in dried blood. I quickly hid it under the sheet, mortified by the memory.

"What kinda game gets your hand tied up?" she asked.

"It doesn't matter now. Anyway, I won," I said. "Get out of my room."

"It don't look like you won, " Carrie said bouncing back up the hall into the kitchen.

ON MONDAY MORNING, I FELT queasy and uncertain as I watched the bus slow to a halt at my stop. I wasn't sure how I would greet Miss Walker. But when the glass doors folded open, at the top of the steps in her high black seat sat an old black man with puffy white hair and a brushy white mustache.

"Good morning!" he said.

I was too surprised to answer him and too shaken by Miss Walker's absence to sit in my usual seat. I walked all the way to the back of the bus and took the empty seat across from Jesse's usual spot. I saw that Davy was absent too and wondered if he freaked out and told his parents about Sherry Walker's story. Maybe he got her fired.

When Jesse climbed the steep steps into the hull of the bus two stops later, he didn't even look up; he was busy digging around in his bag. He finally pulled out a magazine and folded it in half, looked me in the eye with a little smile and cocked it toward me twice before I raised my hands to show I was ready to catch it. Jesse tossed it, then slid in the seat across the aisle and watched my face.

I opened the fold to the glossy cover of Ultimate Outlaw Magazine, the smell of Jesse's dad's cigarettes wafting up out of its warped pages, and there it is.

A blond woman in a white bikini with hair to her waist and black makeup tears streaked down her cheeks was chained to a tree. All around her were men in black leather jackets straddling motorcycles, leering, awful looks on their faces. There was a huge bonfire raging behind them. The biggest man was standing right in front of her, his back to the camera, holding a big silver knife.

"I told you it wasn't true," Jesse said.

VINCENT BLACK LIGHTNING
BY TYLER DILTS

IT WAS THE PHOTO THAT got to Beckett. An old black-and-white eight-by-ten, yellowing around the edges, in a timeworn black frame. In it, a man wearing nothing but a bathing cap, Speedo briefs, and sneakers was lying prone on an ancient motorcycle, his arms reaching forward to the narrow handlebars, his crotch perched over the rear wheel, and his legs extended back into the air while he Supermanned across the desert floor.

The old dead man had the photo in his lap when he shot himself and some of the blood spatter had misted the glass. He hadn't done a very good job of it. The muzzle of the snub-nosed revolver wasn't angled squarely at the center of his skull and the bullet ripped open his forehead. A flap of skin and bone hung down over his right eye. Beckett wondered if there had been enough damage to the brain to kill him, or if he'd bled out. Either way, he was still just as dead.

Beckett took a closer look at the revolver. It was an old Smith & Wesson Chief's Special, with ivory grips and the bluing worn away around the edges of the barrel and cylinder from years of holster carry.

It was the hospice nurse who found the body. She came every Tuesday and Friday afternoon. Drove her Corolla all the way to the far end of the trailer park where the wall backed up against the refinery on the other side. Only two times a week, she told Beckett, that's all they could do with his Medicaid benefits. Should have seen him at least twice as often.

His name was Burke and he had liver cancer that would have ended his life within two or three months if the .38 hadn't done it last night. Judging by the condition of the body, it had probably been less than eight hours, and Beckett wondered if the act had been timed so the nurse would find him before the neighbors detected the smell. It was the middle of winter, but in Long Beach that didn't mean much. Still, it would have contained the putrid odor a little longer, and with the burnt-oil stench drifting over the wall it probably would have delayed discovery of the body another day or two.

Beckett let the crime scene technicians do their work and went back outside.

The uniforms who had responded to the nurse's 911 call had cordoned off the small area outside Burke's door between his dilapidated trailer and the next one up the row. There wasn't much room along the narrow drive that led from the street to the back of the park, only enough for the crime scene investigator's and coroner's vans, so Beckett walked the hundred-plus yards out to Cherry Avenue to where he'd parked his unmarked cruiser along the curb behind the black and whites. He opened the trunk, unzipped his big black duty bag, and dug around inside until he found it—the small .380 in its nylon ankle holster. It didn't see much use anymore. Beckett had worn it religiously when he'd been in uniform, but even then he'd always hated the feel of the thing, the lopsidedness of it, like having an ankle weight on only one leg. He bent over, pulled up his cuff, and velcroed it snugly into place.

Stan Burke, a veteran patrol sergeant who also happened to be the dead man's son, was waiting for him in the driver's seat of one of the squad cars. Beckett bent over and leaned into the passenger-side window. A song was playing on the phone Stan held in his hand. Even through the tiny little speaker, Beckett recognized Richard Thompson's distinctive acoustic finger picking. He'd been a fan for years. The bittersweet motorcycle ballad drifting across the front seat was one of his favorites.

"Hey, Danny," Stan said to him. They'd known each other for years. He'd been the second Field Training Officer Beckett had worked with after graduating from the academy. And the best one, too, Beckett thought.

"Let's talk," he said. There was a little grass area between the chain-link fence and the first row of trailers and they sat at an old wooden picnic bench under a jacaranda tree. A purple trace of the sunset still hung in the sky to the west.

Stan was wearing jeans and a dark-blue fleece vest over a T-shirt.

"You off duty today?"

He nodded.

Beckett crossed his legs. The bottom edge of the ankle holster poked out from under his cuff. "Where should we start?"

"I don't know." If he was upset about his father's death, it didn't show.

"Were you close to him?"

"No," Stan said. "Not at all."

"When did you last see him?"

"Five days ago. That was the first time in over twenty years."

Beckett nodded. "Why now?"

"He called me up out of the blue, said he was dying, asked if I'd come."

"And you said 'yes.'"

Stan shook his head and scoffed. "I told him to go fuck himself."

"What changed your mind?"

"Carolyn." His wife. Beckett had celebrated their twenty-fifth wedding anniversary with them last summer. First time he'd ever had

Cristal and finally learned what all the fuss was about. "She talked me into it. Thought it might give me closure or some shit like that."

"And that was enough to change your mind?"

"Not really."

"Then what did?"

Stan exhaled through his nose. Beckett could see that he didn't want to talk about this but knew he had to.

"There was this stupid old photograph he gave me when I was a little kid. Some idiot setting a motorcycle speed record back in the forties. He asked me if I still had it."

"And you did."

Stan nodded and looked off into the distance. The purple was gone from the sky.

"Tell me about it," Beckett said.

STAN'S EARLIEST MEMORIES WERE OF his father's old shovelhead Electra Glide, sitting in Jimbo's lap, his little knees straddling the fire-engine-red gas tank, not being able to reach the handlebars, his mother saying, "That's enough," and pulling him off, burying his face in her red hair that smelled like apples.

That was his childhood. His father pulling him toward the Harley, his mother pulling him away. How old was he the first time Jimbo disappeared and left his mom bruised and crying, trying to hide it behind sunglasses and a blue silk scarf? Five? He must have been. Because he'd been at school and she brought him back to the empty house and told him father was gone for good this time. "Stay out of the kitchen," she told him, "until I clean up this broken glass."

He remembered being happy the first time his father returned, when he heard the shovelhead rumbling in the driveway, when he tore the brown paper wrapping off the present Jimbo had brought him, the framed black and white of Rollie Free flying across the Bonneville Salt Flats breaking the American motorcycle speed record on his Vincent Black Lightning. "A hundred-and-fifty miles an hour," Jimbo said, "a hundred and fifty!" Together they hammered a nail into the wall and hung it over Stan's bed.

But that memory always bled into the next, his mother's broken eyes when she told him his father was gone again.

Somewhere along the way he learned what colors were and what the winged skull patch on the back of his father's leather vest meant.

The cycle went on and on. After six months, after a year, Jimbo would come back, break everything, then leave again.

The last time he got out of prison and tried to come home, Stan was twelve. He hid in his bedroom while they screamed at each other. "I'll cut you off," Jimbo yelled again and again. But his mother held firm and after what seemed like a lifetime, Stan listened to the roar of the Electra Glide fade into the distance one last time.

His mom went downhill after that, and Stan always blamed himself for not understanding what was going on. A year and half later, when he came home from school and found her dead in the bathroom, they tried to explain to him that it wasn't an overdose, but a tainted batch of black tar. He couldn't understand why that mattered.

At her funeral, his grandparents, her parents, who until that point had only been vaguely remembered ghosts from his toddler years, told him he would be coming to live with them in Pomona. He only took a few things with him—a favorite brush of hers, with a few forgotten strands of her red hair tangled up in the bristles, the faded blue scarf she wore so often, and, for some reason he never understood, that damn photograph.

He only saw his father two times after that. The first was a decade later, when Stan was celebrating the end of his rookie year with the LBPD. He was in a bar downtown with several members of his academy class, when an old biker with a graying horseshoe mustache came up to him and congratulated him. Stan was confused until the recognition slowly washed over him and he broke the beer bottle in his hand on Jimbo's jaw. Before he knew it, his father was on his back on the floor and Stan was driving his fist again and again into the old man's face. It took two of his colleagues to pull him off. By the time the commotion settled and the on-duty cops arrived, someone had planted a switchblade in Jimbo's hand and three off-duty officer had made statements that they'd witnessed the old biker pull the knife and attack Stan with it.

And that was it, until five days ago. He came home to a voice-mail on the landline from his father, pleading with him to return the call. Stan tried to delete it, but Carolyn wouldn't let him. "Talk to him," she said.

The message was so pathetic it nauseated him.

"Ain't gonna insult you asking for forgiveness," Jimbo said when Stan finally caved to his wife's pressure and made the call. "But I am gonna ask for one thing."

"I DIDN'T EVEN REALIZE I still had the photo until I got up on a ladder in the garage and pulled the old box down out of the raf-ters," Stan said to Beckett. "I put it in the dumpster during the last move, but Carolyn pulled it back out without telling me."

"What happened when you saw him?"

Stan shook his head. "Nothing, really. I knocked on the door, he told me to come in. It was a mess, smelled like piss and death." He sat there quietly for a few moments, as if he were replaying the scene in his head.

Beckett didn't press him, he just sat there, a sad smile on his face, waiting for Stan to fill the silence.

"He told me I looked good, I told him he didn't. He was all shriveled, like he'd been ground up from the inside out. But he still had that fucking mustache." Stan knitted his eyebrows and looked down at the ground. "And if I'm going to tell you the truth, I was glad. Glad. I wanted him to suffer. I wish he still had a few months of misery left."

"What else happened?" Beckett asked quietly.

"I gave him the picture. He said thank you. I left."

"What did Carolyn say when you told her about it?"

"'Sorry, I guess I was wrong.'"

Danny chuckled with him.

"Part of me hoped she was right, though, you know? That I'd feel something. Resolution or closure or some shit like that. But I don't. I don't feel anything."

A uniform came up to them. "Detective Beckett?"

"Yes?"

"The coroner's ready to take the body. What should I tell him?"

"Unless he found something else, I'm ready to call it a suicide. Let him know I'll come find him in a minute."

Beckett watched him walk back toward the crime scene. He crossed his legs again.

Stan looked down at the ankle rig. "What do you got there?"

Beckett pulled his cuff up to show him. "Glock .380," he said.

"Good choice."

"Remember that first day I rode with you?"

"That was a long time ago."

"You wanted to see my backup. I didn't have anything to show you."

Beckett saw the memory flash in Stan's eyes. He thought of the photograph of the man on the motorcycle in Jimbo's lap, misted with blood.

"You told me to always have a backup because you never know when you'll need it. Then you pulled out that Chief's Special with the ivory grips. I asked you if you'd ever used it. Remember what you said?"

Stan sat motionless, his head up, eyes fixed on the night sky.

"You said, 'No, but I bet I will someday.'"

Beckett stood, put his hand on Stan's shoulder, and let it rest there for few seconds. "Give Carolyn my best," he said. He turned away and heard the song on Stan's phone again, the melancholy guitar fading away behind him as he headed back.

NO PLACE YOU'RE LIKELY TO FIND
BY ERICA WRIGHT

THE PRIZES WERE TRIVIAL—A ROUND of well drinks, a twenty-dollar gift certificate to the local bowling alley, a T-shirt with the bar name misspelled. Cheap material to boot, not even those soft V-necks Penny liked to wear on buses. And she rode a lot of buses, forgetting sometimes to get off in, say, Montgomery because she thought she was going to Mobile. Or once, confusing Chattanooga with Charlotte. Where was she now? She squinted against the lights, but it was no use. Only the first row of tables was visible in the glare, half-occupied and fully bored. A woman smoked without touching the cigarette, letting the ash drop onto the floor whenever it felt like falling. The microphone smelled of vomit, and Penny turned away to make sure her guitar was tuned. Not that it mattered, she'd decided, after she was announced by emcee Glitter Jacket and his hiccupy laugh. *Ha-a-ha-a-ha-a-ha.*

LOUISVILLE. NO, JUST OUTSIDE. A one-bar town with a talent-show gimmick. It had even been advertised in the local newspaper with a full list of participants. She'd sent the link to her sister who didn't respond. Penny was following a magician with a bag full of birds who was following a ventriloquist with a seasick-looking puppet. *There are worse fluffers,* she thought, then bared her teeth in what might look friendly from the back. If anybody was there. She squinted again and like that—with narrowed eyes and exposed incisors—strummed the first chord of "The Greatest" by Cat Power.

A couple of months ago, there might have been a transformation. Penny might have imagined a hush, the stage lights like tropical sun, crooned herself silly with self-discovery. But the mic really did smell like vomit, and the lights made her sweat, a thin line rolling down her back into her jeans. "Once I wanted to be the greatest," she sang.

The front-row lady's ash finally drifted down, and Penny watched, only partly aware that her voice still sounded out the words of what used to be her favorite song. *So it's like this now,* she thought, wondering if third place might earn her an extra whiskey for her troubles. Third was the best she ever did at these free-for-alls. Third place, and she'd sleep on the bus. It wasn't that hard to stay out all night in most cities. And if she made it to Florida, she could ride out the winter without needing more than the occasional motel room.

The bartender flipped on a blender, and Penny had what seemed almost like her old spark, an irritation at the person who ordered a daiquiri in a dive like this. Her journey had started with anger in a way. She'd slapped a kid for calling her a bitch, and not even the superintendent could get her out of a very public firing. "You should be grateful there wasn't a lawsuit," Miss Tallysee from the Art Department had trilled.

"Once I wanted to be the greatest, Two fists of solid rock," she sang, getting to the refrain. *Bitch.* Penny should have told Miss Tallysee that using a pottery wheel wasn't the same as getting sixteen-year-olds to actually do their equations homework. Maybe if she'd seen the way Calvin scowled at her under his Red Sox hat, cocky to the point of delusion that he was one baseball scholarship away from

being somebody who could call grown woman bitches and be praised for it.

One of the lights went out above her, but Penny kept singing, letting her adequate voice hit all the right notes. Each word died on delivery, no muscle but no mistakes either. *Coming soon to a shotgun wedding near you.*

Her song ended soon enough, and she made her way to a barstool. The whiskey was formaldehyde strong, which kept Penny from gulping the whole thing and being done with it. She rolled a quarter around and watched men watch the pretty young thing on stage high kick to some prerecorded marching band dreck. The girl—just turned twenty-one, according to her rambling intro—might as well have been waving hunks of dead snake at a field full of hawks. Penny would have had some sympathy back in Baltimore or even Charlottesville, but those cities belonged to Angry Penny, not Hopeless Penny. *Who was judging this flea circus anyway?* Sometimes it was hard to tell, but she had her money on the owner's wife loitering by the sound booth in a pastel sweatsuit and rhinestone tiara.

The girl's music ended with a clash of symbols, and Twenty-One (yeah, right) twirled one more time for good measure, finishing two beats after the band. Then the whooping of course, the applause and stomping of predators sounding vicious against the plywood beneath their feet. Penny signaled for another, clapping when her quarter rolled out of reach.

The dancer made her way toward the bartender, beaming at her own triumph. She ordered a strawberry daiquiri and turned toward Penny, expectantly.

"Hey, nice song," she said. "You write that yourself?"

Penny was excused from answering as the blender turned on. The emcee paused, too, shuffling his index cards and waiting for the racket to end. It did, and the bartender slid a dripping pink concoction toward the girl. She took a gulp and pressed at her temple. "Good and cold," she said. "How I like my men."

Penny didn't believe her, but didn't respond either. A girl like that at her former school? She'd have the pick of the litter. No boys with bitten nails and rebuilt junkyard cars. She was quarterback material, at least second string.

"I'm Lark, by the way. You a songwriter?" she tried again.

"Nope, I only play." Penny took a sip of her drink and stared at the initials carved into the bar with ballpoint pens.

"My grandma on my dad's side paid for some piano lessons, but they never stuck. Dancing, though? Dancing came natural. Like your guitar, I bet."

Penny glanced down when Lark gestured toward their feet where a plain black case sat, collecting whatever filth this place had to offer. Penny liked how nondescript it was and refused to muck up the exterior with band stickers. Besides, what was the point of advertising for other people and not getting paid for it? Lark kept talking, ignoring the slick man who sidled up to her and eavesdropped, looking for an opportunity.

"Community college, you know?" Lark said to Penny who nodded, unsure of the question. "Say, you look pretty out of it. They serve food here?"

The hoverer took his opening. "Fries and such. You want I get you some?"

Lark finally turned toward him. "Sure, aren't you a charmer?"

The man smiled and loped off. Penny rubbed her head, knowing she shouldn't get involved and knowing she would. There was something about these girls that always got to her. She never won any teaching awards, but she'd stay late to help the homecoming queen attendants, do her best to get them to look beyond the walls of a concrete classroom, its asbestos hidden like so many well-kept secrets: pot in the tampon dispenser, eight traffic summons in Mr. Mulholland's glove compartment, a first grader who bore a striking resemblance to Principal O'Connor. The kind of place to let indiscretions slide. Just not hitting a kid.

"Watch yourself," Penny said, then cleared her throat to speak more forcefully. "He's no ticket out."

Lark scrunched her delicate features in confusion. "Oh, the fries? Girl's gotta eat."

She laughed, and the emcee seemed to sense her joy from across the room. *Ha-a-ha-a-ha-a-ha,* he boomed into the mic. "The judges have judged, and we have a winner, chickadees."

The burned-out stage light hadn't been replaced, and his face was partly shadowed. He consulted his notes and awarded third prize, a set of shot glasses, to the ventriloquist. Penny held up her whiskey in mock salute, glad she wouldn't have to cart glassware around. The coffee thermos from Richmond took up enough space already. Second prize went to a trumpet player Penny had missed because she was late. The emcee made a spit-happy drumroll with his tongue, and Lark grabbed Penny's hand, hard. Startled, Penny found a small part of herself rooting, as well. When the name of a handsome singer in cowboy boots was announced, she was a little deflated by the faint blush appearing on Lark's cheeks. The girl had planned to win.

"An inside job," Penny said, giving the girl's hand a squeeze before letting go.

"How you figure?"

Penny nodded at the tiara-clad wife-turned-judge for the evening who thought nobody noticed her patting the cowboy's backside in congratulations.

"Oh well, isn't that the pits." Lark tugged at one of her spandex sleeves until it covered her wrist. She let go, and the fabric snapped right back to mid-forearm. "I guess it's like that everywhere."

Penny started to object, but stopped when Lark's attention whipped toward the plate of fries and onion rings headed in her direction. The man carrying them grinned like he was delivering something he killed and cooked himself.

"Watch yourself," Penny said again.

Without turning, Lark scratched at her ankle, knowing Penny's eyes would catch the silver glint of a holster and a doll-sized pistol.

Real enough for its unimpressive size. Penny should have been relieved by a young woman taking care of herself, but instead she was uneasy, sure that at some point her luck would run out. It always does.

The night's live entertainment was at an end, and the jukebox blared to life. Customers began shouting their conversations, but Penny didn't care. She didn't have anything to say to anyone. Her drink was mostly water from melted ice cubes, and she swirled the liquid. Buzzed but not drunk yet, she wondered if she should call it a night, but it was ten, and her bus didn't leave until eight the next morning. As far as she could tell, there wasn't too far to meander in this town. Twenty minutes on foot would take her to the outskirts, and she'd never been that keen on wildlife. *Bugs. They grow giant bugs in the South.*

"A drink for my friend, please?" Lark signaled to the bartender who slung a wet rag over his shoulder and pulled out the cheapest bottle of whiskey available. He served it up neat, and Penny didn't complain. You'd think he'd remember a small thing like ice. *You'd think a middle-aged ex-schoolteacher wouldn't be blowing through her savings to lose a country's worth of talent shows,* Penny reminded herself. She'd gotten better, lately, at perspective.

Lark plowed her way through the food and ordered another daiquiri, everything going on the man's tab. Penny hated to see the scene if she didn't give him her number at the end of the night. Number? Hell, he'd probably expect more than that. Penny hiccupped, surprised to find her glass empty all of a sudden. Not surprised to find she liked how the room seemed softer, the way voices altogether sounded like the whirring of a film reel. Not even the sad country song, something about empty beds and early mornings, dimmed her mood.

She eased herself off the stool and headed toward the bathroom, liking the hot sensation in her cheeks. She was warm, Florida warm, and if she could make it another 1,200 miles, she could survive the winter in Key West without too many motel rooms. Had she said that before?

"Sounds like a good plan," Lark said, holding onto her elbow. Had Penny said that aloud? Must have.

They stumbled through the ladies' room door, and Lark locked it behind them. The noise from outside was still there, pushing in on them, but for a moment, they were cocooned.

"Only us girls," Lark said, pulling down her pants and hovering over the toilet. Penny turned toward the window and listened to the stream of urine. "You mind opening that?"

Penny unlatched the frame, and it groaned up, letting crisp air into the space. The alcohol-induced heat left her skin. She didn't think it was right that she had seen this stranger's panties, but she couldn't say why exactly. Maybe the more and more certain feeling that Lark was a teenager with a fake ID. The toilet flushed, and Penny headed toward the door.

"No, your turn," Lark said.

Penny hesitated then unzipped her own jeans and sat, not up to squatting above the seat. At first, nothing happened, then four drinks took over. Lark swung herself up onto the windowsill— half-out, half-in—and leveled her gaze at Penny. "Better?"

Penny nodded, thinking that the girl might escape into the night, leave the bar flirt waiting for her with a fresh drink. She turned to flush, but the tank hadn't refilled, and the toilet paper swirled.

"Just a sec," Penny said, wanting desperately to be out of the room. She was embarrassed and ready to leave the night behind her. She waited until the familiar suction sound of the flapper, then pushed down again on the handle. She moved quickly to the sink, and that's when she saw that Lark had removed her pistol and was fiddling with the cylinder.

"You should use a stage name," Lark said, squinting at the circle of bullets then popping them back into place.

"Excuse me?"

"Penny McAllister isn't that glamorous." There wasn't any soap, so Penny ran her hands under the water, then wiped them on her pants. "Makes you easy to find, too."

Despite her haze, Penny knew what to expect when she looked up into the mirror. Not the red blotches that had appeared on Lark's face, but her unsteady hands holding the gun in front of her.

Penny thought at first—back in Providence—that she'd been running toward something, each new state a step closer to redemption, a life worth more than a lost pension. But no, aren't we more often running away from ourselves? Aren't we dodging the devil until he's done playing?

"Here's as good a place as any, I suppose," Penny said.

"Calvin and me were going to start a life together. Then he starts losing. Missing pitches, missing practice."

Penny sighed when she should have screamed. Not that anyone was going to hear over the music. "That kid was going nowhere fast. You're better off rid of him."

"Better how, exactly? I've got a 2.1 GPA and a part-time job selling lipstick at the mall. Nobody's giving scholarships for girls in the color guard."

"There are always options."

It was Penny's first lie of the night, and it sobered her. If she were in the mood for honesty, though, she would have told Lark that her boyfriend was an average ballplayer. Oh sure, good enough for high school, but not likely to make a college team. A brat to boot. And that's what made her mad, not willing to admit that you're like everyone else. It sounded too familiar, and Penny finally felt something like fear, that everything she could accomplish, she'd accomplished, that a gift certificate to a local bait-and-tackle store was the closest she'd ever come to success, to being the best at anything.

"What's wrong with a C average and a job?" she finally said, knowing the answer was "everything." The Greatest. Some joke. Penny was smiling when Lark pulled the trigger.

PLAYED TO DEATH
BY BILL FITZHUGH

GRADY SHERMAN CAME TO IN darkness and motion and pain. And from somewhere, music played, a song he'd never heard before. This mattered to Grady more than it would most people under the circumstances because Grady considered himself a music expert. He made a good living telling radio programmers what to play. He knew all the songs people wanted to hear and this wasn't one of them.

But for now, Grady had to let that go. He was in the fetal position, dazed and confused as to how and why he'd ended up . . . wherever the hell he was. He tried to sit up but banged his head on something metal that put him back down.

Then, in the corner of the space, a light blinked four times, accompanied by a sound Grady recognized, the rat-a-tat of tires on pavement markers. Now he knew. Okay, I'm in the trunk of a car, he thought, that's a start, but whose car? My own? Someone else's? Was there an answer to either of those questions that could possibly explain why I'm in the trunk?

He didn't feel so good.

Grady drank too much. He knew that. Didn't need to be reminded. But *this* wasn't the solution. Take my keys away, fine.

Call a cab, whatever, but you don't throw a man in the trunk of a car to get him back to his hotel. I don't care how drunk he is.

He banged his fist on the trunk lid. "Hey! Let me out of here!" The yelling made his head throb even worse.

The song, the unfamiliar song, grew louder as someone in the car turned up the volume, apparently to drown out the yelling. Was this some sort of practical joke? Stuff me in the trunk of a car and play music nobody recognizes? If so, it damn sure wasn't funny. Grady wondered if he had gotten belligerent at the bar. Wouldn't be the first time. He could be a real prick. He knew that, but he didn't care. He banged on the trunk again. "I'm calling nine-one-one asshole!"

Grady felt for his cell phone but it was gone. That discovery forced his pain to yield to fear and a feeling in the pit of his stomach like dread. No, it was more than a feeling, it was dread itself multiplying like ebola in his gut.

A sudden turn off the smooth pavement threw Grady against the trunk's wall as the car made a jarring transition to a rough dirt road. Another song came on. Grady didn't recognize this one either. This song wasn't on any list he'd ever approved. Who would listen to this? None of this made sense to him.

Five minutes later the car stopped and with it, the unfamiliar music. The driver's door opened. Footsteps approached in the gravel. "I'm going to open the trunk now," a man said. "I have a gun."

"Who are you?"

"Don't do anything stupid."

The trunk popped open. A man, older than Grady and sturdier, stood a few feet away, a gun in his hand. The man said, "Get out."

"Who the fuck are you?"

"I'm the guy with the gun telling you what to do," the man said. "Now do it unless you want to die right there. Up to you."

Grady struggled to do as he was told. Good God, his head hurt, a chemical throbbing deep in the folds of his brain rendering him helpless, confused, feeble. Had he been drugged? Nothing else made sense. Hell, being drugged didn't make sense. None of it made a damn bit of sense.

When he finally had both feet on the ground, Grady sat on the lip of the trunk, took a deep breath, tried to focus. The rot of dead fish filling his nose, he turned to see a lake, a wooden pier jutting into a spread of black water reflecting a half-moon. Grady said, "Who are you are? What's this about?"

"I'm a consultant, for lack of a better term."

"A consultant that kidnaps people?"

"I was hired."

"By who?"

"The people I answer to," the man said. "They hired me and I'm taking care of business. It's not personal."

"I don't understand."

"We did some call-out research," the man said. "Results were unequivocal."

"What are you talking about, call-out research?" Grady glanced back at the trunk. Maybe there was a tire iron, something he could use as a weapon.

"You know how it works," the man said. "We had a good sample of the demographic we're trying to appeal to and we asked what they wanted, and this is what they said. We're just giving them what they asked for."

"Which is what?"

"Bad news for you, I'm afraid."

"Look," Grady said, "I don't know who put you up to this but . . ."

"Are you a religious man?"

"What do you care?"

"I'm asking as a courtesy," the man said. "I want to give you the chance to pray if you're so inclined."

"Pray."

"You know, when you find yourself in times of trouble, mother Mary speaking words of wisdom to you, all that. Some people take comfort in it," the man said. "A last rights kind of thing, I guess."

"What are you saying, last rites?"

"Put another way, this is the end of side two for you."

It finally dawned on Grady. "Your research said I should be killed?"

"Yes. Do you want to pray?" The guy smiled and said, "Jesus is just all right with me."

Something in the way the man said it was terrifying. Grady realized these would be the final moments of his life unless he did something. He knew he couldn't outrun a bullet so he mustered all the cognitive skills he could and said, "Maybe you didn't ask the right questions. You know, it's not as easy as people think to get the questions right. To get the answer you need."

"Trust me," the man said. "We know what we're doing and this tested really well. Off the charts, as they say." He nodded, saying, "We've got faith in our research."

"Listen," Grady said, "you can get people to tell you they love whatever it is you're selling, if you phrase the question correctly."

The man shook his head. "You're not doing yourself any favors talking like that."

"Okay, look, I've got money," Grady said, patting for his wallet. "Name your price. I'll make you rich!"

"Grady, don't give me that do-goody-good bullshit."

"What?" The phrase gave Grady pause, though for the life of him he couldn't figure out why.

"This isn't negotiable," the man said. "Now turn around."

Grady held his ground. "Please, no, don't do this! I won't tell anybody. You can say somebody drove up, interrupted before you could do the job. Just let me go!"

"What, like give you three steps, a little head start?" The man shook his head. "Dream on," he said. He motioned with the gun toward the dock. "Now let's go, walk this way."

"I want to live!"

The man paused, as if deeply disappointed. Then he said, "Grady, you, of all people, should know, you can't always get what you want."

The man zip-tied Grady's hands behind his back and walked him down the pier. At the end, a few fishing boats tied off on cleats, including a rusty aluminum skiff filled with straw, a single swivel chair rising in the middle on a post. The man pulled a fat cigar from his pocket, a 60 gauge Maduro. "Open your mouth," he said.

Grady clenched his teeth, shook his head. He wasn't going to cooperate any more.

The man cracked the side of Grady's face with his pistol. "Open!"

Grady let the man put the cigar in his mouth.

The man pulled another cigar and did the same. And another and another until Grady's jaw was locked open from the pressure of it all. "Get in the boat."

Hands behind his back, Grady's balance was compromised, so the man steadied him into the skiff and buckled him into the swivel chair. The man pulled a pack of matches and struck one, tossing it onto the straw. Then he shoved the boat with his foot, sent it gliding onto the lake, like a cut-rate Viking funeral.

"Take it easy," the man said.

A DEPUTY FOR THE COUNTY sheriff's office got a call about a report of some kids having a bonfire out on Greasy Lake. When he got to the pier, he saw how someone might think that. A breeze had blown the skiff back near shore. From a distance, it might look like a bonfire. The deputy grabbed his extinguisher, hopped in one of the other boats and went to see what he could do.

He put out the fire and towed the boat back to shore, called it in. "Send CSI," he said. "Don't know if it's homicide or suicide but the man's dead and I wouldn't call it natural causes."

Wasn't long before there was quite a crowd. Coroner, the sheriff along with more deputies, fire department, some press. They found Grady's wallet in his back pocket, saved from the flames by the swivel chair.

They'd been taking pictures and collecting evidence for a half hour when a black sedan pulled into the clearing. Two men. Agent Yates, fifty-nine, and Agent Ball, mid-thirties. FBI. They got out, went looking for whoever was in charge.

As they approached the command post, Agent Yates was talking to his young partner, saying, "It's deuce, not douche."

"Wrapped up like a deuce? What's that supposed to mean?"

"Revved up," Agent Yates said. "Springsteen? 'Blinded by the Light'? 'Revved up like a deuce,' a '32 Ford, a hotrod. Jesus."

They found the sheriff who told them what they had so far. "Middle-aged white male, mouth stuffed with ten big cigars, buckled into the chair, hands tied behind his back. Probably died of smoke inhalation. Would have burned to death but the straw was a little damp, according to the Fire Chief. Made for a lot of smoke."

The two agents nodded like the whole thing fit a pattern. Agent Yates turned to Agent Ball. "What do you think?"

"Seems pretty obvious," the younger agent said. "'Smoke on the Water.'"

The sheriff cocked his head. "Like the song? Dum, dum, dummm . . . dum dum da da. I love that one."

"Yeah," Agent Yates said. "So did I the first ten thousand times I heard it." He looked at his partner and said, "He's getting more elaborate. He's combining titles now. 'Smoke on the Water' plus 'Have a Cigar' and maybe 'Light My Fire,' too."

Agent Ball nodded. "The Floyd for sure, can't say about the Doors."

"What're you guys talking about?"

"Serial killer," Agent Ball said. "He leaves a signature."

"Ohhh," the sheriff said. "And he's a Deep Purple fan?"

"Not exactly," Agent Ball said. "The victims' deaths are staged to evoke the titles of different classic rock songs."

Agent Yates turned to the sheriff and said, "First guy we found, and I think you'll appreciate this for obvious reasons, the first guy we found had a plastic sheriff's badge stuck on his chest. He'd been shot. That was the simplest one."

"Who was he?"

"Some programmer," Agent Ball said. "Used algorithms to determine the fewest number of songs necessary to get the best ratings for the format in any given market. Didn't want anybody to hear a song they'd never heard before."

"Another guy was beaten to death," Agent Yates said. "Now, usually that's done with an easily identified blunt object, you know, a bat, crowbar, a big wrench." Yates shook his head. "Took the coroner a while to figure out this guy'd been beaten to death by what appeared to be a large cowbell, then beheaded with a scythe."

"A what?"

"The big curved blade you always see with the Grim Reaper."

"Ohhh, yeah, I know the song you're talking about. Love that guitar part," the sheriff said, playing it on air guitar. "You got a name for this guy? Like the Son of Sam or the Hillside Strangler?"

Agent Yates said, "I call him the 'Stairway to Heaven Killer.'"

"I prefer 'Highway to Hell Killer.'"

"It's a generational thing I guess."

"You got any suspects? Motives?"

Agent Yates said, "Our profilers have him pegged as a former FM DJ from the free-form era, which makes him a white male in his mid-sixties, most likely. Guy who worked in FM radio during its heyday, when the DJ selected the music from a vast library, none of which was off limits and you were free to speak your mind. They imagine the guy stayed in radio through the late seventies, the AOR years, then eventually got fired or quit when they whittled the playlist down to the last two hundred songs and gave him liner notes to read."

"You'll have to forgive the Agent of Aquarius here," Ball said. "He's been diagnosed as morbidly nostalgic with a complicating vision problem that makes him see everything from back in the day through rose-colored granny glasses." He put his hand on his partner's shoulder. "I'm sorry to tell you, but those days are gone forever, over a long time ago."

Yates took the ribbing in stride. "Go ahead, hit me with your best shot," he said. "It's not your fault you weren't there, got no idea what you missed. But believe me, FM rock radio was a thing to behold when it was in the right hands. The DJs, the good ones anyway, were curators in a vinyl museum, playing things you'd never know about if they hadn't unearthed them for you. People were passionate about it. People loved it. And if you take away something that someone loves, something that had meaning in their lives, and you debase that thing? You force it to behave in all sorts of degrading ways, like double-shot Wednesdays, all Zep weekends, and twenty-six minutes of commercials an hour? You force someone to watch as you kill the thing they held so dear? Who wouldn't snap?" Agent Yates shook his head. "You can only push people so far."

The sheriff asked about a triggering event.

Agent Yates said, "Profilers can't say, but my guess is, the poor guy snapped after hearing 'Free Bird' one time too many."

"Yeah, I could see that," the sheriff said. "They've played that one to death."

WATCHING THE DETECTIVES
BY A. J. HARTLEY

IT'S FUNNY HOW A SONG can take you back.

In the circumstances, it's kind of hard to believe because I've been working my way to driving Janice home from work for days. It was all I'd thought about, getting her in the car away from everyone else, where we could talk and such, you know? But now she is in, and I can smell the perfume she dabbed behind her ears, and she is wearing the skirt—the blue one that hugs her hips and stops a couple of inches above the knee—and I can't think of anything to say, but I know that when I turn on the ancient cassette player, it will be there: that crooning bassline with the reggae off-beat stutter and the voice insinuating its clever words, jagged as a broken bottle, and I will be suddenly, momentarily back in 1977, hot and sweaty, and loaded with adolescent bafflement.

I say 1977, but Elvis Costello's second UK single wasn't really representative of the time, musically speaking, at least when stacked up against the big sellers of the year. "Watching the Detectives" doesn't even crack the top 100 singles for '77, a list which is dominated by disco, "easy listening," and throwbacks like Showaddywaddy, if you can believe that. Every other song on the radio seemed to be by Abba, and Paul McCartney had long since moved from "Penny Lane" to bloody "Mull of Kintyre." I'd like to pretend I was a teenager hipster, a rebel at the front of the punk revolution blowing the Eagles and the Bee Gees out of the water with the Stranglers and the Sex Pistols, but I wasn't. I was thirteen and I knew nothing. I'd just got my first cassette player for Christmas and the first song I ever recorded off the radio—and this hurts to admit—was "Don't Give Up On Us" by that guy from *Starsky & Hutch.*

Sad.

But a part of me knew even then that that was all kinds of fucked up, and I know that because I'd seen Costello and the Attractions doing "Watching the Detectives" on *Top of the Pops,* and something about it had got under my skin. At first it was just the look of the bloke in his jacket and tie and those huge glasses, pulling faces into the camera and twisting his lip into that pre-Billy-Idol Billy Idol sneer. I couldn't decide if it was ridiculous or brilliant, and because I was a kid who didn't know any better, decided not to like it in case I was wrong. In those days what you listened to said a lot about who you were, so you had to pick carefully.

I was scared of being different.

So I taped the bloody David Soul song and sang along to Leo Sayer and nodded in time—God help me—to the plodding, rubber-mallet-to-the-skull creative genius of Status Quo. Come back Noddy Holder, all is forgiven, right?

Anyway.

It was two, maybe three years before I ditched all that stuff, taped over my collections of whatever the hell Radio 1 thought I should be listening to, and started carving out my own little taste cave in the musical landscape. Over time I stuffed it not just with the Pistols, the Clash, the Dead Kennedys, and the Jam, but with Joy Division, the Cure, the Smiths, early XTC, Echo and the Bunnymen, and whatever else the so-called alternative eighties generated. I built my cave and it was me, and if anyone wanted to know me, they had to come into the cave, right? First thing I'd do when I met a girl was find out what she listened to. It wasn't like they had to have the same taste exactly. I mean, some people just don't know any better, do they? But you have to know where you stand on these things. I'm not going to make a serious play for someone who spends her days listening to Boney M. or—as time passed—Banana-fucking-rama. Stands to reason, doesn't it? Half the time I'd find myself wanting to slit them open just to see what they had inside them in place of blood.

The fact is that not many make the grade, especially when you factor in the other basics you want in a woman, the right kind of eyes, the figure, the way they wear high heels without looking like pigs on stilts, the shade of blond, the right amount of make up. You know what I mean. Makes things difficult.

There was this one girl, Michelle Rawlinson, who checked every box, or so I thought. Not too tall, shoulder-length hair, green eyes which wouldn't usually work for me, obviously, but which she managed to pull off somehow, and this smile that made her look ten years younger than she was. Innocent, you know? But not so innocent that it's not worth the attempt. It was a good combination.

We had met at what you might call a mixer at the local sixth form college. I'd already finished my A levels and was trying to figure out what I was going to do next. My qualifications should have gotten me into Oxford and Cambridge but as soon as I got into the interviews the wheels came off. With this one professor who showed me 'round you could actually see him backing off the more I talked, like he knew that I already had nothing to learn from the likes of him. That's what it's like with universities. They say they want smart, talented students, but they don't. Not really. They want kids who won't challenge them and will write down whatever they say. Society should take a big scalpel and slice the lot of them out, you know? All the worthless sheep people. Make some room for the rest of us.

So yeah, by 1985 my educational career had come to a bit of a hiatus, but I still went back to the college dances and such, and since some of the teachers recognized me no one thought to ask me why I was there. This one woman who had taught me history gave me a baffled look one time, and I just smiled at her and asked her how her husband was, even though I knew she wasn't married, and she got all flustered and left me alone.

Anyway. Michelle.

She'd asked me what I was studying and since it was obvious that she was a literature type, I said English, and then went on about *Hamlet* and *Coriolanus* for, like, ten minutes. I knew what the set books were on the A-Level exams and made sure I was ready to say things about them. It's not hard. Anyone can do English literature. It's a joke subject. So Michelle was well impressed and I suggested we go to see *As You Like It* at the Exchange. She was even more impressed with that. Thought me a real high-culture type. The fact that I could give a definitive qualitative analysis of every act at Live Aid sealed the deal.

But the Shakespeare, it turned out, was a mistake, though I suppose it saved a lot of time, showed me things I wouldn't have seen for a while. The show was weird. The woman who played the lead strode about the stage like she was a man or something, bossing people about and being all clever and funny, or so everyone else thought. Michelle about wet herself at one point, and came out all pink and happy at the end. I hated it. I don't know why, but it felt all wrong. Poisonous. As we walked back to my blood-red Ford Escort she just talked and talked about how great it was so I kissed her just to stop her mouth. I hadn't really meant to, and it didn't really go well, but I was just so angry and she was so stupid and I needed her to shut up for five minutes.

She did too. Actually she went really quiet and sat statue still in the passenger seat, and when I asked her if she wanted to get something to eat or go back to my place, she said she thought she should get home. That made me mad too. Still, it might have been okay if I hadn't turned the radio on, if Elvis hadn't started those biting, slashing lines about the girl who pulled your eyes out with a face like a magnet, the one who filed her nails while the detectives were dragging the lake. I turned it up till the bass made the floor shake, and when she asked me to turn it down I ignored her. Elvis did the bit about the parents bracing themselves for the bad news about their daughter's disappearance, and I gritted my teeth with a kind of furious joy I'd never felt before, something that took all the rage and confusion I had been feeling—had always been feeling—and put a match to it so it burned hot and furious and bright.

There was electrical tape in the backseat, the thick, double-width kind. I don't think she realized what was happening till it was too late. I'm not sure I did either. She never even screamed. The scissors weren't as sharp as I would have liked, but they did the job.

Afterwards I just drove around with her sitting next to me, trying to calm down and find somewhere to dump the body. I hadn't meant it to go like this, even though I'd thought about it before. That's normal, right? I mean, people have these dark ideas, fantasies, but they listen to Abba and Boney M. and somehow that keeps you in line, stops you from being antisocial or whatever. That's how it is. If you feel, really feel, and think for yourself, then you find the monster which is inside all of us. Love will tear us apart, right? At least it's honest. I didn't feel bad exactly, not for Michelle. It wasn't like she was a real person. Not really. But I knew that I could get into serious trouble and that was scary.

I went over the people she might have told who she was going out with, who would have seen us together in the theater, and I knew I couldn't hide the fact that I'd been with her. The best solution, I decided, was to chuck her in the canal and then say I'd dropped her at the bus station because I had to get home. I'd lined the backseat with a plastic tarpaulin before I'd put her back there, so clean-up wasn't going to be a problem, and if the police found any of her hair or anything that would just prove she'd been in the car, which I wasn't trying to hide. I even thought how

I'd play it if it went to court. I was confident that I could put some
doubts in a jury's mind. I'm a pretty good actor, if I say so myself,
way better than the bitch who played Rosalind at the Exchange.

But you know what? It never came to that.

It was a week before they found the body. Some loser walking
his dog and probably whistling Mull of fucking Kintyre found her
the same day—as luck would have it—that another girl went missing from the same school. That one was nothing to do with me,
but the cops thought the two cases were connected, and though
they brought me in for questioning, looked over the car and my
bedroom, even kept a tail on me for a few days, I was never
charged with anything. Two months later they got the perv for the
murder of the other girl—Peterson, his name was—but they
didn't find all the remains. Handy for me, you might say, because
they just chalked Michelle up to that bloke. I resented that a bit,
because he was the lowest of the low and you'd think any halfwit
would have been able to tell the difference between what he had
done and what had happened to Michelle, but I suppose it was
just as well.

I went to the funeral, partly for form's sake, partly because I
wanted to see what I had done. I parked right by the graveyard
and set the cassette player just right before going out to stand a bit
away from the family while the coffin was lowered into the ground.
It's a terrible thing to see parents grieving for a lost daughter.
Terrible and great and I felt it all again, the rush of it, the power.
They saw me there, of course. They were supposed to. I looked sad
and serious and gave them a nod, but Mrs. Rawlinson just gave me
this haggard stare and her husband had to be stopped by some
brother or other from coming over. He was a big bloke who ran a
scrap metal and towing service. Not someone I wanted to tangle
with, to be honest, but he couldn't do anything about it, not that
day, standing there in his funeral black with the sun shining and
everyone watching, and that made me feel powerful too.

Did they know it was me? No. They had thought they had

known right after it happened, but then when pervy Peterson got nicked they weren't so sure. I caught her dad watching my house once, just sitting in his tow truck in the street, not even looking up at the window. I called the cops on him and they made him leave, even came to check on me, apologized for the disturbance.

I liked that.

But when the coffin was in the hole and everyone started filing out I went back to my car, climbed in and rolled the window down before turning the engine on. As soon as I did the music came blaring out—"Watching the Detectives," of course—and I pretended to take a second to figure out how to turn it down. Everyone stared—the parents, friends, relatives, this couple with a baby cradled in her mother's hands who I thought might have been Michelle's elder sister—not so much shocked as knocked back into reality, but I doubt they ever got it. I just wanted them to hear what she heard as she went out, you know? Felt fitting. Gave the whole thing a sense of closure, of ritual. I couldn't help but laugh about it later.

That was thirty years ago. I've not always been a good boy since, but I have been careful. That first time had been an impulse and it was messy. I thought a lot about the next one and made sure that the whole approach was different so that no one would ever connect the two or put me in the frame. The only thing that was the same—think of it as a kind of private joke—was the song I had playing at the end, the same lugubrious bassline, the same insinuating off-beat guitar, the same searing words about how you can't be wounded if you've got no heart. Everything else was different. Maybe not so much the girls. I mean, everyone has a type, right? But the rest was unconnected. After all, I have a life, a career, not quite the way I might have once wanted things to go, but good enough that I wasn't about to jeopardize it by getting carried away.

Then there was Janice. And Elvis on the radio. Like I said, it's funny how a song can take you back.

Right back.

Janice had only been working at Jefferson's a week. I know because she arrived two days after the police visited me for the last time. Remember Pervy Peterson, the bloke who took the rap for Michelle? Turns out he died in prison, and in his last days he confessed to a whole bunch of things. Some of them couldn't be proved, but other things—after he'd written out notes and maps and whatnot could—and the local bobbies were suddenly signing off on a lot of what the police shows on telly called "cold cases." But he went to his grave, apparently, denying he had ever laid eyes on Michelle Rawlinson. So they came to me again, asking the same questions they had three decades earlier. I hadn't expected this but, like I said, I'm careful and had never forgotten a single detail of what I had told them at the time. So I gave them all the same answers and they went away, their duty done. There was a picture in the paper, but the next day the police said the case was no longer being pursued, so that was that. The following day, Janice showed up.

She was older than I usually liked, but not by much, and her hair was just right, and she wore this sparkly pink nail varnish that made you think things. I think I knew she would be the next one as soon as I saw her. She sort of half smiled at me and I thought, yes. There it was. Bashful and secretly wicked.

I gave it all a lot of thought, but when the time came and I actually had her in the car, it took an unexpected turn.

"Don't take me straight home," she said. "Drive me to Longridge."

"Longridge?" I said. "What's in Longridge?"

"Fields," she said. "Trees. It's a nice night and I want to sit where there's a nice view."

I couldn't believe my luck, to tell you the truth. A secluded spot out of her normal routine? It might be just what I needed, particularly if I could avoid the traffic cameras. On my lunch break I had already switched the license plates on my Escort, just for added safety, so even the traffic cameras might not have been too much of a risk.

It was a nice night for the time of year, chilly, as you'd expect, and quickly getting dark, but not rainy, and I found myself warming to the idea, amused by how easy she is making it for me. Even so, I was taken aback when she pulled out a dainty little flask from her handbag and offered me a swig. I stared at her, wondering momentarily if she was not the girl I took her for.

"I'm driving," I said.

"Coward," she teased, waggling the flask in front of me. It was stainless steel but decorated with little pink cats. "Go on," she said. "Be a man."

I flushed at that, and privately decided to make her pay for it later, but I took the flask from her and, just to prove the point, drained the whole thing in three long swallows. The whiskey burned my throat, but the fire was useful. Sometimes I needed a little push. It was not usually the girl who gave it to me quite so directly.

"So where in Longridge?" I asked, already feeling the whiskey starting to work.

"The disused reservoir on the edge of town."

I didn't say anything for a moment, and kept driving, mind racing. I knew the place vaguely: a Victorian stone-edged rectangle with a sloping grass verge and trees. You couldn't see it from the road unless you were way up on the hill, and then you would be too far away to see anything, especially after dark. It might be perfect. I'd need to be careful, of course, but then I always was. I wasn't sure what disused meant. No manned pumping station was, of course, good, but if it had been drained, then that would be no use to me. A well-weighted body could stay lost for a long time in water.

"What do they use it for now?" I asked, trying to sound casual, eyes on the road ahead.

"Nothing," she said. "Fishing, I think."

Fishing meant water, of course, though it also meant snagged hooks on hair and clothing if you weren't careful.

For a moment the dotted white line on the road seemed to shift and blur and I wondered if the whiskey was a mistake, but I fought to concentrate and keep going till she told me where to turn. Even so I took the bend wider than I'd meant to and slowed down deliberately.

Make it last, I thought. I didn't want to rush anything, and not just because rushing makes you careless. Half the satisfaction was in the buildup. Everyone knew that.

So I drove and she told me where to park. I didn't like her giving orders just as I hadn't liked her waggling the flask and saying I wasn't a man, but I let it go for now. She'd know who is in charge soon enough.

It was dark now, and the reservoir was glittering and black, but over on the other side I thought I saw the shape of another car. I didn't like that, even if the people inside were probably too interested in each other to pay us any attention.

"Maybe we should go somewhere else," I said, but she shook her head and took off her seatbelt as if she was getting ready for something. In front of the car the grass fell away into the water, but fifty yards or so across there was a narrow spit of land with a road to some kind of access point, and I saw the way a thick metal cable seemed to run from there into the water and over to us, ending in a big rusting hook no more than a few yards from the passenger-side wheel. I didn't know why I notice it, and it bothered me because I realized how much my mind was wandering. I started to say something, but the words came out garbled, slurred, like I'd had a stroke.

She opened her purse and took out a nail file, using it to trim a cuticle like it was suddenly the most important thing in the world and I felt a weird sense of strangeness, of vertigo, like the world had shifted. But then she gave me that smile of hers and in spite of everything else that felt wrong I thought *yes*. Now. This was when I'd do it. She was perfect. Ready. I had to hold onto the idea though, because my head was swimming and when I reached for the ancient cassette player in the dash—carefully maintained through the years—my hand was unsteady. More than that, the muscles felt loose, disconnected, so that instead of punching the button I sort of flapped at the controls but didn't quite reach them. It was the weirdest sensation I've ever had. My brain was alert, but my hand felt like it was not in my control, like the nerves were dead, turned to rubber or a bunch of sausages stuck to my arm. I tried again, but the feeling was spreading from the wrist now, through the elbow and up, so that nothing seemed to be working properly.

"Let me get that for you," she said, tapping the button precisely.

Here came the bass, the staccato rattle of the snare drum, the voice with its load of spiky, fractured words . . .

"Oh this," she said. "I thought it would be this."

I tried to look at her but my head wouldn't turn all the way and I couldn't stop her as she reached into the steering column and flashed the headlights twice. There was an answering flash from the car on the other side of the reservoir, and moments later it was coming toward us.

"You know the first time I heard this?" she said, nodding at the stereo. "I don't remember because I was very small, but it was at my aunt's funeral. Michelle. You remember Michelle, don't you, Barry? I was too young to understand then, but they used to talk about it, her mum and dad. The way you played a few bars when you turned your engine on at the funeral. Like it was a mistake. But they knew. They always knew. They even told the police, but no one took them seriously. Said a song on the radio wasn't real evidence. You know what, Barry?" she said looking at me with something that was almost a smile, but cold as the girl in the song, "I think if there had been one woman on that investigation—one female police officer—they would have got you in a second. Because you're obvious. Small and obvious."

I tried to turn away, but couldn't. Something wasn't right. And now she was listening to the song as if she'd never heard it before, nodding her head in time to the rhythm.

"Good song," she said. "I wondered if you would have moved on to something else. 'Psycho Killer,' say, or 'Don't Like Mondays,' but those are a bit on the nose for someone like you, aren't they? Too self-aware. You're more the type who thinks 'Every Breath You Take' is a love song, aren't you, Barry? I'm glad you stuck with this. You know what it's about, right?" she said, not flirty now, not playful. "A man whose girlfriend would rather watch TV than have sex with him. I expect you know all about that, don't you, Barry?"

I wanted to say that she was wrong, that it was a sinister study of heartless women getting what they have coming to them, but my mouth won't move right and now I was looking at the flask and wondering if she drank from it at all.

"I can almost remember you at the funeral," she said, thoughtfully. "Almost, but not quite. Michelle's mum and dad remember though. That's them coming now."

I couldn't turn away so I could see that the car was not a car but a pick up truck with a little crane on the back.

"'They call it instant justice,'" she sang along with Elvis, and gave me a grin. "Well, not instant."

And then Janice was taking the brake off, getting out and closing the door behind her and I couldn't move, couldn't turn the engine back on, even as I felt her hook up the chain to the underside of the car. The pickup truck had parked on the end of that spit of land and someone out there in the dark was connecting a winch. I could feel the strain of the cable as it tightened, feel the creak of the car as it began to roll into the water, but all I could hear was "Watching the Detectives" as the car started to fill, cold and black and stifling.

BOY WONDER
BY JIM FUSILLI

IT HAPPENED SO TERRIBLY QUICKLY. Bowie Thomas was spinning after midnight at a warehouse in Sault Ste. Marie; the standard DJ fare, but with a bit more bite and taste: a few EDM hits for the crowd; lots of house from Detroit, 350 miles south; some techno out of Berlin; and then he mixed in a few tunes he'd created using Reason, his Midi keyboard, his Nord synthesizer, and his family's old upright piano, the one his father bought for Bowie's lessons beginning at age six. A good show: tight, fluid, musical. Bowie was pleased, quietly so, as was his way.

As he was packing up his car, bundled against the snapping winter wind, he was approached by Emily, a sophomore at his high school. Bowie tried to place her: a brother off in the Navy; their father hunted elk and whitetail deer with a bunch of steel fitters who were Packers fans; mother? Kind of a loner. "Hi," said Bowie, blowing on a bare hand.

Shy and awkward, Emily sputtered to tell him his set was hot. She tugged at her tuque, which bore the school colors.

"Thank you," said Bowie, as he put a blanket over his gear.

She asked about the tracks she didn't recognize.

He replied with titles.

"All yours?"

"All mine," he said. "No one else to blame."

"They're great," she said with a bright smile. "Really."

Music brings her out of her shell, doesn't it? "Well, I'd better be . . ."

"Okay. Sure, okay." Head down, Emily trotted off toward her father and his mud-caked Grand Cherokee. Stopping suddenly, she turned and shouted: "Really hot."

Bowie nodded, waved.

When he returned home, tiptoeing in 3:30 a.m., he emailed two of his tracks to her. "Don't share, please," he cautioned. Then he Skyped Ramaaker in Breda; Ramaaker chided him for spinning dumbed-down EDM. Bowie had a photo of Ramaaker on his workstation; Ramaaker spinning in Paris, the crowd on fire.

On defense, Bowie told him he'd dropped in a couple of his own tunes too. "Send," said Ramaaker. Bowie did, then climbed under an unruly mountain of comforters. Soon came an IM from the Netherlands. "Better," Ramaaker told him. "Not ready."

He nodded off, purple light bouncing off a mirror ball pinpricking his eyes.

HIS MOTHER KNOCKED ON HIS door. Bowie fought through the fog; his throat frogged as he tried to respond. Cold morning sun pressed against the basement blinds. He draped a comforter like a cape around his shoulders as he toddled across the room, bypassing his beat-up pawnshop Fender Jazzmaster bass.

"Bowie," she stage-whispered. Kim Thomas aspired to fame in the nineties. A glam rock revival. She never played a gig outside of Michigan. "There's somebody—Bowie, get out here. Hurry."

His clothes were in a pile on the floor. As he hobbled into his pants, he tapped his iMac's space bar. He had 178 incoming emails.

He walked in bare feet upstairs to the kitchen. Ionic Strength was sitting in his father's seat, his hands wrapped around a cup of instant cocoa.

Kim fluffed her son's hair. "There he is," she said. "My Bowie."

Ionic Strength, the producer and twice voted the world's greatest DJ by *DJ Mag* back in the late nineties, stood and extended a warm hand. "What are you? Twelve?"

In shock and still half-asleep, Bowie smiled. He had his father's easy manner.

"He's seventeen," Kim Thomas announced. The Damned T-shirt she wore was about twenty years old.

"And a hundred pounds."

"Lanky," she said, running her hands along her hips. Bowie's father was a bear of a man, big, bearded, and flannelled. A hippie cabinetmaker.

"Pack up," Ionic Strength told the boy. Ion wore a silk T under a pearl-gray suit. His midnight-black hair, parted in the center, was an arc around his tanned face. A diamond ring glittered on the middle finger of his right hand. Bowie knew it was a gift from a Super Bowl champ who wanted in. Everyone knew Ion made the tracks that bore the jock's name. As a producer, Ionic Strength was as dependable as Kraft cheese.

"LA?" Bowie said.

"LA," replied Ionic Strength, who had a limo at the curb and a private jet waiting at the nearby municipal airport.

Bowie nodded. "How did you know?"

"They return my calls before I dial," Ionic Strength replied, allowing his perfect teeth to shine.

Kim shivered in delight.

"No. Really," Bowie said.

Again, Ion smiled.

Bowie retreated to his room and, as he packed his duffel, scrolled through his emails. Emily, it turned out, had posted on Soundcloud the tracks he'd sent her. Of the now-189 emails, twelve were from her. She apologized with a torrent of emojis and exclamation points. "I couldn't help myself. I got excited. They were brilliant," she wrote. "Both tracks. Especially

'Euphrosine.' So hot, so chill. Forgive me. Please. Say you do. Bowie. Bowie?"

Angry, not angry, Bowie took up his laptop and returned to the kitchen. Ionic Strength was in the limo, savoring the heat. Late January, in the UP, it was eight degrees on a sunny Saturday.

"Bowie," Kim said, clattering with excitement, "I should go with you."

With a little laugh, he replied, "I don't think you bring your mom to these things."

"But what are 'these things'? Bowie?"

Good question, he thought. Maybe all it is a free trip to LA. "I guess I'll find out . . ."

"And don't sign anything. Bowie, oh Jesus, how can you be so calm?"

Bowie shrugged. He had long fantasized about a moment like this, though Ionic Strength would've been about the last producer he would've put in the picture.

"Message me." Now she was hopping in place, baggy socks sliding up, down.

Bowie grabbed a banana. "Tell Dad."

Yes. But not until the plane is in the air.

He kissed his Mom on the forehead.

"Bowie, jump on it," she whispered. "Get it all."

He walked toward the long white limo, its engine puttering, clouds billowing from the tailpipe.

"AND YOU LET HIM GO?" Ben Thomas said. They were in his storefront workshop on 3 Mile Road, surrounded by the scent of bare wood and steam heat. A converted shoe-repair shop, it was cluttered with unfinished furniture; empty drawers awaited cabinets and end tables. In the backroom, an old radio offered earnest folk music.

"What choice did I have? This could be it."

Ben had his safety goggles high up in his unruly hair. His beard wore sawdust flakes.

"Besides, it's Bowie. He knows what he's doing."

In LA? With record producers who fly a private jet to the UP on a whim? What kind of money is behind that man and what kind of authority does it bring? "He had better."

"I offered to go."

"Kim . . . do we know how to reach him?"

"He has his phone." Ben lived happily without technology. He'd never sent an instant message, never downloaded an app, never owned a laptop. He had a flip phone for emergencies.

He looked at his knobby fingers and knotty hands as if they held an answer.

"He deserves this, Ben," Kim said with a trace of defiance.

He groped for his safety glasses. "Let's talk later."

As she departed, he thought, *Deserve?* All these years together and he hadn't yet convinced her that there was no such thing as "deserve."

NOT THAT HE WASN'T IMPRESSED by the private jet or immune to the flattery of the beautiful pilot and the beautiful stewardess, but Bowie was asleep by the time the flight rose over Eau Claire. Nestled in a buttery seat that reclined to flat, he woke up briefly to find Ionic Strength in his throne-like leather chair and working his laptop. Bowie knew Ion preferred easy-to-use Ableton for his productions.

Bowie rustled, pulling the blanket up to his shoulder. Of commercial EDM, the kind Ionic Strength brought to the market, Deadmau5 had said, "The songs sound the same. I'm surprised the record companies that sign these people aren't just going home and making the music themselves. Cut out the middleman."

Bowie knew how cookie-cutter EDM was made. He would challenge himself to identify, before a track ended, the source of the tones and beats. He tried to do it without judgment—his father told him long ago that people have their reasons for doing what they do, even if they don't make sense to us—but at times he couldn't believe how lazy some producers could be. He wondered if Ion was building a track by dragging and dropping files from Ableton's library or from other cuts he'd already produced.

The stewardess wheeled a cart to Bowie, who had caught the scent of the chateaubriand before she arrived. Kale and purple cabbage with chickpeas and grape tomatoes filled in a glass serving bowl.

Ionic Strength, now in a blue kimono, slipped off his headphones. "No drinks."

She nodded as she lifted the carving knife.

Bowie said, "No. No thanks."

She feigned disappointment. "If you'd like anything, Mr. Thomas . . ."

He was asleep again when they passed high above Grand Junction.

Three hours later, a limo pulled to the curb in Silver Lake. Ion's driver hurried to open Bowie's door. At the airport in Burbank, Ionic Strength told Bowie he could spend $1,500 on clothes. Eyeing Bowie's hoodie, T-shirt, and jeans, he said, "Do like you, but, you know . . . this is this." He nodded toward the flawless Southern California sky. January and it was eighty-five degrees. "And you're wearing me tonight."

Bowie was confused until he remembered Ion had his own rave-appropriate clothing line.

After shopping, Bowie was driven to the Mondrian in West Hollywood. In his orange room, luxurious and Spartan, angles and dull corners, he dropped the shopping bags and opened his laptop. Now there were 314 emails, including twenty-eight from Emily. He hesitated, decided to weed through them later, and then IMed his mom back home. "Arrived," he said. "All good."

He tossed the five $100 bills Ion had given him onto the bed. Digging, he found the bathing suit he'd bought, changed in the gold-plated bathroom, and walked to the elevator in the embrace of the fluffy robe he found in the closet.

Quietly amazed, he fell asleep in a lounge chair by the rooftop pool, the persistent sun his cozy blanket.

"MALIBU," SAID ION'S DRIVER, WHO delivered to the Mondrian the red-leather jacket and waxy black slacks Bowie wore. "You heard of Rakesh Malik?" he asked.

"I have," said Bowie, as he held up the hanger to examine the ensemble. Ionic Strength wanted him to dress up like Tiësto, the Dutch DJ said to be the first $25 million a year man in EDM.

Malik was owner and CEO of RM Global, the international management firm. RM Global had many DJs and producers under contract. It invested in clubs in world markets and provided capital for mega-festivals. RM Global was publicly traded on one stock exchange or another. Bowie hardly knew what that meant, but over in Breda, it annoyed Ramaaker no end. "So you wouldn't mind that your father made furniture for Sears?" he once asked via Skype. "You want the shareholders to pick the wood, the lacquer?"

There were maybe fifty people at the party, maybe one hundred, Bowie couldn't tell. The room was dark; candle lights flickered. People came and went, air kisses for hello and goodbye. A wet bar. Hors d'oeuvres were circulated. The house was out of a glossy magazine. Or, better, a movie. A movie about a party in a home owned by a mogul who wanted to sign a seventeen-year-old from the UP.

Out on the deck, a DJ spun clichés. People dug it, Bowie noticed. They bobbed and shuffled. They were all as beautiful as their clothes: it was as if the mannequins in those Melrose Avenue boutiques had come to life. Perfume competed with the ocean air.

Fizzy water in hand, Bowie sidled toward the DJ, who was working his controller like he was spinning vinyl on two turntables: hunched over, deep in concentration, his headphones around his neck; a well-timed fist pump or two, sly eye contact after the almost seamless segue between tracks. Meanwhile, the unnamed DJ had patched his laptop into the soundsystem: he'd pre-programmed his set. What the crowd wanted, or what the moment demanded, didn't matter to him. He was on autopilot.

This was weak by house standards, thought Bowie Thomas. Make that play in Chicago or Detroit clubs and see that door marked "Lame . . ."? Bowie's parents were sitting on his bony shoulders. Maybe that's the best he can do, son. Go knock him aside, Bowie. Take over—

He felt a hand on the small of his back, and when he turned, there was Ionic Strength, Malik at his flank.

"Here's your boy," Ion said with cheer. He wasn't the only man wearing sunglasses at night.

Rakesh Malik's eyes sparkled when he smiled.

"Hi, Bowie," he said warmly as they shook hands. "Thank you for coming."

Malik was in his mid-forties with a salt-and-pepper goatee. Short, fit, and gleaming, he wore business apparel, gray and lavender. There was a faint trace of India in his accent as he spoke over the booming music.

"I trust Ion is taking good care of you," Malik said.

"He is," Bowie nodded.

"But it's all a bit much."

"It's all a bit much," Bowie agreed. He wasn't sure what he was projecting, but he roiled inside.

"At least there is music," Malik said. He held a champagne flute.

Ionic Strength waited for Bowie's reply.

Yes, thought the boy. One hundred and twenty-eight beats per minutes. Four beats per bar. Here comes the breakdown, right on time. Now the drop. Music by prescription.

"It's very Avicii," Bowie replied. "Late Avicii."

Bowie knew Avicii had signed with a label before he'd turned eighteen. He topped out at twenty-one.

Malik knew Avicii hadn't yet turned thirty and was worth $50 million.

Ion hid his frown. Was this kid from the North Pole probing? Or did he just send Rakesh a sign that he was dotted-line ready?

Ionic Strength had told Malik he had it under control. EDM was ready for a new boy wonder. "Bowie Thomas, he slides right in," Ion had said. The kid next store. The all-American. He's having fun, you're having fun. Porter Robinson, Flume, Bowie Thomas . . .

A woman approached. A goddess. An African queen. She nestled into Malik as if she had reserved the spot. "Rakesh," she pouty-moaned.

Bowie couldn't tell if it was a request or a command.

"I trust we will see you again soon," Malik said.

"Thank you. For the invitation."

As Malik was steered away, Ion said, "Let me ask you something, Boing-Boing. You think you're ready?"

"I can do what I do, so, yes. I'll say yes."

Ion said, "Bold. But you can only get so far by yourself."

Bowie did not reply. He had known what the game would be before he left Sault Ste. Marie, before he put on the Tiësto jacket, before he was in a roomful of mannequins.

BEN THOMAS HEARD THE SHOP door open. The morning mail, he thought when no customer called to him. He kept sanding, the rhythm smooth and easy. But then he realized there was no mail delivery on Sunday.

There was a teenager girl, slight, shy, slumped into her down coat. Mittens.

Ben put the sandpaper in his back pocket.

"What did I do?" asked the girl.

He saw that she had been crying.

"I'm sorry," Ben said. "Are you . . . you must know my son, Bowie."

"It's my fault."

Whoa, Ben thought as he hurried to reach her. Now she was sobbing.

He steered her toward a rocking chair awaiting brush and stain.

It took a while, but she got it out.

She had placed a few songs Bowie had composed—two, actually: "Euphrosine" and "Bonnie Bonnie Holiday"—on the Internet and now he was furious with her. He wouldn't return her emails, her texts. She tried to call. But he didn't— He wouldn't— He excused himself and returned with tissues. She was a child. So was Bowie and now he was in Hollywood, and they were going to try to steal his soul. That's what Hollywood was for. It had no other purpose. Cyphers and vipers.

"Bowie's not home. He's on . . . a business trip, I guess."

"Well, I know that now," she said, dabbing at her nose. "I'm Emily, by the way." She offered a little wave.

Ben watched as she took out her phone. Soon, she was showing him a photo of his son. "That's Ionic Strength. They're at Chalk. It's a club in Hollywood."

The man had his arm tight around Bowie's red-leather shoulders. "So that's Ionic Strength . . ."

"He's huge," she said. "And awful."

Ben sat, balancing on the edge of a nightstand. "How so?"

"He makes the worst—the *worst*—music, and now he has Bowie."

He waggled his finger at the photo on the little screen. "Is there some kind of write-up with that?"

Just a caption, it turned out. Ben saw the word "prodigy."

"I killed his reputation," she said.

"Emily, how can this be your fault? Really."

"When Ion owns you, it's over. Ask—" She rattled off names Ben had never heard. But he could tell they had some sort of purchase in the marketplace. "They haven't made any good music since."

"Bowie's seventeen. He can't sign a contract. No one owns him."

Emily took back her phones and danced her thumbs across the keys.

Now Ben was looking at what appeared to be a magazine article in miniature.

"Who is Ramaaker?"

As Emily explained, Ben read the screed, written by Ramaaker in awkward English. In brief, Ionic Strength was the personification of all that was wrong with electronic dance music. A corruptor. Vile. Took the money and ran. Banal. Void of musical talent; void of music. A parasite. No soul.

Bowie had great promise, Ramaaker railed. Listen to "Euphrosine" and "Bonne Bonne Holiday" and you hear . . .

Not "Bonne Bonne." Bonnie had been Bowie's first piano teacher. Bowie labored, but he never quit.

"Ramaaker sent links to all the EDM websites," Emily said. She looked for a trash can for the tissues. "It's blowing up."

Ben tried to tamp his anger. He remembered he was speaking to a tender heart. "If Ionic Strength is as terrible as this man says, wouldn't everyone already know this? That he's in it for the money, not the art of it?"

Frustrated, Emily said, "That—that right there—says Bowie is dead."

Ben smiled. "Bowie is not dead. I don't know much about that kind of music, but—"

"No one will take him seriously."

"Emily . . ."

She snatched her phone and shoved it into her coat pocket.

"Emily, this is just . . . it's a setback, if that. It never goes smoothly." He shrugged. "It just doesn't." He tapped her soft shoulder. "Let's believe in Bowie, okay?"

BOWIE SPENT MUCH OF THE day in a daze. He had never traveled so he knew nothing about the effects of jet lag. He hadn't eaten much, and he was uncomfortable calling for room service. He turned on the TV. Football at 10 a.m. He bumbled around the room before walking to lunch at P. F. Chang's. He swam in the hotel pool. In January. The sun tingled on his shoulders. Freckles would emerge.

He answered emails, the total now exceeding five hundred.

"It's fine," he wrote to Emily. "No worries."

To Ramaaker, the message was even more succinct: "Have faith."

Then, the next email: "Mom, all good. Hi to Dad. Home soon."

He was napping when the bedside phone rang. *Someone to see you, Mr. Thomas.*

Bowie felt compelled to tidy the room. He brushed his teeth.

He expected the driver, but it was Ionic Strength. Bowie stepped back to let him in.

"I want to show you something," said Ion, who wore a long electric-blue shirt over baby-blue slacks. Barefoot. A gold bracelet rattled on his wrist as unzipped his satchel and removed the latest iPad.

Bowie sealed the door.

"Sit," said Ionic Strength, nodding toward the long, board-like sofa.

Bowie sat as he received the tablet.

"Watch."

Bowie hit the proper arrow.

Oh, no, he thought.

The man in the shaky video footage was slope-shouldered in a long ratty coat as he trundled along a joyless city street. Long-nailed and frazzled, he seemed small against an ancient building's heavy gray stones and invisible to the people who waited for a trolleybus. The man, who oozed suspicion, carried a tattered tote bag that strained to contain a collection of vinyl recordings. A billboard touted an American movie, the glowing actress familiar, but the title now in Dutch.

Now the man stopped to wait for the traffic light to change. He shuffled impatiently, almost angrily. He scowled; he wiped his nose on his sleeve. The camera pushed in: a desperate Ramaaker. He needed a shave, a bath, a meal. He lifted the tote and held the vinyl to his chest, as if to protect it from theft. The trolleybus arrived and soon departed, and Ramaaker remained.

He howled, turned on a battered heel and rushed toward where he'd come from.

"There's more," said Ion, as he took back his iPad.

Bowie slumped.

"Your advocate. It's more than jealousy."

Bowie fumbled for his defense.

"Speak," Ion said, "but it comes down to do or bitch."

"He does." Meaning: he makes good tracks.

"Who listens?"

Bowie was about to say: I do. But he held his tongue. Ramaaker, oh man. Beaten down Ramaaker.

"The earth spins and nobody cares about the crazy man who wants it to stay in one place."

"'Crazy,'" said Bowie, shaking his head. "That's cold."

Ion tsk-tsked. "Paranoid, bipolar, whatever, but functional without the drink." He put the iPad on an end table. "Keep it. There's more. The arrest in Ibiza: bottle through the window, handcuffs? It's on there."

Bowie wasn't sure what he had heard. Ramaaker spun in Ibiza, but blew it?

Ionic Strength crossed the room. "You're on tonight at Chalk. We're gonna set it straight." He nodded toward the iPad. "The playlist is on there too."

"I don't have my gear," Bowie replied.

"Behind Plexiglas, remember? Just let it flow."

Bowie had visited the lounge last night. He would be shielded and on a raised platform. No one could see that he was pushing buttons and sending out Ion's playlist.

"Fake it to make it," Ion said.

CHALK'S MAIN ROOM PULSED AND rattled, and the dancers bounced and squealed. Glee ruled, so did abandon, and laser lights and soap bubbles heightened the dizzying effect. The music wasn't horrible: the DJ had skills, no doubt, if narrow tastes; he kept it moving and given a choice of remixes, he chose close to the most appealing. The crowd: glitter on faces, yes, and Day-Glo wristlets; but not too many hat-imals, no pacifiers to ward off the effects of grinding teeth—alcohol, not E, the drug of choice on the Strip, at least on a Sunday night. Or maybe not. Bowie didn't care. Circling, he looked for people who were listening. Soon, the driver ushered him back to the shadows where Ionic Strength held court with bottle service. The women smiled as Ion pointed to the boy from UP in a $380 hoodie, spanking new skinny jeans, and his Dr. Martens from back home. Bowie couldn't hear the names as Ion made introductions, but no one seemed to mind.

Ion shooed until a space opened next to him on the banquette. Bowie squeezed around the table, bypassing long legs, dimpled knees, and Jimmy Choos.

"You brought your laptop," Ion shouted, his lips inches from Bowie's ear.

Bowie nodded. He wasn't going to tap a button on the iPad and let Ion's playlist represent him. It was dreck. Music as product; music to move product.

"You're thinking you can pull it off," Ion said, as he reached for his glass. "But remember where you are. These people, they want what they want. Don't confuse them. This isn't the Warehouse in 1977, and you're not Frankie Knuckles."

Bowie was surprised that Ion knew the club where house music got its start. But then he remembered that he was in the game way before there was money to be made, before the B-list spun for fame.

"I hear you," Bowie nodded.

Ion threw his arm around Bowie's shoulder. "Rakesh is here. Both of us—me, you—we could have a very sweet week."

"Okay," said Bowie.

HE FLEW COACH AND THEN had to use his emergency credit card to get to Sault Ste. Marie from Detroit. His father drove him home after engulfing him in a hug.

"So . . . ?" asked Ben.

Bowie shrugged as if to remind his father that, as a teen, he had the right to remain petulant. Heat streaming from the vent rode up the leg of his Levi's. Outside the truck, it was silver-sunny and a crisp eighteen degrees.

"Was it what you thought it would be?"

"Sort of," Bowie replied.

"The good? The bad?"

"Something to remember, for sure."

They left the airport grounds, and soon they crossed 3 Mile Road. Ben had left a sign in the window: LONG LUNCH.

"Regrets?"

If Bowie regretted anything, it was leaving behind that hoodie. He was never going to have a hoodie like that again. He thought about keeping the iPad too, as if burying it would protect Ramaaker. But it remained in the booth at Chalk.

"I'm good, Dad," he said, stifling a yawn. "Maybe it was necessary."

Ben tapped his son on the thigh. "All right . . ." he said softly.

They headed south toward home.

At Chalk, the handoff had been fluid: The DJ who called himself Deen Angst ended his set with a pop hit with an EDM platform, so Bowie slid in with a Latin remix of the same backing track. The handful in the crowd who knew the craft caught it, and so did Ionic Strength, who was standing with Rakesh Malik and his African queen at the side of the booth. Bowie popped open an energy drink.

The Latin groove felt right for the room, so Bowie rode it for a while. African queen was digging it. Bouncing along with the rhythms, Bowie looked through the Plexiglas: people were dancing, not fist-pumping and pogoing in place. One a.m. on a Monday and the room was swinging side to side, not up and down. Rhythm ruled happy, happy Hollywood: Bowie knew good music knocked the blasé out of anyone with feels. He had known this since he toddled.

He had in his laptop a version of his "Bonnie Bonnie Holiday" that he sweetened with percussion from an old Deodato track. The beats-per-minute was a tad slower than what he had been spinning so he dropped in a few scratches and a thunder pop, then let it fly. It worked.

But Ion was displeased. Two bars in, he knew Bowie had chosen to spin his own composition, one Ion intended to register with his name as co-composer.

Bowie brought up a seventies disco remix, then, as if to appease Ion, tossed in a Lady Gaga track that drew heavily on retro house music. But Ion guessed what was coming, and Bowie transitioned to funk and disco-influenced house hits out of mid-eighties Chicago and Detroit. And the crowd, which now included people who had been savoring the main room, didn't mind at all.

Malik observed, his eyes reflecting the twinkling lights. He scanned, taking it in with mind, not body: The party was hot; the customers were responding; the boy was in control, certainly, but he acknowledged, as if in gratitude, the energy that was coming toward him. *Politeness is an appealing trait in a newcomer, is it not? There is something about him,* Malik thought. *Natural innocence? Yes, I think so. If he is impressed with his own cleverness, he does not let it show. I like his enthusiasm,* Malik thought. *But why is Ion so upset?*

Bowie had chosen to end his tribute to early house with an obscure mid-eighties track by Cybotron, a group out of Detroit. It had aged well: It percolated; it was still undeniably sexy and fun. As it unfolded, Ion walked toward the steps at the side of the booth. Seeing him coming, his anger gathering, Bowie switched deftly to "Beverline," last year's monster club hit, one that held court from Ibiza to Las Vegas and, apparently, here in LA: Produced by and credited to Ionic Strength, it had ripped off Cybotron. Bowie and Ion may have been the only two people in the room who knew it before the transition.

Ion had to acknowledge the crowd's sudden attention. As he waved and forced a smile, the African queen beckoned him to dance.

Now Bowie was all in. It took him two tracks to get to a place where he could spin Ramaaker. And he did until it was time for him to surrender to the next DJ.

He was soaked in sweat when Malik met him with a warm handshake and a cuff on the shoulder. The African queen blew him a kiss. Ion waited, then pulled him away from the fans who had gathered around him.

Bowie had to call a taxi to take him back to the hotel. He was at LAX well before sunrise.

"I MET YOUR FRIEND EMILY," Ben said as they drove past the old Best Western. "She seems sweet."

Bowie had been reliving the night at Chalk. It took him a moment to understand.

"Emily?" Yes, the girl who leaked the tracks. How long ago was that?

"But maybe you could call her." Ben let out a little, self-depreciating laugh. "Do you guys do that? Do people still call each other?"

"She's probably in class now," Bowie replied.

"Sooner than later, I'd think."

"How did—?"

"She came to the shop. The thing that Ramaaker put on the Internet: it upset her."

Bowie couldn't believe he heard his father say the name "Ramaaker." Then he remembered the video, shot covertly and for spite. Somehow, it explained Ramaaker's rage over learning about Ion, Malik and RM Global. His blog post had been an insulting, condescending screed—but entirely correct about Ionic Strength and his place in EDM.

"Son?"

"Emily," Bowie said. "I'll do it tonight." Then: "Did Mom see the post?"

"Oh yes,"

"And?"

"You tell me."

"I couldn't guess," Bowie sighed. Meaning: Yes, I know.

"It's fantastic. You're a star. How did she put it? 'The little fish hate the big fish.'"

"She is going to be disappointed," Bowie said.

HE DIDN'T HAVE EMILY'S NUMBER, so he poked her on Facebook. She responded immediately.

Bowie Thomas: "Don't worry."

"I did a terrible thing," she replied. "I'm so, so, so sorry."

"Really. It wasn't terrible."

"Ramaaker."

They both hated Facebook Messenger. There was a sense that a billion people were eavesdropping.

"Ion's problem."

Bowie waited for her response. He could see her typing and erasing, typing and erasing. Finally, she asked: "What's he like? Ionic Strength. Ion."

Her took her shift in tone as a sign that she understood she was forgiven. His bed beckoning, he told her exactly what he had told his mother: "He wants to kill music."

Silence.

"Don't you let him," wrote Emily.

"'Night," Bowie Thomas replied.

RAKESH MALIK HAD SUMMONED IONIC Strength to the RM Global Building in Century City. The chairman and CEO had been informed of Bowie Thomas's banishment by Ion's driver, an opportunist who lacked the acuity to be more than useful. To Malik's mind—and he would be the first to admit that everything but the numbers confused him regarding how the world of electronic dance music functioned—Bowie fit precisely the model Ionic Strength proposed for the next EDM superstar, and the crowd at Chalk approved, heartily. His African queen did too. What had occurred in the aftermath made no sense to Malik, who, above all else, was rational.

Ionic Strength crossed Malik's stately office to the strains of a Prokofiev violin concerto. Malik stood and waved the producer into a Louis XVI armchair before his desk. Beyond the chairman's head, Ionic saw an endless blue sky and velvety clouds. Ion was unaware that he had been betrayed.

Malik lowered the volume by fluttering his fingers in the air.

In a blood-orange suit, sandy silk shirt, and Ferragamo python loafers, Ion was in contrast to Malik's business gray and Brooks Brothers four-in-hand tie in Harvard crimson. He noticed that he hadn't been offered tea, a Malik custom.

"They are young," Malik said without preamble, "and they have been led to believe, by the fantasies encouraged by popular culture, that a modicum of undeveloped talent, willfulness, budding self-awareness, and a grasp of irony will deliver success as easily as the sunrise brings a new day. But"—here, Malik clasped his hands—"we have learned that this is not so."

Ionic Strength had come a long way from his childhood in Providence's rough, crime-soiled West End neighborhood, but his street smarts held and he intuited that Malik had learned he had kicked Bowie Thomas out of Southern California. Malik wasn't going to listen to any explanation, especially one that couldn't balance with the income Ion himself had said a new Boy Wonder with the right backstory would generate: "wheelbarrow after wheelbarrow of cash rolling down the Avenue of the Stars right here to RM Global's vaults, Rakesh." That Bowie had mocked Ion with his set wouldn't mean a thing, not after Malik experienced the crowd's reaction while he did his calculations.

"What I see in young Mr. Thomas tells me his focus is aligned with our ambitions."

"Sure," said Ion. "But he has school. He works at Kmart. So, you know, he had to go."

"Ah. He chose to leave."

"What could I do?"

"You have his commitment?"

Shifting in his seat, Ion said, "Well, he's only seventeen."

"I would accept his word as bond," Malik replied. "At this point."

Ion decided to take a shot. "What's on your mind, Rakesh? Really."

"I am led to believe he is excellent. Have we not a stable of people who do what you say?"

Crafty bastard, thought Ionic Strength. *We're raking it in with cookie-cutter tracks, stadium shows and merch, but you're hedging. You're thinking there's an paying audience for good music.*

"To my mind," Malik said, "the best part of what is achieved is when it evolves on its own merit and begins to exist outside ego and sentiment. And fashion."

"He'll probably want to finish high school," Ion offered.

"He will perform in the main room at Chalk on Saturday night," Malik said. "You will make it so."

Malik fluttered his fingers again, and now the music of Bowie Thomas, and not Prokofiev, filled the room.

BEN SNORED, SO HE WAS often dispatched to the living-room sofa, which is where he was when he heard it, coming up through the heating vent. Kicking free of the comforter, he sat up, uncertain if he should intrude. He tiptoed to the kitchen, microwaved a cup of instant cocoa, and went quietly downstairs to the family room.

Bowie was at the upright piano. He played gently, letting the chords linger as he explored notes that added color, tension, aching sadness. Ben didn't recognize the tune, but he imagined it might be one of Bowie's compositions. Ben knew his son wrote his songs on piano and then recorded them in electronic form, layering instrument upon instrument, creating complex rhythms, inventing sounds. Often he would eliminate the original piano in the final mix, but, as he said, it gave the track a musical spine that he believed resonated with listeners. "It resonates." Bowie was fourteen when he made the claim.

Now he turned toward his father. He wore a T-shirt, PJ bottoms, and his Dr. Martens, the laces undone.

Ben handed him the cup. "She didn't mean it," he said.

Kim had been brutal, and Bowie may not have known exactly what she meant when she said: "You are throwing away a dream" and "You don't understand how important this is to us." He was a boy; resolute and wise beyond his years. But what child knows the depth of his parents' disappointments?

Long ago, Kim had imagined an impossibility, given her level of talent and unrelenting anxiety: she wanted to be a rock star, not a rock musician, not a musician. Behind a veil of self-deceit, she hadn't yet, to this day, understood that she had never tested herself against those who had worked for it.

She thought Bowie's gifts affirmed that she had been gifted. She failed to realize, even as she witnessed his effort, that Bowie's music was the result of relentless dedication, imagination, and humility. Living within the music, Bowie expected very little in return but the profound satisfaction of doing the hard thing well. This was beyond Kim's comprehension, Ben knew, and it saddened him that she would never know the tranquility found in creation made only for the sake of creation.

"Stevie Wonder?" Ben asked now, gesturing to the name and face on Bowie's floppy T-shirt. "We intersect."

Bowie nodded.

Ben retreated to the sofa. "Go ahead, son. Play."

MALIK'S SECRETARY TEXTED IONIC STRENGTH. "Kim Thomas called."

He was splayed on a massage table. A naked Korean teen walked on his back.

"Who is Kim Th—"

The mom. *The mom.*

Ion heard it as if she were in the room: "Please. He's young. He doesn't know. I've talked sense to him."

He wondered how deep she would go.

"This thing with Ramaaker. It threw Bowie off. He was frightened. Give us another shot. He needs someone like you."

Hmmm, thought Ionic Strength as he wriggled the girl off his shoulders. *This could jump out superfine.*

Impossible for Kim Thomas, way up there where the buffalo roam, to know that Rakesh was displeased.

And signing Bowie would be in a kick in the teeth to Ramaaker and all those other sanctimonious basement dwellers who think they invented music and dignity.

Oh yes.

Oh sweet.

Oh me.

BOWIE WAS BACK IN SCHOOL, and a few of his classmates had heard what had happened. Something about going out to Hollywood, maybe signing a contract—all abstract; was Hollywood real? Mild interest was stirred, a little bit of a buzz in the halls, though the metalheads wouldn't cross the borderline to ask him about it and the jocks kept on preening, a home game tonight. Bowie was glad: he got off easy. He hadn't processed it yet, at least not well enough to put it in a good place.

He had a parking spot in the senior lot. He figured if he got to the car without having to talk about it, that would be fine. He'd drive off to log in stock at Kmart. At least he'd be some sort of busy.

Basically, it had could down to reality. Long/short: he was in no man's land. He was the guy Ionic Strength turned down and Ramaaker disavowed. Even if neither interpretation was exactly true, that was his legacy. At age seventeen. His story would read: UP kid had his shot, set up at the Mondrian and spinning at Chalk, but he couldn't pull it off. He was willing to slave for the overlords of dumbed-down EDM, but he couldn't make it happen. He's tainted. Boy is a careerist, a suit.

Kim's Volvo purred behind Bowie's car. She stepped into the bitter air when she saw her son in the rearview, and called to him with enthusiasm. Kim in buckskin fringe, jeans, suede boots.

Kim Malczewski Thomas wanted her life back, to be the girl she was when she became pregnant at nineteen, before the drunken hookup with a dewy-eyed hippie carpenter, a man happy to sling a hammer. She could've sworn he said he knew Freddie Mercury. Turned out Ben had built a chiffonier for a man who saw a Queen tribute act eating ButterBurgers at Culver's.

"What's on, Mom?" Bowie said tiredly, as he dropped his backpack.

"Ionic Strength called the house," she said.

Technically true. He returned her call.

"Mom, please—"

"It's good news, Bowie." She smiled and swiped playfully at his arm.

He stepped aside to let a car pass. Soon there would be a steady stream toward the exit gate.

"He wants to see you. He said he's still interested. Isn't that— What, Bowie? What now?"

He shook his head sadly.

"Don't make a face," she said.

"The whole thing . . . It's not—It's not *valuable.*"

"Valuable? Bowie, are you serious?"

"It's a trap."

All he had seen and felt flashed across his mind: the private jet, the limo, the clothes, the hotel, Malik's home, the beauties, the cash: it didn't balance with what he prized. "I don't need it."

"Bowie, this man . . ." She began to sputter. "This man, he represents everything you could ever want. He is—Who is bigger in your field, Bowie?"

Bigger? What is that?

"Could you explain what the options would be? If you say no to this man, where do you go?"

"Mom," he said softly. "The only part of it I enjoy is making music. Spinning is the cost, so I do that too and I don't mind. But all the rest? It makes my skin crawl."

"He will give you everything, Bowie."

"I'm trying to explain—"

"What's your option? You open up a shop on 3 Mile Road where you can sell your little records?"

Bowie said, "Mom, don't. Please."

"You'd better make up your mind, Bowie. Ionic Strength is coming tomorrow. He's coming, and you're going to appreciate what he's trying to do. Or you will live with regret for the rest of your long goddamned life. Nobody gets three chances."

Kim flung open the car door, jumped inside and squealed away.

THIS TIME NO SHOCK AND awe when Ionic Strength arrived, no über-cool staging. To keep it earthbound, Bowie made sure his father would attend. Kim vetoed a meeting in the shop, but otherwise was resigned to Ben's presence.

Neither Ben nor Bowie knew Kim had invited Ion to come back to the UP. Once he agreed to fly east, she envisioned a role in Bowie's management. She saw a house in Venice Beach, and a reserved table at the Roxy, the Viper Room, the Troubadour. Velvet ropes would be brushed aside. She felt clever and delicious. Something had reawakened.

Bowie had gone about his business: homework, too quickly; and then back to the digital work station, where he was tidying up a piece he called "Karlheinz" that he'd been working on for weeks. The piano part had been looped to unfurl in reverse, and Bowie, Fender Jazzmaster in his lap, was trying to insert a kind of wet Bootsy pattern between the notes. Given it would hardly be audible among seventy-two tracks, it didn't matter very much if his playing wasn't perfect—he could fix it with the software—but he wanted to get it right, even if only he knew he had done so. He cursed himself for being such a crappy bass player.

Upstairs, Ben and Kim negotiated in whispers. Their positions, not quite entirely oppositional, were clear. Ben considered it a concession on Kim's part when she agreed that they would do only what Bowie wanted. "I'll go with him this time," she said, "to LA." *Of course*, thought Ben, who wondered if she would return. For years, he had assumed she would leave after Bowie set out for college.

The white stretch limo eased in front of the house at sunset. As Kim retrieved Bowie, Ben stepped outside in flannel and jeans, ignoring the icy chill.

The driver who had betrayed Ionic Strength hurried to open the door.

Rising out of the car, Ionic Strength, mustering gravitas, slipped into a long gray fox coat.

As Ben Thomas thrust a calloused hand toward his visitor, he saw Emily, Bowie's little classmate, marching with purpose, arms swaying, her toque bobbing. She walked directly to the producer.

"You suck," Emily shouted. "Leave everybody alone."

"'Everybody'?"

She raised her fists.

As the driver moved in, Ben held out an arm. He said, "I've got her."

Squeezing past his mother in the doorway, Bowie rushed toward them, crunching rock salt with bare feet. He was bone-thin in a Ramaaker T.

Ben said, "Emily. Emily."

She struggled to escape his bear hug.

"Emily," said Bowie Thomas, arriving. "Dad."

She wriggled and kicked.

Whoa, thought Ben, as he lifted her. *This girl enjoys her music.*

"I'll take her, Dad."

"I suck?" Ion asked no one.

His arm around her shoulder, Bowie led Emily past snow mounds toward the house.

Mortified, Kim stepped aside as Emily began to sob.

"Sorry about that," Ben said. Now he and Ionic Strength shook hands.

"Bah," said Ion. "Teenage drama. She's too young to know."

"Let's get out of the cold."

WITH EMILY DISPATCHED TO BOWIE'S room and the tea kettle about to whistle, Kim Thomas offered to take Ion's fox coat.

"Mom," Bowie said, "he might not be staying."

"Your pop ever work security?" Ion asked. He was remembering the time in São Paulo when a DJ pulled a gun and took a shot at him for knocking his set, the bullet pinging the cash register behind the bar. Then there was that night in New Orleans. . . .

"Ion, I think I'm going to stay home," said Bowie Thomas.

Ionic Strength pointed toward the Ramaaker logo on Bowie's chest. "He stays home. Losers, they stay home."

The producer had a hand to play. He looked at Kim Thomas as he dug into his pocket, produced his cash, removed the clip, and spread the fresh bills on the kitchen table.

Ben Thomas knew men at the Elks who put a twenty around ten singles and called it a bankroll. Hollywood led with a hundred-dollar bill and backed it with at least thirty more.

Turning to Bowie, Ion said, "You think I'm on about that?" He pointed at the cash. "That is nothing. Tip money. I'm talking about opportunity."

Bowie had yet to look at the cash on the table.

"Kid, I know you. You're a stubborn little Eskimo," Ion continued, "spinning in my face at Chalk like that. All right. Be stubborn. You don't bend. Fine. It pays."

Ben inched past the producer and took his seat at the table.

"Bowie," said Kim, as the tea kettle called. "Listen to the man."

The boy turned and cut the flame under the boiling water.

"You spin Saturday night at Chalk," Ion said. "Show Rakesh you respect his tastes."

"He does," said Kim. "He respects. You don't know him like I do."

"Kim . . ." Ben said softly.

Ion shrugged. He was thinking Kim Thomas didn't know as much about Boy Wonder as she thought. The big guy, though: trouble. He sees. Maybe Rakesh would pay out for a million-dollar desk.

Meanwhile, Bowie calculated. Ion was telling him he had to spin tracks by RM Global clients, but the subtext was that he didn't have the muscle to force him to do it. "I respect Mr. Malik," he said. "But it's not my time. Not yet."

"Let the people decide," Ion said.

Kim leaned against her son. "He's right. People know."

Some did, Bowie thought. But five minutes in a crowd while an A-list pop EDM producer spun proved it was the scene, not the music, that they craved.

"You want to advance the culture?" Ion asked. "Win a while and then do what you think you can do."

Ben studied his son. The producer had raised a fair point. Given a platform, Bowie could take it wherever he wanted to once he was established.

"Thank you, but no," Bowie said.

If tarred with an associate with Ion and crass EDM, he knew he could never recover. To the commercially minded, any move toward making original music would seem a step down. And the musicians he admired would view him with suspicion.

"Bowie . . ." Kim moaned.

Ion reached for the cash. "There's always another, you know. Another you."

"Maybe so," Bowie said.

Oh no there isn't, thought Ben.

Ion needed an exit line. "I'll send the plane. Bring the folks."

"I've got a gig," Bowie told him, as he walked toward the door. He was going back to the warehouse. Two sets: all ages at 8 p.m.; and then he'd return at midnight.

As Ben stood, Ion looked at Kim. He had a mind to turn her in, but he saw she was broken. It rarely paid to be kind, but he was thinking he might be coming back to the UP. EDM was going to die one day. Maybe a Bowie Thomas would have a different kind of currency.

Ionic Strength ran a finger along Bowie's cheek. "You want the hoodie?"

Bowie smiled, said no.

By the time Ion's limo pulled away, Bowie was in his bedroom.

Sheepish, her cheeks glistened with tears, Emily stood surrounded by his gear: the synths there, the bass in its stand, his drum pad on his swivel seat. A photo of Ramaaker was his screen saver. His bed was a tangle of comforters and sheets.

"Emily," said Bowie. "You are one harsh critic."

"Did I—"

"But not wrong."

ABOUT THE CONTRIBUTORS

GALADRIELLE ALLMAN is the author of *Please Be With Me, A Song for My Father Duane Allman*. She studied writing at Sarah Lawrence College and lives in Berkeley, California, where she is working on a novel about teenage love and punk rock music.

A lifelong New Yorker and recovering journalist, **PETER BLAUNER** is the author of seven novels, including the Edgar-winning *Slow Motion Riot* and the *New York Times* bestseller *The Intruder*. His short fiction has been anthologized in *Best American Mystery Stories* and on NPR's *Selected Shorts from Symphony Space*. He has been a writer for several television shows, including *Law & Order: SVU* and *Blue Bloods*. His novel, *Proving Ground*, will be published in summer 2017. Website: www.peterblauner.com

Called a hard-boiled poet by NPR's Maureen Corrigan and the "noir poet laureate" in the *Huffington Post*, **REED FARREL COLEMAN** is the *New York Times* bestselling author of Robert B. Parker's *Jesse Stone* series. He has published twenty-five novels in several series and standalones including the acclaimed *Moe Prager* mystery series and the *Gus Murphy* series. He is a three-time recipient of the Shamus Award for Best PI Novel and a three-time Edgar nominee in three categories. He has also received the Audie, Anthony, Macavity, and Barry awards. Website: www.reedcoleman.com

DAVID CORBETT is the author of five novels: *The Devil's Redhead, Done for a Dime* (a *New York Times* Notable Book), *Blood of Paradise* (nominated for numerous awards, including the Edgar), *Do They Know I'm Running* ("A rich, hard-hitting epic"—*Publishers Weekly*, starred review), and *The Mercy of the Night* ("Superlative"—*Booklist*, starred review). His novella, *The Devil Prayed and Darkness Fell*, appeared in 2015, and his story collection *Thirteen Confessions* was released in 2016. His book on the craft of characterization, *The Art of Character*, has been called "a writer's bible." He's a contributing editor for *Writer's Digest*, and his nonfiction has appeared in *The New York Times*, *Narrative*, and *Zyzzyva*, among others. Website: www.davidcorbett.com

TYLER DILTS is the author of the *Long Beach Homicide* series of crime novels featuring Detective Beckett. The son of a policeman, he grew up wanting to follow in his father's footsteps. Along the way, his career goals changed, but he never lost his interest in the daily work of homicide detectives. Now an instructor at California State University in Long Beach, his novels include *A King of Infinite Space, A Cold and Broken Hallelujah*, and, most recently, *Come Twilight*. Website: www.facebook.com/tylerdiltsbooks

BILL FITZHUGH is the award-winning author of nine novels, ranging from comic thrillers to social satire to humorous mysteries. He has written for radio, television, film, and the theater. He lives in Los Angeles. Website: www.billfitzhugh.com

JIM FUSILLI is the author of eight novels, including *Closing Time* and *Tribeca Blues*, and several books of nonfiction about music, including *Catching Up: Connecting With Great 21st Century Music*. He is the rock and pop music critic of the *Wall Street Journal* and is the founder of www.ReNewMusic.net, a music website for grownups. He lives in New York. Website: www.jimfusilli.com

USA Today bestselling author **ALISON GAYLIN** has been nominated for the Edgar, Anthony, and ITW Thriller awards and won the Shamus award for her *Brenna Spector* suspense series. Her ninth novel, *What Remains of Me* (William Morrow), is out now in hardcover and paperback. Website: www.alisongaylin.com

A. J. HARTLEY is the British-born international bestselling author of mystery/thriller, fantasy, historical fiction, and young adult novels, including *The Mask of Atreus, On the Fifth Day*, the *Darwen Arkwright* children's series, and, most recently *Steeplejack*, a young adult alternative detective series. He is currently the Robinson Professor of Shakespeare studies at the University of North Carolina, Charlotte, where he specializes in the performance history, theory, and criticism of Renaissance English drama, and works as a director and dramaturg. Website: www.ajhartley.net

CRAIG JOHNSON is *The New York Times* bestselling author of the *Walt Longmire* mystery series, which has garnered popular and critical acclaim. Titles include *The Cold Dish, Death Without Company, Another Man's Moccasins, The Dark Horse* (*Publishers Weekly* Best Book of the Year), *Junkyard Dogs, Hell Is Empty* (*Library Journal* Best Mystery of the Year), and *As the Crow Flies*. The *Walt Longmire* series is the basis for the hit A&E drama, *Longmire*. Johnson lives in Ucross, Wyoming, population twenty-five. Website: www.craigallenjohnson.com

DAVID LISS is an Edgar- and Macavity-award winning author of ten novels, most recently *Rebels*, the second book in the *Randoms* trilogy. His previous bestselling books include *The Coffee Trader* and *The Ethical Assassin*, both of which are being developed as films, and *A Conspiracy of Paper*, which is now being developed for television. Liss is the author of numerous comics, including *Mystery Men, Sherlock Holmes: Moriarty Lives* and *Angelica Tomorrow*. Website: www.davidliss.com

VAL McDERMID is a best-selling, award-winning Scottish crime writer best known for her mystery, detective, and suspense novels including series featuring Dr. Tony Hill, Kate Brannigan, and Tony Hill with Carol Jordan. Her recent novel *Out of Bounds,* is *The Sunday Times* number one bestseller. Website: www.valmcdermid.com

Born under a bad sign, **GARY PHILLIPS** must keep writing to forestall his appointment at the crossroads. He writes comic books, novels, short stories, novellas, scripts, and anything else he can get away with. He is currently president of the Private Eye Writers of America. He lives in Los Angeles. Website: www.gdphillips.com

NAOMI RAND has published three *Emma Price* mysteries including *The One That Got Away, Stealing for a Living,* and *It's Raining Men.* Her fiction and literary criticism appears in many small press magazines, among them *The Flexible Persona, Other Voices, Melus,* and *North Dakota Quarterly.* She has contributed to *Hard Boiled Brooklyn* and has written for numerous magazines and newspapers including *Redbook, Parents, Ladies Home Journal, The New York Times,* and the *Boston Globe.* She lives in Montclair, NJ, twelve miles west of New York City. Website: www.naomirand.com

PETER ROBINSON is a Canadian crime writer born in Britain. He is best known for his crime novels set in Yorkshire featuring Inspector Alan Banks.

Several of the novels have been adapted for television under the series title *DCI Banks*. His work has received a number of honors including the Edgar, Anthony, and Arthur Ellis Awards. Website: www.inspectorbanks.com

ZOË SHARP opted out of mainstream education at the age of twelve and wrote her first novel at fifteen. She began her award-winning crime thriller series featuring bodyguard Charlotte 'Charlie' Fox after receiving death-threats in the course of her work as a photojournalist. She now writes fiction full-time, interspersed with stints as an international pet-sitter. She lives in the English Lake District. Website: www.zoesharp.com

MARK HASKELL SMITH is the author of five novels including *Moist, Delicious, Salty, Baked,* and *Raw: A Love Story,* as well as the nonfiction books *Heart of Dankness: Underground Botanists, Outlaw Farmers and the Race to the Cannabis Cup,* and *Naked at Lunch: A Reluctant Nudist's Adventures in the Clothing Optional World.* He lives in Los Angeles. Website: www.markhaskellsmith.com

WILLY VLAUTIN is the author of four novels: *The Motel Life, Northline, Lean on Pete,* and *The Free.* He is also the main songwriter for the bands Richmond Fontaine and The Delines. He currently resides in Portland, Oregon. Website: www.willyvlautin.com

ERICA WRIGHT's latest crime novel *The Granite Moth* (Pegasus) was called "brisk, dark, slinky" by *USA Today.* Her debut, *The Red Chameleon* (Pegasus), was one of *O, The Oprah Magazine*'s Best Books of Summer. In addition to crime writing, she is an acclaimed poet, and is the poetry editor and a senior editor at *Guernica Magazine* as well as an editorial board member for Alice James Books. Website: www.ericawright.typepad.com

RECENT AND FORTHCOMING BOOKS FROM THREE ROOMS PRESS

FICTION

Lucy Jane Bledsoe
No Stopping Us Now

Rishab Borah
The Door to Inferna

Meagan Brothers
Weird Girl and What's His Name

Christopher Chambers
Scavenger
Standalone
StreetWhys

Ebele Chizea
Aquarian Dawn

Ron Dakron
Hello Devilfish!

Robert Duncan
Loudmouth

Amanda Eisenberg
People Are Talking

Michael T. Fournier
Hidden Wheel
Swing State

Kate Gale
Under a Neon Sun

Aaron Hamburger
Nirvana Is Here

William Least Heat-Moon
Celestial Mechanics

Aimee Herman
Everything Grows

Kelly Ann Jacobson
Tink and Wendy
Robin and Her Misfits
The Lies of the Toymaker

Jethro K. Lieberman
Everything Is Jake

Eamon Loingsigh
Light of the Diddicoy
Exile on Bridge Street

John Marshall
The Greenfather

Alvin Orloff
Vulgarian Rhapsody

Micki Janae
Of Blood and Lightning

Aram Saroyan
Still Night in L.A.

Robert Silverberg
The Face of the Waters

Stephen Spotte
Animal Wrongs

Richard Vetere
The Writers Afterlife
Champagne and Cocaine

Jessamyn Violet
Secret Rules to Being a Rockstar

Julia Watts
Quiver
Needlework
Lovesick Blossoms

Gina Yates
Narcissus Nobody

MEMOIR & BIOGRAPHY

Nassrine Azimi and Michel Wasserman
Last Boat to Yokohama: The Life and Legacy of Beate Sirota Gordon

William S. Burroughs & Allen Ginsberg
Don't Hide the Madness: William S. Burroughs in Conversation with Allen Ginsberg
edited by Steven Taylor

James Carr
BAD: The Autobiography of James Carr

Judy Gumbo
Yippie Girl: Exploits in Protest and Defeating the FBI

Judith Malina
Full Moon Stages: Personal Notes from 50 Years of The Living Theatre

Phil Marcade
Punk Avenue: Inside the New York City Underground, 1972–1982

Jillian Marshall
Japanthem: Counter-Cultural Experiences; Cross-Cultural Remixes

Alvin Orloff
Disasterama! Adventures in the Queer Underground 1977–1997

Nicca Ray
Ray by Ray: A Daughter's Take on the Legend of Nicholas Ray

Stephen Spotte
My Watery Self: Memoirs of a Marine Scientist

Christina Vo & Nghia M. Vo
My Vietnam, Your Vietnam
Vietnamese translation: *Việt Nam Của Con, Việt Nam Của Cha*

PHOTOGRAPHY-MEMOIR

Mike Watt
On & Off Bass

SHORT STORY ANTHOLOGIES

SINGLE AUTHOR
Alien Archives: Stories
by Robert Silverberg

First-Person Singularities: Stories
by Robert Silverberg

Tales from the Eternal Café: Stories
by Janet Hamill, intro by Patti Smith

Time and Time Again: Sixteen Trips in Time
by Robert Silverberg

The Unvarnished Gary Phillips: A Mondo Pulp Collection
by Gary Phillips

Voyagers: Twelve Journeys in Space and Time
by Robert Silverberg

MULTI-AUTHOR
The Colors of April
edited by Quan Manh Ha & Cab Trần

Crime + Music: Nineteen Stories of Music-Themed Noir
edited by Jim Fusilli

Dark City Lights: New York Stories
edited by Lawrence Block

The Faking of the President: Twenty Stories of White House Noir
edited by Peter Carlaftes

Florida Happens: Bouchercon 2018 Anthology
edited by Greg Herren

Have a NYC I, II & III: New York Short Stories;
edited by Peter Carlaftes & Kat Georges

No Body, No Crime: Twenty-two Tales of Taylor Swift-Inspired Noir
edited by Alex Segura & Joe Clifford

Songs of My Selfie: An Anthology of Millennial Stories
edited by Constance Renfrow

The Obama Inheritance: 15 Stories of Conspiracy Noir
edited by Gary Phillips

This Way to the End Times: Classic & New Stories of the Apocalypse
edited by Robert Silverberg

DADA

Maintenant: A Journal of Contemporary Dada Writing & Art
(annual, since 2008)

MIXED MEDIA

John S. Paul
Sign Language: A Painter's Notebook
(photography, poetry and prose)

HUMOR

Peter Carlaftes
A Year on Facebook

FILM & PLAYS

Israel Horovitz
My Old Lady: Complete Stage Play and Screenplay with an Essay on Adaptation

Peter Carlaftes
Triumph For Rent (3 Plays)
Teatrophy (3 More Plays)

Kat Georges
Three Somebodies: Plays about Notorious Dissidents

TRANSLATIONS

Thomas Bernhard
On Earth and in Hell
(poems of Thomas Bernhard with English translations by Peter Waugh)

Patrizia Gattaceca
Isula d'Anima / Soul Island

César Vallejo | Gerard Malanga
Malanga Chasing Vallejo

George Wallace
EOS: Abductor of Men
(selected poems in Greek & English)

ESSAYS

Richard Katrovas
Raising Girls in Bohemia: Meditations of an American Father

Vanessa Baden Kelly
Far Away From Close to Home

Erin Wildermuth (editor)
Womentality

POETRY COLLECTIONS

Hala Alyan
Atrium

Peter Carlaftes
DrunkYard Dog
I Fold with the Hand I Was Dealt
Life in the Past Lane

Thomas Fucaloro
It Starts from the Belly and Blooms

Kat Georges
Our Lady of the Hunger
Awe and Other Words Like Wow

Robert Gibbons
Close to the Tree

Israel Horovitz
Heaven and Other Poems

David Lawton
Sharp Blue Stream

Jane LeCroy
Signature Play

Philip Meersman
This Is Belgian Chocolate

Jane Ormerod
Recreational Vehicles on Fire
Welcome to the Museum of Cattle

Lisa Panepinto
On This Borrowed Bike

George Wallace
Poppin' Johnny

 Three Rooms Press | New York, NY | Current Catalog: www.threeroomspress.com
Three Rooms Press books are distributed by Publishers Group West: www.pgw.com